HARD TO WIN

I. M. PRICE

HARD TO WIN

I. M. PRICE

This book is dedicated to:

Garrett Baski

Without whom I would have starved to death in the back of my van.

You are a SUPERSPORE

Garrett Baski

Michael Price

GREATER
WOLVES

Blair Lovern
Chad Zerangue
ChristaCarol Jones
Dave and Donna Larkin
John and Donna Larkin
Michael and Julia Price
Praveen Thirumurugan
Stephanie and Arlo Frost

AnimeRules!
Ann Hulett
Annmarie Penello
BJ Sloan
C.D. Britt
Colin Holmes
Deborah Sandin
Jessica Price-Richardson
Matthew Rollins
Morgan Whitney
Paul Pizzella
Riordan Frost
Russell Connor
Samuel Morgan Wiseman
Sandy McKinny

I. M. Price

ian.price.author

impriceauthor

IMPriceAuthor

I M Price Author

Play List

A sample of what I listened to while writing this novel:

Feet of Flames (Hyde Park, London)	Michael Flatley
Khoya Hain (Bahubali: The Beginning)	Kaala Bhairava & Neeti Mohan
Croí na Saoirse	Celtic Pub Brotherhood
Dance the Wild Eire Way	Celtic Pub Brotherhood
You'll Never Beat the Irish	Celtic Pub Brotherhood
Noel's Creamy Pints	The 2 Johnnies
Ebudae	Enya
Malhari (Bajirao Mastani)	Vishal Dadlani
Running in the 90's (Initial D)	Max Coveri
Forever Young (Initial D)	Simone Valeo
Corridors of Time (Chrono Trigger)	Masayoshi Soken
Dance of the Fireflies (Final Fantasy XIV)	Masayoshi Soken
Sultana Dreaming (Final Fantasy XIV)	Masayoshi Soken

For extended listening checkout the OST of Initial D (anime), the OST of Final Fantasy XIV (video game), top Bollywood soundtracks from 2000-2020 (movies), and the extended discography of Enya (artist)

Acknowledgements

Acknowledgments? Acknowledgments!

Yar-har and fiddle Deedee (punctuation/capitalization is fun!), a bookish life is a life for me. I really want to add "it seems" after "life for me," but I'm sure many people I know would assure me it needs to be cut to improve readability, ~~or some such~~.

To everybody I was going to thank in this section, thank you for revealing your heart to me so I know to remove you. Good luck.

And because it's my party and I can cry if I want to, I'm going to pretend I'm up for a particularly pretentious Oscar and keep going. They're tears of joy, I promise, because these people 'like me, they really like me,' almost as much as I like them, and while 'I ain't people,' such a volume of 'liking' is really saying something. So here's to the baiz!

You've heard of the Justice League? The Fellowship of the Ring? The Powerpuff Girls? Then beg mercy for, and salvation from, Blair, Drew, and Stas!!!—Word benders of a caliber so extreme, Aang ducks for cover. They've got plot twists harder than Shyamalan (and not only at Night); descriptions to knock your socks off; and mood-setting skills so fine, they're a fine thing indeed. Like a Who down in Whoville on the first of Octember, they've the dialogue of champions: "Quite yes, sir?" "Quite ever."

I'm blessed to have these men in my corner. The greatest actor, the world's premier modern philosopher, and a New York Times best-selling author of fantastic, quirky fun. The feedback, help, and encouragement they've given me over the course of pushing for victory has been irreplaceable. It's no small statement to say I would not have made it this far without them, especially Blair, who fought through two different dog-shit versions of Hard to Win like he was a fucking Navy SEAL, deep-diving my brain and busting out all the bad story in there with Bad-Story Bunker-Busting Bombs.

Don't tell them, but I've snuck into the Secret Laboratory of Gratitude with my left hand bound, and since I'm wondering "What does this button do?" let's find out together as I press it with all my dexterity. This is from me, boys, to you: thank you.

To the man who's been my best friend for ages: "Get me a Dr. Pepper!" Hahahaha! To the world's best support both on and off the map, Garrett: from leveling my head mid-match with a 'winnable' to pushing me to take bigger risks and try, you've always been there for me. You're a winner, man. I don't know how many people will read this book, let alone this section, but if I can get any one thing across to readers from this book, it'd be that when people in the world come to meet you, man, they show you the kind of love and unconditional kindness you've shown me these past many years. You deserve it. Thank you, G.

Then to RodC, whose real name, much like Batman, is actually the name of the alter ego he likes to keep shrouded in mystery. Rod and I met years ago when I first commissioned some art for my characters. I have serious difficulty envisioning things in my mind's eye—I don't seem to be able to do it. He not only stepped up to do the art for Saoirse and my other characters but also became the kind of friend I could confide anything in and resonate with on a deep level. For those reading, I have a personal goal of earning enough from writing to finally visit him down in Argentina and see him face to face. He brightens my day and makes my life better with every conversation and stream. Thank you, Rod—you a beast.

And to my beta readers Chad, Meera, Karoline, Matthew, and Brian (from Dublin): I know you sacrificed a lot of your psyche on really awful versions of my book that didn't quite hit the mark. I'm both sorry and thankful. Without all the hard work you put in catching my mistakes, despite how the previous versions of the book made you feel, I'd never have refined it to a worthy piece of art. Thank you ^^

Now for a pair of legends, Kate and Joe Zimmerman. Many of you won't know this, but I live in a broken van. It's got no engine, no transmission, a dead battery, and I live every day praying everything I own isn't stolen and that I'll wake up to see tomorrow. I almost didn't several times. I've found black mold growing under my bed; I've had wasps move into my car; and when Texas hit a cold snap, I told myself I was all in on hoping to make it through the cold—that was until the big hearts of Kate and Joe opened their home to me and quite literally kept me alive. Neither I nor this book would have made it without you. Thank you for looking out for me. And for all the tea. I never thought I'd like tea.

This part's going to read as a bit unorthodox. Or maybe it won't. I won't lie, I don't read acknowledgments in books (am I alone in this?). So maybe this is completely normal, but I wanted to say thank you to some of the people who inspired me to put myself out there because they've already put themselves out there, and in ways I still don't think I'd ever dare, I have to thank to Nux Taku, Smug Alana, Asmongold, Projekt Melody, and Maximilian Dood, thank you. I'm sure this is coming across as parasocial, but I promise you I don't think of you like that. I enjoy your content. Without it, I might never have gotten the courage to create my own. Thank you.

And last but certainly not least are the people without whom this specific book would never have been written—the people who helped me understand (or at least pretend to understand) Irish culture. YouTubers Candlelit Tales and The Fortress of Lugh were indispensable in understanding the ancient cultures and myths; the lecture series on the 'Ulster Cycle,' taught by Elizabeth Baldwin; the Lord of the Dance himself, Michael Flatley, whose Feet of Flames show in Hyde Park, London, I think I've seen a few thousand times now; Naoise Hurling, whose instructional videos helped me actually learn hurling; and the single most important man in my Irish inspiration, Martin G-L.

Martin was a childhood friend of mine and brilliant at Irish step-dancing. Even as a kid, you'd watch him in the talent show and know, 'there goes a man who's truly got it.' Now, thirty years later, and having no idea where he is or what he's up to, I've written a book inspired by deep memories from when I was five. Ha! How the world comes full circle, eh? Thank you all for helping to inspire me about Irish culture. I hope I did it any justice.

I don't know how to wrap all this sappy malarkey up, yeah? So just consider yourselves acknowledged, thanked, and awesome. Because you are.

—I. M. Price

Contents

Irish Hurling

This book focuses on a fantastical, magical version of the wonderful sport of Irish Hurling, the national sport of Ireland. Coined 'war in shorts' and 'the fastest game on grass,' Hurling combines the best aspects of lacrosse and field hockey into brutal fun.
Since it's possible you don't know much about Hurling or Camogie (the women's version), what follows is a quick six-page info graphic on the basics you'll need to follow along with the novel.
Enjoy!

PARTS OF A HURLEY

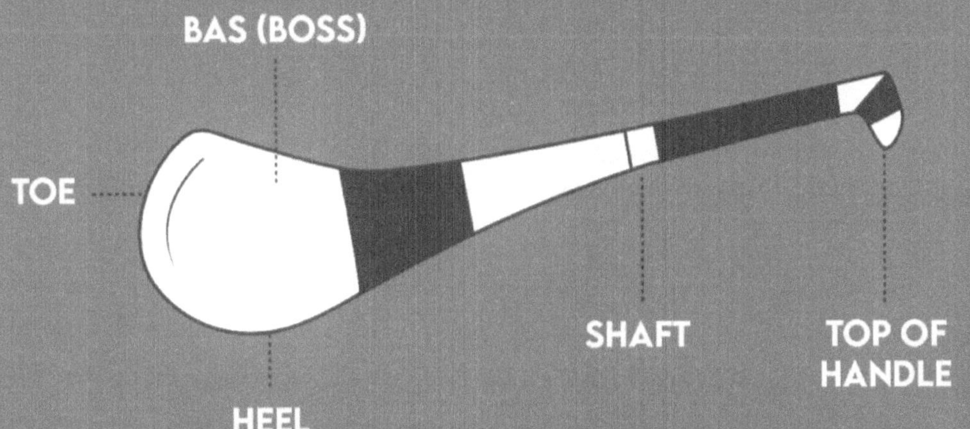

SIZE OF A SLIOTAR (slit-er)

Leather-stitched balls with cork centers: a sliotar's diameter ranges from 69mm to 72mm (2.7-2.8 inches). They weigh between 110 and 120 grams (3.9-4.2oz).

HURLING - RULES & MAGIC

SIZE OF A FIELD

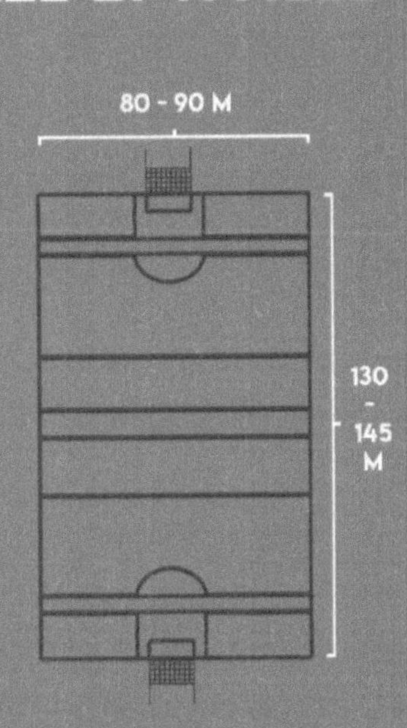

SIZE OF A GOAL

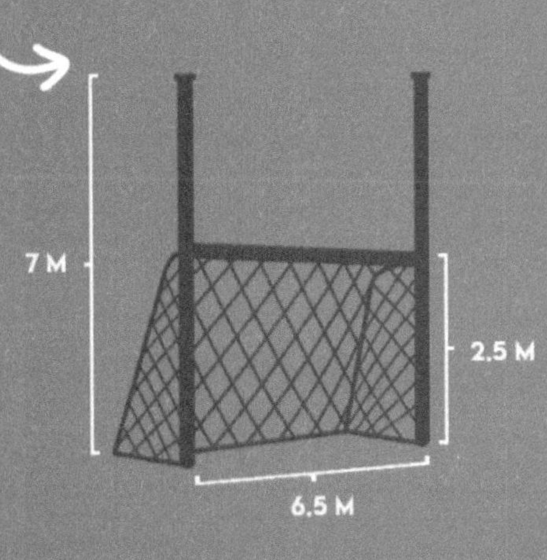

PLAYERS AND POSITIONS

EACH HURLING TEAM HAS **15** PLAYERS

DEFENSE	OFFENSE
Goal Keeper	Midfielders
Full-Backs	Half-Forwards
Half-Backs	Full-Forwards

HURLING - RULES & MAGIC

SCORING

GAME DURATION:

30 minute halves with
a 10 minute half time

1 point
over the bar

1 goal 3 points
under the bar

Example: 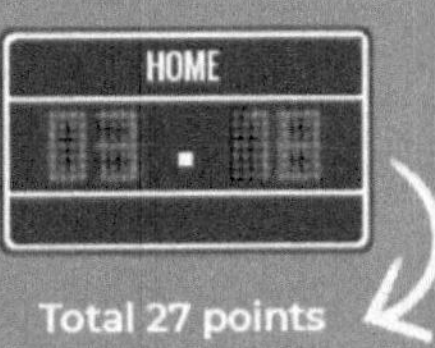

Total 27 points

WHAT'S A SOLO?

A player runs down the field
balancing the ball on their hurley.

HURLING - RULES & MAGIC

WHAT YOU CAN DO

CATCH:

HAND PASS:

RUN WITH THE BALL:
Up to 4 steps

STRIKE:

KICK:

WHAT YOU CAN'T DO

Pick up the ball with your hands

Throw the ball

Carry the ball down the field

HURLING - RULES & MAGIC

JAB LIFT

A technique used in hurling to lift the sliotar from the ground by 'jabbing' the hurley under the ball, and lifting it into the air.

ROLL LIFT

A technique used to lift the sliotar by rolling the ball onto the hurley, and lifting it into the air.

SIDELINE CUT

How the ball is put back into play when it goes out of bounds

HURLING - RULES & MAGIC

WHISKEYS

Whiskeys - Whiskeys are the term for the magical
spells available to players. Each player may have
only 1 Whiskey per match. A player can use their
Whiksey at any time during a match.

Whiskeys are as numerous as spores in the sky. With them,
players can run faster, jump higher, create temporary clones
of themselves, and much more!

Players who use their Whiskey gain a temporary boon of
enhanced focus after use, but soon suffer intense feelings of
fatigue, often enough to induce sleep (right there on the
field!). Most players can only use a Whiskey once per match.
The stronger the magic, the stronger the aftereffects.

. . . .

Any kind of dispute in Éire can be solved
by winning a Rite of Ritual Hurling,
where a challenging player must win a
"reasonable" hurling trial set out by the
challenged. Nearly every problem is
solved this way.

If you wish to encourage your opponent with a friendly show
of sportsmanship, simply say, "An evening star shines down
upon you," to which the reply is, "May it be."

Now, "Let's Hurl!"

HARD
TO
WIN

I. M. PRICE

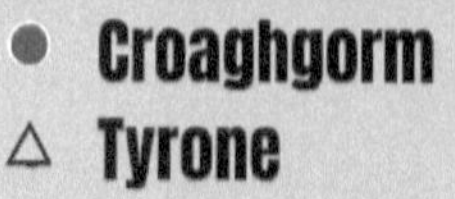

Croaghgorm
Tyrone

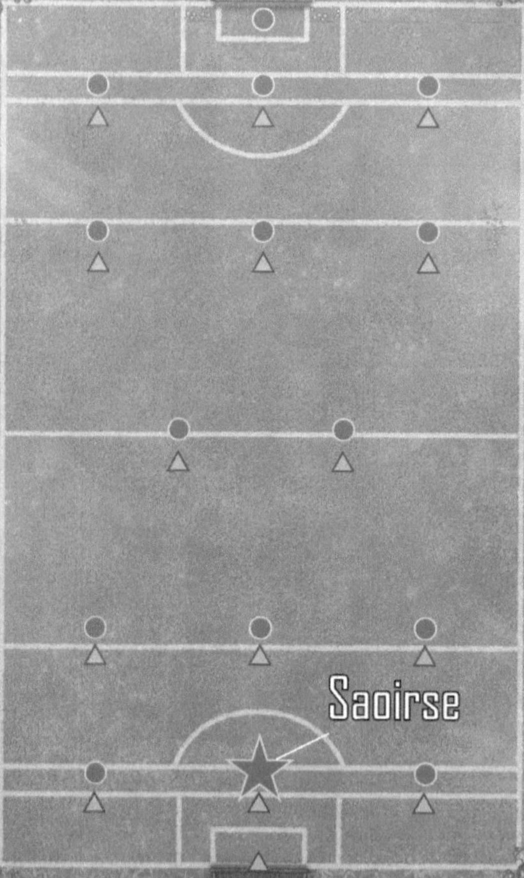

CROAGHGORM
GOAL
Saoirse
TYRONE CAMOGIE
GOAL
LOW BRANCH
STADIUM

Saoirse Storm

Eight Days Remain

Two kinds of fans filled the stadium tonight: those cheering for County Tyrconnell and those who were wrong.

Roars raced down seats. The crack of sticks sang through the dusk. An ornery old grandpa had smuggled in a watermelon. Nobody knew how this feud started; they only knew how it ended, and fruit salad was not included.

County Tyrconnell hated County Tyrone.

And the last match of the season—"Ends in ten minutes' time!" the announcer barked over the crowd, voice amplified.

There was just one problem...

The crowd cheered her name:

"Saoirse, you're the greatest!" a man shouted.

"Best player in years!" a woman said.

"Three goals! She's scored three goals!" a kid.

...She had to throw the game.

"Not good." Red hair shimmering, blue jersey stuck with sweat, Saoirse scraped across the field, battling a heavyset Tyrone defender.

I scored too many goals!

Glowing, slimy green mushroom grass squelched beneath her studs. A bit of hardwood was shoved up her backside.

"Anxious?" the full-back sneered.

Saoirse pushed back, maintaining position. "Sorry, Noreen. I don't play for Tyrone."

"County Tyrone shoots!" the announcer called.

The sliotar—a ball about the size of Saoirse's palm—sailed high toward her team's uprights. Hope filled her chest. If this went between them, Tyrone would get a point.

They'd be tied!

"It goes wide!" the announcer called.

"NO!" Saoirse yelled.

Noreen eyed her.

"I mean, yes!" *Spores*, she cussed. Slashing her hurley through the mushroom grass, green shroom guts splattering the ash wood. The one time she needed her opponents to score, they couldn't do it! Tyrone Camogie struggled with the unusual terrain. Fresh dirt and grass weren't the same as worn red bark covered with green fungi.

The keeper took her sweet time getting another ball.

Saoirse's pointless fight with Noreen resumed. The ref let them shove it out.

SHE'S DEFINITELY OUT HERE FEELING GUILTY, FOLKS, her inner voice chided her.

Stuff it, Satirical, she shot back at the old-timey broadcaster.

OH, SURE, IT'S MY FAULT, Satirical said.

In Saoirse's mind's eye, Little Hurler—a cute, mute, mini-her with stubby appendages and a big head—made a rude gesture at Satirical.

FECK OFF, LITTLE HURLER.

Saoirse shook her head. Neither 'Saoirse Satirical' nor 'Little Hurler' was real. They were mechanisms she'd developed during therapy to explain her emotions in hurling terms, but at times the 'broadcaster in her brain' and the 'little menace in her heart' seemed more real than wood.

HURLING IS THE GAME OF THE GODS, Satirical said.

Yeah. That's the problem, Saoirse thought back.

Bioluminescent mushrooms bathed the hazy field in salmon-pink shimmer.

The Croaghgorm goalkeeper put the sliotar back in play. It was seized by a Tyrone player, who made another attempt for a point over the bar but missed, thanks to a lovely block.

The crowd roared their approval.

Their hope, their excitement, crackled across Saoirse's skin; she refused it. If she could let herself bask in the crowd's fervor, sup on their hope, she would. Saoirse shook her head. A better girl would be cheering.

"You're going to lose, girl," Noreen sneered.

Saoirse shouldered her into the bark. "Hatch snatcher."

This was home: County Tyrconnell. A place where, for twenty-six years, every team in their county lost to teams from County Tyrone. Home: a tree stretched from the base of the ocean to well past the sky—the canopy sealed off all but a sliver of the setting sun—home: a place she had to betray.

Come on, Tyrone.

I'D LIKE TO RETIRE AS YOUR IN-HEAD COLOR COMMENTATOR.

Little Hurler threw her hurley through the broadcast booth window in Saoirse's brain.

"Ow!" Saoirse seized her head.

YOU'RE GONNA PAY FOR THAT WINDOW, HURLER! Satirical shouted at their heart.

The mini-her didn't care.

The Camogie Cunts made a stellar block on another attempt to tie the game. Her teammates were in rare form. It was clear they could taste the victory. Their blocking was the reason Tyrone kept sending it wide.

Tyrone got the loose sliotar.

Noreen and her continued scrapping. All the play was down on the Croaghgorm team's end.

Saoirse squeezed her lucky hurley. She didn't have a choice. She had to get in there and mess up the defense. She had to lose.

DON'T!

I will not be like those women!

Tyrone tried again. Missed again.

The dead eyes *those women* had, the hateful expressions *those women* wore—Saoirse would not join them in their regret. She would not participate in her people's sacred rite!

Her keeper played it short, and it was stolen almost immediately.

"Little Hurler!" Saoirse said. "Let's do this!"

Little Hurler locked eyes on the sliotar, pumped her arms, and heat, like molten bronze, flooded through Saoirse from her core.

There was only one way forward. One way out of the death pact she'd made with her religion: go pro. With professional trials in a few weeks, and the rite in only eight, she'd only get that chance if she threw. This was her one hope. Her one shot. She could not miss her chance to go. She'd lose herself in this movement, this moment; lose her gods' favor by losing this game. She would, or she'd never be free.

"It's fifteen girls against fifteen women!" the announcer said. "Will the Camogie Cunts of Croaghgorm Mountain finally put an end to the terrible terror that is Tyrone?"

No.

A whistle blew. The final match of the season went into extra time.

"Go!" the stadium announcer was losing his mind.

In the stadium pews, fans in their blue for the Croaghgorm girls drowned out the white and red for Tyrone. Last-minute music pumped through the black speaker mushrooms.

"The sliotar's been knocked free!" he cried. "Now the ball's rolling across the barks!"

"Tyrconnell!" the fans screamed.

"Defense!" cried another.

"Watermelon!" The grandpa.

A Tyrone girl got the sliotar.

It's good-guys up one, Satirical said. *We can win, folks.*

Saoirse tugged at her heart. Little Hurler egged on her betrayal.

If you just play, Satirical said, *you'll be a heroine!*

I'll be doomed! Saoirse charged toward her side to 'play defense.' She had size on most women—height and width; she'd throw her weight around. Would this look terrible? She didn't want to run afoul of the league. Match-fixing carried a fifteen-year minimum sentence ever since that one cow incident, but there were precious few moments left. Nobody in their league could afford—Saoirse skidded to a stop—"MAGIC!"

Bright white light erupted from far in front of her goal. A Tyrone forward hollered something she couldn't make out; it didn't matter, she knew what it was: magic. An enchanted power move. A legal cheat.

"YES!!!" Saoirse leaped for the sky. The nearby defenders watched her, looking stupefied.

Little Hurler broke out the pompoms, dancing to the top of her heart, cheering with all her might—despite being completely mute.

It couldn't be! Yet it was.

Saoirse tried to save her outburst with a look of mock horror as the mists seeped onto the field from the mushroom seating, draining the stadium pews of their bioluminescence and flooding the pitch. Black. Violet. Salmon. A rushing river of magical power. A vortex. The blessings of the gods.

And being given to County Tyrone!

"FOUL HER!" she roared, then dropped her voice to a bare whisper. "But don't, though."

She needn't have worried. The shock seemed to have gripped her teammates. In the momentary lapse, the mist swirled toward the County Tyrone player, her hurley raised, glowing white.

She cried, "TYRONE TACKLE!"

The glow transferred to the woman's shoulder. She lowered it toward the Tyrconnell half-back Kate, who controlled the ball.

"Kate!" But it was too late.

With a sound like thunder, the spell worked its magic and sent Kate soaring through the air and into the stands, where she landed with a crack into a pile of home-county gold and green.

"NO!" Saoirse screamed. There was nothing she could do from here. The opening gave County Tyrone the chance to shoot, and they did.

The sliotar sailed past the Tyrconnell keeper, under the bar, and into the back of the net—three points.

Tyrone Camogie up two.

"Spores!" She fist-bumped Little Hurler through her chest. County Tyrone had done it. The pressure was off. At any moment, the ref would blow the whistle. Her team would lose. She'd be safe, she'd get to have her whole hurling career, nobody would pick her flowers, and best of all, it didn't even look like it was her fault.

I CAN'T BELIEVE YOU, Satirical sighed.

Zip it, cú, Saoirse thought back. *Besides, I've already scored three goals!*

YOU'LL BE IN A DUNGEON! WE'LL BE IN A DUNGEON! YOU'RE MY LEGS, YOU KNOW!

The Primary Éirish National Institute for Sports was the judge, jury, and executioner in Éire.

Saoirse eyed the stands where a large cohort of PÉNIS members stood erect near the Tyrconnell supporters. The organization was on stanza as having chosen the acronym to represent virility and strength, which, as far as she knew, made sense.

They likely traveled to see her, the rookie sensation, in her last match of the season.

Satirical sighed with the name of their gods, *TUATHA DÉ DANANN.*

They got what they wanted to see.

I DON'T GET WHAT SHE'S SO AFRAID OF, FOLKS, Satirical said as if announcing to an invisible audience.

The ref's whistle blew.

Afraid of? After her chieftain had rolled their religious artifact to check her luck? The word: 'Yes.' It always came up 'Yes.'

"Saoirse!" her coach boomed from the sideline.

Saoirse snapped to attention. "What?" She'd been completely zoned out after the goal, convinced her con was over at the whistle, but the sliotar had been put back into play, soaring upfield in her direction!

Shite! The match was still on? And she was entirely out of position! This could look bad.

Red dust. Scuffed boots. Hurley held tight between her fingers. One hand free to catch the sliotar. She spared a glance at the game timer.

Gods salm it! She could totally score! And she was her. She'd be expected to score!

Her teammates joined from the bench.

"Yes! Saoirse, save us!!"

"Come on, Saoirse!
"No girl is better at handling balls!"

"Saoirse!" the coach shrieked.
"Two hands on the shaft! Get that goal!"

The crowd roared. Knots sank in her stomach, but she had already jumped. The sliotar sailed into her palm, knocking free a bit of golden dust—the hint of her own magic ability... if only she had it. Right now, it was better that she couldn't use it. It might make her failure look less obvious.

I can't trip right now. That'd be too egregious.

Still at midfield, when her boots hit the bark, she spun—and fast—tossing the ball in front of her, bouncing it in the air on her lucky hurley as she ran upfield, hassled by her defender.

GO FOR THE GOAL. SCORE!

I can't.

"There she goes! The best player County Tyrconnell's seen in years! She's our champion!" the stadium announcer roared—a total homer.

She couldn't stop the tears forming at the corners of her eyes, tears she was certain no one could see.

"She's taking the ball by herself," the announcer said. "Bouncing it on her hurley—a solo!"

It'll be fine.

If she had any one skill in this, the sport of the gods, it was soloing.

Please be fine.

"SAOIRSE STORM!"

They called her the Dancer.

Take it home, Twenty-Seven!

Majesty. Clarity. Purpose. When a hurley hit her hand, she was one with the mists themselves, one with the storm, one with the star.

The corner-backs closed in on her from the left and right. Saoirse skidded forward, cleats kicking red dust.

Gold: her rhythm. Her hurley: her hand's hard shoes.

The girl goes dancing there.

She cradled the ball against the flat of her hurley. When the defenders bit on her feint, she let her cleats catch, the momentum of her dash carrying her forward as she twisted and split the defenders, leaving them in a heap of white and red pelts behind.

She couldn't stop after that either! *Shite!*

"Score!" her teammates were shouting now. "Put that biscuit in the basket!"

She had a free pitch—just her and the goalkeeper! Little Hurler was freaking out.

For women, her religion outlawed dance. She wasn't exactly pious...

Saoirse raced full speed, red hair streaming behind her—little more than a pale blur of freckles and pride.

...She loved dance more than anything. More than hurling, more than life. They let her get away with it on the field, because hurling was not dancing—even if sometimes...

She couldn't score, she thought. She couldn't be the heroine. She couldn't be the girl to break the twenty-six-year-long losing streak for Tyrconnell against Tyrone!

...it felt like it.

Three meters out.

The keeper flinched.

The crowd held its breath.

She popped the ball into the air—just one clean strike would do it.

"Saoirse!" her teammates bellowed. "You're you. You deserve this!"

> *They're wrong, you know.*
> *You don't deserve it.*
> *You don't deserve to score.*

It was her body, her choice.

Three meters out.

She froze—refusing to shoot.

The sliotar clattered to the bark—a free ball. After an uncomfortable amount of time, the Tyrone keeper scooped it up as if she couldn't believe her luck and sent it soaring back up the field. A few seconds later, Saoirse heard the whistle. Tyrone scored another goal.

The stadium went silent.

I'm sorry. I'll beat them next season. I promise. I'm so sorry.

She jumped, letting out a shriek when a pair of guards in dark blue uniforms cuffed her wrists.

"Saoirse Storm," said one of the men. "You are hereby under arrest for conspiracy, sabotage, and match-fixing."

"WHAT!?" How could they know? Could they read minds? "But I haven't done anything."

"Let's go." They shoved her toward the exit.

Her hope had cratered. If they found her guilty, if PÉNIS declared her a *Bad Girl*, she'd never be allowed to play pro for the County Tyrconnell Hurling Club, and she only had this one chance to avoid her people's sacred rite. She tried speaking again, but her voice was failing. "I-I'm a *Good Girl*."

They hauled her off the pitch, studs scuffing along the ground. She was bound in blue fuzzy cuffs, watching what little of the freedom she'd thrown away set beyond the horizon.

Don't Skip the Song!

HEARD A GOOD RECITATION LATELY, FOLKS? SHE ASKS THE VOID. Satirical Sighs. I DON'T KNOW WHY I DO HALF-TIME SEGMENTS AND STORE THEM IN SAOIRSE'S MEMORY FOR NOBODY. ONE DAY, SATIRICAL, ONE DAY SOMEBODY WILL APPRECIATE YOUR BROADCASTING—MANIFEST IT.

ANYHOO. WHERE WAS I, FOLKS? THAT'S RIGHT, RECITATIONS! SAOIRSE, LITTLE HURLER, AND I LOVE 'EM. IF THERE'S SOMETHING GOOD BEING SPOKEN, WE'VE GOTTA GO HEAR IT! DRUIDS, BARDS, AND SATIRISTS, LIKE ME, TRAVEL ALL OVER ÉIRE AND RECITE ALL KINDS OF WONDERFUL POETRY.

ONE THING I HATE, THOUGH, IS WHEN DRUIDS GET ALL JEALOUS OF BARDS AND TRY TO SING. WHO NEEDS THAT? IF THEY HAD STORYTELLING CHOPS, THEY'D AT LEAST MAKE SURE THEIR SONGS MOVED THE PLOT, BUT NO. YOU GOTTA SIT THERE AND LISTEN. YUCK.

MAYBE ONE DAY SOMEBODY WILL DO IT RIGHT. THAT'LL BE GREAT; I'D DEFINITELY LISTEN THEN. IN FACT, IF THERE WERE CRUCIAL PLOT AND CHARACTER INFORMATION IN THERE, I'D EVEN ADVISE STRANGERS: "DON'T SKIP THE SONG!"

UNTIL THAT FATEFUL DAY, I'M AFRAID WE ALL MUST SUFFER. NOW TO START THAT MANIFESTATION BOARD... OH, LOOK, A MIC-SPORE!

Manifestation Board

I Want to Score

S aoirse sank deeper into the hot tub, massaging where the fuzzy cuffs had bound her wrists, glad to be out of the full-body suit they were required to wear under their uniforms.

She had done it. She'd gotten away with everything. She'd thrown. When she made the pro team, the law would force her religion to drop her death pact. She would avoid becoming one of *those women*, and she would be allowed to dance! Nothing could stop her now.

What about the fact that you're banned? Satirical asked.

Suspended, Saoirse corrected her.

That sounds like a big deal.

The investigator said she has to carve out some notes and send them up to the official investigator. That's nothing.

You're the queen of denial, you know that?

It's not a big deal. Relax.

Little Hurler disagreed. Being denied the ability to play hurling left her in tears.

Saoirse had been in and out of the interrogation in less time than it took to shoot a sliotar. Conspiracy, sabotage, and match-fixing? Her scandal wasn't that big. A devious smile worked its way across Saoirse's face. *Success*. This time in a few weeks, she'd be doing the tryouts for the County Tyrconnell Hurling Club, score so many goals it would fix the team's broken magic, and be the heroine of the county. Bards would sing about her, satirists would construct poems, and druids through the ages would recite her glory.

I hope this works out the way you think it will.

It will.

Saoirse loved coming to the Warm Pools—a series of pools and hot tubs carved into the branch of a great tree. Everything here was county-colored, the colors she'd be wearing in a few short weeks: gold and green. The walks, the chairs, the pool toys all screamed, 'Get some goals, we hate being the worst team in Éire!'

Little Hurler seconded that opinion.

Satirical seconded Saoirse's opinion that these massage shrooms were hitting just right.

"That feels amazing," Saoirse said.

"I'm a great therapist," Aisling, her eternally benched best friend, sat in the opposite corner. A bush of brown curls hid most of her mousy features, the rest concealed beneath an exfoliating bear dung face mask. "Oh, you meant the hot tub."

"Both."

Her friend was a dedicated student of therapy. Aisling knew modules for dealing with all kinds of traumas: abandonment, internalized worthlessness, post-hurling stress disorder, and more. After the session just now, Saoirse was confident there was no reason to feel guilty. So, she wouldn't.

An enormous mural, ten meters tall, depicting the County Tyrconnell Hurling Club starting fifteen, each holding a milkshake, spanned the length of the complex. Saoirse looked up into the face of her soon-to-be captain.

Lorcan.

So handsome.

Heart eyes filled Little Hurler's big face.

The captain was by far the best-looking of the Wolves, which was actually saying something. Spores, he was so—*ugh*. Every bit of 6'9" and built like it. He had hairy, muscular forearms cracked with veins; long brown hair spilling over his shoulders with the occasional braid; and a mighty, angular-cut beard. His face was like a wolf's, with piercing yellow eyes, extra-long canines in his scowl, and that presence—even though it was a painting—Captain. Commander. Nobody second-guessed who was in charge.

That's where his nickname came from. He didn't just look like a wolf. He didn't just sense like one. He was one. He was: "Aware Wolf."

"And if the gods say no?" Aisling asked.

"I just don't see how a world with such wonderful hurling could be bad."

Aisling laughed.

Saoirse eyed the mural. Little Hurler set a tempo.

"Here. We. Go. Yes."

SAOIRSE:
"Our county has the worst team
in all professional hurling."

AISLING:
"We only watch because they're hot,
and get our toes a'curling."

SAOIRSE:
"There's Lorcan, he's so dreamy,
Mr. Bearded, hot and steamy."

AISLING:
"Or Sean the gambler,
with a spore or dice."

BOTH:
"Mmhmm."

SAOIRSE:
"Nolan's big and broad and buzz cut—
a full defensive hunk."

AISLING:
"Or even flippant Cian,
surgeon-druid with a trunk."

"There are a whole bunch more,
and they're all attractive rakes."

Saoirse thumbed at the mural featuring the players holding drinks from the pool cabana.

SAOIRSE:
"And based on their pictures,
they like our big milkshakes."

"For years and years, we've lost our games
no matter who was playing."

AISLING:
"The Shitty Forward line?"

SAOIRSE:
"Yeah, that's what I'm saying."

"I'm going to replace that trash
and help the men I love.
I'll give them what they're missing
so they'll give me tons of hugs!"

SAOIRSE (CHORUS):
"I want to score. I want to score.
I want to score and score some more.
To have my flowers picked by Lorcan.
It wouldn't be a bore.

"I want to score. I want to score.
I want to score and score some more.
Let them give me sticky buns—
from the Cook Street baker stores!"

"I'd be there for them every day.
I'd be there for them every way.
All we'd do is play, play, play.
Hurling is the way!"

Everybody knew the Wolves had no magic; she'd fix that with all her goal scoring.
"We kinda forgot about something when we wrote this," Aisling said.
"What?"
"*Sexplosion*? Pregnancy? Death!?"
Saoirse, Aisling, and Little Hurler all traced a prayer around themselves in the shape of a shamrock.
Saoirse shrugged. "It's a fantasy."
Shamrock Violet, their religion, taught that engaging in any _Intercourse_-related activities with a man outside of one's clan would lead to sexplosion. That is, the man would explode and die. She wasn't really sure how they could both explode and die; one seemed to indicate the other, but it didn't matter. She wasn't a murderer.
"Seriously," Saoirse asked, "why did the gods even invent sexplosion?"
"No kidding. Ready?"
"I've got the words."
"Go!"

SAOIRSE:
"In our religion, there's a festival,
and we're bound to it by death.
To *Intercourse* everybody—"

AISLING:
"And at the gods' behest."

SAOIRSE:
"They told us it meant 'carnal,'
but we heard 'carnival.'"

"Whoops," said Aisling.
"No kidding." Saoirse laughed. "But it makes a fun headcanon till they tell us what actually happens!"
"Agreed."

SAOIRSE:
"Playing games and winning prizes
with a genuine article."

"Games like Hide the Hurley."

AISLING:
"Or Ovens Full of Buns."

SAOIRSE:
"Underwater Basket Weaving."

AISLING:
"Bear-back rides sound fun!"

SAOIRSE:
"The only problem is with
all the ugly boys in town.
When 'me-want-do-the-thing'
with the Wolves from all around!"

AISLING:
"Ah!"

There was no way *The Violet Intercourse* actually matched up with their awesome headcanon. The Carnal Carnival? A place to go on dates like that couldn't possibly exist. It'd be too amazing.
"Seriously," Aisling said, smacking a mushroom to restart her massage, "I wonder what actually happens during *The Violet Intercourse*."
She spoke the name of the rite with careful emphasis. They all made shamrocks again.
Very little was covered in Shamrock Violet teachings. She and Aisling only knew the basics: get picked by the gods, spend a month with others chosen doing fun events and games, and somehow end up pregnant, but they didn't have any specifics. It was illegal to inform girls about *The Violet Intercourse*. The punishment for doing so was death. So, they'd come up with their own headcanon.
Little Hurler paused her timekeeping.
"What if we're accidentally right?" Saoirse asked.

"The Carnal Carnival?" Aisling asked. "That'd be wild."
"I still say it has something to do with men picking your flowers."
"And I say it's on bear-back rides."
What would it be like to zoom around the Great Aurum Forest on the back of a grizzly bearfly? She worked with the creatures at the jobbery, but she'd never been bold enough to ride one. "You know, what happens if they pick our flowers while we are up high in the sky on a bearfly?"
"Twins?" Aisling suggested.
That gave her pause.
Hurler restarted her drums.
"Huh," Saoirse said, "Okay."

SAOIRSE:
"But then they up and told us
the worst news of all."

AISLING:
"An evil sickness we could catch.
It makes a girl's skin crawl."

SAOIRSE:
"One to end a career."

AISLING:
"That gets worse as you mourn."

SAOIRSE:
"The wicked 'pregnancy,'
its evils should be scorned."

"How to avoid 'pregnant?'"

AISLING:
"Is it stinky feet?"

SAOIRSE:
"Coming down with 'pregnant' is such an
awful cheek—"

AISLING:
"-y thing."

SAOIRSE:
"It's like I'd lose my chance at hurling."

AISLING:
"And I PÉNIS therapy!"

BOTH:
"Pick the wrong event
and you spend nine months in defeat."

SAOIRSE:
"I want to score..."

Saoirse hit the chorus once more, this time with her wishing 'Sean would shuck her little seashell while sitting by the shore,' or 'Padraig would roll her through hay till his butt got sore.'

"...All we'd do is play, play, play.
Hurling is the way!"

SATIRICAL:
Yo, it's Satirical,
let me get up on this mic.
You fools need to listen.
Imma tell this story right.

In Shamrock Violet, it's illegal
to tell us anything.
The Éirish people die of shame
any time that we speak.

"Hey!" Aisling cut in. "You know I love her, but it really sucks that Satirical's our rap bardist. I never get to hear her. If you're not going to sing her part, then it's just you over there doing this shite." Aisling jerked around in funky spasms. "For thirty seconds."
I'm sorry.
"She's sorry."
"It's not anybody's fault. I just wish I could hear her." Her shoulders slumped. She must have been feeling left out. "Let's try something else."
"Yeah."
Awe...
Sorry, Sat. Next time.
Inspired, Saoirse popped out of the hot tub for a quick dry and wrap—Aisling on her heels, wrapping herself in a towel against the cold.
"What is it?" Aisling asked.
"Come here."
She pranced to a mushroom stool outside the bar, where a large leaf-board cutout of Lorcan offered a milkshake. His likeness was probably trademarked, but eh. After a quick reposition of Lorcan, Saoirse sat on the stool and, one hand to her forehead, fell backward—but the cutout was life-sized, so she missed his shoulder and landed on the drink in a sprawl.
Aisling snorted and shifted a small lightshroom on the bar to give her a spotlight.
Saoirse spoke,

"When I heard I'd been banned from PÉNIS,
I thought my life was through."

"You're a goofball, Superspore."
"Thank you."
Still kinda is if we don't get unbanned.
True.
Saoirse continued her speech with slow flair.

"For a girl to get onto the Wolves,
what was I supposed to do?"

She turned to stare up at the mural—her heroes whom she'd never even met. Together, she and Aisling walked to the wall. Saoirse placed a solemn hand on the county's failing pride, and her overacting fell away. She sang so softly it was almost a whisper.

"I hear what they say about Tyrconnell.
I hear what they say about our team.
I hear all the rumors and the whispers."

"I hear the people speaking.
I hear our rivals laugh.
I hear the complaints of all the sisters."

"Superspore?"
"I'm okay." Saoirse fell into the mural, her back flat against the wall, looking out on the beauty of the forest. "It's just..."

"I have so much hoe-
p even in my little toe.
People think I'm crazy,
but I know we're worth a go.

"It seems like doing basic life
with a man on hand
is the most dangerous thing
that any girl could plan.

"But the team are the only men
who can understand
what it's like to lose and not give up,
so I say, 'Yes, we can!'"

She spun out from the wall, hands wide, belting back at full tempo to the forest so every tree could hear.

"So, I will score. I will score.
I will score and score some more.
Sausage gobbling competition?
I could eat them till I'm sore!

"I will score. I will score.
I will score and score some more.
I want to play around with all the men.
I swear I'm not a—..."

"Shite!" Saoirse froze. What rhymed with score?
"Defender!" Aisling sang.

"Defender~!"

"Thanks."
"Gotchu."
AND DEFINITELY NOT A GOALKEEPER, FOLKS.
"What are you?" Aisling asked.
A round of small mushroom stools faced a fire pit near the mural. Saoirse pulled Aisling onto one, then took up a stance just below the piercing yellow gaze of Aware Wolf, where she spiked her towel into the ground and struck a heroine's pose, hands on hips, picking a slow, ramping march.

SATIRICAL:
This feels like the climax!

SAOIRSE:
"I'm a full-forward born and bred,
and something-something kept."

"Nice."
"Thanks."

"With all my being full and frontal!"

AISLING:
"Fill that empty net!"

SAOIRSE:
"I wish to receive them all—
their passes coming through.
It'll be something like this.
Now watch me what I'd do."

She ran as if with a hurley down one of the gold and green paths, slipping between the pools.

SAOIRSE:
"It's a long pass in from Connor!
He's moved to my inside!
Two balls deep from Padraig,
and I bury them with pride!

Donncha slips me his,
but it goes up my backside.
I handle it with ease,
and it's a goal for all time!"

AISLING:
"She wants to score."

SATIRICAL:
She wants to score.

???:
"She wants to score."

????:
"She wants to score!"

SAOIRSE:
"Yes!"

SATIRICAL:
Chip and bauble.

AISLING:
"Strike the cobbles."

???:
"Co Tyrconnell."

NARRATOR:
Hurler wobble.

SAOIRSE:
"Are your forwards' sliotars poor?
Mine will always score!"

ALL:
"Yeah!"

THAT WAS AWESOME.
Agreed.
Little Hurler was tuckered out from all the fun and passed out face down at center pitch.
Together, they laughed their way back to their scented hot tub and collapsed.
"I'm going to save them," Saoirse said.
"I know."
She loved all the team equally, except the Shitty Forwards. She'd memorized all the good players' stats for each year going back since she'd been born, even the ones who weren't on the team anymore. They lost every game—almost literally—and had been doing so for twenty-six years, but—
They never gave up.
No matter the losses, they came back each season; no matter the defeats, they came to every practice. They still tried and tried and tried!
For all of her life, she'd been at war with her people's magic totem, the literal voice of the gods; they called it the Magic Eight Ball. It could answer any question: "Yes," "No," "Try Again Later." Blasphemers claimed it was all luck, but she knew better, as never—not once in her whole life—had it come up with the answer she was looking for. Nobody could be that unlucky. No. Lately, it did nothing but roll the worst answer of all: "Yes."
"I just wish they had magic." She'd do anything to help them.
"Maybe give them some therapy."
"Nah. That's your thing, cú."
"I don't know," Aisling said. "I think you'd be particularly good at it. You care so much."
"YOU WILL ALWAYS SCORE!?" a woman's voice boomed through the forest.
Saoirse swallowed all the laughter she'd been enjoying. The air grew cold. The forest darkened as the mushrooms surrounding the grove dimmed, the magical energy drained by danger, and pairs of monstrous, wicked yellow eyes popped into being all around them.
One set howled. Another followed suit. Then a third.
They'd been surrounded.
Only now did Saoirse realize others had joined their singing—and who.
THIS WASN'T THE MESSAGE WE'D HOPED FOR.
It was *her* entire pack.
"THEN WHY DIDN'T YOU!?" the voice bellowed.
A bolt of pink lightning struck the branch.
Saoirse and Aisling screamed.
As a living goddess of Ulster province, humbled their presence: Melak - The Wolf of Enniskillen.
"THANKS TO YOU," Melak bellowed. "THE COUNTY TYRCONNELL HURLING CLUB HAS BEEN FORCED TO CLOSE!"

Geas

The words reverberated through her head. Saoirse's knees shuddered beneath her. She collapsed into the water. Close? Her one escape: closed?! It couldn't be. She clutched at her chest.

Aisling rushed to embrace her. "Saoirse!"

"Traitor," Melak snarled.

There were things far worse than being banned from PÉNIS.

Little Hurler came to, exhausted.

Saoirse forced herself to look up at the goddess. A woman who'd always been her friend. Saoirse had never seen her so angry.

Even standing, she didn't reach the base of Melak's little toe; kneeling as she was now in the dip of her pool, the goddess seemed even more impressive.

A wolf fit for the size of the Aurum, Melak towered over all the wolves in her pack. Her coat was whitening with age. Deep scars, cuts patterned in the endless knots of their gods, ran the length and breadth of her body, crackling hot pink with the magical power of the mists. Great bronze manacles, dragging broken chains big as the mushroom cabanas, braced her forepaws, stained with the multicolored blood of crushed mushrooms. Her eyes, colossal, solid pink orbs that leaked trails of magic like smoke from the corners, glowered down at her.

Melak - The Wolf of Enniskillen, living goddess over Ulster province.

In the dimmed light of the mushrooms, the rest of the pack loomed into being. Surrounding them on every side, lounging, leering at her from the neighboring branches of the Aurum Great Woods—those that had joined them in their song—wolves the size of mountains.

Melak lowered a vicious snarl to their level, tooth all Saoirse could see, and spoke. "I shall escort you directly to the Primary Éirish National Institute for Sports. You will tell them you are a Bad Girl, and you will do so right now."

"Superspore?" Aisling asked in a soft voice.

Saoirse braced herself. *How? Why?*

TWENTY-SEVEN? Satirical asked.

Little Hurler was up, holding Saoirse's heart, squeezing all she could hug.

Warmth filled her.

"Uilleann," Melak demanded, using her nickname for Saoirse as she always did. "There is little time to waste. The balance of Ulster hurling must be preserved!"

"Why?" Saoirse asked.

"I don't have to explain anything to you," Melak said.

"Please! I need to know." It wasn't that simple. *I had a way out. We had a way out.* She'd be released from her geas, her death pact, and avoid *The Violet Intercourse*. Under the water, a current of purple mist twirled around her hand, forming a triskele, a symbol made by joining three swirls into a triangle.

SOMETIMES LIFE SUCKS.

All Saoirse had to do was throw the game, call the gods, and make the pro team—a team that no longer exists...

Aisling held her by the shoulders.

Her gods, the Tuatha Dé Danann, picked who qualified for *The Violet Intercourse* based on their hurling skills, but Ulster law said any person would be let out of their geas if they made it pro. A catch twenty-two.

Play well enough to make the team.

RISK INCREASING THE CHANCES OF BEING PICKED.

If Melak forced her here and now to turn herself in, and she missed getting rejected from the rite, she wouldn't just be put in a dungeon. She'd die.

YOU KNEW THE RISKS.

I didn't know this.

"Can my chieftain roll our totem?" Saoirse asked.

"No." Melak's words were not as angry but carried no less weight of command.

The goddess was usually so friendly, but... but Little Hurler's eyes? Those were some hard eyes. The tiny woman was center pitch in Saoirse's emotions, out in front of her heart, defiant glare locked on the wolf goddess.

"Come on." Aisling helped her to stand.

"You are the one who made this mistake," Melak said. "Why are you so afraid, Uilleann?"

Why? Saoirse couldn't meet the goddess's gaze. It was simple.

The word 'violated.'

She'd talked to Aisling about it, but her friend didn't remember. Saoirse did. Maybe it wasn't a real memory; she didn't know, but she remembered a kindly woman from when they were kids. The ritual had just finished when Saoirse found her in the corner of Croaghgorm, makeup running from her eyes. Saoirse asked what happened during *The Violet Intercourse*. The woman was crying, shaking; she said she'd been violated.

Later, the heads of Shamrock Violet ushered the woman off to the Library of Lived Experience for an emergency Sisterhood Healing Circle. She'd confessed to the crime of telling a child what happened during *The Violet Intercourse*. Saoirse had never seen her again, and when she'd asked about it later, everybody in the village had been cagey about the whole thing. She'd never gotten a straight answer and eventually stopped asking. The head of her *Color* began binding adults in geas to stop the information from spreading.

Death or being defiled.

Her heart knew that was what every woman in Shamrock Violet was picking between, whether they knew it or not. She was one of ten women chosen for this festival, among more men than she could count. She may not have all the answers, but if she were going to participate in anything, she'd do so on her own terms, not the terms her society set for her.

The clincher, Satirical pointed out, was that if it was actually so good, they wouldn't have to bind all the children in death pacts to make it happen. Saoirse would not go through with it. She would not be like *those women.*

"Superspore," said Aisling. "You're shivering."

The problem is she just threw a game to lose the favor of the gods so her roll on the Magic Eight Ball would seem legitimate, but if her plan to escape Melak's ire worked, everything she'd just thrown for would be undone. She'd lose her chance to escape *The*

Violet Intercourse, but if she didn't go through with it, jail would stop her from living the life she dreamed of. Match-fixing, conspiracy, and sabotage, the investigator had said, carried twenty-five to life.

"Stall any longer, Uilleann, and friend or not, I shall drag you away myself."

Saoirse understood. She forced herself to look up at Melak. If she couldn't make it past the Magic Eight Ball, it meant one thing. "I invoke the sacred rite! The Rite of Ritual Hurling!!"

The wolf barked with derisive laughter. A snide smile curled at the corners of her mouth. "You would challenge me while standing in the water?" She lowered her snout to her. "You may have his light, Uilleann, but you are not him."

"Ritual Hurling," Saoirse repeated.

"Fine." Melak pulled back with a growl. "I agree to the rite."

"You agree?" Aisling said, stupefied.

"I have to. I am a god."

Spores. Saoirse had bought herself a chance. "Bushbaby?"

Aisling held fast to her arm. "On your left, Superspore. Always on your left."

Little Hurler had her hurley high.

TIME.

Little Hurler?

Her heart responded.

Saoirse focused on her mind's eye. On her inner world. On Spirit Stadium, the home of Little Hurler, the great theater of her emotions. Little Hurler was there, standing at center field, hurley at the ready, helmet on. Her heart nodded. It was time to merge. Time to combine the embers of her magic with her will to win.

DANCING, FIGHTING, MAKING LOVE—

Saoirse shouted, "Uilleann!"

—THAT'S HER NAME!!!

The magic flowed. A warm fire burned in her breast. Little Hurler began to glow bright white; hot fire filled Saoirse, fueling her. The water rippled around her. Her hair fluttered in non-existent wind. Saoirse, pulled free of Aisling's grip, reached up and clapped above her head, showering herself and her friend in her special golden dust.

Her heart set, a warm crackle of energy danced about her skin. She called it "Hurling Sense." It wasn't a Whiskey, but it was a step.

Together, she, Satirical, and Aisling joined Little Hurler in staring down death.

She wasn't playing for her freedom from _The Violet Intercourse_. She was playing for her very life.

LADIES AND GENTLEMEN, Satirical called.

"Bring it on."

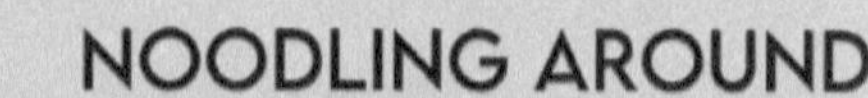

NOODLING AROUND
Saoirse and Aisling must score three goals on the pool cabanas before the wolf pack puppies can clear the pool of toys

GIRL'S SCORE ZONE
Wolf Puppies
Aisling
Saoirse
WOLVES' SCORE ZONE

THE COUNTY TYRCONNELL
HURLING CLUB

THE WARM POOLS

My Spirit

W olves howled. Pool noodles slapped. One of the wolves ate some watermelon. This match wasn't going at all how Saoirse expected.

It was not supposed to be this hard!

"Fetch!" Saoirse shouted and sent another inflatable pool ball soaring to the wolves' side of the pool.

Melak's challenge was simple. The wolf goddess emptied a mushroom full of pool toys into the pool and charged them: score three goals on her team's cabanas before her puppy pack cleared the area of play.

It hadn't seemed so bad...

"Go fetch!" Aisling bellowed, sending yet another pool ball soaring over a puppy's head. The six-foot-tall wolf puppy did the paw prance, then dashed off after the ball. "This isn't good!"

...Until Melak informed them, they wouldn't be allowed normal hurleys.

"These hurleys are trash!" Saoirse smacked a waterlogged cloth ball with her pink pool noodle. It went maybe a foot. "How am I supposed to play hurling with a limp noodle and full balls?!"

Their improvised sticks were just so awful. That was the thing with the Rite of Ritual Hurling: the challenged could set the rules, and any rules went as long as they matched the severity of what was being played for. That meant no lucky hurley.

They played in the complex's main pool, an expanse of waist-high water about the size of a hurling pitch. Fungal cultures grew along the bottom. At this angle, their luminescence tinted the mural of the County Tyrconnell hurlers, and their glorious milkshakes, shamrock green.

They'd thought about hand-passing the heavy sliotars up the pitch, but the wolf puppies would have quickly outscored them. Instead, she and Aisling worked together, doing some serious ground hurling—or in this case, water hurling—whacking away at inflatable balls floating atop the surface, sending the balls sailing to a distant sideline. With each ball sent, one of their opponents would chase them down in a merry scamper, but they were running out of balls to pull on.

TEAM BIRTHDAY SUIT BESTIES HAVE WORKED THE MATCH TO A STALEMATE!

We might be about to die, and you're calling us Birthday Suit Besties?

IT'S ACCURATE.

They barely managed a single goal so far. It'd taken everything she had just to solo a pool-otar while her limp noodle flopped along the surface. She'd only gotten a goal by making the opposing goalkeeper 'roll over' and kicking it in the net, but she wasn't sure that would work twice in this insane knick-knack paddy whack.

"I find myself wishing I had my Whiskey." Aisling pulled on another inflatable toy, and several wolves chased.

Thankfully, there was no time limit. In theory, they could play fetch forever, but she was confident they'd tire before the wolves did.

"I agree." Saoirse's 'Hurling Sense'—the magic of her merging with Little Hurler—pumped through her, a constant warm assurance. It gave her strength and better sliotar control, and helped her stay aware of her surroundings, but both were tiring after playing a double-header in one night. Little Hurler herself was already down on one knee, sucking wind.

The geas coalesced on the back of Saoirse's palm.

I'M SURE THERE ARE RELIGIOUS EXEMPTIONS, Satirical said.

I won't be like those women.

IF WE GO DOWN?

Then we enjoy our last dance!

Little Hurler had her tutu on over her hurling kit.

Saoirse looked apprehensively at the flaccid length in her palm. Her own Whiskey? Her own power move like the County Tyrone girl had done earlier that night? What if it was the only way out? Her size did nothing against the wolves. Could she even use a noodle to make magic? Saoirse let some of her golden dust fall free from her palm.

"Whiskey." Nothing. "Shite."

She shortened her grip and slipped it under a pool-tar, raised it, then lost it thanks to the long end of her noodle dragging in the hot water. She smacked her useless hurley on the tension. "This feckin' thing is worthless! I'll show you." She seized both ends, smooshing them together so the noodle resembled half a shamrock leaf and smashed it into the water, where it thwacked the surface with... strength!? "Rigidity! Aisling!" She wobbled her somewhat workable noodle.

Aisling quickly followed suit, doubling her noodle over it and forcing it to maintain its shape with a fierce grip. "Thank the gods."

The puppies were on their way back.

Saoirse dunked her new half-shamrock noodle into the water and popped up a ball with comparative ease. "I can score!"

"Do it, Superspore. I'll cover with all the balls I can pull on!"

Saoirse balanced the heavy pool-tar on the end of her bent noodle and took off through the water. The change in strategy did not go amiss.

"Stop the girl!" an older wolf barked.

Three of the puppy pack shook themselves free from playing fetch and doubled back toward the cabana goals at their end of the pool.

Saoirse's sham-nood sagged from the weight of the ball.

Stay together. You salm noodle!

WHOA NOW.

Even Little Hurler was taken aback at her outburst, but she couldn't lose the noodle. They had to win! She would not die! Aisling wouldn't be able to keep the whole pack from getting toys to the edge. If she lost this, she'd have to pick between death and being defiled while locked in a dungeon.

The race to win was on.

At the pool's edge, the wolves waited, growling over the gold and green, having pulled pool chairs into the shallows to shrink the field of play.

I can do this! She broke free of the pool and raced up the paths.

A wolf approached. Saoirse popped the ball into the air, then spun, swinging her pool noodle like a club. The sliotar passed through the noodle's open center. She caught the first puppy on the nose, knocking it aside, and heard a sound like something ripping. "Sorry."

She spun again, doing the same, sending the second wolf tumbling onto a pool chair, which snapped closed, taking the puppy harmlessly out of play before she caught the ball on her shamrock, the tearing sound growing louder. Was that her noodle? "Shite!"

Little Hurler bit her nails.

THIS NOODLE! Satirical joined in the panic.

Saoirse threw a shoulder into the last wolf, knocking it aside, and ran for the cabanas. Three mushrooms, one green, one white, one orange, 'lifeguarded' by a three-story-tall wolf relaxing in a red life preserver bed.

STUPID NOODLE!

"This time I won't!" the wolf-keeper screamed as if to convince himself. "I won't roll over!"

"There were five on the bed, and the little wolf said," Saoirse shouted.

"No!"

"Roll over!"

He almost did. "I refuse!"

"Roll over!!"

"Nooo!" the wolf cried as his own body worked against him once more, rolling over to the side, freeing access to the cabanas.

Saoirse shot with her rigid noodle and—*tsssssp*—It ripped in half. "Feck!!"

The strain of bending it in half while soloing the pack had proved too much for its fibers. Her knee-jerk reaction was to scream 'worthless,' but something in the tear made her sad. She kicked for another goal, sending the pool-tar into the heart of the white cabana, and found Little Hurler frowning in her heart, staring at her own noodle, also ripped.

TALK ABOUT A SERIOUSLY STRANGE WAY TO SCORE TWO GOALS.

No kidding.

But then, it was a strange game of hurling.

Play stopped after the goal. Saoirse and her heart took time to place their broken noodles reverently out of play. "Thank you," she spoke to the noodle.

MAYBE WE SHOULDN'T HAVE BEEN SO MEAN, Satirical said.

It did try its best for me. Being so close to death didn't mean she should treat others with malice. "I'm sorry." She'd treat her next noodle better.

A wolf leaped down from a nearby branch to help their little one out of the pool chair trap. The wolf-keeper made it back on the branch, but turned toward the trunk, whimpering, as if it was guilty of ripping up a huge cushion.

The mountain-sized wolves lounging on nearby branches barked their opinions:

"Domesticated!"

"Bowow wow!"

"Who's a good disgrace to the pack? You are!"

"I'd like to see you try!" the goalkeeper protested, but the others were having none of it.

HE'S GETTING THE CURLY PAW, FOLKS, BEING PULLED FROM THE MATCH.

The keeper-wolf scowled and retreated to a particularly distant branch, replaced by a grizzled female of equal size with a cut over one eye.

Saoirse returned to the water, but not without sparing one more glance for the torn noodle.

Aisling came to greet her with another soft hurley—County colors.

Saoirse took it. "Hey, little noodle," she said Let's win." She rubbed the foam in her fingers with care. It seemed... apprehensive? Could noodles be apprehensive?

WIN? THAT'S EASIER SAID THAN DONE. LADIES AND GENTLEMEN, WE'RE DOWN TO THE LAST BALLS.

"I know you won't break on me. You want to score, right? Tell me what you need."

"Usually I'm all for therapy," Aisling said, "but it is a noodle."

Saoirse didn't heed her. "Come on, little noodle, be hard for me. I know you're a winner. I know you want to score. I want to score too!"

The wolf puppies lined up on their side of the pool. Saoirse didn't need to understand Wolf to know the goddess was miffed.

"Superspore?" Aisling asked.

"I can't risk bending another noodle to my will." If this one tore, there weren't enough toys. Whichever one she got would be her last attempt on goal.

"I did my best," Aisling said.

"I know you did."

Aisling whispered, clearly thinking along the same lines. "We can't get more than one or two puppies to play fetch. These hurleys are useless."

Were they? They'd had more uses than she'd been initially willing to admit. They'd handled the inflatable balls well and managed her two goals despite it all.

The noodle rocked with the water. There was something about this noodle: it was... right. Warm. Full. Eager. Like it belonged in her hands, rising and falling in the undulations.

"Are you ready?" Melak asked.

Saoirse closed her eyes, took a deep breath, and focused on the water. This was it. Her life or death rode on this limp noodle.

Maybe death wouldn't be so bad. We could swim the Shannon. Who knows, they might even have hurling in Tír na nÓg.

Little Hurler sat in Saoirse's emotions, drawing shapes in the milieu with her new noodle. She seemed uncertain.

Would it be alright to die? Let it all go? She'd been okay with it before she'd found a way out of her geas. Small waves lapped at her waist. The ebb and flow of heat kissed her skin. No. There was a time when she'd have said yes, but here and now...

I want to win.

You sure?

We are going to win.

The history of Éire was one of invasions, but she would not let death invade her heart. She'd just have to find another way to avoid the rite—another way to dance.

Ladies and gentlemen, you heard her.

That got Little Hurler back on her feet, the determined expression she'd used to stare down Melak firmly back in place.

Saoirse opened her eyes. "Yes," she said to Melak.

We're here to win.

"I mean, they're either too floppy or they break." Aisling flopped her noodle about.

And it all made sense. "I'm an idiot! That's it!"

Melak howled.

"What's it?"

"Aisling!" Saoirse bellowed, seizing her friend by the shoulders.

The wolves charged.

"Stop using it like a hurley!" Saoirse seized the noodle. "See it for what it is instead of what you wish it to be!"

"Tuatha Dé Danann!" her friend screamed, holding hers at arm's length. "A noodle!"

Saoirse and Aisling both turned toward the toys.

The last play. They had something new—hope.

Heat and floppy hurleys propelled their belief through the water. They raced for the last of her life. The wolves closed in.

Aisling, with her fresher legs, reached first, grabbed her noodle by both ends, used it to corral the toys into a line, slipped her noodle beneath several balls at once, then yanked the ends away from each other to pop multiple balls into the air together, bent her noodle double, and screamed, "Go fetch!" She swung, released one end of the noodle, and a crack like a whip broke the evening air, sending multiple toys scattering across the pool. It caught up nearly half the wolves.

Not all, but enough.

"It worked!" Aisling yelled.

"We have a chance!"

"No!" Melak bellowed. "She cannot be allowed to win! Stop her!"

The lingering wolves raced for her. Several larger wolves bounded from their branches in a last-ditch effort to join the game.

"Cheaters!" Aisling shouted.

Saoirse didn't care. Her eyes were on the prize. One pool-tar remained—a golden apple embroidered with silver twigs and purple leaves.

The heat rising from the pool gave way to mist.

Green. White. Orange.

Come on, Little Hurler, let's do this!

LADIES AND GENTLEMEN, THERE SHE GOES, YOUR NUMBER TWENTY-SEVEN AND MINE, DANCING WITH WOLVES—

Her heart thumped an answer of explosive power.

—SAOIRSE STORM!

Tide. Depths. Surface.

When a noodle hit her hands, she was one with the oceans, one with the rivers, one with the gods.

The wolves lunged in from all sides, jaws mere inches from the last pool-tar.

"This one's mine!"

With a deafening crack, she brought her noodle down in a blur of gold and green. It slapped the water and caught the golden ball flush. The ball dipped below the surface in a haze of mist; the splash caught the wolves off guard, hot water stinging their eyes, and they recoiled.

The salmon: her life. The eel: her death.

She dove.

"My girl."

Fingers gripped the wooden bottom of the pool, pulled her through the paws.

She caught the pool-tar on her toes, bringing it forward. She resurfaced and kicked, launching the ball through her opponent's waiting maws, sending it soaring meters and meters into the sky.

"You are my light."

On the leaf-sown, new-mown, smooth.

Strength of the salmon! Manannán, guide my feet!

Saoirse braced herself against the bottom of the pool. Strange heat—something more than just the weight of water—pushed through her thighs, a sensation she'd never felt before: a feat. In this moment, she could have fought a whole army on behalf of Ulster...

"They know my son."

...And won.

"For Éire!" She leaped, erupting from the surface of the water. She was higher than she'd ever imagined, soaring meters above the pool as she was propelled by it, thrust forward by a golden geyser of water and light.

"They will now know my spirit."

Saoirse raised the noodle above her, spinning it in wild circles over her head. Was this a Whiskey? Had she earned a Whiskey!? She roared, "AAAAAAAH!" Skin bristling with heat, her mouth opening more, more, more till her jaw unhinged.

WHISKEY! Satirical shouted. *NOODLE STRIKE!*

"AAAAAAAAAAAAAAAAAAAAAAAAAAAAH!"

Cries rang out around her:

"Swing!"

"No!"

A blistering flash of gold and green ripped past her vision.

"Uilleann!"

And struck hope.

"Saoirse!"

The apple flew—straight and true—soaring through the attempted snatches by the eager pack, many of whom over- or underestimated their last-minute jumps from neighboring branches and began tumbling out of sight to the forest below.

Chips of bark.

Flecks of red dust.

A trail of gold.

Infused water traced the arc of her shot through the sky.

Aisling, Satirical, Saoirse, and more roared, "Roll over!!!"

The wolf almost did. She jerked awkwardly, one shoulder collapsing before she snarled and caught herself, barely managing at the last second to reach—

Shouts reached her from all around:

"No!"

"Yes!"

A whistle.

A howl.

The toys?

Silence.

Then...

GoooooooooooooooooooooooooooooooooAL!

"Winner," Melak growled. "Uilleann and her Bush."

Spores

Did you see my manifestation board? I figured if my legs are going to walk around manifesting, I will, too. Gotta pin all my interests.

Anyhoo, let's talk about the greatest word ever added to the Éirish lexicon: "spores." There's an awful lot of these feckin' things all over the place. The Aurum is the name for the great forest that grows across Éire, and that forest is covered with mushrooms.

The mushrooms are huge! Only a few varieties are small, like the mushroom grass at Low Branch Stadium or chihulooshrooms. Most mushrooms are so massive their spores are the size of a sliotar.

Spores are so common, "spore" became the go-to word for "thing": pool spores, water spores, "the spores over there," "get those spores off the table"—you hear it all the time. It doesn't necessarily mean it's made from a spore. Like, in the case of 'water bottles,' it's 'water spores.' They're bottles, but nobody says that. Water bottle. That's so weird-sounding. Water spore is where it's at.

I added a cool-looking water spore to my board.

The Forgotten County

"Yeah!!!" Saoirse raced for the water, where she leaped and tackled Aisling to the bottom of the pool.

We did it! We won! Satirical cried.

A sweaty Little Hurler smiled contentedly from the stands in Saoirse's stomach, a green and gold noodle draped across her shoulders.

Saoirse was alive! She wouldn't be escorted to PÉNIS. They'd survived! And she would not have made it if her friend hadn't been there.

Aisling pulled her tight, and together they resurfaced, sending ripples through the water. The mists that'd taken over the surface of the pool were once again little more than the usual steam.

But who was that voice she'd heard? *Satirical?*

DON'T LOOK AT ME.

If it wasn't you, who was it?

I'M NOT A MEDI-DRUID OR ANYTHING, BUT IF YOU'RE HEARING VOICES, YOU MIGHT WANT TO GET THAT LOOKED AT.

"Thank the gods!" Aisling spluttered, crying through a big smile. "I thought for sure we were gonna lose till you did all that." She waved her hands as if spinning a noodle. "You know, that thing! How did you do that? You were flying through the air." Aisling gestured in awe. "Meters and meters, swirls of gold!"

AND GLOWING! added Satirical.

"Glowing?" Saoirse looked herself over.

"You've got to be a magical girl," Aisling squeaked. "You've got to have a Whiskey!"

Saoirse seized her noodle. There was no lettering to indicate magic. Had that been a Whiskey? Didn't she have to yell the word? Satirical had shouted the words inside her head. Did that count? Saoirse hadn't been able to speak—her mouth. She checked to see that her jaw was in place. It was. "I don't think so. I have no idea how I did that."

"And," Melak spoke above them, "you probably won't for a long time." The wolf goddess loomed over them.

"That's an annoying answer," Aisling said.

"I expect," Melak explained, "the stress of the situation triggered something latent in your potential, Uilleann. It may very well be that you were very close to unlocking a True Whiskey."

A True Whiskey? Saoirse stared at the spent noodle. Her own magical power move. Whiskeys were legal 'cheats,' great feats of magical ability that came with intense drawbacks. People paid druids massive sums of money to carve Ogham lettering down the shaft of their hurley and used the power of the spell to wield the mists, but these spells were false. A True Whiskey, on the other hand, was something a player earned all on their own. Nobody really knew what it took to unlock one, so they were exceedingly rare. But if you did unlock a True Whiskey, the resulting power would carve the spell into the shaft.

Could she really be like Queen Maeve and earn her own? Saoirse rolled the noodle over in her hands. No lettering. So, it wasn't a Whiskey.

Saoirse hummed. "And that voice...?"

"What voice?" Melak huffed in terse tones.

"In the mist, I heard a voice."

"Never trust a voice you heard in the mists, Uilleann."

"But—"

"NEVER TRUST A VOICE YOU HEARD IN THE MISTS."

"Fine." Saoirse dropped it. Even if she was curious, she knew better.

"Like as not, it was a dangerous fae coming for your soul," Melak said.

"A chaun?" Aisling shuddered at the implications.

Chauns were the most terrifying of fae. Leprechauns, clúrachán, and their other cousins besides were always best avoided.

"Perhaps," Melak said. "Best put it from your mind for now, Uilleann. If there is no lettering on the noodle, then your Whiskey is as of yet out of reach, and, should it be some other magic, I cannot say for certain. You will never know till you truly put yourself out there."

"I do put myself out there. You're the one giving cryptic answers," Saoirse said, looking up to the eyes of the goddess, who was now lying down so that her face sat inside the complex. Even at rest, she dwarfed the enormous mural of the county's starting fifteen.

"I cannot say more. Not right now. Your actions have vexed me. It's taking a lot to talk with you now."

"That wasn't ominous," said Aisling.

"Please. Anything?" Saoirse asked.

The pack came to her defense:

"She played for her life."

                                                                              "She was brilliant."

              "She called us dogs."

Melak sighed. "And clearly, for some of you, it was deserved."

Little Hurler silently went "Oooh!"

A few wolves whimpered at that. Not the pups—they were busy receiving a dressing-down from a coach wolf at the far end of the mural in hushed growls. They didn't look too pleased about it.

Been there.

That we have.

"I shall," Melak said in her usual elegant tone. "I knew one who could do such magic, in a different cycle, a different age. A Warp Spasm, they called it. He was more fearsome in the water than outside of it, and that is saying something, Uilleann, but I **cannot find him**!" she suddenly shouted the last words. "Nobody can now. He is supposed to spawn on the pitches of Ulster. He *always* spawns on the pitches of Ulster, but..."

Saoirse asked, "Who, cú?"

"Yes." Melak was distant.

Saoirse passed some side-eye to Aisling, then down in her heart to Little Hurler. Both seemed just as confused.

"It is... worrying." The wolf huffed.

Aisling waved for them to return to their preferred hot tub.

"So much is different this time," Melak said. "This whole cycle is wrong. Events are happening out of order; some things are not happening at all. He should be on the fields!"

Melak shouted it, then calmed some, watching them as they crossed to the pool that had massage-shrooms and bubble streams and—ahh—she definitely deserved them this time.

Saoirse nestled back into her spot. In her mind's eye, Little Hurler was there relaxing with her, stuffed in her cleavage like it was her own personal massage nook.

She slapped a palm-sized mushroom nearby; bubbles filled the pool, slips of purple mist swirled across the water.

"As you have won," Melak said, "I can only ask that you still go, Uilleann, and today."

Her stomach sank. She'd been so caught up in the win she'd forgotten. Somehow, some way, her throw had caused the County Tyrconnell Hurling Club to close. It was as if the gods themselves had betrayed her. Now she had to face the prospect of rolling the Magic Eight Ball. She'd thrown the game to convince her gods to roll her a no. Even if she had... insurance. Now that she'd beaten Melak's pack, word of her victory would run through Tyrconnell. The puppies were yappers. Nobody would believe she'd roll a no after that.

"I want to," Saoirse said, side-eyeing Aisling, who was thinking the same thing. "I really do, but I'm sorry, Melak, I can't."

"It matters not to you that the balance of Ulster hurling must be preserved?"

"I'd like to, but with the win against you—" Saoirse held her right hand, and, thinking of her death pact, mist swirled about her wrists.

Melak's breath blew across the complex like a stiff breeze. This sigh was different—an understanding. "I should not have pressed you so."

Good thing even gods understand geas.

She agreed.

Taboos at their most extreme were geas or death pacts. While geas were rare outside of her Color, taboos were a crucial part of life in Éire. They permeated every aspect of the culture. The most famous and common were "freely offered hospitality," "eating dog meat," and "sporting wagers," though there were tons. If a person made a social misstep, like turning down freely offered hospitality or eating dog meat, they'd be punished by the gods with a guaranteed bout of cosmic bad luck.

She knew what her bad luck would be.

Violated. She'd be violated.

"You can always still go through with the roll," Aisling said.

"And risk being found guilty of whatever PÉNIS thinks I've done?" Saoirse asked. "I don't mind the ire of everybody in Croaghgorm, but the law?"

"Salm it," Aisling cussed.

In death, a person's warrior spirit turned into a salmon and was forced to swim against the Shannon, slipping between all your life's sins in the hope of making it to Tír na nÓg and reincarnation. It's where the term 'salmed' came from, which is precisely how she felt—salmed if she did, salmed if she didn't.

"Why did my throw force the team to close?" Saoirse asked. And why was her life going along with it.

"I suppose," Melak said, "as victor, it is your right to claim a Champion's Portion."

Saoirse and Aisling shared worried looks.

"Ulster's Druids at Law, the bumbling buffoons, concocted a stupid agreement years ago," Melak explained. "Any team that loses for twenty-six years in a row can be put to a vote of removal under the non-competitive clause of 201 by the other counties in the province. At face value, it's a pointless rule. After all, how could such a thing ever come to pass?"

And yet here they were.

"But," she continued, "because of the verbiage, it didn't specify if they had to lose every game or every game to one specific county."

"Tyrone." She and Aisling scowled together. County Tyrone only existed to be hated.

"Correct," Melak said.

"What an obscure rule," said Aisling.

It was little wonder nobody told Saoirse what was at stake tonight. Any druid so advanced in druidic law would spend their time in Emain Macha, Ulster's capital.

Drawing from CSI: Enniskillen again?
Always.
She was sure this would be an excuse for Aisling to go on one of her tirades about why writing was useful. Saoirse was glad she didn't.

"You were the last game of the season in every regard. PÉNIS showed up to ensure that no matter what happened, it all went smoothly, but with your final act—"

"No wonder she hated me," Saoirse said, her investigator's actions finally making sense. "Everybody must hate me. This is a super high-profile case."

"Everybody in the county probably hates you, Superspore."

She looked up into the yellow eyes of Lorcan in the mural, hoping for some reprieve, and found none. She'd cost the county its hurling club. There could be no greater dishonor.

"They may, Uilleann, but there is hope—a clause in the small carving. If you are declared to be a Bad Girl, that is, found guilty, then there is to be a rematch between the county's premier clubs: the Wolves vs. the Sperrins." The goddess leaned forward with an eagerness, as if to inspire hope, but both she and Aisling only sank deeper. A scramble told her Little Hurler was working to stay above water.

"A matchup we've lost for twenty-six years," Aisling said.

Saoirse fully submerged, leaving her heart behind.

That's an awful turn of events, folks.

You said it.

The only way for the Wolves to maybe continue was if she turned herself in? They were the whole reason she threw! To get out of her geas, she had to turn pro.

If she rolled a 'Yes' on the totem after winning this game, it was only eight days until she'd be committed to *The Violet Intercourse*. Eight days. Eight days! Trials—even if the team hadn't gone belly up—were several weeks away. Her extra time from dodging *The Violet Intercourse* to attempt going pro was up in smoke.

They'd had twenty-six chances.

Think that again, then look at the mural. Saoirse resurfaced to "Superspore?" and a comforting hand from Aisling.

"Emergency staves," Melak said, "have already been dispatched to every corner of Tyrconnell on the hope that you were a plant, which is ironic, Uilleann."

"How?" She wasn't a plant, but Melak didn't seem keen to elaborate.

"These Emergency Trials," Melak said, "will put together the single best team this county can possibly field for this last chance to save you all. Two weeks, with only the very best champions being allowed to compete from each city across Tyrconnell."

"A last chance trial!" Aisling jumped for joy. "Saoirse!"

But if this wasn't the worst news she could have heard—"You've got to be joking!" Saoirse twisted back into the scar. A game she'd dreamed of, and she couldn't even compete!

"Is this not good news?" Melak asked.

"I'm banned from PÉNIS!" she whimpered.

Suspended.

"Suspended from PÉNIS," Saoirse clarified.

Drops fell in her heart, Little Hurler sniffling again.

The gods had betrayed her, hadn't they? They'd set this situation up on purpose just to ensure she couldn't escape! Saoirse picked up a pool-tar and hurled it at a nearby mushroom. It didn't help. "With my ongoing investigation, I'm legally barred from any professionally sanctioned activities, locations, and personnel. Besides, I couldn't even play. I'd be in a dungeon during the final match."

Melak sighed. "I should have beaten you myself."

"That's your answer?" Saoirse couldn't believe it.

"I will do what I must to keep the team alive. I will not make the same mistake as those fools in Ossory."

"Where?" asked Aisling.

"Precisely." The wolf goddess stood. Her pack followed suit. "Things are happening out of order. Creatures invented across the seas are a part of us now. The Fianna have come at the time of Mac Nessa. We've Bricriu but not the Light of Lugh. They wear yoga pants with tunics, setter boots with spears—it is as if time itself has compressed. Something has gone so very wrong. Should I ever get my paws on the Swan, I swear, Mother Danu, to tear its wings apart one feather at a time."

Saoirse didn't have a clue who most of the people Melak had just named were. The wolf sounded like she was talking to herself. Something was clearly wrong, whatever it was. "The Swan?" she asked. Her dad talked about such a monster in the old stories, but it wasn't real.

"The Swan?" Aisling repeated, hopeful.

Inside Saoirse's heart, Little Hurler held up a leaf-board cutout of a creepy white monster.

All three shared a disappointed look while Melak continued her gaze toward the middle distance. Well, Aisling missed Little Hurler's look.

The goddess rose. "This time, I will not let Tyrconnell be the Forgotten County."

"Melak," Saoirse said.

"Forget what I have said, Uilleann. Know that I was unaware of the death pact involved in your choice. I thought you merely wished not to live life in a dungeon."

"I don't."

The goddess nodded. "Be true to your heart. Go, see to it that they roll this artifact, remove yourself from _The Violet Intercourse_, then go to prison. You'll live, and so may he." Melak turned to go. Her pack followed suit.

Saoirse called after her. "What do you mean by forgotten county? What's going to happen to Tyrconnell?"

The Wolf of Enniskillen paused, one paw hovering off the branch. She set it back and fixed Saoirse with a meaningful all-pink stare. "Ulster law. Any county without a professional hurling team immediately forfeits the right of territory to its neighbors."

"Forfeit?"

"You'll become part of County Tyrone."

Satirical Story Time
Spirit Stadium
Saoirse's Emotional World

SATIRICAL'S
BROADCAST BOOTH
She's almost always up
here shouting about some
nonsense

THE COUNTY TYRCONNELL
HURLING CLUB

LITTLE HURLER'S
HOUSE
Complete with a
field, goals, locker
room, jacuzzi, and
lots of spare snacks

THE
SNACK STANDS
The psyco
Spectators, Satirical
sells tickets to,
gotta eat something!

THE
STADIUM PEWS
Stomach the action

Manifestation Board

Chastity!

S he had not planned on using her insurance. If she did, if she pulled a trick on the Magic Eight Ball, the voice of the gods, it'd ruin her with the Violet. She could be ushered off to the Library just like the woman she'd seen crying—the girl who'd never come back, the one who'd been violated. Now? Going to trials risked ruining her life with the law. But it was either that or be a part of, mother-feckin' Tyrone! If only her people felt the same way.

THAT COULD HAVE GONE BETTER.
Yeah... it sure could've, cú.
"Fuck you!"

"Cheater!"

"Traitor!"

"We hate you!"

"Kill yerself!"

The moment she'd gotten back from the game against Melak, she'd been swept away by a current—this river of hatred. Saoirse stood in the courtyard of Croaghgorm Hollow, her city. The only thing shielding her from her people's anger was a podium made from crumbling rock and the tiniest sliver of hope that, somehow, some way, she'd win a round of her worst holy ritual.

Croaghgorm Hollow was a city carved inside the cavity halfway up the trunk of an Aurum Great Wood. The city stood seven stories tall. Carved in the round, county colors hung off every banister. Faces loomed at her over every rail. Stairs sagged under the weight of games lost. Croaghgorm was a city of pride. Saoirse had underestimated their anger at her failed shot.

One person can play for Croaghgorm, Satirical said.

She'd gotten details on Emergency Trials, too. They were a two-week affair; cities from across Tyrconnell were allowed to send a limited number of hurlers based on population. That way, the event logistics were manageable given the timetable. And Croaghgorm got one. Everybody knew it would have been her.

SHOULD HAVE BEEN.
Should be. But she'd thrown.

MAYBE THAT'S WHY YOU'RE BEING CHALLENGED TO CHASTITY!, Satirical said. *AN EXCUSE TO WASH AWAY YOUR SINS?*

That went some way to lifting her spirits, especially after she'd been stripped of her lucky hurley and Aisling had been whisked away. *I'm still suspended.*

YOU AND I BOTH KNOW WE CAN'T LET THE COUNTY BE ABSORBED BY TYRONE!

True.

Her *Chastity!* proctors stood across from her. Affectionately called Triple K, the Kwality Kontrol Kouncil were the Mothers Superior of Shamrock Violet. Mother Uilefaoimo O'Gasm, whose face was a pudgy, lopsided blob; Mother Mai Kleetoris, who wore a manic expression, a nose ring, with blue hair picked out from beneath her wimple; and Mother Karen About, an otherwise kindly face contorted in rage, were a three-meter-tall, three-headed triantess dressed in a Violet habit with the symbol of the feminine upside down in the center of their bandeaus.

They looked like they were having a good day. Maybe Satirical was right, and this was an attempt to cleanse her of her sins and send her to trials on a high note.

Several sums—high-ranking women of Shamrock Violet, wearing Violet habits that marked their status—busied themselves with setting up the balloon arch and ritual game board. Saoirse tried to catch her father's eye.

Chieftain Cathal, a skinny man in robes a bit too short for him, had just finished chatting with the triantess. When he caught her eye, he gave her a big smile—the kind that said it was fine.

Her worry melted away. After everything that happened, this game was rigged in her favor!

Triple K held their arms out to Croaghgorm, and Mother Uilefaoimo O'Gasm, who always sounded like she was complaining, spoke. "Ladies and gentlemen, let's play, Chastity!!"

The crowd booed something fierce.

THEY CLEARLY DON'T WANT YOU TO WIN.

Saoirse rested her hand by the big red button set in her podium.

Chastity! was a Shamrock Violet test. Women competed against one another to prove their faith by answering a series of questions from a large board. Usually, there were five categories, each with five questions, and three women competing. Today, only one square denoting one question sat on the board, and she had no competition. It was all or nothing between her and representing the city as Croaghgorm's Champion for Emergency Trials.

"As always, I'm thine blessed with the blessed-est—best. Whatever. Mother Uilefaoimo O'Gasm, a non-trinary, druidically affirmed, hearing-impaired, sexually frustrated, autistic, with robes disease."

Applause greeted the introduction.

What even is robes disease?

Saoirse shrugged. Who knew.

Little Hurler pointed at her knees.

Nah, I doubt it's chafing.

Triple K waved the city down and regained control of her sermon. "Today the lordess has brought-eth-est us thine, Saoirse Storm. Saoirse is being-eth given-est this decree by the gods. A best one...eth. Ah feck it."

Triple K's left-side head started foaming at the mouth.

"Forgive Mother Mai Kleetoris," Uile said. "She's testy until we rub her out. I'm sure those of you unable to participate in *The Violet Intercourse* understand."

The entire Hollow cast a shamrock over themselves. Saoirse quickly did the same.

"Now," Mother Uilefaoimo said, "should Saoirse be given unto answering correctly, she will represent Croaghgorm as Champion in thine Emergency Trials."

More jeers.

The other women in her Color seemed to hate her on principle. They were probably most eager to see her be humiliated. The ugly girls and many of the older women nodded. They were among those who hated her the most. They, like her, probably thought the event was being put on to punish her. She was famously bad at it.

Mother Karen About shot furtive glances about the crowd. She whispered something to Mother Uilefaoimo O'Gasm.

Triple K turned back to the crowd. "We have another surprise."

THIS IS FISHY.

"Should she lose," Uilefaoimo said, "she will be banned from playing for the Camogie Cunts forever."

Several whoops met this announcement.

Mother O'Gasm continued, feeding off the crowd. "Her hurley will be snapped!"

"What?" Saoirse shouted.

"And," Triple K spoke in unison, "she will be forced to roll her fate on *The Violet Intercourse*!!!"

They all shamrocked again, and Croaghgorm cheered. Men and women gripped the banisters with savage anger.

This is absurd! They can't just spring this on us!

This was supposed to be rigged in her favor! She shot a look at her father, who seemed equally appalled, his jaw hanging open in pure disbelief.

Little Hurler made an extra shamrock just in case.

"What do you mean by 'banned'?" Saoirse asked. "Like a few weeks or—?"

"Forever," Mother Mai Kleetoris spat.

"This is unfair!"

"To-eth thine category," all three heads said together.

"Wait!" Already!?

"Satirical Trivia!" Triple K shouted.

The crowd hollered at this.

Saoirse's stomach churned like the gods were using it to clean their sliotars. Satirical Trivia!? She ran her fingers through her hair. This was her worst holy category!

Little Hurler was seriously reconsidering her nightcap.

FECK. LADIES AND GENTLEMEN, THIS IS BAD, Satirical said. *GET UP ON THE EDGE OF THOSE SEATS AND LOCK IN! IF WE CAN'T LAND THIS QUESTION, WE'RE DOOMED.*

Little Hurler made up her mind. She shook out her arms and legs, stepped up to her own makeshift Chastity! podium.

Saoirse did the same, gripping the crumbling rock hard. If she could prove herself chaste... She flashed a quick glance at her dad. He'd recovered. He tapped his breast pocket.

Her heart skipped a beat. He had it on him, and they were going for it. Okay. She might not only get to be champion but also skip the rite!

OR LOSE EVERYTHING.

Little Hurler had on her boxing gloves. Saoirse balanced on the balls of her feet, shifting her weight, ignoring the crowd. If this was how it had to be, "Bring it on."

"Very well," Triple K said in unison. "Pick your category."

"I'll take Satirical Trivia, please, Mother Uilefaoimo O'Gasm."

"Satirical Trivia! Admittedly, it's the only square we have on the board."

A shapely Violet sum sashayed in front of the board, arms out wide to indicate the square, which magically turned into an image of hope. Saoirse knew that symbol anywhere: a curve like a crescent moon, an éireconda slithering, and a long, straight mark!

The logo for CSI!

Her heart roared. Her haters groaned. Satirical stayed on edge.

They'd wanted to see her fail, and she was as famous for being bad at Satirical Trivia as she was for being a nerd about CSI!

This point is free! She'd almost forgotten the game was originally rigged in her favor!

DON'T UNDERESTIMATE THE KKK!

Mother Karen About's eyes kept a firm watch on the crowd.

Mother Uilefaoimo O'Gasm read from a stave in her hands. "In CSI: Enniskillen, when Colleen Sherman, voiced by Rita Righta, is offered a chance to become the principal detective, why does she turn it down?"

All the tension fell right out of her body.

HERE I WAS, AFTER THINKING WE WOULD DIE OF HUMILIATION.

Right? This was too easy!

CSI: ENNISKILLEN. RECITALS IN BALLYBOFEY, TUESDAY NIGHTS AT NINE, FOLKS. LISTENER DISCRETION IS ADVISED!

She knew the answer. *She didn't want to join because she'd become pregnant and wanted to care for her child.* More proof that pregnancy killed careers. She wasn't against having kids one day, but she was only eighteen! She could worry about kids after she'd won a few All-Éires and a couple of All-Star competitions.

Little Hurler agreed with a high-five through her heart.

BUT IS THAT HOW TRIPLE K WANTS IT PHRASED? Satirical asked.

Shite. Good point. They'd be expecting something Violet.

Saoirse slapped the buzzer on her podium. A bit of the rock crumbled away.

Everybody leaned in to hear her answer.

Saoirse asked, "What is the Paddyarchy?"

The onlookers gripped the banisters. Kids leaned past the rails. The whole Hollow held its breath. The three heads of the KKK debated in hushed whispers.

This is taking a while.

IT MUST BE REALLY CLOSE TO THE RIGHT ANSWER.

Thank the gods they didn't ask about something like Kin and Cow or Mother Kathleen.

HEY, I LIKE KIN AND COW.

What?

LITTLE HURLER AND I LISTEN SOMETIMES WHEN PRACTICE IS SLOW.

You? Listen? She must be more tired than she'd thought if her alter ego was starting to have a life of her own.

"Good people of Croaghgorm," Mother Uilefaoimo O'Gasm complained, "we've decided. Thine Paddyarchy is indeed sinful. Oppression brought unto us by men named Paddy—each day we interact with the Paddys, we dare a dreadful dance of disaster." Triple K held their arms out in a sermon. "It is because of the Paddys dance is illegal to the women of the Violet, as it takes two to tango."

Many people nodded in solidarity.

What does this have to do with our question?

I HAVE NO IDEA.

"All this is to say," Triple K said, "you got it wrong."

The crowd roared. Cheers rang hollow. The Camogie Cunts shook proud fists at her.

Saoirse couldn't believe it. "How is that not right!? It is the Paddyarchy!"

Triple K sneered across all her faces. "We were looking for the answer: What is the group of men named Paddy who conspired to create a system that would oppress her? Not: What is the Paddyarchy?"

"They're the same thing!" Saoirse shouted.

"I don't see how," Mother Uilefaoimo sneered. "You're not going to get the Champion's stave. We agreed that any champion sent to represent Croaghgorm should represent Shamrock Violet ideals, not be a good hurler. You might be surpassingly gifted on the pitch, but now you will roll the Magic Eight Ball."

Satirical was quick to get her attention. *Saoirse!*

The leader of their Color held out a hand toward the sums.

No! Her head snapped to her dad in the corner. "Chiefy?" Saoirse asked. "The Magic Eight Ball?"

Chieftain Cathal popped into action at once, seizing the artifact from his breast pocket.

"Not his." Triple K waved dismissively. "We will roll our very own!"

No. No, this couldn't be! Saoirse's eyes went wide. She glanced at Chiefy, who flashed her a signal, but despair overwhelmed her as Triple K dropped the Magic Eight Ball and kicked it at her.

"Well? Roll," Triple K spat.

The ball clacked across the wood and came to rest at her feet.

Don't do it!

The Magic Eight Ball—a black ball painted with a white circle that surrounded a black éireconda in twin loops, eating its own tail. The eyes of the snake on Triple K's ball were set with violet gems. On the inside: the voice of the gods. All one had to do was ask it a question, shake it with the magic words, and roll the spherical artifact. Your prayers would be answered.

"Pick it up," Mother Karen About whimpered eagerly.

Saoirse didn't move.

Triple K commanded, "Pick. It. Up."

She did so, shaking it softly between sobs.

"Do it right!" Mai was frothing at the mouth again.

Saoirse did. Desperation moved her arms in manic circles she couldn't control. She choked out the words. "Hey yadiyada, hey yadiyada, hey yadiyada, and a hoiyoiyoi."

The gods hated her.

"Abra kadabra alakazam! Come on, baby, mama needs a shazam. Must I participate in *The Violet Intercourse*?"

She rolled.

Her whole world held its breath.

The ball stopped. She didn't even bother to look. It'd been the same answer for several years.

"As Mothers Superior of Shamrock Violet," Triple K said together, "you are hereby banished from the Camogie Cunts for life."

She could not stop the tears.

"Sums," Uilefaoimo complained, "bring me her hurley."

Violated.

She only had seven days.

The Library of Lived Experience

Seven Days Remain

Her gods had abandoned her.

It was the next morning, and admittance assaulted Saoirse from every direction. Nameless voices spoke:

"My truth is, I lied. I did see the kelpie. I didn't warn him. He... he—"

"As a womb-bearing being—"

Saoirse rolled her eyes. "Tuatha Dé Danann," she cussed. Womb-bearing being was one of the KKK's dumbest ideas.

"—I am upset. I want him to give me more. He refuses."

"My truth is, I once stole from him."

"My truth is, I attacked her."

"My truth is..."

"My truth is..."

"My truth is...
I'm a bad girl."

That last one made her squirm, but that's how it always was in the Library of Lived Experience.

The Library was a thicket of thorny rose bushes with buds the size of her head. The thicket had grown into a dome that sheltered the buds as they slithered across the wispy, shimmering mix of pure black and bright white bioluminescent mushroom grass. As she walked, blades squished beneath her bare feet, releasing their shroom blood and coloring her skin violet.

They'd snapped her lucky hurley. Saoirse dabbed away a tear, tested the bruise on her thigh where she'd been walloped by the sums and their wooden spoons. She'd have been fine with being banished—she'd have run to the trials the same, crossed her fingers that she'd not be instantly put in a dungeon for breaking the terms of her suspension with PÉNIS, and tried to save the team—but her lucky hurley?

In Croaghgorm, hurleys picked their player at birth. They said the magic imbued in them by Shamrock Violet meant they'd never break unless you broke your covenant with the gods. Triple K had shattered hers to pieces.

I'm sorry, Twenty-Seven.

It's not your fault I went from one lose-lose situation to another. But I have to know why the gods abandoned me.

Little Hurler threw a rude gesture at the sky.

They both wanted to give the gods a piece of their mind.

A rose bud slithered after her, eager to eat her confession.

Ladies and gentlemen, I hate these things. You know, Little Hurler and I think we should challenge them to two truths and a lie. What do you think?

Go for it. Saoirse answered, smacking the bud as it came too close.

I bet we'll win. Hurler's great at reading people. It's practically her Whiskey, folks.

Little Hurler gave Satirical a cheeky wink before returning to solemnity.

Several rose buds rose up from the shroom grass, dripping violet blood. The heads followed her, pouring out garbled approximations of the human voices who'd confided in them their deepest secrets and truths.

"She told me this..."

"They arrived on black clouds "from the stars!"

"I took his cookie!"
"You have to say 'my truth is.'"
"My truthest."
"No, not like that."

Shamrock Violet claimed this place had the power to heal and forgive. People came here to unburden their sins and move forward. It's what she needed. She needed the voices of her ancestors past and friends present to hear and understand her. To hear and understand why they were *wrong* and should let her go play at the Emergency Trials. *Feckin' hatch snatchers.*

Penance trod inside her: Little Hurler had matched her dress. Violet robes, bare feet, and the typical offering—a dead rat to feed the buds that never bloomed.

In the middle of the dome, Saoirse stopped at the altar, a simple, proud stone marked with a triskele. Ogham lettering etched into the stone surface read—she'd been told—"forgiveness of another is really forgiveness of the self that let itself be harmed."

Dumb quote. It should say forgiveness is the strength to outscore those who oppose you.

Doesn't sound as poetic.

She set her dead rat on top of the altar and waited. Little Hurler did the same. They sat back on their knees in shroom grass. Saoirse added some of her golden dust, just for fun, to the shimmering glittery silver sparkle of the grass.

Everyone would rather I serial-<u>Intercourse</u> twenty-seven sets of twenty-seven men for Shamrock Violet than swing a hurley for glory.

It's times like this that you not being able to count past twenty-seven is really weird.

Sure look.

It didn't take long for one of the hungrier buds to slink its way through the air toward the stone, where it snatched up her offering with a quick tongue-like petal and an eager maw. When it finished its chewing, its petals opened up to her, bathed her in a spotlight—ready to capture her confession.

Saoirse craned her face to the light and closed her eyes. How did she want to phrase this?

Whatever it is, make it snappy. This place gives me the heebie-jeebies!

"I know." Saoirse cleared her throat and stared down the plant, ready to address the gods. When exactly the right words came to her: "Fuck you."

Oh yeah, that's going to inspire forgiveness.

Little Hurler raised both hands in rude gestures to the plant.

"Fuck you!" Saoirse shouted, the weight of all that had happened welling up in her chest. All the frustration. "Fuck you! Fuck you for everything. Fuck you for creating Shamrock Violet. Fuck you for saying girls can't dance. Fuck you for saying we can't gamble, that we can't wear dresses, that we can't bake sourdough bread!"

I thought this was going to be about hurling.

"Fuck you for making County Tyrconnell suffer! Those boys try so hard, but you make them lose. Why? They don't deserve it. They try. Where is their magic? Where is my magic? Huh? You make no sense. Make it make sense. And sexplosion!? What's that all about? If you're going to bind me to some hatch snatch ritual, you'd think you'd at least have the proper decency to let me pick whose hurley I'm hiding!"

Twenty-Seven, calm down! The gods aren't familiar with your head-canon. They won't know what Hiding the Hurley even means!

"Calm down!?" Saoirse seethed, staring into the light escaping the rose bud's open maw.

Calm down. Take some breaths. None of this has anything to do with getting you banned.

"It has everything to do with it. If these freaks didn't make it illegal—"

What? You wouldn't play hurling?

Little Hurler looked up at her with a stunned expression.

"No." Some of her anger escaped her. She deflated. "No, of course I would. I just wouldn't have to hide the rest of me. I hate it. I hate it so much."

Little Hurler kicked her in the gut.

"I can't get rid of the gods, Hurler."

Good.

Hurler shook her hurley at Saoirse.

"I just can't."

She could sense Satirical pondering this in her brain. Little Hurler sniffled. At the end of the day, her heart agreed with her on everything; she just didn't need to use that tone.

As well, you shouldn't. If you can't give up on them, maybe you should say the actual truth?

I can't. Could she?

What would life be like without worshiping the Tuatha Dé Danann: the Mother Goddess, Danu; the Good God, An Dagda; the Crow of Battle and Goddess of the Rite of Ritual Hurling, An Morrígan; or even the Lord of the Sea himself, Manannán Mac Lir? There were more gods in the pantheon, of course. Those were the most important four. Living gods like Melak were wonders of the Great Aurum Forest, but they were nothing like the gods above all. She wanted their blessing. Now more than ever. For them to be with her, to say it was okay to go to the trials and save the county from Tyrone—but, given recent events, maybe it was wrong.

What's the risk? Nobody is around.

Saoirse shot a glance at the entrance to the Library. She was alone. Maybe.

It starts with 'my truth is.'

Should she? If she lived her truth, wouldn't the gods abandon her?

Try.

Saoirse squared herself to the flower, bracing herself against the light. Why not? Why should she lie?

Little Hurler encouraged her from her heart.

Saoirse took a deep breath and spoke. "My truth is—"

"That you did it," an angry woman's voice called from the entrance.

Saoirse whipped round to find Kate, the half-back who'd taken the Whiskey tackle from the Tyrone player, flanked by several other women in Violet robes. Kate was on a crutch now, one leg heavily bandaged, one arm in a sling, a holier-than-thou smirk smeared on her broad little face.

"Go on, say it," Kate spat.

"I didn't do anything," Saoirse said, and the flower snapped closed behind her, cutting off the light.

"Can you help me?" Kate said in a mock tone. "I need to tell somebody they suck, but I'm not evil like you."

"What are you even doing here?" Saoirse asked.

"It's time for a Sisterhood Healing Session," said one of the other women.

Grand. A ritual for helping people confess to their wrongdoings. She hated these things. At least she'd finished telling the gods they could feck off. "I'll go then."

"No, stay," Kate said with an evil sneer. "I want to see you in the Gratitude Circle."

THIS FEELS LIKE A TRAP, FOLKS.

I can't just leave. What if Kate makes up a story for the investigator?

Hurler, on the other hand, was game to sprint for the exit.

"I'll stay," Saoirse said.

"Good."

The rest of the girls filed into the room, seven all told, mostly her age. Saoirse found a place among them in the circle, nearest the entrance, so she could make a quick break for it.

"Recite the poem," Kate said.

"Verse 2:15," the women chanted in chorus. "On this day, the Lordess doth come upon a cheater."

They all paused to stare at her.

Saoirse squeezed her fists, white-knuckled at her audacity. First she cuts her off her prayer, now this? "You're ridiculous, Kate."

"You're hating on our religious recitations?" Kate asked. "This came from Mother Mai Kleetoris herself."

"And it's out of context!"

"You're supposed to say," Kate explained, "'Thank you for your courage to hold me accountable.'"

"Yeah, how about 'this moment's going to swallow you in the Shannon'?" Saoirse snarled across the grass.

TELL 'EM!

Kate made a mock expression of outrage.

"You'll be safe as long as I score," Saoirse said.

"We'll get saved if you're a good Violet," said another woman.

"The County Tyrconnell Hurling Club hates you more than we do," said another of Kate's cronies.

Was that true? This girl couldn't know that, but—"Whatever." Saoirse threw Kate a rude gesture and headed for the exit, but her ex-teammate called after her.

"You may want their jersey," Kate said. "But the gods don't want your goals."

Saoirse rounded the exit of the Library.

Jobbery

S aoirse spiked the crate of sugar spores into the dirt.

Don't listen to Kate, Twenty-Seven.
Listen? I'm going to be the biggest sin she's ever seen! Slip me in the Shannon, Kate.
The grizzly bearflies burrowed their den into the back of their exclosure. The thick smell of wet fur hit her in the face. They weren't kidding. He was down bad.

Her stomach twisted, not so much for Kate, but in compassion for the bearfly. In Saoirse's inner world of Spirit Stadium, she had a section of stadium pews in her stomach where Saoirse Spectators, even tinier versions of Little Hurler, and all with a serious case of the munchies, liked to watch her play hurling or dance. Though several often showed up when she was working. Today, the little groupies had big, sad eyes for the pained grizzly.

Inside the den, the father of their local bearfly family lay in obvious discomfort—a big, hairy beast with six wings and two large insect eyes. He snuffled at her. Something large was lodged in his furled black proboscis.

"Hey there. Let's get you taken care of, big boy." Saoirse shook her box of sugar spores with one foot, rather more aggressively than usual.

Little Hurler rapped a warning against Saoirse's collarbone. She took a deep breath. The last thing she needed was to let her rage spill over into the fly and get mauled. She snatched up one of the sugar spores—white balls about the size of a sliotar. It worked a charm. The bear flopped his large paws dramatically, one after the other, on his way to the pile where he lay down at an angle that was easy for her and pawed a spore.

"Nice."

You're doing awfully well, all things considered.
I'm feckin' seethin'.
What little mid-morning sun reached Croaghgorm lit the jobbery. Saoirse sat down in the tall grass at the head of the grizzly, her shield of wood at the ready. Grizzly bearflies were notoriously territorial, and Mama was only a few feet away, licking sugar spores with her cubs.

The exclosure was made from a large floating "plate" of dirt and green grass that'd long since been tied up to a branch just outside the Hollow. There were many similar nests in the jobbery. They didn't trap the flies, hence the term 'exclosure.' Large walkways, closed off with ropes and nets, protected visitors from the creatures, who were welcome to fly anywhere and return. They always did; they knew where they were taken care of. Flies were smart like that.

Time to work the blockage out of his nose.

AND RUN FROM MOM.

"Let me see." Saoirse reached for the dad fly's proboscis when the mother grizzly bellowed in an ornery rage.

HERE SHE COMES.

Yep.

Saoirse gripped her shield and leaped back. The mother bearfly charged and was cut off with terrifying speed and power by the dad.

HE'S ALL FUR, FOLKS. THE DAD GRIZZLY GOES FOR A RIGHT—NO, A LEFT PAW. THE MAMA GOES DOWN!

Nice call.

THANKS.

The Spectators cheered.

Saoirse put her shield by the rock. Fights were over and done with quickly. It wasn't every day the mother grizzly got up in arms. She walked back to the cubs with extra sass in her swagger, then escorted her little ones up and over the netting with their spores. Saoirse still never figured out why female flies just did not like her.

SERMON ON COMPASSION—TRIPLE K: A WOMAN'S IRE IS IN DIRECT PROPORTION TO HER INADEQUACY COMPARED TO YOU. NEVER LET MISPLACED EMPATHY STOP YOU FROM YOUR GOAL.

I'm just trying to help.

I KNOW, AND YOU'RE NOT EVEN A FLY.

Saoirse grabbed the large bear's proboscis with some grumbling from the insect and began to work the blockage out of it.

She'd gotten this job almost instantly. The older women took them out for 'Jobbing Day' during Little's School. There were Hunt Jobbers and Craft Jobbers, even Sales Jobbers and more, but there was only one thing that matched her affinity: the Hand Jobber. And she wasn't just any Hand Jobber. Saoirse let some of her golden dust flow free from her fingertips, and the fly relaxed—she was a Golden Hand Jobber. She'd been able to get any blockage or kink out of an insect proboscis with little more than a proper rub and tug.

The grizzly bearfly collapsed into ecstasy at the foot of her rock. Relating to him, Saoirse leaned into his fur and murmured, "You and me both today. You and me both."

Other than the grizzly bearflies, they had a pig clan, a púca, two changelings, an elephantfly, a horsefly, and even a housefly, which were always fun to see. Plus one milking cow, a small nest of camelflies—the two-humped kind—and a ton of good snacks. Great place to work.

Saoirse picked up the pace with two hands, using liberal dust as the proboscis became fully extended. A good hand job was tiring work, but eventually—"Boom."

The grizzly bearfly sneezed out the broken mash of spore shells, like shards of pottery covered in green mucus and blood.

"Top left, where dad keeps the sugar spores."

The Spectators whooped and clapped, and one even adjusted the scoreboard to read 1-0 for the goal.

"That's got to feel better, right?"

The bear huffed.

"Here, snort this balm and wait a bit before you start eating." She moved the crate into position and heard a—"Woo!"—that meant Aisling had arrived. Sure enough, her friend appeared above the tall grass, smiling beneath her bush of brown curls.

"Your hand jobs must feel amazing," Aisling said. She had a basket under one arm, cradling a baby pigfly in the other. The little insect's wings weren't yet able to take flight. Its giant bulbous eyes were covered in contented lids while it suckled on a spore of sugar water through a tiny proboscis. Aisling set aside her basket.

Saoirse shook her head. This could be her in nine months and seven days. It sent shivers down her spine.

"Superspore?" Aisling asked, sitting down beside her.

"It's nothing."

"You know," Aisling began with the tone of 'hey, let's not talk about that thing that you don't want to talk about,' "I've been reading up on this scary disease called 'erectile dysfunction.' I don't really get it, though. I feel like the druid who carved the stave wrote it in code. They said it's when a man can no longer use his Whiskey."

"His magic?" Saoirse asked, finding herself actually interested, for once, in Aisling's preferred field of PÉNIS therapy, or as her friend called it, 'sports medicine for the mind.'

"Right? At first, I thought it might explain the Wolves, but no—it's only for ages fifty and older."

And with that, it was no longer so interesting. She mentally let go—so much for a quick fix to the professional hurling team's magic.

"Disappointing, right?" her friend asked.

The baby pigfly suckled on the bottle.

"Somebody would have thought of it by now," Saoirse said.

Her friend gave her a knowing look. "You're still banned."

"Thanks for the reminder." It made her Spectators glum.

"Now, if the team's hurlers had a blockage in their proboscises, that would be a different story. You could give them Golden Hand Jobs for days!"

"Sure, look." Saoirse sighed. "Even if men had proboscises, I doubt a hand job would fix erectile dysfunction—even a golden one."

"You mean their Whiskeys."

"Yeah."

"They'd probably need some kind of medicine from a medical druid."

"Spores." There had to be some kind of loophole to her suspension.

"Kate?" Aisling asked, gently rocking the baby pigfly.

Leave it to her friend to hit the sliotar in the sweet spot. "Do you think the team hates me?" The gods were one thing, but what Kate said was getting to her more than she'd thought.

"You're the best full forward in all of Ulster camogie, you know. Maybe even all Éire." Her friend bent to catch her eye and held her gaze. "I can't give you a golden hand job, but I can hand job your soul."

Therapy. Saoirse grunted. "Nah, I'm good, cú."

"Figured. You couldn't score under this *pressure* anyway." Aisling set the piglet aside and let it run free, where it immediately went for the large grizzly bearfly and climbed him like a mountain.

Saoirse knew full well what Aisling was doing: trying to goad out her frustration. And, spores, it didn't sound so bad right now.

Aisling grabbed her shield and held it before her, mockingly dancing about. "You have entered my No-No Zone."

Saoirse almost laughed. Aisling was giving this her full focus.

"This isn't going to work," Saoirse said.

"Isn't it?" Aisling kept dancing. "I brought sliotars!"

Saoirse checked the basket. Aisling had indeed brought sliotars. Plenty of 'em. "Fine." Saoirse spilled them across the grass.

"Goal's the hall to the feed room?" Aisling asked.

The large hall set into the wall behind Aisling was way too big to be readily defended, but it was the best they had. "Sure."

"Think you can score?" Her friend teased. "No-no!"

This time, Saoirse did snort. Aisling's favorite player was a legendary Cork Camogie captain from a generation past. She kept her collectible player stave in her room—Captain Pressure. A full-back whose defense was so legendary they said any time you got caught inside her trap, you'd entered her No-No Zone—a place from which no player could score.

Saoirse sighed. Captain Pressure never went pro. She'd played only one year, then disappeared. Saoirse's geas formed on the back of her hand. What if that happened to her?

TAKE HER DOWN, TWENTY-SEVEN.

Little Hurler cheered her on.

If she couldn't, then—"I hate the KKK!" Saoirse hurled an angry sliotar at Aisling, who blocked it with her shield.

"No-no!"

The Spectators groaned and gave Aisling a point for the block.

That felt good. "I hate PÉNIS!" she hurled another.

Another block. Another round of sad Spectators.

"Number twenty-seven, the boldest full forward in all the stars!" Aisling called.

DO ANOTHER!

"I hate the fact that they trapped me with this!" A third.

Block. "Elaborate! Tell me more!" Aisling said.

"Feck the Tuatha Dé Danann!" She threw hard for a goal!

The Spectators cheered.

"I hate that everybody blames me for something that's been happening for twenty-six years!" Saoirse threw.

"No-no!" Aisling danced.

And Saoirse just—"I hate..." she just—"I hate..." she just couldn't anymore. "I hate that there's no point in getting good at something because the gods can just take it away!" She collapsed.

Aisling wrapped her in a hug. "Superspore."

"If I stay, the team can't possibly win. I have to turn myself in. If I am found innocent, I can play, but there will be no team or county left to play for! If I go now, I risk being found guilty by PÉNIS before I can even save them. No matter what I choose, I lose! What do I do?"

"Maybe breaking your suspension won't look so bad if you prove you're innocent."

"It fixes nothing," Saoirse said.

"Why do you care what the gods think so badly? Or Kate?"

"I can't throw them away. I can't throw away Shamrock Violet. If I did, it would be like throwing you away, throwing away my people, throwing away my clan."

"And if society sucks?"

Saoirse balked.

"Given what's happened lately, I think it's a legitimate question."

If they sucked? This had to be punishment for playing fast and loose with the rules—watching dance performances, doing 'trick shots' as an excuse, and baking sourdough. Why was it a crime to be herself? If she did go, despite having no hurley, despite her suspension, despite not having the gods, she'd be stealing the spot from whoever Croaghgorm sent to be their champion. All because of that one word: violated.

"Bushbaby?" Saoirse asked.

"Hmm?"

"When I die, will I make it up the Shannon?"

"Depends. Is there hurling involved?"

Greensleeves

Hurling: gone. Hurley: gone. Her out: gone. Her gods? At this point, there didn't seem much reason to hide this last, but she had to. Saoirse had left behind Aisling at the Jobbery because perhaps there was nothing the gods wouldn't steal away. Or would they steal this, too? Would they steal away dance?

The 'Secret Spot.' Her dad found it. A place away from Violet eyes where she could fulfill her 'special needs.' A place where she could cheat the gods. It didn't look like much, just a clearing, a patch of empty red bark where the bioluminescent fungi blocked the path from view. The speckled mushrooms, twenty-seven or so feet tall, tilted into the clearing, creating a canopy that blocked views of her from above. It was secluded, serene, and had the world's best view.

When her dad brought her here, she'd thought it was for her hobby. She loved to 'collect vistas.' Aside from scoring, it was her reason for wanting to play pro: to travel, to see things, to collect beautiful scenes she'd never be rich enough to see otherwise. She'd not realized the true view wasn't out into the Great Aurum Forest, but down.

The music slipped softly on a strange breeze; it always had.

Ankle hooked into a strap so she wouldn't fall the mile-long drop to the forest floor, Saoirse lay on her stomach, listening, watching what she never got to do—dance.

It was beautiful. They were beautiful—three-by-nine dancers of the Ardnamona called Greensleeves. Every facet of their being was illegal—elegance, grace, poise. She couldn't imagine being such a bad girl. Some of them even wore heels or sports bras instead of chest wraps, and no bodysuits! Saoirse had a flowery apron with a ruffled hemline she kept buried at the bottom of her equipment bag, but she'd never been able to bring herself to wear it. She'd be excommunicated—that was even before she dared to bake sourdough bread. She'd die if she ever wore the pro camogie skort! Just thinking about it made her hot.

Gods. She knew she was casting a net over herself by watching. This habit of hers would be a big sin to slip in the Shannon. She didn't care. Greensleeves practiced here to keep their new dances secret. She couldn't hear them speak, even though she'd always tried. Her secret spot was just too far away, nearly a quarter mile. But it didn't stop her from watching, learning, and trying.

Smooth motion. One traced an arc with her foot; the rest followed. The leader walked them through the steps while a man played the harpsichord. Today, Saoirse couldn't even join. Dancing was illegal for women in Shamrock Violet. She only got away with dancing by playing hurling, got away with dancing by practicing 'trick shots,' got away with the blasphemy that had cost her with the gods. Without her lucky hurley, she could only watch.

The gods don't need your goals.

The words clawed away at her gut. Maybe Kate was right. Maybe playing fast and loose with the rules was the reason she'd been thrown overboard, but she couldn't be one of *those women.*

YOU DON'T KNOW THAT. IT COULD BE GOING OUT ON FUN DATES, AS YOU'VE ALWAYS IMAGINED.

Now look whose coping.

A pair of kicking feet in her heart told her Little Hurler was trying some of the new moves, hurley-less.

Saoirse gave her a little shake to knock her off. She might not want to do *The Violet Intercourse*—she and Hurler made shamrocks—but rules were rules. She didn't want to risk doing the trials without the gods' favor either.

When the Greensleeves took a break, she did too. Saoirse stood, unhooked her foot, and found she wasn't alone. Her dad was sitting on the bench of broken hurleys, watching her. A thin man in a set of robes a bit too short for him, he had a sullen but determined look today. Of course he did. Only he knew all her secrets, and she'd let him down.

"I thought about bringing the pieces of your hurley for the bench, you know," her father said with a wink, "but then, you aren't dead."

"Yeah."

"We can't roll now," he said. "The gods wouldn't change their minds that fast."

"Yeah."

"It's about what people believe is true."

"Yeah."

"And it would have been a hard sin to slip in the Shannon."

"I thought—" she said, the pain of it all finally hitting at once.

"No. Good call."

Saoirse's eyes filled with tears. Shite. She'd been hoping to avoid this. "I'm sorry, Dad! I'm so sorry! I didn't mean to get banned!" She lunged for him like she was a little girl again and buried her face in his chest. Each croaked sob seemed heavier than the last.

"Shh. It's okay." He pulled her into a warm hug. "You did your best."

That made it worse.

"You'll always be my Special Needs."

Saoirse cried. All the tears she'd thought she'd gotten out for the failed scandal. All the tears for Chastity!, for the team, the county, for her hurling pride. Nobody in Croaghgorm knew who their father was. Nobody wanted one, so nobody picked. She did. She'd picked Chiefy, head of all Croaghgorm. She could still remember his smile the day she'd told him. 'You're my dad, and I won't do no other cause I wanna one.' She'd been five. His was the best smile in all the world. She'd let that smile down.

Her dad rubbed her arm. "The rest will come around in time."

"What time?"

"Probably next season when they realize we can't win without you."

That made her laugh. *Spores.* She sniffled.

"No matter how mad everybody is, the rest of the county had to spend twenty-six years losing to County Tyrone for you even to be put in this position. They just haven't put that together yet. It's still too fresh, too painful." He moved a lock of hair out of her face.

Saoirse pulled back and smiled. "You think?"

"I know."

SOLID DAD ADVICE THERE, FOLKS.

Little Hurler nodded.

They listened to the harpsichord drift up from the dance practice, where it seemed to get trapped in the mushrooms surrounding them—loud again despite the distance.

"It's a high-profile case," her father said. "Everybody in Tyrconnell knows by now. I don't doubt they'll have the same reaction."

"I feel like I'm trapped in the middle of a river of hate, with a current sweeping me away," Saoirse said. At least here she had peace. Her dad was like a rock in that river, something to keep her from drowning.

"I think I can do something about that," he said, and smiled.

"Like what?" Dare she let herself hope he had an answer?

"I'm going to turn myself in."

No. "Dad, you can't!" she shot to her feet. The harpsichord screeched to an uneasy halt.

The deepest cut. Little Hurler shattered to pieces. Satirical whimpered on the loud-spore.

A gale of wind ripped their clearing.

He was smiling. How could he be smiling?!

"It's done," he smiled.

"No."

"When the investigator comes—"

"No!" This wasn't possible! How could they! How could the gods take him too!

"Special Needs." He stood. "The only way we save the county is if *somebody* is declared guilty. And that somebody doesn't have to be you."

"But you're not bad—you didn't even throw!"

"There is no other choice. I'm told the clause in the small carving insists-"

"I'll ask the investigator."

"And admit guilt?" He took her hands in his.

She wrenched them away. "I refuse to believe it. There has to be some other way! At least give me time to think."

Her father laughed. How could he laugh? Her rock in the river. He was going away!

"When it comes to dealing with PÉNIS," he said, "there is no time to think. They always come too soon."

Saoirse paced. Threw herself on the bench. Then paced again. All this because of one little choice. Her choice. She couldn't let him do this. "How can you turn yourself in? You know the team will just lose!"

"They need a girl like you."

"I don't want to be that girl if it means I lose you!"

Her father took a deep breath. When he exhaled, she exhaled with him. The calm stopped her feet.

"When you win the All-Eire," her dad said, "The High King at Tara is bound to give you a Champion's Portion. You can ask for my safe return."

THAT'S NOT A BAD IDEA, TWENTY-SEVEN!

Little Hurler jumped for joy.

She had to admit it was sound. "But getting to inter-county alone will take years." Her father would be trapped in a PÉNIS dungeon. She knew what those were like, what they did to people as well as he did.

PÉNIS forced their incarcerated to wear three-piece suits; to get up in the morning with an alarm; to sleep off to some godsforsaken work site and waste their day, their week, their lives on the promise of three meals a day, a cell to sleep in, and a future freedom they'd be too old and decrepit to enjoy. It wasn't hardly a life at all.

Triple K had a sermon titled 'Working for PÉNIS.' The tale was horrifying. Saoirse couldn't let him, but then, she couldn't stop him.

She met his gaze. There was a fire there. A prick of light in the back of the pupils. He'd not given up in the slightest. He really thought it was the best shot they had. She forced back tears when a loud buzz cut the tension. A striped fly zipped its way overhead, freezing only a few meters above them. Green and black, the creature looked like a large cat with a long, striped tail.

"A tigerfly!" she yelled, recognizing the tail from lessons. She'd never seen one before.

"Not just any tigerfly," her father said, practically shouting over the buzz. "A Celtic tigerfly!"

Sure enough, she could make out its blocky features. Its face looked as if it were designed in the endless patterns of their gods. These creatures were exceedingly rare.

Is this some kind of sign, folks? Satirical called.

Little Hurler looked in wonder.

"Incredible," Saoirse whispered. It was so close.

The tigerfly scratched its face, and a lone whisker fell to their feet.

Her dad picked it up as the fly zipped away. "Saoirse." He took the whisker and threaded it through one of her braids. "One day you'll learn, you don't swing a hurley to escape a life. You swing it to save one."

She met his eyes.

Suddenly, her dad whipped round to face across the mushroom enclosure and pointed at nothing. "Watch it, it's a rogue half-back!" he called, as if seeing an invisible hurler closing the distance to their bench.

Saoirse, clued in at once, joined in the charade. She leaped over the bench and juked past the invisible defender.

"A long pass in!" her dad called as she ran.

She leaped and turned in midair, expecting to catch nothing, but instead a small pouch soared toward her. She caught it and heard the unmistakable clink of coins.

"It goes through!" he said.

Saoirse paused. This was so much copper. She looked to her father, who was looking the other way.

She clutched the pouch to her chest. Then rushed back up the bark and hugged him from behind. "I promise I'll save you." But just how she would was up to the gods. Gods she simply had to get back on her side now.

He gripped her forearms. "Give them a show, Superspore."

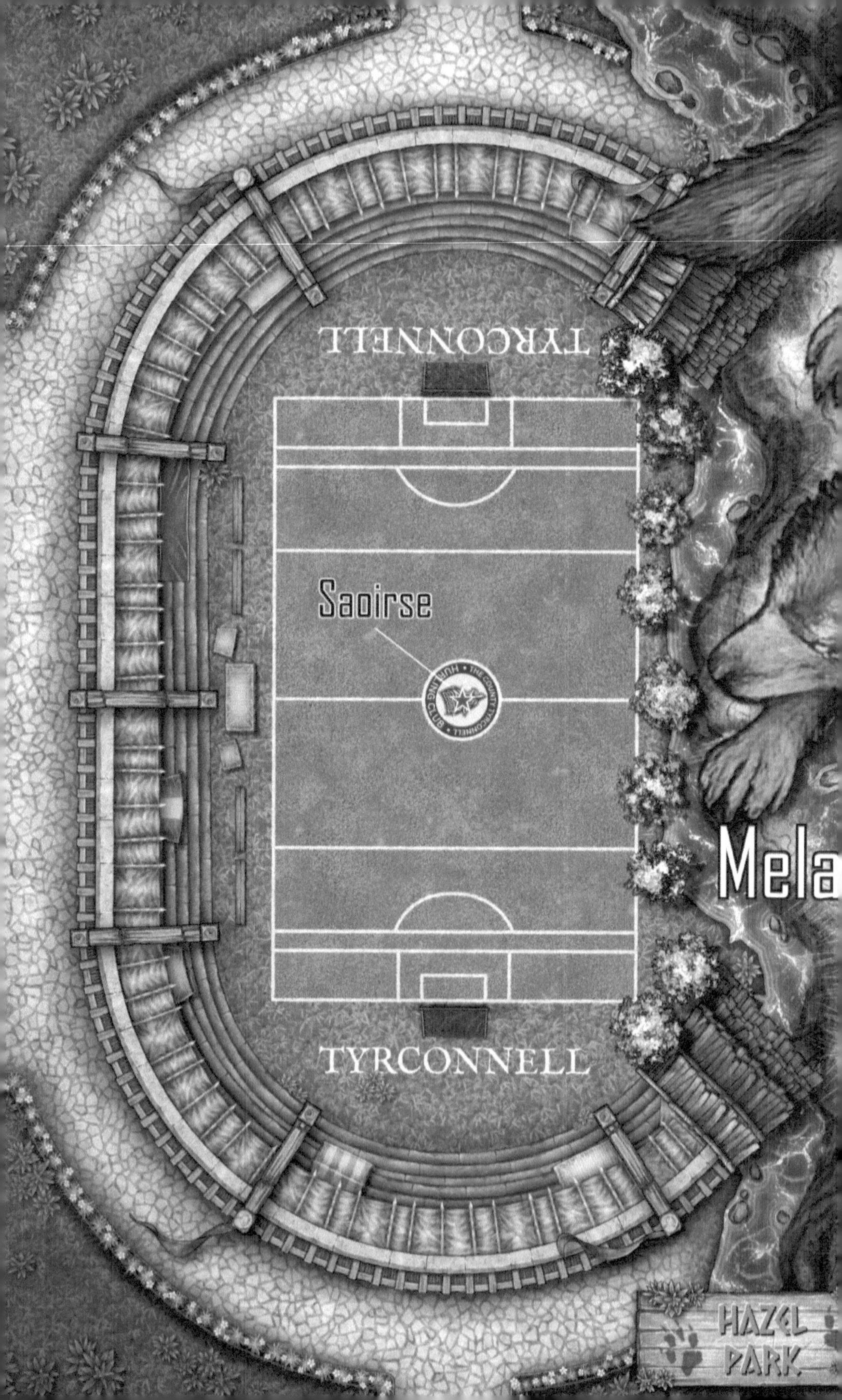

TYRCONNELL
Saoirse
THE COUNTY CLUB · TYRCONNELL HUB
TYRCONNELL
Mela
HAZEL PARK

Center Pitch Line

"**D**ad, I'm going to play hurling till my hurley wears out."

Coming down to the Ballybofey plate always struck Saoirse as strange.

In the Great Aurum Forest, rivers of colorful mist flowed through the air between the trees. On said mist floated isles made of dirt and real grass. Most 'plates' as they were called, were a few paces across. She and Aisling lost many an hour riding along through the forest, snacking, enjoying the views from on high. Ballybofey was a different beast; the plate was huge.

It went on for miles in every direction, trapped halfway off the forest floor between the boughs of the woods. The druids said it was the largest expanse of open sky in all of County Tyrconnell, short of going to the coast. Nobody was meant to see so many stars at once. If the gods wanted them to see stars, they wouldn't have grown such big trees. Yet at the same time, there was something comforting and deeply satisfying about running through the grass with bare feet. As if she was supposed to be here, and not inside the Hollow. Maybe it was why she loved hurling so much? Maybe not. Who knows.

Saoirse rode the back of a three-story-tall wolf, the one who'd rolled over to let her score. His penance was to shepherd her around for trials. He'd brought her to the only place she might be able to intercede with the gods—Hazel Park.

Two large banners of gold and green framed the entrance, and a large bronze logo for the County Tyrconnell Hurling Club stood beyond. The stadium itself was lit by a series of green and gold glowing mushrooms.

Her ride walked slowly along a thoroughfare of pavers that led to a bronze statue of Melak with one paw resting on an enormous sliotar, letting her take it all in. Pathlight mushrooms, tall, spindly black fungi whose bioluminescence was contained to a single bulb in the tip, hung over the path like upside-down fishhooks, spotlighting low garden boxes of honeysuckle flowers and simple chain fencing.

All those nights she'd stared through her vision-enhancing lenses from up in the forest had never done it justice.

The wolf took her around the side of the building. Hazel Park's stadium pews were a semi-circle. Both ends backed up to a sheer cliff, a fault line in the plate that cut right through River Eolas, where, instead of the water flowing down in a waterfall, the mists took the river up the cliff, rising to the upper tier of the river, where the water burst in soft spray.

She petted the wolf. "Is she up there?"

"She is," he said.

The large creature lay down. Saoirse slipped his nose like a slide to the safety of the surrounding grass, then shouted as loud as she could, "Melak!"

"Uilleann?" boomed the voice of the goddess. A moment later, Melak appeared standing atop the cliff face, feet caught in the spray of River Eolas. "Spores, girl. What are you up to now?"

"Finding out if I should preserve Ulster hurling. Can you give me a lift?"

Melak barked several happy laughs. "That I can."

Without leaving the cliffside, the wolf goddess easily placed a paw on the ground at Saoirse's feet. Saoirse wrapped her hand with several strands of her fur. The wolf pulled her up over the wall and into sacred ground.

Saoirse unwound herself and waved.

The wolf smiled.

We made it, Satirical said.

Yes.

Now? She just needed her answer. Were the gods with her? If she asked and they said no, she'd go right to PÉNIS and turn herself in before her father got the chance, but if they said yes, she'd make her promise. She'd save the Wolves. She'd save her dad.

You realize that means you can't dance, you can't gamble, you can't wear dresses, show skin, or—

I know.

Little Hurler donned sacred violet robes. She was center pitch in Spirit Stadium.

Saoirse matched her heart and took the center pitch line of Hazel Park, right in the middle of the Wolves logo, and inhaled. The fresh-cut grass, the sweet spray. *Yes.* Perfection. "If I promise to be the perfect Shamrock Violet, will you save me? Will you ensure PÉNIS declares me a Good Girl and still give the team a second chance? Will you help me make the team? Will you let me save them with my goals?"

Little Hurler?

Her heart responded, hurley at the ready. It was time to merge. Time to combine the embers of her magic with her will to win.

Dancing, fighting, making love—

Saoirse shouted, "Uilleann!"

—That's her name.

The magic flowed. A warm fire burned in her breast. Little Hurler began to glow bright white; hot fire filled Saoirse, fueling her. Her heart set. A warm crackle of energy danced about her skin. The wind gripped her chest, pulling from her an explosion of golden dust, a release of her latent powers.

Croaghgorm's women agreed 'the shakes' were when they came closest to their gods. Saoirse didn't need to shake, standing on the center pitch line, surrounded by the emblem of the Wolves. She didn't need to ask for any more signs.

She'd give them everything. She'd be the perfect Shamrock Violet as payment for their help. She'd follow the teachings to the letter. She'd be the woman they so desperately wanted her to be.

A sharp breath. Spray. She shuddered.

In that one moment, that one breath, she had her answer. Tears filled her eyes.

Her gods were with her.

With her in the wind that wielded her hair, decorating the pitch with a flowing ribbon of red pride, that rode the roars entangled in the grass, and scuffed the groans entrenched in each white line; with her in the soft, constant spray from the reverse falls that misted the northern lip of the field, in River Eolas, on the scoreboard mounted high up on the cliff face, the hazel trees lining the lower bank; and dancing in the purple swirling mists of the Aurum, slipping in spirals to nowhere, blown away by the silent anticipation of a crowd not yet arrived.

She didn't need to roll the Magic Eight Ball for their favor. She needn't pry.

Hurling belonged to glory.

Glory to the gods.

And the pitch to Saoirse.

This was the way—even if she'd been lifted in to find out.

"Okay," Saoirse whispered through her tears. "I forgive you, Great god Manannán—Lord of the Seas; Goddess Danu, my All-Mother; An Dagda, the Good God; An Morrígan—Crow of Battle; and the rest. For this moment, for this vista... I'm thankful. I promise from this day forward, I will never transgress again. Not for anything."

Number Twenty-Seven

I LIKE BROADCASTING WHEN SAOIRSE IS ASLEEP. SHE'S ONE BIG SLEEP POD. SO THAT MAKES IT A POD-CAST. HA! I'M SO CLEVER.

SPEAKING OF CLEVER, LET ME TELL YOU ABOUT THE TIME SAOIRSE WON THE RIGHT TO WEAR THE NUMBER TWENTY-SEVEN, THEN BROKE ULSTER HURLING.

SEE, OUR GIRL'S KINDA FECKIN' GOOD AT THIS WHOLE STICK-PLUS-BALL-EQUALS-VICTORY STUFF, BUT HURLING HAS SET PLAYER NUMBERS, YEAH? WELL, IN ÉIRISH CULTURE, YOU CAN WIN A 'CHAMPION'S PORTION' FOR SUCCEEDING AT MAJOR EVENTS AND MAKE 'REASONABLE REQUESTS.'

WHEN YOU'RE NUMBER TWENTY-SEVEN AND MINE—SHE WAS NUMBER FOURTEEN AT THE TIME—WON THE TYRCONNELL CAMOGIE JUNIORS AT ELEVEN, SHE ASKED TO WEAR THE NUMBER AS HIGH AS SHE COULD COUNT. THEY WEREN'T KEEN, BUT TOLD HER IF SHE EVER MANAGED TO PUT UP TWENTY-SEVEN POINTS IN A MATCH, SHE'D BE ALLOWED.

THOSE POOR, POOR GIRLS FROM DONEGAL...

ANYHOO, AFTER SHE GOT A SPECIAL NUMBER, EVERYBODY WANTED A SPECIAL NUMBER, AND THE BIGWIGS IN EMAIN MACHA GOT SO MANY ANGRY STAVES, THEY CAVED AND SAID: "IN ULSTER, ANYBODY CAN HAVE ANY NUMBER THEY WANT SO LONG AS IT'S TWO DIGITS, BUT ONLY SAOIRSE CAN HAVE TWENTY-SEVEN."

The First Twenty-Seven (Kickstarter)
Thank you,
Stanislav Lukashevich

Fighting Flowers

Six Days Remain

T he perfect Shamrock Violet. Sure, other Colors might not have the same rules; Sure, their teachings varied plenty; Sure, she and Aisling made up that whole bit about the Carnal Carnival, but now, if they were right...

She might get pregnant!

Magee's Public House screamed 'wicked hive of spores and villainy.' A bright, colorful thatch roof made from a wild assortment of 'spore feathers' covered a series of grey rock walls with small windows. A set of wide-open double oak doors, flanked by frosted glass panes, perfectly framed the danger.

These feckin' hatch snatchers had gone and planted *flowers*! Roses!

PETUNIAS!

Unia chunia bunnia dunias! And more besides.

I'VE NEVER SEEN A PITCH WITH STRONGER ZONE DEFENSE, FOLKS!

How was this even possible? In her made-up headcanon for *The Violet Intercourse*, Saoirse was certain it was flowers that got a girl pregnant!

OR CAUSED SEXPLOSION!

Little Hurler slid into ref's colors and pulled out her first card of the evening—a red—against the pub.

LITTLE REF'S ALREADY GIVING A WARNING, FOLKS. THE UNSHIN RIVER PUBLIC HOUSE HAD BETTER WATCH ITSELF! HURLER'S SCARY IN 'REF MODE,' FOLKS.

Saoirse backed into the High Street, eyes transfixed on the flowers. How was she supposed to go in there!? She'd sworn to the gods not but a few minutes ago to be the perfect Shamrock Violet: no drinking, no gambling, no dancing. It would be difficult, sure. She knew from recitations of CSI: Enniskillen that all three of those things were considered sacred to Shamrock Green, which most Éirish people were, certainly all of Ballybofey. Yet her choice had been the only choice that made sense.

I AGREE. AS LONG AS YOU'RE A GOOD GIRL—VIOLET SPEAKING—WHEN PÉ- NIS SENDS THEIR INVESTIGATOR DOWN, THEY'RE SURE TO FIND YOU A GOOD GIRL—LEGALLY SPEAKING—AND GIVE THE COUNTY A SECOND CHANCE.

Right. She wasn't taking any chances. None of 'her' were. Satirical even promised to stop gambling on kelpie races, whatever that was about, and deep in her heart, Little Hurler had shoved her tutu away in a locker and barred it up with every conceivable constraint known to man. Which really just boiled down to a feck ton of hurleys, glue, and willpower. The only problem was just to get her name carved down on the Champion's rolls for the Emergency Trials—she'd have to be with men AND flowers! She would have to be bad.

Saoirse stared through the open double oak doorway. This practically was *The Violet Intercourse*!

YOU'RE THE ONE WHO SAID SHE WANTED TO SCORE SO THEY'D HUG HER AND TAKE HER TO COOK STREET.

That's different.

PRETTY SURE ONE OF THE STANZAS EVEN MENTIONS LORCAN PICKING YOUR FLOWERS.

That's definitely different! Saoirse flushed. *What about sexplosion?* Her epic adventure would end with murder—and less than a day after starting! Dare she test her luck? What if it was one of the good players? What if it was Lorcan? She could kill Lorcan!

CSI: Enniskillen (Ballybofey special)—'Wolf Man.' She could hear the recitation now:
'Looks like he died from sexplosion, detective,' A MAN WOULD SAY ON THE SCENE.
'Tried to pick flowers with a woman outside the clan?' THE DETECTIVE WOULD ASK.
'Indeed.'

PIECES OF LORCAN LAY STREWN EVERYWHERE, HIS HURLEY STUCK IN A TREE. A GARDEN OF DAISIES GROWS NEARBY.

'Guess he couldn't handle...' (THE DETECTIVE ADJUSTS HIS TINTED LENSES) 'The Violet Intercourse.'

Bowowowow! She and Satirical finished together.

The last bit would be the cool horn sound effects that complimented the recitation. Feck. She didn't want to go to regular dungeons just as much as she didn't want to be in PÉNIS ones!

Bunch of messers! Whoever owned this business should die!

Little Ref pumped a tiny fist under fierce, determined eyes.

You really think we've got this?

WE'D BETTER. YOU'VE ONLY GOT SIX DAYS LEFT BEFORE EVERYTHING ENDS. TRIALS MIGHT LAST TWO WEEKS, BUT IF YOU'RE NOT ON THE TEAM IN HALF THE TIME—

She'd die to her geas, and her dad would be lost to the dungeons for life. Saoirse sized up her chances. Men in setter boots with jeans and spears inside, women in bonnets, frocks, and Doc Martens outside. Was that really so strange a sight as Melak had mentioned?

THERE ARE WOMEN INSIDE! LOOK!

Saoirse peeked through a window. Satirical was right. There *were* women inside. Settled at several tables on a raised platform. They looked like they didn't have a care in the world. They didn't seem like players.

Maybe it's a safe zone?

I mean, I could be wrong about the whole flower thing. Saoirse set her jaw. *We're going in. I can't turn back now. If I don't claim the spot as the Croaghgorm's Champion and Triple K sends another player, I'll never be able to play for the Wolves.*

Little Ref nodded.

Saoirse seized somebody's hurley from a rack near the entrance. "Let's do this."

HERE SHE GOES, Satirical cried, *YOUR NUMBER TWENTY-SEVEN AND MINE, READY AT THE DOOR LINE. WILL SHE BE ABLE TO PUSH THROUGH THE SMELL AND SOUR FLOWERS?*

She traced a quick shamrock prayer. Little Hurler was on defense. Ready for anything, Saoirse crept in a low, ready stance over the threshold. Salm, it was loud. She scrunched up her face. Man stank. The pub was full of rough, grimy hurlers who didn't give her a passing glance. Bioluminescent shroomlight strings laced with honeysuckles hung from the ceiling. She maneuvered inside, battle-ready.

Let the flowers come. Let them taste my ash! Let them see the strength of my shot! Saoirse's eyes darted about the dangerous ceiling for falling petals.

She headed left toward the women on the raised platform. If she could just make it to them before anybody started picking flowers, they'd be safe. But spores, it was as terrifying as it was exciting. She was with the team! Her knack for memorizing player stats let her identify any number of incredible men.

Her Spectators pointed eagerly as they passed faces they'd only ever seen from miles away.

There was Connor Mac Cairbre, their long-time left corner-back. His long, lush green hair was the kind of thing women dreamed of. He had a penchant for seeing the little details on the pitch.

Seamus! Oh! He was an incredible left half-back, distinguished by his bright pink ponytail. He had an intense air about him she'd never captured from far away.

Tuatha Dé Danann! She squealed softly to herself, recognizing a man described by his deadpan expression and bright blue headband, which he wore to show off his proud brow. It's Ronan mac Eóin! From Malin Head! He's supposed to be amazing at center half-back. He had been sent to the trials?! *That's amazing.* And it wasn't just him. The carve downs were a who's who of all the best minor league players from across Tyrconnell. One man held his hurley like a club. The boy in the corner had a strange, fish-like appearance, eyes so far apart he looked like a trout.

Wow. The energy in this room. The hurling skill. It radiated out from each man like the glow of a mushroom. They weren't afraid of the stakes facing the county. They were hot. Ready. Dance partners for her scoring show. *These trials are going to be amazing!*

Something brushed her elbow.

"Excuse—"

"Roses! Aaaah!" Swinging like she was trying to puck one over the bar, Saoirse turned and struck the man speaking hard across his face.

GOAL!

"Ah! Feck!" he said, recoiling to grab his cheek, steadying himself on a table.

"Shite! I'm sorry!" Saoirse said, reaching a hand. "I thought you were a flower!"

"What?"

The man spun around, and she honestly considered another gobsmack—he might actually be a flower. If Lorcan was a beast, this man was a beauty. *Tuatha Dé...* he was so pretty!

Smooth, handsome features, a cocky smile, a wave of blue hair trimmed short at the sides, with deep blue eyes to match, and devious, fox-like features. Her body must have been a fan of Captain Pressure because a warm tingle flooded her no-no zone.

She readied her hurley.

"Easy, Little Shroom." He smiled.

The way he spoke, so relaxed—being in this man's presence was like soaking in the Warm Pools. Oh, she could not think those thoughts! Saoirse turned and smashed a light string of petunias like it had left her on Cook Street without sticky buns. **Crack!** "Piece of shite petunia!"

THAT'S SIX POINTS, TEAM SAOIRSE! LET'S GO!

A rowdy Little Ref ran to each kill with a yellow card, her Spectators cheering for more dead flowers like she was killing Fomorians in a coliseum. Saoirse would oblige.

"CSI: Enniskillen — Petal Crime Unit. Dead petunia."

"Whoa," the man said. "Nice strike."

Saoirse huffed, still active with her sword hurley—but when she went to wield it again—"Oh no..." It had cracked, split right down the bas.

Halfway into another yellow card, Little Ref's eyes started tearing up. Saoirse sniffed.

THAT'S NOT GOOD.

Some poor man's hurley. They were in trouble.

"I'm sorry," the man said, rubbing his temple. "I'm too hard-headed. Here, let me take a look." He reached for her hurley, but she yanked it back.

Her gaze fell to his slender, very distracting neck, where he wore not one, not two, but three bronze torque necklaces. Her mouth fell open. This man was loaded! He wasn't just rich—he was rich-rich. Who had the money for three full torques!? Probably wasn't very good then...

"I'm not buying my way in, thank you."

"Sorry." Her judgment must have been all over her face. Feck, she looked like a fool—a hurley-less fool.

"All is forgiven," he said. "As long as I'm not implicated in the murder. It'd be different if you attacked honeysuckles. They're my favorite flower."

This piece of shite.

DOES HE KNOW THAT'S OUR FAVORITE FLOWER?

He couldn't right? Either way, she needed to get out of here before anybody sexploded.

"Here, let's start over." He snapped off a honeysuckle from a dangling string of flowers and moved to her ear!

Saoirse screamed.

She swung for the flower with all her might. The man recoiled, and she sent the flower soaring into the ceiling, further splitting the hurley.

"No..." she whimpered, torn in two directions from the near-fatal attack and her further ruined hurley.

"What's going on back there!"

That voice. She'd never heard it before, but she didn't need to look to know that presence. Captain. Commander.

"You! What's your name?"

Saoirse turned and saw that everyone in the bar was facing them. Including the man himself, even more impressive in person—every inch of 6'9"—the definition of perfection: Lorcan Maguire, Aware Wolf.

SO MUCH FOR BEING SAFE, FOLKS.

"S-Saoirse Storm."

Throwing Shapes

S aoirse faced down a legend. The man in charge of her destiny, the person who had final say on if she lived or died—and spores, was he attractive: Captain of the Wolves—Lorcan, feckin', Maguire!

Under the heat of the light shrooms, surrounded by flowers, her knees didn't just buckle—they attempted retirement and a plaque in the Hall of Fame. Saoirse had to grab a nearby table to stay standing.

"Saoirse Storm," Lorcan growled.

Audible murmurs ran through the crowd:

"Say no!"

"She's the reason we're in this mess in the first place."

"Kick her out!"

"Cheater."

"Match-fixer!"

Saoirse chewed her lower lip. Her stomach churned. Not more than a few steps into the Unshin River, she was in another trial like the one against the KKK. The same angry expressions jeered her from the pub, the same hate, except unlike then, where she'd had a crumbling rock with a big red button, or a father to be her shield; now, she had no one.

Saoirse moved through the watching trials for an open space at the base of a small stage near the back of the pub, hoping Lorcan might say something, but he just stood there.

IT PROBABLY CAN'T BE HELPED. HE CAN'T DEFEND YOU IN FRONT OF EVERYBODY SINCE YOU THREW.

Yeah...

She stopped just shy of the stage, trying—and failing—to hide the stolen, broken hurley. "Sup, cú," she squeaked. "I'm the champion for Croaghgorm..?"

JUST LIKE YOU PRACTICED.

I don't need sass right now.

Little Ref hit Satirical with a yellow.

"Hey, that's mine!" someone shouted.

Saoirse flushed bright crimson and set the hurley behind her with a mumbled apology. Somebody snatched it. She braced for the reprimand—the part where she was kicked out, or forced to face some kind of something.

Lorcan growled deep, from the chest—low, so low it traveled down the podium and through Little Hurler. It shook her. This was... this was... she cringed.

Lorcan stopped growling.

THAT WAS IT?

Is he really not going to do anything?

I DON'T KNOW. THAT'S SUSPECT, RIGHT?

I guess?

Spores, this whole situation was so strange. Shouldn't Lorcan be acting like a captain? Taking charge? Dishing out punishments? She'd never gotten to meet the Wolves in person—but they weren't living up to her fantasies at all.

"Stave?" Lorcan said. He was so tall he had to stoop to keep his head from sticking out the thatch roof.

"Um. I lost it."

THIS IS AWKWARD, FOLKS.

You're telling me.

"How unlucky," said a man to the captain's right. She recognized him instantly—Sean, assistant captain and midfielder. Dreamy, he lounged in his chair, rolling a coin across his knuckles, his 'lost-in-the-wind' blonde hair complementing his cocky smile and his loose white tunic.

"Cheatin's deadly, cú." On Lorcan's left was Nolan. As big and broad and buzzcut as the song she and Aisling composed would suggest, he seemed even bigger and broader and buzzcutter in person—as tall as Lorcan and nearly twice as wide.

The Wolves might lose every match, but these three men were the reason no team in the last few years scored more than fifteen points. They were some of the best hurlers in Éire trapped in a bad team.

Sean probably meant 'cheating' with regard to the fact she'd shown up without her city's Champion Stave thanks to the Chastity! debacle with Triple K, but it was clear that this conversation wasn't going to progress unless she said what they didn't want to hear.

"I didn't fix that match," Saoirse said, her voice small. "Though I understand if you hate me... I just dropped the ball."

There were more grumbles.

"You have to be found guilty," Sean said.

"Maybe," she said.

Sean leaned forward. "The clause in the small carving clearly states it."

And if she clearly stated her father was taking the fall, she could get looped back into the conspiracy. "If it's all the same to you, I'd rather wait to worry about that until after the investigator tells me personally." She could feel the judgment at her back. She'd have to win the All-Éire. The Champion's Portion legally required the High King at Tara to grant any one request. "I know you have no reason to let me participate, but I do actually think there's a way around the clause that still lets us participate in a redemption match. I want a chance for redemption, too."

Sean shared a look with Lorcan, who sighed. His behavior was a mystery. He still hadn't taken charge of the situation. He was supposed to be a terrifying wild beast! Not this sad... thing. The flowers hanging from the ceiling terrified her more than this man. Aisling ought to give him some PÉNIS therapy. Maybe then he'd act like a man again.

Sean took her stave.

"Welcome to trials," Lorcan said.

Yay?

SOMEHOW WE MADE IT, FOLKS. IN THIS AWKWARD, CRINGE-INDUCING CARVE DOWN.

Saoirse fist-bumped Little Hurler through her chest.

"Thank you." Provided everything went well, when her father took the fall, she'd be let out of her suspension, and her being here would be seen as no big deal. She'd have to keep up appearances till then.

She turned to leave when a voice shouted over the grumbles. "Weak!"

She found the source of the voice immediately—the Shitty Forwards sat at a nearby table. Roudan, the speaker, had buck teeth and a twitching nose like a rat. Then there was Michael, a weasel of a man, and Seanan, who looked like he might be part ugly trickster fae. All three of them were total shapers on the field. Always making it look like they were something when they were really nothing.

Little Hurler gave them a rude gesture.

LOOKS LIKE THEY'RE THE SAME WAY OFF THE FIELD. FECKIN' SHAPERS.

"Any girl prettier than your Wife and you'll just roll over!" Roudan said. "Doggy want a bone?"

Astonished gasps met this statement—Saoirse was one of them. How dare Roudan say something like that! And to the captain! Little Ref gave Roudan a yellow card.

Come on, Lorcan! Fight back! Tell him off! But he didn't.

One of the women on the raised seating, a lady with brown curls, stood and shot a piercing gaze at the captain, who hadn't budged. Lorcan just... sighed. Again.

What? He might look terrifying, but he wasn't all bark or all bite—he was neither! Where was Aware Wolf she'd been hoping for?

"Roudan. Shut up," Sean said, though he didn't look like he was about to do anything either.

"You shut up," Roudan sneered.

A different woman from the raised section made a strange gesture at Roudan. The rat-like man immediately caved.

LADIES AND GENTLEMEN, WHAT IS GOING ON?

Saoirse didn't have words for it. The women on the platform seemed to have impunity to shame the best men in the county for absolutely no reason. This was egregious!

"Quiet. It's not funny. Shuddup!" Roudan snapped at the onlookers.

No one was laughing. The pub cringed, several of the hurlers exchanging awkward glances. Saoirse, too, despite her standing with the others, got more than her fair share of looks from men who were upset with what they'd come in on. Nobody liked their team's forwards. They'd gone a whole season with a grand total of fourteen points—as a group. But this? This had to be the worst team atmosphere she'd ever seen! No wonder the county was losing. For feck's sake, all this was happening in public! If the team was used to being attacked, it would have to be affecting their play.

The captain, through all the hullabaloo, had not moved—just sat nonchalantly—but now she looked more closely... she saw them. His eyes. They sent a shiver through her soul. They were dead: defeated, destroyed, ruined yellow orbs, staring at nothing. She couldn't look away.

THIS IS WHY THEY SAY NEVER MEET YOUR HEROES.

Saoirse noticed other things about the team: They were kinda fat, that one stuffed his hands in his pockets, a few in the back corner curled like they were afraid to be seen, two over there stuck to the shadows; spores, the whole team looked... sad.

"Weak, Lorcan," Roudan jeered. "You want an excuse to replace me with a girl."

"There's nothing we can do for your wounded pride, Roudan," Lorcan said.

Is that really all he's going to say?

"Sure, there is," the woman who'd shamed Roudan spoke up. "They could learn to play better."

The whole place seemed to turn in on itself. Her own stomach squirmed as a few errant voices, of all things, came to the Shitty Forwards' defense with "shut it, woman" or "leave him be," but they gave up just as quickly.

Saoirse cleared her throat and spoke to the women on the raised platform. "Maybe this isn't the place?"

The woman balked at her.

"Think I'm weak too, huh?" Roudan snapped. "I can fight me own battles, kid."

"No, that's not—" Saoirse said.

"I'll get you on the pitch. I'll—" he cut off.

The woman leaned over the rail around the raised platform and whispered something in Roudan's ear, and a wicked, evil smile curled his face. "With a bet!" Roudan shouted. "A sporting wager!"

Noooooo!

Of all the things... Gambling was a transgression! Worse, it was a taboo!

She knew from CSI: Enniskillen that there were certain things you didn't say no to: hospitality freely given, sporting wagers, and you couldn't eat dog meat. If you picked wrong on any of these things, they said An Morrígan herself would curse your fate with bad luck. So often, these very triggers were the reason people ended up dead in the recitations!

"Best tally takes it, loser legs it," Roudan said. "First day only. No Whiskeys."

Her stadium screamed no. Her Little Hurler looked at her like she was nuts. Satirical came on over her loud shroom.

PLEASE DON'T TELL ME YOU'LL SAY YES. IS THIS GIRL SERIOUS? ARE WE SERIOUS? AM I SERIOUS? ARE WE GOING TO THROW AWAY EVERYTHING AGAIN FOR A BET?

Of course not... she had to be a good girl. She'd promised the gods. Even if a part of her wanted to take Roudan on.

"Well?" Roudan jabbed.

Saoirse took a deep breath and gave the only answer she could. "No."

The tension grew so thick she could have cut it with her hurley.

Sean looked straight at her. "You don't refuse a sporting wager."

"Refusal's deadly, cú," Nolan said.

"I'm... Shamrock Violet."

Lorcan looked taken aback. Several did. They started hand-passing hate Roudan's direction, but—

"Nobody cares!" Roudan shouted, gleeful as all get out. "You're a hurler!"

Wouldn't anybody come to her defense? Lorcan? The captain remained mute. *Tell him off. Be my shield... please.* She could have sworn his eyes flashed to the woman with brown curls on the raised platform—but nothing. Saoirse was alone in the Unshin River Pub with not even a hurley to hold back the odds; she had nothing more than hate and shame.

YOU'RE ON YOUR OWN IN THIS PLACE, TWENTY-SEVEN.

She shook her head. "I'm sorry. I won't."

It was the correct answer, but that didn't stop the murmurs. She walked in as an outcast, and now in their eyes, she was something worse—tainted.

I CAN'T SAY SHE MADE THE WRONG PLAY, FOLKS, BUT AT THIS RATE, IT MIGHT BE TIME TO START CHEERING FOR OUR OPPONENTS.

An errant tiny hurley got thrown through the open broadcast window in her brain. Satirical ducked for cover. Little Hurler thumped her chest.

I'M JUST ADDING SOME COLOR!

"Afraid are ye?" Roudan asked, not bothering to contain his sneer. "No shame in it, really. You'd get your hoop handed to you!"

The Shitty Forwards cackled over their clays.

Saoirse squeezed her fist. "Careful where you're stepping, cú. Keep throwing shapes, and you're likely to walk over a corner."

A few people cheered up at her trash talk.

Lorcan raised a solemn hand. "Let's just finish," he said. "If I'm not mistaken, Violets are allowed to sing. So—favorite drinking song. Even though I know you can't drink."

"Sure." This was her chance to get their respect. Without their support, how could she hope to make the team? Especially when she only had a week, while they all had two. Not to mention, she had no idea what trials actually entailed. Pressure pushed in on her from all sides. She couldn't mess up here. She needed a winner. Something strong. Something really Éirish. Something everyone would know. She ran through everything she could think of.

"Out with it!" Roudan slapped the table.

She couldn't wait to kick that hatch-snatcher off the team.

But what? She spied the bar in the corner—ha! She got it! A song so Éirish it should be illegal.

"This is just for all of you," Saoirse said to the room. She cleared her throat. Her Spectators got to their feet. Satirical cracked fiddles over her loud spore. Little Hurler took to center pitch, stick out to the green, white, and orange.

"Come guess me this riddle—what beats pipe and fiddle,
what's hotter than mustard and milder than cream?"

Why wasn't anybody joining? She even looked around like some might, but they all pulled back. What's worse—they seemed to hate her.

"What best whets your whistle,
what's clearer than crystal..."

She let her voice trail. Even Spirit Stadium became unsure. Satirical stopped the music she'd put on blast in her emotions. But it didn't make sense. Sure, everybody knew 'The Humors of Whiskey.' It could get the High Branch singing for hours!

She looked to Lorcan, who just shook his head like he couldn't believe her audacity. "Conspiracy, match-fixing, and sabotage."

Everybody pulled back from her—the other hurlers, even Sean and Nolan.

How was that a bad song? That song was brilliant! And why react like this?

The Shitty Forwards let their laughter bounce off the light shrooms.

Saoirse ducked into the crowd, trying to wade through the onslaught of negativity, realizing the man she'd thought would be a shield—the man she'd idolized—was little more than a crumbling ruin.

Roudan called after her, "Good luck walking home—and good riddance to ya as you do!"

The Wives

When Saoirse finally found the wall, she slumped against it, praying the ceiling of flowery death wouldn't make this worse than she already had. How was she supposed to make the team when they hated her? Nobody wanted poison in the lockers. And what exactly was wrong with 'The Humors of Whiskey'?!

Little Hurler had spiked her hurley in the dirt and was on the bench in Saoirse's heart, slumped with a frumpy expression.

Despite it all, she'd watched Lorcan make her a player's stave and toss it in the barrel with the others—a gesture that hadn't gone over her head. He was giving her a chance, even if she was on thin ice. She'd just have to prove that, despite the Shamrock Violet restrictions, she was worth it.

JUST MAKE SURE YOU GET RID OF THAT BAD LUCK BEFORE THE TRIALS TOMORROW.

I will.

Removing the taint of a taboo wasn't difficult; you simply had to experience bad luck. Lots of people in Éire were known for making dangerous or reckless choices on purpose to remove them. She'd have to find something like that to do soon. Somewhere.

LAUNCH OFF A JUMPSHROOM BLINDFOLDED?

And hit an insect mid-air as my bad luck? No. A one-mile drop to the floor of the Great Aurum Forest wasn't something she was keen on taking. There would be something better.

The atmosphere in the pub came back around now. Other hurlers from near and far took their turn, announcing themselves and where they were from, her fiasco all but forgotten. Saoirse pulled her eyes from the hurlers. Something made even less sense to her now than before she'd entered—the women in the corner.

On a raised platform on the opposite side of the pub were roughly twenty-seven women, engaged in conversation and sparing furtive glances for the proceedings. They definitely weren't players, and they seemed to know many of the players on a personal level. The one in particular—a short woman with locks of brown curls under a pink beanie—seemed particularly aghast at the fact that Lorcan made her a stave, but she'd been aghast at all of Lorcan's actions. It was a sentiment Saoirse was coming to understand.

HE ISN'T THE HERO WE THOUGHT HE'D BE.

A fact that left her heart wounded.

Do you think the gods are still with me?

The Tuatha Dé Danann are always with you.

She looked back at Lorcan—Aware Wolf, barely surviving. It didn't feel like it.

Those women up on the platform, somebody needs to tell them that they shouldn't shame the team during carve downs.

DON'T YOU MEAN IN GENERAL?

Aisling said thinking about mental health is a fairly new branch of Druidry. *The women can't have meant what they said, or maybe they don't understand what this does to the team. If I explain this correctly, they'll realize they went too far.* She couldn't expect the team to win if they were constantly being harassed.

FIGHTING IS AGAINST THE VIOLET RULES.

Fighting might be, but not confrontation. If anything, Triple K preferred it when women were hostile and combative. *I'll try a Sisterhood Healing Session. If I can get them in a Gratitude Circle, I bet they'll change their minds.*

GOOD PLAN.

Her heart agreed.

Saoirse crept under the potentially dangerous—though seemingly less so—strings of flowers, passed the other hurlers, and onto the raised platform of women. Dressed in colorful, elegant dresses of the kind Saoirse had often dreamed of wearing while wandering about town, they didn't seem like bad people, but what they did wasn't right.

She cleared her throat. "Sup, cú."

In perfect unison, all the women turned to stare at her with the exact same expression—one eyebrow high—and some serious attitude that made her falter.

"I'm Saoirse. I—well—I think maybe you might... not want to talk to the players like you just did. Uh, and... we could do a Sisterhood Healing Session? Form a Gratitude... Circle..."

The women burst into laughter, but the players ignored them as the women jested her: "How cute."

"You're a doll."

"I love your freckles."

Saoirse shrank under the sarcasm, but Little Hurler was ready for a brawl.

"Hey there!" In the middle of the group was the woman Lorcan had been wary of. Her pink hat framing a cute face. Next to her was a thin, bubbly woman with her hair in dirty-blond waves, and a third woman with shoulder-length auburn hair.

"I'm Lauren," the first noted. "This is Lauren, too, and this is also Lauren."

The others waved.

Saoirse said, "That's nice."

"You haven't heard of us?" asked the main Lauren.

"Uh. No?"

"But we are a not-so-secret secret organization!" said the Lauren with dirty-blond waves as if this fact were plainly obvious.

"Should I know you?" Saoirse asked.

All the women balked.

It didn't seem so offensive a statement to her; she'd never met them before.

The twenty-seven women put their heads together, then, after a moment, sprang into action.

"Allow us to introduce ourselves!" The primary Lauren quickly issued several wordless directions to the other women, including those not in on the conversation. Suddenly, there was a large backlight; two rows of women on either side of the three Laurens, every woman in the rows clapping in rhythm; and another set of women twirling hurleys in march step.

THE FECK??? THESE WOMEN ARE CRAZY.

Saoirse nodded, but Little Hurler was totally into it.

The first Lauren struck an epic pose in front of the backlight.

Lauren One
"Prepare for headaches."

The second Lauren came to meet the first.

Lauren Two
"With life-altering stakes."

They changed poses.

Lauren One
"To destroy all husbands, we shall not cease!"

Lauren Two
"Our insecurities will ruin world peace!"

The backlight changed colors as the other women cheered: "Wives! Wives! Wives! Wives!"

Lauren One
"We'll lock ourselves in the bathroom to cry like adults."

Lauren Two
"Our emotions are your fault."

Lauren One
"Prime."

Lauren Two
"The Fun Wife."

Lauren One
"Prepare to play hurling and be distressed."

Lauren Two
"We are the Wives—"

Lauren Three
"And I'm the Third one, I guess."

The last of the trio struck her pose, despite speaking in a complete monotone.

YOU KNOW, FOR SOMEBODY WHO DOESN'T SEEM THAT INTO IT, SHE REALLY HIT THAT POSE WITH SOME PIZAZZ.

I'd say.

The rest of the women leaped into the super group pose, each with their own unique flair, a few unfortunate girls in the back trying to continue supporting the 'backlight from nowhere' with outstretched feet. It was wobbling a bit.

"Hint," said Wife Prime. "This is where you're supposed to be impressed."

"Oh—uh—," Saoirse joined in the energy. "So, you're the Wives!"

"That's right, Saoirse-tron," Wife Prime said, optimally.

Spores, city folk were strange.

Though Little Hurler clapped enthusiastically.

IT'S NOT OUR PLACE TO JUDGE. THEY ARE WIVES.

Satirical had a good point. The Violet taught that Wives were pets. Women gave up their humanity the moment they bound themselves to a man. They hardly even were women anymore. The only thing to offer such creatures was pity.

The women broke free of their pose. Saoirse spared a glance for the rest of the pub; nobody had even blinked. Either this occurrence was commonplace, or they couldn't be bothered.

"Lorcan," said Prime.

"Sean," said the one with dirty-blond waves.

"Nolan," droned Wife the Third.

"Ours." They said it very, very slowly.

They must think I'm dumb.

WELL, YOU CAN'T COUNT PAST TWENTY-SEVEN.

How about you shut the puck up?

But her heart couldn't help laughing.

Fine. "What's up?"

"We enjoyed your song," said Prime. "It can't have been easy going up there with all that hostility."

"I'm getting used to it."

"I'll bet. Look, I'd like to be nice. You're the only female hurler—where are you staying?" Prime asked.

"The Puritan." Her father set it up for her. She'd already put up her stuff.

"That won't do. Why not stay at my family's place, the North Tree Hotel? It'll be free."

"No thanks. I really just came over to see about a Gratitude Circle." Again, the Wives didn't bite.

"Look, we appreciate you trying to treat our husbands well—in *your* opinion—but we aren't willing to change."

What a stubborn lot Wives were. They'd always seemed such in CSI, but any time they had their 'cookies stolen,' somebody ended up dead. She'd always thought it was a euphemism for something, but now she wasn't sure if it was literal. Still, she wanted the team to win, and that wasn't going to be easy if their pets kept putting them down.

She might not be allowed to dance, but if they weren't going to do a Gratitude Circle, "Then I challenge you to a Rite of Ritual Hurling."

The women perked up.

"If I win, you treat them better. If you win, I'll stay at this place."

The Wives reconvened.

ARE YOU SURE ABOUT THIS, TWENTY-SEVEN?

It'd be tough with her leg bruised from where the sums walloped her. *Easy, cú.*

Little Hurler was already hitting warm-up stretches.

The Wives turned back around. "Okay, we agree to stand down for twenty-four hours if you beat us in a Rite of Ritual Hurling."

"You're on!" Saoirse reached for her lucky hurley... and of course it wasn't there. It was still in pieces in her gear bag at the hotel. "But I don't have a hurley." *Spores.*

YOU IDIOT. NOT BEING ABLE TO ACCEPT THE RITE PUTS US UP FOR ANOTHER TABOO!

Shite!

"No hurley, you say?" said the Fun Wife.

"It's okay," Prime cut in. "I won't hold it against you—no bad luck for being unable to participate in the rite."

Saoirse exhaled the worry. "Thank you."

WE GOT LUCKY.

No kidding. She did not need another bout of cosmic bad luck.

"Since you were so willing to participate, how about we repay your earnestness with a little freely offered hospitality?"

Another Éirish taboo. "Thanks, I'd love that."

The women shared a look, then turned back to her. "Well, it's a good thing we had this prepared then." Wife Prime snapped, and a young girl rushed over with a silver tray.

"We'd hoped there would be some other female trials," the Fun Wife explained.

"But you're the only one," said Wife the Third.

They spoke at once. "We didn't want our efforts to go to waste."

"What are you talking about?" Saoirse asked.

"Solidarity," said Prime. "As women. This is for you."

The young girl took the silver cover from her tray, and Saoirse nearly lost it. Standing there at the edges of the Unshin River, they'd offered her free hospitality of another taboo: dog meat.

Trick Shot Champion

Weighing in at 130 lbs, standing at 5'5", unable to count past twenty-seven, she's your full-forward and mine, Saoirse Storm!

That's the intro I gave her when she took the stage at the All-Central County Tyrconnell Trick Shot Competition the first year she competed (and won). She's sixty pounds heavier now and six inches taller, but she still can't count past twenty-seven. She never will. I think she must have been dropped on her head when she was a baby or something, but thankfully, she doesn't need to count past twenty-seven to kick butt at hurling!

You should have seen her at that competition. Girls and boys get dressed up and put on a performance. Some go for shot quantity, some go for the number of bounces—our girl went for skills; her ball control is unparalleled. She fused the dance moves she got from the Greensleeves with her innate sense of balance and then smashed it right through a tiny hoop. It was mesmerizing!

My favorite part, though, was watching the crowd watching her and Little Hurler. Saoirse couldn't hear me at the time, and she didn't understand her hurling sense was her fusing with Little Hurler, but we did, and it was amazing.

Finley Man Domhnaill

S he couldn't hold offense against the Wives. Wives were emotionally compromised creatures, basically half-fae, but spores, she couldn't help but think that if she had her lucky hurley, she wouldn't be in this position. The only blessing was that it had been faux dog meat, a vegan mushroom approximation, but it still counted. That gave her the taint of two taboos.

In Éirish culture, not accepting hospitality was the far worse sin than eating dog meat, even if that meat was fake. In order to avoid a third possible bout of cosmic bad luck, she had to agree to Wife Prime's request: to stay at her chosen location for the duration of the trials, the North Tree Hotel. Which, honestly, wasn't so bad. This place was an entirely different kind of stayover.

The North Tree Hotel. Carved deep into the trunk of an Aurum great wood, a dozen shroomdaliers hung at intervals through the ceiling, plush couches filled the seating area, a long bar to her right looked to be a pub of some kind, and doors against the wall closest to the center of the trunk would 'ding' and slide open to reveal boxes of people.

Unbelievable.

TUATHA DÉ DANANN. WOW.

Little Hurler slipped off the bench and into inspiration. They'd never even imagined a place could look like this.

MAY I? Satirical asked.

Go for it.

LADIES AND GENTLEMEN! WELCOME TO OUR FIRST-EVER AWAY GAME AT THIS 'STADIUM,' THE NORTH TREE HOTEL! YOUR NUMBER TWENTY-SEVEN AND MINE, THE BEST PLAYER IN ALL THE STARS, HAS JUST STEPPED OFF THE STAIRCASE AND INTO THE LOBBY. WILL SHE BE ABLE TO FIND THIS FOALAN AND FULFILL HER TABOO? YOUR GUESS IS AS GOOD AS MINE.

We don't have this in Croaghgorm.

OR BALLYBOFEY. YOU'D THINK 'DING-BOXES' WOULD MAKE AN APPEARANCE IN CSI: ENNISKILLEN.

'Elevators.' I'm glad they don't. Saoirse couldn't have smiled bigger if she'd tried. Nobody had spoiled her on the vista—one more memory for her collection. Boxes that carried people up and down the Great Aurum trunk. She'd have to try them on the way back down.

A pool chair popped open at the center pitch of her heart. Little Hurler joined in, admiring the view.

Class, yeah?

Her heart nodded.

You know we're not on vacation, right?

Little Hurler nodded, then put a tiny faux shroombrella into her drink.

Though she wasn't sure how much she ought to hold the catch-twenty taboo against the Wives. This place *was* terrific.

Saoirse adjusted her leather gear bag on her shoulder. She was even more grateful for Aisling's help in defeating Melak's pack. Without her wolf ride, she'd have been bound to a hotel a six-hour walk away. With the wolf's help, the distance was a breeze.

Let's find Foalan.

Agreed. After I put this pack down, we can find some way to ward off the two taints. All she had to do was have a bad or terrifying experience. There were always ways to do that, and if she didn't, she'd be carrying the threat of cosmic bad luck into trials. That was something she couldn't bear in good conscience. She only had six days—five, really, once this day was over—to make the team or end up violated. Just as bad, she'd never be able to win the Champion's Portion from the All-Éire and save her father.

Saoirse swallowed down the pressure. She couldn't end up like *those women.*

Spectators slipped into her stands, occuls—vision-enhancing insect lenses wrapped in twigs—pressed to their eyes, making them even wider and more adorable as they took it all in, calling for their friends to hurry to their seats.

I sold extra tickets. Knew nobody in Spirit Stadium would want to miss this.

I'll explore later. That way it's worth it.

Lines formed at the snack stands in her lungs. Pitch-side service ran Little Hurler a cup of pretzels to go with her drink. She held up a thumb without looking back at the broadcast booth.

Saoirse wasn't really sure what her mind was on about—selling tickets to her made-up stadium—but then Satirical had mentioned similar weirdness before. Aisling said part of her subconscious really enjoyed putting on a show. Saoirse disagreed.

Little Hurler urged her deeper into the stayover when a familiar voice popped up behind her.

"Well, that could have gone better."

Saoirse spun and found the man from carve downs with fox-like features. She winced when she realized he had a red mark on the side of his unbelievably gorgeous face.

Warning! Danger! Aurum to us! Flower!

What?

Saoirse snapped to with a slap from Little Hurler just in time to realize the crazy moron had a flower in his hand, headed straight for her ear again!

Alert, sexplosion imminent in three, two—

Without thinking, she snatched his wrists.

"Wow, you really do have a thing with flowers," he said, pulling his hand away. "Or is it just honeysuckles?"

"What do you want?" she asked despite herself. Tuatha Dé, that was so close.

He tossed the danger on a seat, extended a flowerless hand this time. "I'm Finley, Finley Man Domhnaill."

"What do you want?" Saoirse asked again with a step back. Spores, each tooth of his smile sparkled like they committed tax fraud.

"To talk CSI: Enniskillen," he said. "Even if I personally prefer Kin and Cow."

"Kin and Cow?"

I don't trust this guy.

Neither did she, but her Spectators were too busy going gaga at his pretty features for her to trust her gut. "Look," she said, "I'm just trying to find the person I'm supposed to meet here. I don't want any part in your weird schemes. If you're going to have that much trouble making the team, leave me out of it."

Finley acted like he didn't even hear her. He just hummed and handed a small coin from a pouch at his waist to a bellhop who scuttled off and out of sight, bowing so energetically he looked like he couldn't care if he broke his back.

"I wanted to talk at carve downs, but the only thing that happened was you kissing my face with a hurley." He smirked.

THAT'S SOME SUSPECT PHRASING.

"You mean you followed me here?"

"No and yes. I've business in the gardens," he nodded toward a large window across the foyer. "Meeting some contacts. I saw you when I arrived and considered it a stroke of luck. Now, I don't have to wait till tomorrow."

Do we trust him or not?

DOESN'T EVERYBODY HATE YOU?

True, it was weird that this Finley didn't treat her with scorn, and she had her own pressing issues. Helping this man might leave her unable to deal with her taints. If it came to that, she'd have to say no. Her stomach growled.

Finley raised a brow.

And she needed some food. "What do you want?"

"Help solving a mystery."

At this, Little Hurler raced for the lockers. She loved a good mystery.

SHE'S LOOKING FOR HER TRENCH COAT, ISN'T SHE?

Yep.

He waved as if to brush off her expression. "Not a murder; not committing one either. Which, I don't think you could even begin to understand how strange that is for me."

PLEASE DON'T BUST OUT YOUR SAOIRSE NOIR MODE HERE. WE JUST HAVE TO STICK TO THE PLAN. BE A GOOD GIRL, SCORE GOALS, REMEMBER?

I'm going to, but there's nothing wrong with a little mystery.

OH, GREAT TUATHA DÉ DANANN, WHY DID YOU HAVE TO SADDLE ME WITH THIS MYSTERY-RECITATION JUNKIE?

Little Hurler returned with her noir trench coat ready.

But when a groan came over her loudspore, Saoirse thought, *Fine, Sat, you win.* "I can't," Saoirse said. "I'm sorry, I just want to get out of the situation I'm in and get onto the Wolves."

"The Wolves won't exist unless you accept your situation."

"I'll find a way." Or her dad would.

Finley furrowed his brow at her. "I'm not trying to hand-pass you any hate, cú," he said. "I'm with the boys on the team. It's unfair how much everybody is putting this on you. But the clause in the small carving is very clear. If somebody is found guilty, there's a second chance. PÉNIS has to declare you're a Bad Girl."

The team thought that the way she was being treated was unfair? That made her flush. Some people in Éire understood. It went some way to restoring the image of the team she'd held in her heart. Still, she couldn't tell Finley about the plan with her father, or it could loop her into the conspiracy. Then nobody would be able to get him back out again. "That's what you say."

"That's the truth."

"Are you a Druid at Law?"

"No."

"Then how could you know?"

Finley gritted his teeth. "You don't have to be a Druid at Law to know the codes. My family's business requires us to be more knowledgeable with the clauses in the small carvings than even most druids."

"For your enterprise?"

"The aggressive repatriation of foreign cattle."

Grand...

Business jargon.
Spirit Stadium went dizzy-eyed at the strange business words.
Ding! One of the elevators arrived at the sliding doors. Little Hurler reluctantly gave up on the idea of doing noir and returned to her pool chair.
"Mater Finley!" a new voice called across the hall.
A bouncy old man, balding with wizened teeth, bounded toward them.
"Foalan!" Finley smiled.
"Welcome to the North Tree Hotel, yes, yes, yes!" the old man said in a sing-song voice.
Foalan? As in the man she was looking for? Saoirse expected Finley to bow, but instead was surprised when Foalan bowed to Finley.
Finley's got three torques.
Ah. Money.
Finley took her gently by the wrist and pulled her forward. "We need to check in an unexpected guest of your granddaughter," he said.
Saoirse found herself stumbling into place at his side.
The man's eyes fell on her face.
Saoirse smiled. "Uh... sup, cú," she said with a little bow.
Foalan looked her up. Foalan looked her down. Then Foalan stared her straight in the face and said, "No."
"What?" Saoirse asked the happy old man, now scowling.
"No." He laid it on thick. "Saoirse Storm."
At the mention of her name, the whole hall ground to a halt.
Nobody moved. Nobody spoke. Nobody did anything but stare at her with hateful reproach.
You could have heard a hurley hit a cotton spore, folks.
"This establishment is full," he said.
"But, sir, your granddaughter bound me in a taboo."
"Not my problem."
"I have to stay here!"
"But you're not welcome here. Go." Foalan didn't stay a second longer. He merely swept away, into the ground, leaving her holding her overstuffed gear bag, now ripping at the seams with the added weight of a third bout of cosmic bad luck.
But...
I'm sorry, Twenty-Seven.
It's not your fault.
Eventually, the hotel returned to function. Saoirse worked hard to keep her head above the hurley as people passed with dark expressions. Why did everybody blame her? Could they not see how little their situation was her fault?
"You really have a knack for getting into easily avoidable trouble," Finley said.
She jumped so hard that Little Hurler spilled her drink all over her trench coat.
Sorry, she said to her heart. *I forgot he was there.* "Couldn't you have helped?" Saoirse asked.
"Why should I pass to a girl who doesn't shoot?"
"I thought you said you didn't care about my scandal."
"I don't, but you didn't help me either."
Her stomach grumbled as she put her gear bag between herself and the outward hostility and made for a couch out of the way by the far wall.
Shite. Three taboos. She needed three bad experiences! Where did she go now? Back to the Puritan? She'd agreed to the terms of Wife Prime's taboo. It wasn't her fault she'd been blocked from staying here, but taboos had no loopholes. No ways out. Once you were stuck with one, you had to see it through to the end. Saoirse tossed her things on the couch.
Finley meandered after her. "Saddled with cosmic bad luck and no place to stay."
"I will stay here."

The blue-haired man cast a bemused look around at the hatred being hand-passed in her direction. "Seems nice."

She threw her hands out in frustration and thought about defending herself, but considered better of it and collapsed on the couch.

"So, where will we go?" asked the too-handsome man.

She eyed Finley with suspicion.

"Hey, I'm not some kind of bad guy. I mean, I am, but it's a different kind of bad." He winked. "You need a place to stay, right?"

"I'll just go back to Ballybofey."

"Suppose that's fair, but at least hear me out."

I DON'T KNOW. HE'S SUSPECT.

Finley raised his hands innocently. "Not everybody is so stupid as to blame you for a quarter century of our county losing games."

HE IS REALLY SUSPECT.

Her stomach growled again.

Finley smirked. "I'll buy you dinner."

"Deal."

THAT'S LIKE THE MOST SUSPECT!

Saves us money, and if we've got to stay at the Puritan, we'll need every bit of what he gave me.

HURLER, BACK ME UP HERE.

Her heart shrugged.

We can at least hear him out for a free meal.

FINE.

"Then come with me." Finley threw her gear bag over his shoulder and offered her a hand, but she couldn't be too careful. "I got rid of the flower."

"It's not enough."

"Heh. This way." He nodded toward a large archway from the foyer in the direction of what he'd called the gardens. She couldn't see any mushrooms from here, just light, but her stomach led the way, her hunger trumping her ability to find Finley attractive. That was right until they reached the threshold.

It wasn't flowers stopping her from crossing this time...

"Welcome to," Finley threw his arms wide to the towering buildings lining the silver walkway.

It was...

"The Carnal Carnival."

Hurl-ectile Dysfunction

*T*he Carnal Carnival? The Carnal Carnival?! An Dagda... Saoirse sighed with the name of a god. *Aisling, we were right!*

There, framed in an archway—a threshold between herself and <u>*The Violet Intercourse*</u>—she saw it all. Quirky, lopsided mushrooms and wacky wooden buildings bent into a tunnel, making it impossible to see out into the forest. At the base of the fungi tunnel was a long road of silver insect sinew, a walkway from the hotel's exit into the haven of heretics. But the carnival didn't just go down the sinew—no, it sprawled out to the sides.

Several of the floating islands hovered in space on amber mists. They'd been roped into place, attached to the path, the mushrooms, or each other, each boasting fluorescent lights, each with people shouting into the packed throng filling the street, looking for customers. The result was a complete maze of debauchery.

Saoirse almost collapsed where she stood.

GODS. GOOD GODS! DO YOU SEE THOSE TWO? SAOIRSE, THEY'RE HIDING HURLEYS!

Sure enough, a pair of women were putting several hurleys into a barrel next to some kind of sign.

AND THEM! THEY'RE ROLLING HAY!

Two women were indeed rolling hay into bundles of shame.

AND THEN, HER! OH, GREAT GODDESS DANU, HER!!! Satirical cried.

Saoirse couldn't look—but she could. The woman was churning butter!—*oh great goddess Danu!*—Wearing a frock and bonnet, the woman had a hurley in some kind of sticky, sloshy mix and was really going at it.

Goddess Morrígan, watch over me as I battle these sins! Aisling, I think I need some therapy.

This counted as bad luck for the taint of one taboo.

"Have you ever played? It's a lot of fun." Finley held a hand out to the scene, as if he'd not a care in the world, a devious smile stretched across his face. "They call it Balls Deep, you—"

But she didn't hear the explanation.

GIRD YOUR LOINS! LOIN YOUR GIRDS! ALL HANDS, DEFENSIVE STATIONS! SAOIRSE! SAOIRSE!!!

Little Hurler pointed noiseless directions at the Spectators, who ran screaming all over the place.

"Saoirse?" Finley asked. "Saoirse, are you okay?"

"I can't go."

"You need to sit down."

"I can't go."

"Here." Finley took her by the shoulders; she was too weak to protest as he pulled her through the portal and along the outside wall of the hotel to a small bench. Then he picked up the flower beds hanging off the windowsill and threw them, where they shattered at the base of a shop.

Saoirse shivered.

"You were going down pretty hard, Little Shroom."

Hurler's eyes were swirling.

"If you'd like to stay here at the hotel for our chat, then go back to the Puritan. I can take you there, or if you want to try one of the other hotels, they're in the other trees." He indicated. "Waaay over there."

We should go back to the Puritan.

Her breathing came heavy deliberate.

Little Hurler slapped her tummy defiantly.

It's true they didn't get pregnant in the Unshin River.

We could have gotten lucky!

"Personally, I still think you'd love the carnival," Finley teased. "It will be fun. We can play games, win prizes."

"I don't think I can."

"Don't worry, you're with a genuine article." He threw an arm around her. Saoirse instantly whipped her hurley from her bag. It was still broken and worked more like a sharp spear. "Stay back!"

"Whoa there, Little Shroom. I was just trying to rub your back. You look sick."

"At the end of the hurley."

Finley didn't move. "Why?"

"One hurley length to stop the spread," she said. How could this man not know? It was core Violet doctrine.

"The spread?"

"Of cooties!" she shouted. "If they reach critical mass."

"Shamrock Violet..." Finley closed his eyes, nodding to himself.

"What's that supposed to mean?"

"Nothing. I've heard stories of your Color. I now realize they were true. You're very... pious."

"Thank you."

Finley set a finger atop the broken shaft and pushed. "I'll stay a hurley away as long as you don't point it at me. None of my cooties will pass the bas. Okay?"

She bit her lip. How many times had she and Aisling sung 'I Want to Score' over the years? They had been too accurate. They'd never considered it manifesting. Hay rolling *and* hurley hiding. What if Finley got the chance to 'shuck her little seashell'?

We'll have to tread carefully. Spectators, keep an eye out.

The panic in her gut quieted some. Several Spectators ran to the top ledge of Spirit Stadium to stare out into the courtyard. She got the distinct impression they really could see what was behind her.

She stared at the stall near the smashed flowers. A man was haggling with a woman over an innocuous counter, the entire shop lit with some kind of orange lightshrooms. He sold food. She remembered how hungry she was. "Fine, I'll stay and listen. As long as we don't go in."

"Do you want sticky buns?"

"Ahhh!" she swung her spiked handle.

"Hey!" Finley barely ducked.

Heat flushed her face. "Sorry."

"I told you I'd buy you dinner. You can't get upset at me because I figured you can't read."

"Sorry."

"Look," he pointed. "Over there's Ovens Full of Buns. That's Sausage Gobblers. They do this thing with mustard. It's to die for."

"Die!?" Saoirse fought to keep her hand down.

"Okay, so not sausage."

Casually dropping sexplosion? "I'll... take buns."

"Sticky or not?"

"Not sticky!"

"Okay. Give me a sec." Finley made a movement as if to say he were reconsidering his choice of mystery partner. It stung.

She slumped in her seat. He walked to the nearby stall he'd called 'Ovens Full of Buns.' A kindly woman had a clay hearth behind her counter, a set of large tools for stoking the fire and handling the buns inside. It was strangely normal, but Saoirse didn't trust it.

SMOOTH. Satirical teased.

You can't do any better. Talking to Finley normally was hard enough, let alone with the added pressure of being so near her headcanon of *The Violet Intercourse*. Finley wouldn't violate her, would he?

Little Hurler put her beach chair out of the way and hung the stained noir coat on it, having washed out the mess so it could dry.

Saoirse tried to understand the nature of the real Carnal Carnival.

A man nearby shouted something about having cheap game coins for 'the House.' Another sold women's garters in broad shroomlight. There was a man down the way taking bets on something, and a seedy-looking older woman with loose skin telling men she'd 'give them a horn' for just a few copper coins.

Hurler wanted to check it out. They did have enough coins, and how cool would it be to have a horn?

WE HAVE TO BE GOOD GIRLS.

Right. The investigator could arrive at Croaghgorm at any time; her father might already be in custody. If she couldn't heed her gods, they wouldn't give her favor during the trials. Favor she desperately needed when she had only a week to make the team. The trials lasted two weeks, and she had no clue what they entailed. Not to mention her broken lucky hurley. That alone put knots in her stomach.

ONE STEP AT A TIME.

Yeah. We'll hear Finley out, then get rid of our other two taboos. In that way, the Carnal Carnival had already been a blessing. The bad experience meant she only had two taints left.

Finley returned, holding out the golden-brown bun, wrapped in a small snipping of a leaf. "Here, one sticky-less bun."

"Thanks," she said.

"Don't worry about it."

Finley sat on the bench, far enough that it didn't bother her. She peeled back the leaf and tucked into the bun—a potato dough filled with pork that almost burned her mouth. She huffed and puffed several times to cool it off before she took another bite. Who'd have thought, her first time at the Carnal Carnival, she'd spend it sitting on a bench with a strange man eating his buns? She wasn't complaining. The meat in the center was tender and delicious. The brown sauce? A treat. This better not count as a sin when she swam the Shannon. At least it was more wholesome than churning butter. That woman was exhausted.

"Gonna fill me in on this mystery?" she asked.

"Absolutely," Finley said.

He lowered a hand and dropped his voice. "But we've got to keep this part down. This is a very sensitive topic, and I mean *very* sensitive. Thankfully, it's pretty loud here."

That it was. The sinew street was incredibly busy, not to mention the voices drifting through the windows of the North Tree Hotel.

"Look," Finley whispered.

Saoirse leaned in secretively. Whatever Finley was about to say was clearly very secret and very important. She could not afford to miss it.

This better be good.

Even Little Hurler was all ears.

"My family thinks the County Tyrconnell Hurling Club is suffering from," he paused, "hurl-ectile dysfunction."

"Hurl-ectile dysfunction?!"

Several heads turned their way, with pity-filled eyes. "Shh!" Finley flushed. The people moved on.

"Sorry," Saoirse said. Hadn't Aisling been researching hurl-ectile dysfunction? Or was that something else?

"It's okay, just—"

"Right," she whispered into another bite.

Finley checked the surroundings, stood, and looked through the windows.

Was it really that sensitive a topic?

Finley took a bite from his own bun and then sat back down. When he finished, he continued. "It means they can't get their Whiskeys hard—their magic's gone flaccid, which is why they can't wield their mojo out on the pitch!"

Saoirse's eyes went wide. Finley's mystery was why the team couldn't use magic?! That was *the* crucial problem to solve. If they could use magic, they'd have a good shot at winning the redemption match against County Tyrone. That meant her dad's sacrifice to be found guilty of match-fixing wouldn't be in vain! She attempted a reply through all the meat filling her mouth, but didn't manage. "Spo-ahwasf."

"You could say that again."

She swallowed. "Spores."

"I didn't mean literally."

If he was asking for help, didn't that mean he had a lead?

"My father thinks defeating hurl-ectile dysfunction requires a woman's touch. If you help, we can get their Whiskeys hard!"

Hurler ran for her stained trench coat, but put it back down when Saoirse sighed.

"I'm sorry," Saoirse said. "I'm going to say no."

"But why? It could fix the team. Save the county!"

"Yeah, it probably could." Salm, Shamrock Violet. "But I'm in a bind." Saoirse set down her sticky-less bun and held up her hand. As she thought about her geas, the mists swirled about the back of her palm, connecting in a triskele. "In six days, I have to join a sacred rite. I don't want to. I have to make the team to be free. There's... other things I can't tell you about, too.

"I want the team to have magic, I really do, but I have to play for my goals first. I think I have a way for PÉNIS to both realize I'm a Good Girl and give the county a second chance. Once I'm on the team, I can help, maybe."

"There is no second chance unless you turn yourself in," he said as he had before.

"There will be." She met his eyes. For a long moment, he didn't look anywhere else. She saw a sincerity in him she'd not seen before.

"I hope you know what you're talking about," Finley said.

She did too.

You really are the queen of denial.

"I'm sorry," she offered.

They sat for a while, she eating, he staring into the carnival, lost in thought.

That really bungled his plans.

I guess so. I wouldn't mind helping after I made the team, but that comes first.

"Well," Finley cracked his neck with one hand, "it is what it is. One thing still confuses me, though."

"What?"

"I don't know how you even planned on seeing the dancing if you can't go up the street."

"The what?!" she shouted. "Dancing?!"

DID HE SAY DANCING?

Her whole stadium had turned back to face the gorgeous man, heart on high alert. What did he mean by dancing? What kind of dancing? Were there dancers here? In the carnival!?

"The dancers," he said. "I mean, isn't that why you'd choose to stay outside of Ballybofey?"

"I didn't choose. The Wives catch-twenty tabooed me."

"Salm, the Laurens." He shook his head.

"But what do you mean by dancing?"

Finley caught her gaze with his deep, piercing blue eyes. "You're really into this, aren't you?"

She nodded eagerly.

"Alright. On the other side of the Carnal Carnival is a place famous for its dancers. They do all kinds, but most people either know it as an Éirish step-dance burlesque cabaret and gentlemen's club, or as the home of the Daughters of Dagda, an Éirish step-dance fusion troupe famous for their skill and style-blended dance performances. I figured with your nickname, 'The Dancer,' going to a show would be a given."

Saoirse reeled back. *Dancing! Professional dancing! We have to see!*

No! Satirical was adamant.

Yes!

IT'S ON THE OTHER SIDE OF THE CARNIVAL!

That's okay. It's like the flowers—I'm not participating, I'm just nearby.

AND THE DANCING?

There's never been harm in watching before. Come on, Sat, think about how good my goals will be if I can learn from professional dancers! Imagine the color commentary. Go on.

YOU PROMISED TO BE A GOOD GIRL, TO BE THE PERFECT SHAMROCK VIOLET—SWORE IT IN FRONT OF THE GODS!

That... was true. Her gods were with her. Now she wanted to run off and *almost* transgress?

"Let me guess, transgression?" Finley asked.

"Yeah."

He toyed with his perfect, smooth chin. "What if I can get you out of your geas?"

Saoirse froze. He couldn't do that. Could he?

ISN'T THE BETTER QUESTION: WHY IS HE OFFERING NOW?

Not if he can do it. "How?"

"My family has ways of connecting with people in a manner they find agreeable. I'll go get a promise stave from the head of your Color that if you fix the team's hurl-ectile dysfunction, they are bound to free you from your bonds."

"I can't read."

"Put me in a geas then. If I don't return with the stave tomorrow, then you don't have to help me. If I do, you still won't have to help me, but you'll have the option to."

THAT SEEMS FISHY.

There's no downside to this deal at all! Even if he does return, I still don't have to help.

HE ONLY OFFERED IT AFTER HE KNEW YOU WANTED TO SEE THE DANCERS, SAOIRSE. THIS GUY IS A BAD MAN.

How can a bad man be so good?

Her heart was certainly on her side. "What's in it for you?" she asked.

"While yes, it's true that my family is the largest donors to the County Tyrconnell organization, something we only started contributing to this year. I'd be lying if I said money was why I wanted to help." His deep blue eyes. He was either a great liar or intensely honest. "I spent my life coming to matches, following the team, memorizing the player staves," he said. "Even though they never won. I don't want to see them go. More than that, I want them to win."

It was honesty.

"What do you say?" he asked.

A completely optional way to get one over on Triple K for breaking her hurley? "Deal."

Man Domhnáill Enterprise

Aggressive Repatriation of Foreign Cattle

Carnal Carnival

They called her The Dancer. Everyone who attended her matches—all the announcers, even some of her opponents. Saoirse had never asked them to. She'd never called herself The Dancer, for obvious reasons. It wouldn't fly with Shamrock Vi. As her dad always said, she just had 'special needs'—the need to dance. Trick shots were one thing, playing hurling and incorporating the moves into her solo style quite another, but being up on the branch, in her secret spot, watching the women below flow like water—that was something else. Now, Finley was saying a troupe of true professional dancers was on the other side of debauchery? Saoirse stuffed the last of Mr. Three-Torque's buns in her mouth and faced the prospect of crossing the Carnal Carnival.

I KNOW YOU WANT TO GO, BUT WE LITERALLY JUST PROMISED THE GODS WE WOULDN'T TRANSGRESS, Satirical said.

The tutu in her heart couldn't disagree more. Hurler was already hitting a plié.

I THOUGHT YOU'D STUFFED THAT IN A LOCKER!

I'm not going to participate. Just looking at the carnival made her tremble. We pass through and stay at another hotel.

Plié.

AND IF WE GET STUCK? IF WE'RE TOO AFRAID TO WALK BACK?

You mean without Finley?

YES.

Plié.

She hadn't thought about that.

Plié.

NOT JUST THAT, BUT PREGNANCY, DEATH, WHAT IF YOU SEXPLODE SOME POOR MAN, AND WE END UP IN A DUNGEON? OH, SAOIRSE, FLOWERS ARE ONE THING, BUT HALF THE SONG YOU AND AISLING WROTE HAS TO DO WITH THE CARNAL CARNIVAL! THIS IS DANGEROUS.

The daunting tunnel of heretical debauchery was somehow even worse and yet even more tantalizing than she'd dreamed up with Aisling all those years ago—the towering fungi, the neon signs, the lights that wouldn't quit. An orange sin, all stretched over a path of silver insect sinew.

Hurler couldn't keep her eyes in one place too long. She had a coin in her hand and the desire to spend it.

Finley stood, waiting for her. He had her gear bag slung over one shoulder with his own. It made her smile.

"Now," he said, "about getting you that place to stay. Are you going back to the Puritan, or do you want to try some other hotels?"

Yes, that's right, he's got transportation. We're saved.

Yeah. Saved. Then why did she feel let down? "Don't you want to give me your leads?" she asked, thinking of how little she knew before they'd made a geas.

"I might not actually, but we'll get to that as we travel. I need to make the right arrangements. I've got business first, and the gardens are on the other side of the Carnival."

Heat flushed her skin. She didn't know why, but the fact that Finley was so capable somehow made her want to walk the carnival even more.

Sexplosion!

It's just a fantasy.

"How are we getting to the hotels?" Saoirse asked.

"I've got a bearfly."

"No!!!" she screamed, then caught herself. She could not ride bear-back with Finley. "I mean no. Don't you have anything else?"

"Not right now."

Transportation's out.

I'd say.

And I don't want to walk six hours back to Ballybofey.

Satirical hummed in her mind.

"You won't ride the fly?" Finley asked.

"Never."

"That's a shame. Ewe's really cool." He glanced up the street. The dinner rush noise was a feckin' cacophony. "I can't take you back to the Puritan until after. I don't know if I can find another fly. Will you wait here, or—?"

Wait here? In the hotel of haters or next to the carnival on her own? Neither option was any good. All this because she'd been unable to beat the Wives in Ritual Hurling. "Do you think the other hotels will take me?" she asked.

"You really want to see the dancers, don't you?"

"Yes."

It's not like we have many good options.

A couple of well-dressed lads slipped past them and into the North Tree Hotel.

Finley ran his free hand through his wavy blue hair. "I don't really want to say this, but there might be a lady willing to give you a place to stay."

"Really?"

"I can send her to you, but you'd have to earn it, and she's a real piece of work."

"But I'll get to watch the dancers?"

He scoffed. "You could join them."

"I just want to watch."

"Alright." He shrugged their bags. "I hate to break it to you, but if you don't want to ride bear-back—"

"I don't."

"—We'll have to go through the Carnal Carnival." He indicated the silver sinew.

When she'd gone in search of her gods' favor after being banished from the pitch by Triple K, then decided to be the perfect Shamrock Violet, she'd never imagined in all her life she'd have to fight flowers, much less entertain the idea of cavorting through the Carnal Carnival while being offered bear-back rides. Like the pub, Shamrock Violet didn't teach anything against the Carnal Carnival specifically—it was another part of her headcanon with Aisling—but...

Satirical found a new apprehension after seeing the sinew. *There's a hive nearby.*

Must be some kind of docile swarm.

There is no such thing as a docile swarm.

As long as we don't touch anything or look. I don't see how we're bad.

Look?

Just to study. If dancing helps me score, who knows what I could do with <u>Intercourse</u> *moves? I might even earn a Whiskey.*

Her mind droned. Satirical was putting serious thought into this, but Hurler hadn't let go of her bronze coin or her hope to spend it.

The bright orange lights were calling to her—the strings of rope lights. One man slid down a chute, another woman climbed a ladder. This place was wild.

She turned to Finley. "Will I get pregnant?"

"Not unless you want to."

"I don't want to."

"Then you won't."

Give me a good reason that doesn't have to do with dancing.

We still have to work off the taint of two taboos before trials.

Satirical groaned. She knew Saoirse had just made a good point. *The only way out of a taint was with a bad experience. There isn't a much better place than on the other side of this debauchery. We'll still be good. We're only bad girls if we're participating, just like at the Unshin River.*

Alright. But let it be known, I hate this.

It's known.

Saoirse stood. "I'm okay with the carnival."

This calls for a proper intro.

Not on your life.

Her Spectators were cheering: '*Satirical. Satirical. Satirical!*'

Her brain got flustered.

"Are you sure?" Finley asked, clearly noting her apprehension.

"No. I'm terrified, but I want to know more about hurl-ectile dysfunction."

"Fast learner?"

She shook her head. "Take it easy on me."

"I'll be gentle." Finley unsheathed his hurley and held it by the tip. Saoirse grabbed his shaft and made sure they had one length between them.

Spores, the man over there was fisting cake—batter. *Come on, Sat.*

Fine.

Ladies and gentlemen, Satirical droned, *boys and girls, it's the moment you have been waiting for. It's the moment you have been cheering for, the moment you've been singing for. With her next step, your number twenty-seven and mine, the best full forward in all the stars, is going to score and score and score some more—she's Saoirse Storm!*

One hand firm around Finley's hurley, shivering, Saoirse took her first step onto the silver sinew and into the Carnal Carnival.

Meh.

Hurler wiggled her hand as if to say 'you could have done better, Sat.'

Satirical rolled her formless eyes.

The street seemed a blur as they passed, but Finley helped her make sense of the shops, which went a long way toward calming her down. There was a small merchandise stall for the dance troupe, the Daughters of Dagda, their emblem—a woman with starlight hair against the green, white, and orange—plastered on a variety of nifty spores. Another stand sold stuffed éirecondas, not unlike her own stuffed animal, Honeysuckle. There were all kinds of food—she could smell roast mushrooms, corned beef, pork cutlet, a winter veggie stew, and still more she didn't know how to describe.

The more they walked, the more her shivers subsided, and what had initially frightened her seemed okay.

I'm telling you, this false bravado won't last. You always underesti-mate your opponents. <u>The Violet Intercourse</u> *won't be any different.*

I've already eaten the food.

That's not the same.

She let go of Finley's hurley, but didn't get any closer. He re-sheathed it in his gear bag.

"I never got out of Croaghgorm much," she said. "Any time we did, we were chaperoned the entire time. Aisling and I only managed to slip away from our purveyors for a few moments, and anytime we asked questions, we were shamed."

"That's too bad. There's a lot of amazing world to see out there. Lots of amazing cows, too."

"You must really like cattle."

"It's the family business." Finley smiled and threw his arms wide. "I suppose I'll be the first to welcome you to a new city, then. This is Rath Hoe—the Fort of the Hoes."

She and Little Hurler giggled. Satirical did not.

"Officially, it's Rath Bhoth, the Fort of the Huts, but everybody slurs the pronunciation."

Eager eyes and a hungry finger from Little Hurler aimed at a stand where a man shouted, 'Lick the Stick, Suck My Sausage,' in front of several skewered meat sticks with an enticing spiced aroma.

"Can I?" she asked Finley.

"Of course."

Finley flipped the man a copper coin for a sausage and handed it to her. She took it gratefully. That sticky-less bun had not been enough. The little gremlins in her emotions were practically drooling. Goddess Danu, it wasn't just Little Hurler—all her Spectators were zazzin'.

An ornery old man ran up the road with a watermelon.

"So, hurl-ectile dysfunction?" she asked, taking a bite of the sausage. Feck, it was hot—but so good. The spice bit the back of her tongue.

"Well," Finley said, "let's just say I think those carve downs are a little odd. For one thing, did you notice they didn't ask anybody about their Whiskeys?"

"Huh." She had to agree that it was odd. Shouldn't they want to know what magical powers a player possessed? Especially when Tyrconnell didn't have any? "I suppose it is."

Finley whacked the gear bags. "The Case of the Curious Whiskeys."

"The... what?" she asked—but she was distracted by a group of men and women who were—picking flowers. Together. The hair on the back of her neck bristled. An island floated by beneath the sinew street. Saoirse almost fainted and steadied herself by grabbing hold of Finley.

There were dozens of them—men and women in matching bright pink uniforms, gardening outfits, kneeling and working on honeysuckle flowers nestled in a forest of spindle trees, gooseberry plants, witch elms, and poplars. Every woman down there was bound to get pregnant!

THEY DON'T HAVE HURLING CAREERS TO WORRY ABOUT.

Even still!

Her heart agreed as a pair of giggling lovers flew past on a bearfly.

Saoirse clutched her chest. "Tuatha Dé Danann. Goddess Danu, An Dagda, Manannán, An Morrígan!"

"I don't think they'd hang around a place like this."

I TOLD YOU YOU COULDN'T HANDLE IT!

Saoirse tried to recover by looking to Finley.

He pointed at his shoulder. "Cooties?"

She yanked her hand away. How had she gotten so close!? This was more dangerous than she'd thought. She started sucking wind. Her mind was dizzy.

"Suck the sausage and lick the stick. Focus on the taste. It'll help anchor your mind."

She did. At Finley's suggestion, she focused. The taste grounded her. After a moment, she calmed down. "Thank you."

"No worries."

You're right. This place is dangerous.

FINALLY! YOU JUST GOBBLED A SAUSAGE! YOU COULD BE PREGNANT. LET'S TURN AROUND.

"Am I pregnant?"

"What?"

"I just… gobbled that sausage."

Finley went pink, muttering something about Violet teachings. "No. You didn't even come close."

HE'S SUSPECT.

I know you think that, but he's not so bad. She still wanted to see the dancers.

"You can sit over there," Finley said. "Take a moment to rest."

Saoirse sat on a bench between two stalls. People passed, laughing their way down the sinew. A girl in a lovely dress talked about gambling with her friend in a blue bonnet. A man in a tweed suit passed next, then a young boy in ragged jeans with a spear strapped to the back of his plate armor. This place attracted all kinds. Was it really for her?

You're right, she thought to Satirical. *I'm scared, but we have to get rid of these taboos, and that wasn't big enough.*

Her brain knew it was true.

I don't want to stay scared. Maybe there's a way to participate without being a bad girl. Then the gods won't betray me to PÉNIS.

YOU CAN'T BE SERIOUS.

I want to try something.

WHAT?

Something wholesome.

WHY?

You already said it. Finley's not always going to be with us. If we have to go through the Carnal Carnival every morning just to get to Ballybofey, it seems like a good idea to be less afraid of it.

HMM.

"About being a genuine article?" she asked.

"Want to try Hide the Hurley?"

"Spores, no."

"You say the word, and I'll cover you."

"You shouldn't spend so much on me."

"There isn't much of a point in being rich if you aren't spending it on everyone else."

The walk was a bit wider here—a kind of square. Finley explained that they were at the center of the carnival, with many of the most popular attractions and pubs readily accessible.

A tall stage nearby held a busker. "Come one, come all, try the latest and greatest in gadgetry!" he shouted. "It's called the blow dryer!" The man showed off a stall lined with various mushrooms. "Step up if you dare—we'll drench you in water, and you'll find we can dry you just as quickly!"

"Perfect."

"That?" Finley laughed. "He's been here for weeks."

"What?"

"It's got to be the most normal, mundane thing in here."

"Then, yes."

I'M STILL NOT SURE.

Come off it, Satirical. If you can tell me what's <u>Intercourse</u>-related about a girl getting wet, then being blown, I'll give you a bronze harp.

YOU DON'T HAVE A BRONZE HARP.

You're just stalling.

Her brain didn't have a comeback.

We've sung a song for years about scoring—just so we could do this with the team.

FINLEY ISN'T ON THE TEAM.

No, he's not—and I hate that—but if I can't do something as simple as get blown at the Carnal Carnival by myself, then I'm not sure I'm worth the Wolves.

YOU'RE DOING IT ON YOUR OWN?

Yep. Just you, me, and Little Hurler.

THAT'S A RELIEF. ALRIGHT, AS LONG AS WE AREN'T WITH HIM, I'M OKAY WITH IT. GOOD GIRLS GET BLOWN SOMETIMES, TOO. I'M SURE OF IT.

Let's do this!

Finley paid the man to take Saoirse, which delighted the busker. He had a pair of skinny assistant girls take turns splashing her with water from a nearby barrel. She smiled and waved at Finley. "I'm wet as feck, cú."

Several people in the audience nearly died of laughter.

Then she was escorted into the stall lined with mushrooms. The busker said some spiel, then smacked a button.

Whoom!

The gadgetry roared to life. Hot wind danced about her, rushing up her pelts, slipping through her fingers, playing with her hair. She leaned back into the heat and wind. The force of the gust coming through the floor was strong enough to support her as she let her feet rise off the floor, her hair tossing above her.

The feeling was just... amazing.

"Good gods!" someone shouted.

"Are you seeing what I'm seeing?" said another voice.

"It can't be!" a third.

After a moment, the blow dryer finished. Saoirse slowly touched back down and found herself dry except for her hair, which was still a touch damp.

THAT. WAS. AWESOME! DO THAT SHITE AGAIN!

Satirical?

AGAIN!

She did. And did. And did. Again. Then one last time, melting into the warm embrace of the Carnal Carnival, when Satirical of all her voices came over the loudspore:

THIS ISN'T ANYWHERE NEAR AS BAD AS I'D THOUGHT.

Social Suicide

T he heat, the power—Saoirse couldn't keep the smile off her face. Blow dryers were amazing, cú.

Saoirse sat with Finley at the end of the Carnal Carnival, where a row of benches backed up to an enormous wall that cut right across the sinew, blocking the forest from view. The lights at this end of the carnival took on a pink hue. The kinds of shops had also changed. They didn't seem as friendly. Their wares, however—dresses, lace, frills, and fabrics—she could make sourdough bread in an apron like that. Maybe one day she'd have the courage to buy it. For now, she'd continue sucking on Finley's popsicle—a thick white éireconda on a stick. Its body had been coiled into two balls near the base, and its head had a smiley face—only one eye, though. What was that about? She licked the tip of her popsicle, then had to switch when she realized its balls were dripping.

JUST BECAUSE I HAD FUN BEING BLOWN DOES NOT MEAN I'M WRONG ABOUT THE CARNIVAL!

Saoirse rolled her eyes. Satirical had jawed all the way up the sinew after they'd been laughed at. Apparently, there was something really funny hanging over Saoirse's head, though Finley assured her she'd just attracted a harmless 'frizzy sprite.' A kind of fae she was unfamiliar with that made her hair a bit heavy and awkward. She sure was getting a lot of attention.

AND WHAT HAPPENS WHEN WE DON'T HAVE HIM?

We made it through the blow dryer.

IS THAT ENOUGH? I'M JUST SAYING, MAYBE WE SHOULD THINK ABOUT WHERE WE ARE STAYING. THAT DANCE LADY SOUNDS NICE, BUT A DIFFERENT HOTEL MIGHT BE SAFER.

That was a good point. *We still have two taboos, and it's not like we have to stay with the lady Finley mentioned.*

Her Spectators were at ease right now, fat and happy on new sausage; she wasn't interested in riling up her stomach with the queasy notion of being stuck on the other side of the Carnal Carnival.

There will be a way out.

THERE BETTER BE.

"You ready?" Finley asked, getting up from the bench.

"Ready for what?" That smirk was definitely hiding something.

He urged her to join him, pointing to a set of wide sweeping steps that led off the side of the wall and down to a large island floating in the mists. Saoirse joined him, trotting down the steps, finding herself strangely excited.

"Prepare your heart," he said.

"For what?"

Finley escorted her down the steps, around the wall, toward a large wooden platform overlooking the forest. "For Social Suicide."

Saoirse took the last step and lost her heart to awe.

If her gods spoke to her on the pitch, they were screaming at her now. Saoirse threw her whole weight against the redwood banister and into a masterpiece of a vista. Every bit of her being dove deep into disbelief.

THAT SUCH A PLACE COULD EXIST, FOLKS!

"Tuatha Dé Danann," she whispered. "It's a hive!"

Silver strands of sinew stretched from the Aurum Great Woods all around them to the open center of the grove, where they supported a structure the likes of which could only have been made by the gods.

The building was an insect hive turned into a palace—a masterwork of carving, craft, and care. Many floors taller than Croaghgorm Hollow and many times as wide, the outside of the hive boasted carvings—bands of the unbreakable knot designs of their gods.

And it didn't stop there. Three great gardens joined at the base of the hive, tethered to the spit and sinew. The way the islands were arranged formed giant shamrocks, each half-leaf a differently themed bioluminescent botanical fungal garden. They glowed back at her, the closest shamrock gardens pink, brown, red, green, purple, and black.

And that music! Special drum beats she'd never known blasted from the hive itself. It seemed to pulse with it, glow with the rhythm, each snippet of luminescent shroom decorating the palace strobing to every change in the bronze dord horns, every stroke in the fiddles, every pump of the uilleann pipes.

"This is incredible!"

"Social Suicide," Finley said, joining her at the banister. "Twenty-seven floors of pure fun. Gambling, drinking, fighting, girls—and yes, dancing."

"Those are all transgressions."

"You don't have to partake, but they don't call Rath Hoe Sin City for nothing." Finley smiled. "That's the home of the Daughters of Dagda."

Saoirse sucked on her popsicle. The single greatest vista she'd ever seen. The very best dancers. Could there be a place more amazing?

Finley escorted her to a smaller platform off the first that had a viewing area with cushioned seating and a fire pit. Saoirse took the hint, sinking into the cushions, stretching her feet to the fire. Finley set their bags down.

"You never did finish telling me about the Case of the Curious Whiskeys, cú."

"You were a bit distracted."

That was fair. "Still, I want to know. Even if I can't help yet."

Finley nodded. He was sucking on his own popsicle—pink. It looked like an open slip of peas with one left. "The thing is, about their Whiskeys, is everybody has tried everything already. Every conventional method to help them get their magic back. Every technique. Every idea. Of course they did. It's been twenty-six years."

A swarm of giraffeflies zipped by overhead. They had such long necks.

Saoirse thought about what Finley said. "If nobody else figured it out, how are we supposed to? I mean, I know the basics—ogham lettering, mists in the hurley, druids, stuff like that—but I don't know what to do or where to start with the team. Like, if a Hard Whiskey is how the magic works, how hard do they have to be, cú?"

At this, Mr. Three-Torques-Rich snickered something fierce, the edges of his smile curling in on themselves.

"What is it?" Saoirse asked. That had seemed a perfectly serviceable question.

"Shamrock Violet," he snickered. "It's just... It's not a proper conversation for a man and a woman."

"Lame, cú. Tell me!" She punched him playfully on the arm.

Finley controlled his laughter, pressed his palms together, put his fingers to his nose in thought for a moment, then looked back to her. "I'm not saying they are flaccid—not yet. I don't know for sure. If my father's conjecture that hard is, well... hard—that's where I need you. It might not be the case—spores, they're only twenty—but if it is, someone who can help me figure out whether they are flaccid and, if so, why, is critical. For the life of me, I've never heard of a man with a flaccid Whiskey. Even me old gaffer's holding strong, and he's in his seventies."

"I've never heard of it either."

"To be honest, if anybody would know, it would be the women here." Finley gestured to Social Suicide.

"Like the Daughters of Dagda?"

"At least some of them."

How curious. She might really be the perfect person to help Finley. No wonder he was so adamant. If the secret to solving the team's hurling lay with the women in this dance hall, it stood to reason they'd be more willing to tell her than help him.

She lost herself to the strobing lights for a while, feet warm at the fire pit, sucking the rapidly shrinking éireconda.

Hurling's always been a way to make my dancing better.

AND NOW YOU THINK DANCING IS A WAY TO MAKE YOUR HURLING BETTER.

Not mine—but the team's? After seeing them at carve downs, it wasn't a stretch to say they needed all the help they could get. She still wished she could get Aisling to give them some PÉNIS therapy, but she couldn't go back to Croaghgorm.

"I've been thinking," Finley said. "This entire walk—about how much to tell you. Remember when I said I might not fill you in on what I know? Well, I think it's best if you figure it out yourself, and not just because it's improper or sensitive. If everything we already know is wrong—if my dad is right about the overlap—well, maybe it's best to get a fresh look at things. Even if you only have six days."

She nodded. "I'll do some, but I'm still going to play for my goals, cú."

"You've made up your mind?"

Saoirse nodded. "I'm staying at Social Suicide."

"Then we're on the same side." He held up his opened pink pea pod—what was left of it. "In the spirit of things, we've got to start this off right. Cheers over an official mystery satire title."

"With popsicles?" She looked at her half-eaten one-balled éireconda. "You know what? To us."

"To Finley Man Domhnaill and Saoirse Storm in: The Case of the Curious Whiskeys."

They tapped popsicles.

Together, "To the County Tyrconnell Hurling Club!"

The Colors

The Shamrock religion is split into seven colors, one sect, or Color, for each color of the rainbow. The most popular color by far is Green, but Orange is also common. There's a popular religious figurehead for Blue who wears blue robes and is making waves right now. I don't know much about him, and I know even less about the other Colors. I mostly get our Color, Shamrock Violet: Color of Innocence and Ownership!

That's why we have things like The Library of Lived Experience and Sisterhood Healing Sessions with Gratitude Circles. When you're feeling guilty or shameful, you give that shame to your sisters and the plants. Then the sisters will tell everybody in town what you're ashamed of, and the whole city can hold it against you. The healthiest way to deal with your repressed and dangerous feelings is to give the responsibility of those feelings to others so that you're too afraid to act on bad feelings again.

It's also why nobody is told about <u>The Violet Intercourse</u> until the last moment. That way, you can remain innocent of the true cost of your fealty to the gods until you're ready to take ownership of that shame.

Genius, right? Anyhoo, check out my manifestation board! It's getting cool.

Strumpets

S ocial Suicide's fung-tanical gardens were broken up into districts based on their color. The woman Saoirse needed for her place to stay would find her, Finley said, so she took his suggestion to enjoy the gardens to heart, wandering the darkened grounds while he dealt with his business. And after wandering through the Black Light District full of rare goghshrooms, and struggling past the Purple Light District dedicated to equally expensive escherooms with gardens that'd messed with her brain, she was happy to be in the Red Light District. It just felt like home.

Saoirse meandered from a crimson and gold garden, under a rock archway, and into an avalanche of new color. Ornate burgundy chihulooshrooms, cultured into elaborate interlocking shapes that reminded her of blown glass, hung from tall bronze yard ornaments of stacked faces. Between them, piccashooms, a rare breed of mushroom that appeared to be 'sliced' in blocky angles, added a flash of contrasting waxy color. This particular assortment was going through a blue period. *Spores.* Saoirse paused to take it all in. *I could stay here forever and never run out of new vistas.*

I KNOW WHAT YOU MEAN.

"That's why I'm asking," said a woman's voice.

What was that? The voice came through another archway, leading to a new color—hot pink. Somebody was in an argument. *Wanna check out a new district?*

Little Hurler was definitely game.

"Are you saying something I was supposed to be listening to?" said a different woman's voice. "Or something else?"

"On An Dagda, Four," said the first.

I DON'T KNOW, STEPPING IN ON AN ARGUMENT SOUNDS LIKE A BAD IDEA.

What if it's them?

DANCERS, YOU MEAN?

That nice old man said we could find two in the pink and one in the Sphic.

I'M PRETTY SURE HE WAS DRUNK. LET'S JUST WAIT FOR THE LADY, TWENTY-SEVEN.

"Don't on An Dagda me, skank," said the second.

"TDD!" The first voice shook with anger. "Give me my list!"

Curiosity got the better of her. Saoirse swept through the burgundy and blue for the Pink District. What were they arguing about?

I DON'T LIKE THE FEEL OF THIS PLAY, ME.
We made it through the Carnal Carnival.
SUSPECT RATIONALIZATION.
Just be with me on this.
SPORES.

Heart hyped, Saoirse crept to the threshold, hiding just around the corner to the pink fungal district, and saw *everything!*

SURE, LOOK!

There were dead trees wrapped in glowing, neon pink, vein-like fungi that radiated sweltering heat, like a sauna; there were beds of smooth black river stones; and there was something else as well: a rock archway. Suspended over the curious conversation, the entire length of stone was covered with painstakingly curated, glowing neon stencils of women... in the nude.

Hurler almost fainted. Saoirse's nostrils flared. Who would depict such a thing!

THE TAINT OF A TABOO?

Was it? Her heart beat like it was fist-fighting for a free sliotar, but just because something was shocking didn't necessarily mean it was bad luck or a bad experience. *I don't think so.*

CAST A NET ON ME!

The two women stood beneath the... archway.

AND THEY DO NOT LOOK LIKE FRIENDLY PLAYERS BY ANY RIGHT, Satirical said.

Hurler nodded, though her heart seemed enamored by the first, which struck Saoirse as strange, because her heart was wrong. Never in Saoirse's life had she ever laid eyes on a person and instantly jumped to hate, but she was jumping now. This woman was a... a... strumpet!

Framed right there in the center of... the action—*spores*—stood a tall girl with stunning features, arms crossed, head a voluminous spill of tight blond curls. Which, what, when, where, and why, in all the names of the gods, had decided that making *this girl* was a good decision? Just the way she stood was a sin she'd never slip in the Shannon! Saoirse would like to get her in Rite of Ritual Hurling and bury her on the pitch—for no good reason other than somebody ought to!

AGREED.

Hurler made a rude gesture at each of them.

Saoirse ignored her.

The other woman, though, seemed alright. Standing off to the side of the archway in a shadow by three large oak barrels, she was shorter than the other, brunette, with long, attractive arms.

Both women were dressed in skin-tight, stretchy black pants and massive, puffy winter coats that reached their knees; *they must be sweltering.*

"Well? Any time," asked the awful one.

Salm, she was bossy.

OUR HEART'S LOST IT.

"Fine, Fiadh. If your highness demands," said the one by the barrels.

"I do," said Fiadh.

The other growled at her. "There's Hater, Bob—"

"Not Bob."

"Fine."

"Jiggly?"

"We call her Sinead, and she doesn't want to."

"TDD," Fiadh said instead of Tuatha Dé Danann. "She's a blindfolded chaun in a coin factory! Who else?"

Clack!

The women snapped to look in her direction.

Saoirse groaned.

Little Hurler face-palmed.

Satirical was losing it over the loudspore.

Saoirse had accidentally kicked a loose river stone. She winced at each loud smack against the garden walk.

SMOOTH MOVE, ME.

Slip me in the Shannon, Sat.

There was a long moment of uncomfortable silence in which both girls looked over Saoirse's head, raised a brow, then looked back at her again.

Feckin' fizzy sprite.

WELL, ARE YOU GONNA LET THIS BE ANY MORE AWKWARD? I CAN FILL THE SPACE WITH BROADCAST CALLS IF YOU LIKE. THERE GOES SAOIRSE! CLUTZ EXTRAORDI-NAIRE! HOW'D SHE GET A FAE STUCK IN HER HAIR? HOW'D SHE GET THAT STONE RIGHT OVER THERE?

Sometimes I really hate you.

YOU'RE WELCOME.

There was nothing for it. Saoirse took a deep breath and crossed from the Red Light District into the Pink, which was surprisingly comfortable once she got into it. "Are you two dancers?"

Fiadh flipped her curls. "One of us is."

The other girl looked like she might explode.

Saoirse's hair stood on end. Dancers. Professional dancers! Spores, how long had she dreamed of being this close to the Greensleeves?

The woman in shadow broke the silence. "I love the outfit."

"I'm sure you do, Four." The blonde smiled. "She both looks and smells like a hobo." Her eyes flicked to Saoirse's hair again. "Who got roped into the blow dryer, like, what, six times?"

How had she known it'd been six? "I wasn't roped in."

"Ignore her," the girl named Four waved her in. "She's not important."

"Projection."

Yikes. Saoirse dared herself closer to the arc of puffy pink poom-poom power. "Nice to meet you. I'm Saoirse."

"You idiot!" Fiadh steamed.

Why was she so upset?

"Introductions?" Four pepped up.

And Saoirse understood at once why Fiadh was upset. She should have figured it out from the name.

"Prepare for headaches!" Four cried.

Four was a Wife.

NOT THIS AGAIN!

The brunette scooped up a pair of river stones and began clacking them together as she maneuvered about the grotto in some kind of interpretive dance routine. "With life-altering stakes!"

Saoirse sighed, ignoring the rest of the routine. "Do they do this every time?"

"Oh yeah," Fiadh said, looking equally done with this shite.

"That's stupid," Saoirse said.

"Our insecurities will ruin world peace!" ***Tap-tap!***

Fiadh shrugged. "They are *the Wives.*"

"I'm Wife Four!" Wife Four struck an interesting pose, one knee up near her face.

Little Hurler applauded; she was the only one who'd really been watching. Saoirse remembered from last time that the Wives would remain frozen in their final pose unless she played along. While a part of her wanted to just leave Four there, she did feel pity for the poor creatures, and she could flex something Fiadh couldn't. Saoirse let her palm fill with her special magical golden dust and threw it at Four.

When—Fiadh threw a fistful of glitter too! ***AND HERS WAS PINK!***

This feckin' cow! Saoirse spun on her heel to face the strumpet. Fiadh did the same, facing her. "Glitter is my thing!" they shouted at the same time. "Your thing?! It's my thing!"

How dare she? "What do you do?" Saoirse asked. "Carry it around in your purse?"

"Yes," Fiadh said with a pop of her curls. "You?"

Saoirse smirked. "It's my Whiskey."

"Your Whiskey is glitter?"

"Jealous?"

"What do you do? Spin on stripper poles in the sky?"

"I don't even know what that means."

"A kelpie with a dried-up mane..." Fiadh shook her head.

"But I know that was an insult!"

"At least you know when you're being insulted."

"At least I know how to play hurling."

"At least I don't have your ridiculous fecking hair."

Hair? Her hand flew up to her... hair. Saoirse's eyes went wide. She turned to Wife Four. "What is she talking about?"

The brunette looked like she didn't want to say.

"What is she talking about?" Saoirse demanded. But she could already feel the answer.

Four pointed at the three water barrels near the arch of fungal fannys on frightful full display.

Saoirse rushed to the barrels and looked into the dark water—and lost her salm mind. "A frizzy sprite!"

UH OH.

"A FRIZZY SPRITE!!!"

DON'T LOOK, LITTLE HURLER!

It was too late. Her heart had already gotten it full in the eyes. Saoirse looked like a puffy red cotton spore on the end of a stick!

I'm going to kill. I'm going to. Saoirse gripped the barrel, fingers white-knuckled on the oak; she screamed, "RAAAAAAH!" Her jaw unhinged. "AAAAAAH!" She spasmed. "I'm going—!" she groaned, unable to hear, rage flushed full across her skin. "RAAAAAAH!"

"What's going on?" asked Four.

"I don't know!" Fiadh said.

HER JAW'S FULLY UNHINGED, FOLKS. OUR GIRL'S LOST THE PLOT!

"HURLING!!!!!!!!!" Saoirse roared.

Clack. Clack. Clack.

Sound? Sound! Woman.

CALM DOWN, TWENTY-SEVEN!

Saoirse clomped to the archway where terror swept up the sinew—terror she was going to beat with her broken hurley.

Warp Spasm

"Hair. Woman. Hurling!" Saoirse roared.

Twenty-Seven! Hurler!

"Hurler. Tutu. Hurley!"

I don't know what to say, folks. Our girl has lost it! She's like a hulking monstrosity. Her skin's turned red, her jaw's open!

"RAAAAAAAAAAAAAAAR!!!!!!!!!"

Her breath is stinky!

Saoirse stare at new woman.

That she is, folks. A new opponent has taken the stage. And what an old brood she is. She's a tall and thin old brood dressed in an outstanding green gown, huffing a long, slender white pipe about as big around as she is, and her pale hands are covered with arm-length orange gloves. It's got to be the most Éirish 'hurling kit' of all time! One thing is clear with every clack of her heels on the silver sinew—this woman is the best player here.

Several Spectators rushed for seats in the Stadium; a few had turned with Saoirse and were throwing a mushroom-and-sausage food fight in the stands.

That energy, though, folks. What a lady this woman is! She's stepping into the fungal grotto. Even though she doesn't match the district color—pink—she dominates the area. It's as if the dead wood and the heated pink shrooms in their beds of black river stones bow to her.

Little Hurler joined the angry Spectators. It was a full-on brawl. A tiny Saoirse caught a right hook; another caught cleats to the face.

"HURLING!" Saoirse bellowed.

"A Warp Spasm," said the woman.

"Stay out of this, hag," Fiadh said. "I'm going to teach this match-fixer a lesson."

"RAWR!" Saoirse seizes a river stone and hurls it at Fiadh. Fiadh dodges to the side! "Bimbo!"

"What do we do?" Four shrieked.

The women dive for cover! You can hear 'em yelling. Look out, Four! That stone was a near miss, folks.

"There are only two ways to get rid of a Warp Spasm: intense hurling and shame," the old woman shouted from behind a large installation of shroom-covered deadwood. "We don't have enough men for the latter."

THE OLD WOMAN MAKES THE CALL. SAOIRSE HURLS ANOTHER STONE.

The woman tsked her tongue. "What a nuisance. Púca Súcca!"

Snap!

THE SOUND OF TWO POWERFUL FINGERS RINGS THROUGH THE GROTTO. IS THAT A REAL PÚCA? AND ACTING ON COMMAND? WHO IS THIS OLD BROOD, FOLKS? I AM DEFINITELY NOT THE ONLY ONE IMPRESSED!

Girls. Hurleys. Now.

IT'S TRUE, LADIES AND GENTLEMEN, FIADH, FOUR, AND THE OLD BROOD HAVE HURLEYS! THEY MUST HAVE COME FROM THE PÚCA'S MAGIC. HELP US, OLD LADIES! PUT OUR GIRL DOWN!

Spirit Stadium stopped its fight at the sight of the hurleys. Little Hurler lowered her gaze in hyper-focus.

The Spectators roared. *'Hurling! Hurling! Hurling! Go!'*

"RAAAAAH!"

"Protect yourselves!" the woman cried.

Saoirse. Scoop. Stones.

AND IT'S A SLURRY OF STONES FROM SAOIRSE—BUT THESE STRUMPETS ARE SURPRISINGLY GOOD! FOUR'S BEHIND THE BARRELS! THE OLD BROOD TUCKS BEHIND A NEW BIT OF DEADWOOD—BUT FIADH! FIADH'S JUST OUT IN THE OPEN WORKING AWAY WITH HER BAS! SHE'S A CONTENDER! SHE CAN MOVE! SHE CAN BLOCK THE STONES! SHE CAN PUT IT ALL ON DISPLAY! DARE I CALL HER A RIVAL?

"Why are you even here, hag? Didn't you have business?" Fiadh shouted. *DARING A DANGEROUS DANCE WITH OUR GIRL!*

"SAOIRSE LEAP!" *FIADH SLIPS AWAY.* "FIADH BAD PLAYER!"

The old woman spoke again. "Master Finley wants us to give her a place to stay."

"This thing?" Four shrieked from behind the barrels.

"ME STAY," Saoirse bellowed. "ME LIKE PRETTY DANCE!"

"Me like pretty dance," Fiadh teased. Saoirse threw a stone at her. She gave the old brood one look. "I hate you for this."

"You hate everything," Four shouted from her hiding spot.

"And I expect to use *my* hurley." *THE SAUCY STRUMPET FACES OUR GIRL IN THE ACTION!* "Match-fixer, I challenge you to a Rite of Ritual Hurling!"

WHAT A CALL! I DIDN'T SEE THAT COMING! ...SHITE, ACTUALLY... DON'T SAY YES. IT'LL FECK UP MY TICKET PRICING!

"HURLING!" Saoirse lunged forward and screamed with her open maw.

"Gross," Fiadh said.

"I ACCEPT."

Spirit Stadium lost its salm mind.

OH, COME ON, I ONLY CHARGED VISTA PRICES FOR THE HOTEL LOBBY, NOT A WHOLE GAME! I COULD HAVE MADE SO MUCH MONEY... I MEAN—HURLING, YAY!

"Púca Súcca," said the older woman.

Snap!

"HAIR. WOMAN. HURLING!!!" Saoirse growled.

Little Hurler ripped up turf in her heart, her eyes a bright glowing red.

"That is one bad hair day!" *FIADH SAYS. PÚCA SÚCCA'S GIVEN THIS GIRL A NEW HURLEY AND, SPORES, IT LOOKS LIKE IT'S MADE OF PURE BRONZE. I'VE NEVER SEEN A HURLEY SO EXPENSIVE!*

'Oooooo,' said the Spectators.

"How do we get her to set the challenge?" Four asked.

"LITTLE HURLER?"

"Who's she talking to?" Fiadh asked.

Little Hurler tossed her hurley high and caught it.

"I have no idea," said the woman.

"TRICK SHOTS."

"Fine by me," Fiadh popped her blond curls. "When I win, you leave the premises forever."

"HURLEY!"

Monster Saoirse holds her hand to the side—but there's nothing there! Her hurley is still broken from Triple K.

"She's just standing there," Fiadh said. "Where is her hurley?"

Four shrugged. "I don't know."

"Check her bag," the woman demanded.

They do. Four is tearing through the side pockets now. She's got a hankering for a hurley. She's found it!

Four pulled back to reveal the bits of Saoirse's lucky hurley—"It's in pieces."—*and Saoirse's lost her salm mind... further.*

"MY LUCKY HURLEY!" Hot liquid fire raced through her body.

She brute-forced a merge with Little Hurler! Gold sparkles fly everywhere—it's not nearly as majestic when she's angry.

"Oh, shite," said Four.

"Run, Four!" Fiadh shrieked.

Four did.

Saoirse's on all fours FOR Four, forward, full-forward, fore Four, forcing her forward! I'm amazed I got out that mouthful, folks. Four's dashing through the installation now. Oh—Saoirse singes herself on a hot, hot pink tendril. She's howling.

'Hurling!'

The Spectators are howling, too!

"Toss the pieces!" Fiadh cried.

Four did not need to be told twice. She ditched the shards of Saoirse's lucky hurley into the three barrels!

Saoirse dives.

"HURLEY!"

She comes up. She looks a bit stunned, folks.

"The water barrels!" Fiadh cried. "They stunned her!"

"Dunk her!" the old brood ordered.

Three pairs of hands seize her, flip her round, and shove her hair-first into the barrel.

She screamed and fought her way up. "Get out and hurl!"

"It's boiling!" Fiadh cried.

"Ow! My hands!" Four whimpered.

The old woman: "Again!"

They plunge her waist-deep into the second barrel, folks.

Even under the water, she screamed. Her mouth growing wider, pure rage kept her from drowning—but it was... colder. She came up. "Me no like me hair?"

"Again!"

For a third time, the others slammed her backward, hair-first into the last barrel. By the time she came up, her rage had subsided, her mouth refigured itself. She checked with a hand. It was just like in the game against Melak. Saoirse fell, coughing and spluttering, to her knees.

"What was that!?" Fiadh shouted, her puffy jacket soaked. She flicked her arms out.

"I thought those only happened in the old stories," said Four.

Saoirse hung her head. "Sorry..."

Water and Gold

A Warp Spasm? Isn't that what Melak had said? So it wasn't her Whiskey, and apparently, it was really easy to tell a woman had hit the blow dryer six times.

YOU LOOKED LIKE A PUFFY RED COTTON SPORE STUCK ON A HURLEY!

And you didn't tell me it wasn't a sprite!?

IT WAS PRETTY FUNNY. I DIDN'T KNOW IT WOULD DO ALL THIS, THOUGH.

The two girls continued flicking out their jackets. The woman stared at her with an unreadable expression, then took a puff on her pipe. She exhaled, and a pair of smoky éirecondas with ruby red eyes slithered their way out of the woman's mouth. The embers flashed across her eyes.

"Was I glowing?" she asked, thinking about what Sat commented on last time.

"No," Fiadh said. "But I could see right down your throat. It was gross."

The old brood studied her.

Saoirse stood resolute, wringing the water out of her hair and, with it, her frustrations. "I am sorry."

"You're in the middle of a Rite of Ritual Hurling," the old brood said. "For an offer of a place to stay."

It took a moment for everything to register: the other girls, their hands red from the hot water; the grotto; the stones all over the place. She'd really done a number. "I'm sorry about your hands."

"They'll heal. The water wasn't actually boiling—just hot," the woman said.

Spores, but she liked this old brood. Saoirse took in the tight bun, the imperious glare. She had the swagger of a right deadly defender.

"I think I remember." She racked her brain. "Trick... shots?"

"Yes," the woman said.

Her Spectators cheered half-heartedly, many of them only now recovering from the brawl they'd had with Little Hurler.

"It's your turn, when you're ready. Four, Púca Súcca, and I will judge."

Saoirse nodded. As bad as she felt for putting them all through such an ordeal, if this fell through, she'd have to return all the way back to Ballybofey for a place to stay, which would eat up the rest of her night. With two taints left, she'd be likely to face the cosmic bad luck on the pitch. She could only imagine how terribly that would go—not to mention missing the dancing, or the chance to ask the women here, as Finley suggested, about getting back the team's magic. Goodbye, professional hurling. Hello PÉNIS dungeon. Or worse.

DOESN'T THAT COUNT FOR THE TAINT OF A TABOO?

I didn't have a bad experience, Saoirse thought. *I was the bad experience.*

FECK.

"Scared?" Fiadh asked.

"I don't have a hurley."

"Jacket." The woman held out a hand to her.

Saoirse struggled out of her wet leather and handed it to her, leaving her upper half in only her blue Camogie Cunts bodysuit.

The woman flicked it out and wrung it several times. She was strong for such a bony old thing. The other girls shot Saoirse annoyed looks for the preferential treatment. "I was under the impression," the woman said, "Shamrock Violet girls were picked by their hurleys at birth. Hurleys with magic so strong they would never split."

How did this woman know she was Violet? Finley must have told her.

"I... well..."

The woman held out a slender hand.

Snap!

The pieces of Saoirse's lucky hurley were suddenly in the woman's hand.

A trained púca?!

I KNOW, RIGHT?

The snakes stared at the broken pieces.

"Interesting bas." The old woman tapped the ash bits with her pipe.

"It's not illegally curved, if that's what you mean."

"Don't see a lot of wave ash, and shaved so thin." She rolled it over in her hands. "The only flat is in the middle."

"Because I only strike with the middle." Did that earn a smile?

"Now I'm really interested. Púca Súcca!"

A malicious little giggle sounded from somewhere to her right. Saoirse jumped.

"Don't be afraid, girl. Our local púca simply likes to find himself wherever the most interesting things are happening." The woman held up the pieces of her hurley, then spoke as if talking to the púca. "If you would."

Snap. The snap of two impressive fingers echoed about their little fungal grotto.

Saoirse blinked. Her hurley was whole. "Tuatha Dé Danann!"

"He only heeds the hag, you know," said Fiadh. "Try being thankful."

"Oh, I am! Thank you, Púca Súcca!" Wherever he was. Saoirse leaped for the hurley, seizing it from the old brood's grasp, which made the others gasp so loudly she half expected them to faint.

"You must really like that thing," the old woman mused.

"More than you know." She let her hands run the length of the grain with her wrapped fingers. Whole again! It was as if a piece of her soul slotted itself back into place. "Púca Súcca!"

The wicked little giggle returned; it seemed satisfied.

Her lucky hurley reformed, Saoirse plucked a smooth black river stone from the bed of a nearby garden. A bit awkward, but she could manage. "Thank you."

"I'm sorry," Four said, "but are we all going to pretend like what just happened was normal?"

It was abnormal? Melak hadn't given her much information before.

Everyone turned to look at the Wife.

"It wasn't my first Warp Spasm," Saoirse said, hopeful, though it was only her second... Maybe your Whiskey is getting close?

Maybe.

"I don't know enough to make a judgment," said the old brood. "I'll have to speak with Bricriu, till then I see little point wasting time on thinking about something I don't know much about. Especially when the relevant information no longer matters. She's calm, and there's a Rite to complete."

Four seemed annoyed, but she put her head down. "Yes, Madame."

So, she doesn't know either.

Little Hurler was more than a touch disappointed.

"Who cares?" Fiadh popped her hip. "Hurry up and take your turn already."

"That eager to lose?" Saoirse asked.

"As if. I'm eager to get out of here and rest my burnt hands."

Saoirse gripped her reformed lucky hurley. Spores, it was good to have it back. "Alright I'll go." It was the least she could do after putting them through all that.

"I've heard you're something special," the old woman said.

Saoirse beamed. "Just you watch," she said. "I'll put a river stone right through the gap in those two fungi past the arch."

FIFTY METERS. YOU'RE FEELING YOURSELF.

"Deal." The woman and her snakes backed out of the way, as did the others.

She didn't know how much these women knew about hurling, but it'd be an impressive feat—one she'd make more impressive with her favorite stylish solo, the same she'd won the All-Central County Tyrconnell Trick Shot Competition with years ago.

She'd promised she wouldn't transgress, and thankfully, trick shots were not dancing. They were hurling.

SHOW HER HOW IT'S DONE.

Her heart hit the splits, getting ready. Saoirse took a moment to flex out the bruise on her left thigh.

Here goes. Little Hurler, you ready?

They fist-bumped. Little Hurler grabbed her own hurley, pulling her own wet hair into a púca-tail so it was out of the way.

It was time to merge. Time to combine the embers of her magic with her will to win.

Dancing, fighting, making love—

Saoirse shouted, "UILLEANN!"

—THAT'S HER NAME.

The magic flowed. A warm fire burned in her breast. Little Hurler began to glow bright white. Hot fire filled Saoirse, fueled her. The pink fungi flickered around her. The nude women of the rock arch appeared to dance. The bossy girl whooped. Saoirse reached up and clapped above her head, showering herself in her special golden dust.

Her heart set. A warm crackle of energy danced about her skin.

Both corners of the Madame's mouth curled into a smile. Wife Four looked aghast.

LADIES AND GENTLEMEN, ON YOUR FEET. THIS MOMENT IS SPECIAL—THE TRICK SHOT THAT TOOK FIRST PLACE.

Her crowd rose in her honor.

Grass plot of the garden. "Let's go."

Saoirse flicked the stone into the air, soloing it. The odd shape made it bounce irregularly, but she kept up with it without breaking a sweat. She smiled a bit; she'd always used hurling to practice her dance. Now she was trying to win so that dance could help the team's hurling. It only seemed right.

Now to show off.

Golden dust shook free of her wrists as she popped the stone up high, then tapped it down, sinking low to barely brush it back into play before it hit the sinew. The move earned Lauren's awe and even a whoop from Fiadh. She could tell they were enchanted by her dust.

She did it again, this time dropping into the splits.

Wife Four let out an "oh my." Surely even the Madame was impressed.

Saoirse caught the river stone on her head—*ow*—then rolled it down her spine as she went into a handstand. The stone passed between her legs; she tumbled forward, still in the splits. The stone continued its path up the front of her body; she popped it into the air with her chest.

"Tuatha Dé," Fiadh whispered.

While the rock was in the air, Saoirse popped up to her feet and whipped her body beneath the sliotar—total hairography. The water in her hair made it crack like a whip, leaving a sparkling golden trail of spray swirling around her. She let the momentum of the move carry her into a spin, bending back, rolling her neck. The sliotar fell, she effortlessly caught it on her bas.

She'd have to hit the shot.

The Madame snapped. Her éirecondas slithered into a hoop ring for Saoirse to aim through—an extra test.

"Don't worry, I never miss."

The show was over.

YOU'RE TWENTY-SEVEN AND MINE—

Smack!

"Boom. Top—oh no."

There was a sharp ***thack***, and Fiadh doubled over in laughter, her blonde curls bouncing in tiny shimmies. Four joined. Even the old brood went pink.

"It would've hit if it were a normal sliotar," Saoirse grumbled.

Little Hurler covered her eyes.

The rock's awkward shape had sent it at a bizarre angle.

It didn't go through the arch.

It didn't even go past it.

Instead, it had gone and stabbed, with a hard thunk—right up the eager vagina of the neon nudist display.

SPIT
WAX YOUR HURLEY

A Sensitive Topic

S aoirse was so stupid. She'd agreed to the condition of her Rite for an 'offer' to stay at Social Suicide, not a guarantee, which meant the Madame had been allowed to add conditions. Saoirse didn't complain, not after the fiasco she'd put them all through with her Warp Spasm. That was until one of those conditions was to give away her soul: the Madame had needed collateral until she got confirmation that Saoirse's story was true, and the only thing she'd had was her lucky hurley.

Without it, Saoirse felt naked standing in her new dorm room with Wife Four. The rest of the Madame's deal was harmless enough: don't tell any other girl why you're here, and join the Daughters of Dagda's morning exercises. Since she'd get her hurley back before tomorrow's trials, it probably couldn't have turned out better. Yet she was sure it was worse.

Which makes the Madame as suspect as Finley.

Stop being so judgmental.

Even the Little Hurler in her heart was hurley-less, but too enamored with her tu-tu to do much about it.

I suppose it could be worse. At least it's fixed.

Púca Súcca's pure class. Unlike Fiadh.

The brazen strumpet had backed out of her half of the challenge, claiming the pain in her hands from the hot water was too much to do any real hurling. Four called her out on it, but by that time the strumpet was already gone, and the old brood had returned to business.

Her new dorm room had a bed, a wash basin, a simple closet, and one window looking out onto the endless ribbons of green, white, and orange fungi flowing into the distance along the forest floor. She'd set her bag near the foot of the bed. She could put everything away later. The Madame said Wife Four would give her a tour of the grounds—and hopefully lead her into some bad luck.

Four watched her from the door.

Despite the state of the place, what with the naked neon women and fungal fanny archways, Saoirse was eager. She was about to be one-on-one with a woman who wasn't just a professional dancer, but a Wife. Which meant Finley was in luck. If anybody knew how to make a man on the team hard, she probably couldn't do better than her. She'd just need to get on this Wife's good side.

"Right, well that's your place," Four said. The tall brunette, also named Lauren, watched her from the doorway. "I know it's not much, but I don't expect you to be spending much time in here. It sounds like you're going to be pretty busy."

Saoirse finished getting most of the water out of her hair with a towel and tossed it on her basin. "Thanks for sticking up for me."

"Yep."

"Time for the tour?"

"Oh yeah."

WHAT DID WE DO?

I have no idea.

The other Wives sure were friendly enough people. When they weren't degrading their husbands. "Do you spend a lot of time with the other Laurens?" she asked.

"Loads." Four held open the door.

"I'm sorry?"

"Let's just go."

Where had the sudden flip come from?

SHE PROBABLY DIDN'T WANT TO HAVE TO SHEPHERD YOU AROUND.

Yeah. She could still try to be nice. What would you call so many Wives? A swath of Wives? *Nope.* A swarm? *Nah.*

"You're an interesting one," Four said, leading her through the dorms, past the door at the far end of the hall, decorated with glistening star spores—little clear balls with a crackling white light in the center. "I don't think most women would so easily entertain playing guest to an Éirish step-dance burlesque cabaret—let alone a gentlemen's club."

Saoirse shrugged. "I'm not a gentleman."

"No," Four said. "You most certainly are not."

They headed outside. The dorms were in a small village unto themselves just for the staff that ran Social Suicide. Three-story wooden long houses nestled amongst a series of leaves from the Aurum Great Wood. Leaves that had been pulled down and pinned to the outside of the branch to serve as privacy walls from prying eyes, giving the feeling that the whole place was inside the bud of some great flower.

Four strode for the exit at the end of a long walk of clay bricks laid on top of the bark and lit by tiny cultures of green shamrock shrooms. Saoirse followed, wondering just what was in some of the other buildings, but Four didn't seem keen on being a good tour guide.

When they hit the long strand of silver sinew at the entrance, Four got onto the nifty gadgetry they'd taken on the way up, which still hadn't lost its cool factor—a chair lift, a slew of ornate bronze benches on a loop of rope that ran the whole strand of sinew to the complex below.

Saoirse sat next to her, enjoying the different-angled view of the shamrock gardens, music from the palace pumping all the way up the grove, and wondering just where to start with all her questions. Since being flaccid was apparently a sensitive topic, she should probably save it for last so they wouldn't have an awkward ride. "What's that old brood's name?"

Four stiffened. "That is Madame Orla: owner, proprietress, mistress, and Madame of Social Suicide. Take your pick. She's always on the lookout for young talent."

"And a broken step-dance cabi-neigh?"

A smile stretched across her lips. "Well," Four said as their chair passed the edge of another large leaf, "we dance."

She pumped a fist.

Little Hurler cheered.

"Are you a Daughter of Dagda?"

"I am the best."

What confidence.

Even Little Hurler was impressed.

The Wife was a bit shorter than her, but that made her taller than most girls. Her frame was so petite. Saoirse wondered what Four might look like if she had been one of the girls on the branch dancing with the Greensleeves.

"Don't think I am?" Four asked.

"I wouldn't know."

"No, you wouldn't." She flipped her hair.

This isn't going well.

TRY A JOKE?

"We do a mix," Wife Four explained. "Ballet, river dance, or step dance—same thing—acrobatics, jazz step, interpretive, and show stoppers. Some women even experiment with more modern styles of step and music—rockspore n' roll, grunge—we have a few that just call themselves head bangers."

"Sounds painful."

Four didn't laugh.

Shite.

"Myself?" said Wife Four. "Acrobatic, expressive, step dance—with kick lines. Lots of kick lines."

"Uh-huh." Saoirse nodded along as the chair lift slid down the sinew. Yep, those were terms. What terms? She had no idea, but it sounded impressive.

I DIDN'T CATCH ANY OF THAT EITHER, FOLKS. DANCE IS JUST DANCE.

At the look on her face, Four added, "We do a big show."

"People called me the Dancer," Saoirse said, trying to find common ground before the big question. "Because I solo so well."

"Yeah..." Lauren did not sound impressed. "We stop the show in other ways."

"What about a gentlemen's club?"

Lauren scoffed as if she couldn't believe it.

BAD PICK.

"Sorry," Saoirse flushed.

The pair stayed silent for the rest of the ride while music vibrated through her feet.

They stepped off at Social Suicide's jobbery. The yard here wasn't so different from hers back home. The smell of horsefly and wet bearfly was strong. Part of the yard had been carved out of the very base of the hive. Winding sets of wooden bridges and stairs hung from bronze wires, connecting the yard to the fungal gardens.

Saoirse joined Four in the outer yard, another sprawl of islands roped and bound in place to expand the landing pad. Men in bright pink wrangler uniforms darted to and fro, taking mounts from patrons and settling them in appropriate stalls hidden beneath lime-green awnings. She supposed if she were ever missing home, she could come down here and give a few golden hand jobs. The men here, hopefully, wouldn't mind her handling their flies.

Now she just needed to pop the big question. It only made sense that the topic was so sensitive. Even teasing the tip of it like this left her wanting, yearning, desperate for more—hinting at the danger. Unfortunately, her tour guide still looked upset.

Saoirse rubbed the brim of her nose. Finley had been serious enough to take on a geas to get her asking about hurl-ectile dysfunction. She needed to take some risks.

"Um, Lauren?" Saoirse asked, dropping her voice so no one could hear. "How can you tell if a man is flaccid?"

Wife Four exploded. "It's not my fault!" she screamed, throwing her hands to the sky, drawing a number of concerned looks.

Whoa!

TUATHA DÉ!

Hurler dove for the cover of the lockers.

She hadn't meant to provoke that! "Sorry." This topic was *way* more sensitive than she'd realized.

"Don't blame me for my husband's failure!" Four screeched at her. "I should've known that's why you're here. Prime!? The moment you hit the splits, it was obvious. The Hoe is strong with you."

"I don't understand." And what was the Hoe? She shared some side eye with Little Hurler, who shrugged.

Lauren stared at her with a wild expression, the fungal glow reflecting malice. "You want to know...? That makes no sense!" she said, prattling to herself. "Why would they send her if she was a problem? What if she's the one? Does Prime think she would destroy our relationships? Or worse, balance them completely?"

Four ran a shaking hand through her brown hair like she was losing her mind—which, to be fair, it sounded like she was. Saoirse only came here from a taboo. She didn't care what kind of relationships these people had with anybody at all unless it interfered with their owners' ability to play. She should have paid more attention to Triple K's sermons on the matter.

"Four?" Saoirse asked. "I'm sorry. I didn't know it was that sensitive. You know I made a deal with Madame Orla, I just don't really know what I agreed to."

A wicked grin flashed across Wife Four's face, quickly replaced by the kind of broad, helpful smile that could capture the sun. "How about I show you?"

Saoirse side-eyed Little Hurler again. "Four?"

LET'S LEAVE!

But she couldn't. Four had a death grip on her arm, towing Saoirse up the winding wooden walk from the jobbery to the side of the palace.

"We call this building the House," Four said, indicating the hive and stopping at a small door.

The music shook her soul.

"Welcome, Saoirse," Lauren threw the door open, "to Social Suicide."

Four shoved her in the back, and Saoirse tumbled into a tangle of velvet curtains. She grappled with them before falling to the ground. "Ha. Ha. Very funny, Four. Four? Where did you go? Four!"

Saoirse turned and came face to face with real debauchery.

"Social Suicide!"

A girl pranced past her, the front of her step dance in belled pleats—but the back! It was cut into little strips all the way up her bum that swished with each sashay!

Saoirse grappled for purchase on the carpet.

ALERT. ALERT! ME!

A girl passed by with her skin on sinful display! Men grabbed her!

SAOIRSE, RUN! RUN!

No! What is this? What was she? She spun. The world blurred—gold, green, brown.

She couldn't see any shapes. She couldn't make out any sounds; it was all one big mass. She scrambled in some direction, clawing at air.

Spirit Stadium was in a full-on crash-out.

LOCATE YOUR NEAREST EXIT AND RUSH AT IT IN TERROR!!!

"Ahhhh!"

Somebody shoved her. She found a wall. She slapped it. She didn't even know if it was the door. "Four! Open the door! Four!"

People were laughing now.

"Four!"

"Are you okay, miss?" a young boy in a proper suit—pink with black accents—bounded up to her.

"Get me out of here!" she bellowed.

The usher boy's eyes went wide. He did just as she bid.

Sock Head

That counted for the taint of her second taboo! Tuatha Dé Danann! Skin! Heretical blaspheming! StRuMpEtS!!!

Saoirse raced back to the dorms as fast as her feet could carry her. She threw the door to the dorms open the moment she made it and stormed up the small staircase to the third level.

Most of her crowd had fainted. Little Hurler's eyes spun with a tizzy swirl.

Run! We've got to run!

When Four had opened that door, several women—

If you could call them that!

—had been congregated on the other side. But all Saoirse could see were—

"BARE ARMS!" and,

"CLEAVAGE!" and,

"ANKLES!!!" she shrieked. "This is a HOUSE OF WHORES!"

Her heart finally succumbed to the overwhelming realization and passed out.

Hurler, are you okay, Hurler!? Get a stretcher to the pitch, stat!

Several Spectators answered the call.

Saoirse burst into her room, sized her things, and took off down the hall, paying no heed to her surroundings. She'd promised to be the perfect Shamrock Violet—not to drink, not to gamble, not to dance, not to wear dresses, to represent the gods in a way that wouldn't cause her to lose—but now? There was no way to avoid any of those things!

She absolutely could not stay. She'd have to risk the bad luck during trials. She could still win. She could still score. Shamrock Violet warned her about women like these: loose women, sensuals, strumpets! Girls who tried to participate in *The Violet Intercourse* without the permission of the Magic Eight Ball! "Outrageous!"

"A lot to take in, huh?" said a voice.

Saoirse slammed on her heels toward a girl's voice she recognized: Fiadh—wearing *absolutely nothing*, blonde hair tied up with well over twenty-seven sets of floosy socks—

Bang! Fiadh slammed shut the door to Saoirse's room and leaned casually against the wall.

In. The. Nip. In public! Not even a bath! And her hands were perfectly fine!

This woman's nuts, folks!

"Don't worry if you crash out," she jabbed. "You won't be the first." With that, the outrageous strumpet popped off the wall and walked away.

"Crash out?" Saoirse faced her full on. "I don't crash out! I win!"

"And you'll never make them hard."

Saoirse's nostrils flared, her red hair almost crackling behind her, but Fiadh was already down the hall, disappearing into the room at the far end—the door lined with glittering star spores.

Make men hard—what could she possibly know about making men hard?!

Administering medicine to Little Hurler. Three, two...

That girl? That loose woman!

A jolt struck her heart. "You—you... sensual!" she cried.

Fiadh merely waved a single hand from behind the wood. "Thank you!"

Bang! Fiadh's door shut with a shimmer, leaving Saoirse standing in the hall. Did she always have to bang doors?

Another jolt.

"Thank you?" She'd said thank you!?

After a moment, Little Hurler came to. She rolled over to stare down the insane girl's door with the same angry fervor she'd shown Melak.

Saoirse couldn't help but agree. Spores on that dog meat! Spores on her refusal of the sporting wagers. This should count for her bad luck! But it wouldn't. Not even a single good quip came to mind.

Me, I—

"This is a really long crash out," Fiadh shouted through the door.

Saoirse threw a rude gesture at it. She wasn't sure which was worse, the ankles or the fact that Fiadh was right. If she left, she'd have one more taboo, no place to stay, and...

And...

She didn't have her lucky hurley!!!

Saoirse ran maddened fingers through her red hair. How could she have forgotten? Orla took it as collateral! "This is so wrong."

"Really long!"

"Póg mo thóin!"

Yeah, kiss her ass, bitch.

Satirical?

"Now we're getting somewhere," Fiadh called in a muffled jibe.

I'm not apologizing. That woman probably couldn't get a man hard if her life depended on it!

The thought made her smile. Hurler agreed, barely awake, intense eyes locked on the door.

Right, she couldn't trust a woman like that.

Usually, I'd counsel we do the right thing and go back.

Yep.

Shamrock Violet and all.

Yep.

Cosmic bad luck and such.

Yep.

Being a good girl.

Oh yeah.

But fuck that girl.

Absolutely.

Hurler mooned her doorway.

Hurler!

Saoirse threw a shocked hand over her heart, but if this was how it was going to be—one taint left and no hurley—she had to stay.

The door to her room opened on its own. Something hung on the back—something on a hanger, something way too glittery to be allowed—cosmic bad luck from the taint of her last taboo.

She screamed.

Slipping Sins

I love all the sayings that come from salmon, folks. Slip me in the Shannon, big slip, small slip, you're casting a net on yourself, one free leap to you, salm it. They are easily some of my favorite sayings, and they all stem from the Shamrock idea of death.

Shamrocks of all colors believe that when you die, your warrior spirit is transformed into a salmon and forced to swim River Shannon. They say the river begins in Tír na nÓg and flows to the sea, the domain of Manannán mac Lir, first son of the sea and ferryman of souls.

While swimming this river, anything you did that was sinful in life will manifest in the river as a branch, a rock, or some other obstruction to bar your path to rebirth. In fact, several Colors in Éire practice Sin Day, where they put sins to slip into the river during the great migration of the salmon. The trial is seen as a celebration of all the greatest warriors from the past generation.

Every year we travel to the Shannon Pot to celebrate the warriors that make it all the way, but one year I'd like to go further south and see how many fish leap the sin I set up for them.

Special Needs

Five Days Remain

*"Y*ou can't, Saoirse."*
"But it looks so fun, Chiefy!"
"Dance is illegal. That's that."

"I've figured it out, Saoirse! Trick shots!"
"Chiefy, that's cheatin'."
"Only if you're caught."

"And first place in this year's
"All-Central County Tyrconnell Trick Shots Competition
"goes to..."

Goddess Danu. Spare me.
She'd struck a deal to dance. What's worse? For the taint of her last taboo. They'd given her the dress to do it in.

A sequined, glittery, solo dress. Madame Orla must have hung it on the back of her door. Saoirse refused to wear it correctly. She crammed it over her winter furs like a one-armed sash. It was the best she could bring herself to allow. Wearing dresses was illegal in Shamrock Violet.

Saoirse stood in the corner of an enormous dance hall, its tall, vaulted ceiling hung with simple lightshrooms that shimmered on the waxed wooden floor, giving it a brilliant sheen. If she'd never made that dumb deal with Madame Orla, she'd still have her lucky hurley, she wouldn't have to be here.

Her heart counted out the beats to Little Hurler's stretches, but she could not, would not join. The only good thing was that she was finally free of her taints. She could focus exclusively on scoring goals and saving her father from life in a PÉNIS dungeon. But... If these dancers were as good as Finley said... learning their moves would help with that. No. Not at the expense of breaking the covenant she'd made with her gods.

Satirical came over the loudshroom with an ad:

Today's match is brought to you by thongs! Crack a spore. Spread that crack. Thongs—the single string to break your back! Who needs panty lines when you're already showing your ankles? Go the extra step in sensuality today. Available in different colors, patterns, and promiscuous personalities. You can walk, you can talk, you can help an ornery old grandpa smuggle in his watermelon! Be sure to drown after death when swimming the Shannon. Buy a thong today.

I thought you'd be back to your usual self.

Oh, I hate this, but I've got to commentate something, or I'll go insane. We should still leave.

A sharp scream and the sound of a bouncing sliotar in her brain said, Little Hurler disagreed.

Hurler!

Her heart snickered.

Don't worry. I know we can't participate. We're only staying to get my hurley, then getting out.

Good. That ad was hard to say.

She knew where Satirical got the inspiration for that ad. If dance itself wasn't bad enough, the hall was a whole jobbery of *those women.* Girls spread across the floor in little groups, stretching—if you could call it that, folks—in tight black flexing pants and oversized loose tops they'd cut off at the belly button.

The audacity.

How many men had they murdered with sexplosions?

Too many.

Gods, could they stretch, though. Saoirse forced herself to look away before she transgressed. The *truth* was, the only thing impressive about these sensual sleaze bags was the length of their legs!

Spores. The human body can bend that way?

Satirical!

It's hard not to stare.

Not that either of them was watching or anything.

The Daughters of Dagda. Leave it to strumpets to pick a blasphemous name like that. Like the Wives, these women seemed to move as a unit, so she'd taken to calling them *the Leggies* for the obvious reason: she could tell them apart by their arms, except that one by the mirror.

Gods, Aisling, if you could see her butt. Just look at her, her butt is so big. She looks like one of those rap bardist's girlfriends. Who understands rap bardists anyway? Spores, it's just so big. So round. So out there.

Tuatha Dé! She could see that other woman's whole calves!

Breathe, me. Breathe.

Little Hurler put a steadying hand on her heart.

Saoirse forced her eyes away from the Leggy doing a splits, her full fanny—feck it—fupa fastidiously fastened to the feckin' floor, and stuffed herself as deep into the corner as she could go, trying to blend in with the dance bags and stupidly tall water spores.

The Daughters of Dagda's water spores came in a ton of colors. Every girl seemed to have one. Tall cups with long straws and a logo of a mouth, tongue out, balancing a cherry.

You totally want one, don't you?

What I want is to get out of here.

And that's why she wore the scream, folks.

You ought to be fired.

I'm literally you.

She let her head fall against the back wall. She had to get out of dancing. The problem was that the one person she knew in here had spent the morning evil-eyeing her from across the room. After Wife Four had thrown her into Social Suicide, she didn't want to know any of the Wives anymore. It couldn't be helped. For the first time in her life, she needed to fake an injury and get off the field.

A sad frown creased Hurler's face, and yet there was no other option.

Reluctantly, Saoirse kicked off the wall and meandered her way between the legs.

Wife Four stretched in a group of seven would be murderous strumpets. Her long brunette hair spilled over a black top with golden ogham Saoirse couldn't read. The Wife was attached at the hip to a similar girl with a black bob cut. The rest, well, they had distinguishable enough arms.

"Sup cú," Saoirse tried. And then, to her surprise, it was carve downs all over again.

All the women in Wife Four's group leaped into action, forming an arc of threatening jazz hands.

What in the world? Oh, right.

FIADH SAID THIS IS GOING TO BE A THING EVERY TIME.

Little Hurler sure hoped so.

Don't talk about that girl.

"So you deigned to walk over," said Wife Four

"Yes? I—"

Four struck an impressive pose.

Wife Four:
"Prepare for headaches."

The woman with a black bob cut, who looked like she was out for blood, stood back-to-back with Wife Four in front of the jazz hands.

Wife Bob:
"With life-altering stakes."

They changed poses.

Wife Four:
"To stop you from dancing, we shall not cease!"

Wife Bob:
"Our insecurities will ruin world peace!"

The women behind them formed a really intense kick line.

Wife Four:
"We know what you're up to, you evil cat."

Wife Bob:
"You won't save our husbands, we're not down with that!"

Wife Four:
"Four."

Wife Bob:
"Wife Bob."

Wife Four:
"Prepare to play hurling and be distressed."

Wife Bob:
"We are the Wives"

BOTH
"And we're the best."

With some final pizazz, they all froze in one amazing pose.

My glitter is feckin pink! Salm Fiadh! Saoirse stuck a tongue out then threw some of her golden glitter at them to restart the poor creatures, and they all sat back down as if nothing had happened.

I'm beginning to see why Triple K said being a Wife was so scary, folks.

Must be their pre-hurling psyche out? Last time the Wives challenged her to a Rite of Ritual Hurling by the Wives she couldn't accept.

Little Hurler clapped enthusiastically.

"Unfortunately, I don't have a hurley," Saoirse said, getting ahead of the challenge.

All the women turned to look at her. Four raised a brow, but other than that, they acted as if nothing from last night had happened, which was a relief.

"So, this is the county killer you told us about?" one girl asked Four.

"I didn't kill the county..."

"Love the outfit, very... neamh-hemian," said another with knobbly elbows.

Saoirse shrugged. "Yeah?" Clearly, Wife Four had told everybody about her, but only Wife Bob gave her a holier-than-thou sneer as she spread her legs like a frog. So, Saoirse pressed on. "I need a favor."

Some of the Leggies in the room were watching now. A particularly proud-looking trio with serious winner energy, including a girl with a broken leg, seemed particularly keen.

Grand.

"What is it?" Four asked, harmless as a half-forward without a hurley.

"I don't think I can do practice today." Saoirse placed her hand on her deeply bruised thigh, where the sums had walloped her with the wooden spoon. "I'm injured."

"That's awful," said Four.

"My thigh. It's in bad shape." She tested it gingerly.

Wife Bob rolled her eyes. "Loser."

Good Girl energy, Satirical warned. Big Good Girl energy. Our dad's life is on you, remember?

Saoirse bit back a retort. "Yep."

"You're so funny, uh, cú," Four laughed. "Look, I wanted to introduce you," she said, indicating the bob-cut frog girl. "This is *another* Lauren! Wife Bob."

We got that from their little speech.

Just play along. Wives give up their humanity when they get married.

Apparently, they give up a serious portion of their brains, too.

Wife Bob tipped at her hips with an aggressive lean.

"Sup, cú." Saoirse said, hoping to break the tension.

"Give me a moment," Four said to the other women before she stood and pulled Saoirse away from the packs of curious strumpets.

She was more than happy to follow out of earshot. They stopped at the far corner of the dance hall near the exit. The Leggies, from what Saoirse could tell, returned to their own conversations.

"Look. You're only here for pretend, right?" Four asked. "Well, we're really good, like-" She raised a hand as if swearing on a name. "On An Dagda, good. It'd ruin the lie if you participated."

"So, you'll help me get out of it?"

"I got you."

"Yeah. Stay in the corner, baby," Bob called across the room.

Her heart put up its dukes.

Good Girl. She dropped her tension with a deep sigh. *It's okay, Hurler, we'll get ours back on the field tonight.*

Little Hurler didn't like it but pulled back.

Four placed a small hand on Saoirse's arm. "We wouldn't want you to feel dirty from all this dancing."

"Thanks."

"And as a gesture of good faith, you know, since you're trying to help our husbands and all," said Four. "We thought we could give you a few pointers."

Saoirse didn't trust her at all. They just said they didn't like the idea of her helping their husbands. Was that whole sequence some kind of strange out-of-body experience, or what? But if it got her out of dance, she'd at least humor the pitiful creature. "Pointers?"

"Right." Four dropped her voice conspiratorially, glancing over her shoulder at the trio of girls with the good energy, who still seemed keen on their conversation, before she continued. "If you want them to get hard, you're going to have to do some difficult things."

"To be honest, I just want to score, but if I find time to try out your suggestions, I will."

"I mean... they aren't that difficult. See Hard is all about chaos and control. Men love to fight monsters, right? They hate peace. Tyrconnell doesn't have as many dangerous fae, or Fomorians, to fight, so the men can't get Hard."

Saoirse gently bit the tip of her thumb in mock concentration.

"So," Wife Four urged her. "You have to create that chaos and disorder. Then you have to control it."

"How can I do that?"

"Men love it when you nitpick them. Or chastise their play. And I don't just mean trash talk. Belittle them, ruin their spirit. And Hard will rise from the ashes."

"From the ashes..." She paused.

Four nodded eagerly.

"Thanks."

"You're welcome. Now, I'll get you with Madame Orla. Hang out in the corner, okay?"

Four headed back to her group. Saoirse stuffed herself back in the corner, absentmindedly watching the trio her heart was drawn to. One had particularly long arms, the girl in the cast had slightly flabbier ones, and the other, well, there was no reason to remember what she looked like; she just looked like a hater.

The Wives must think I'm stupid.

WELL, YOU CAN ONLY COUNT TO TWENTY-SEVEN.

You and I both know that's different... somehow. But be cruel? Insult them?

NOBODY LIKES THOSE THINGS.

Little Hurler nodded. The last thing they'd do is belittle Lorcan. If casting shame on them worked, the team had already gone through twenty-six years of it, and last she'd checked, it hadn't been going so hot.

Though she would still run it by Finley when she arrived at trials, just to be safe, if the way to get men hard was to treat them like trash, it's not like they liked her much anyway.

The Daughters of Dagda

"C an I take classes, Chiefy?"
"It's too dangerous."
"But Triple K are in Meath."

"Saoirse, I've found a way."
"To fulfill my special needs?"
"Come with me."

"Wow! They're beautiful."
"If we watch from this branch—"
"I can practice with them!"

...And never be seen.
THE ANSWER IS NO.
What if I am good enough?
IT'S NOT ABOUT THAT.
I know...

It was one thing to watch the Greensleeves practice dancing, lying down a quarter mile above them, interpreting their moves. She'd spend all day listening to the music, practicing with her hurley, then try to design a trick shot using what she'd seen while Aisling read medical staves on PÉNIS Therapy. It was another thing entirely to be in a room with professionals. But how good could they be? The gods didn't have to torture her like this.

The dance hall had warmed up from the body heat of so many women. Several of the Leggies had progressed from stretching to prancing across the floor in simple combinations, practicing moves in the mirror. Seriously, how did they do that ankle one? Surely their feet could break. Saoirse'd never managed to figure it out on the branch, but she wasn't about to ask a bunch of *those women*.

She'd taken to sitting in the corner for the last few minutes, since she and Four had their chat.

Together, she and Little Hurler drew shamrocks around themselves, but Saoirse still hadn't figured out what she'd done to make the Wives so angry. The only thing Wife Four knew about her was that she wanted to make her husband hard. Wasn't that a good thing?

If her husband couldn't get hard, and she got him there, everybody would be the better for it. It's almost like the Wives wanted the county to go under.

MAYBE THEY DO, Satirical said.

That's absurd. Nobody wants to be from Tyrone.

They wouldn't have to worry anyway. Not for long. Saoirse's chest rose with a sudden surge of manic anticipation and pride—'cause she'd be on the pitch! She'd score! She'd save everyone from their fate with her goals, whether anybody got hard or not. Spores, but she was excited for trials! Even if she didn't have a clue what they entailed. Finley meant well, but the team's hurl-ectile dysfunction was the least of her problems. Her problem now was getting her hurley and getting out of here before it became the kind of sin too big to slip in the Shannon.

Tuatha Dé. Her penance tonight would be brutal.

She marveled at herself in the mirror. Floor to ceiling and wall to wall, she'd never seen a mirror so big before. She could see everything from here, including her not-nearly-as-bad hair day—thank the gods. She still couldn't believe nobody told her about the blow dryer.

I look—

INSANE, YEAH.

Grand. The haphazard dress sash—no. Saoirse took it off and spiked it on the ground. She didn't care what Madame Orla wanted; it was too much.

Little Hurler prodded her heart. Tu-tu on and legs ready.

You're not helping.

She prodded again.

Please. Stop.

Prod.

"Hurler—!"

"Girls!" A single powerful clap echoed through the hall, along with a voice that could only be Madame Orla's.

Instantly, the room snapped to attention. The girls raced to form five lines at the end of the hall.

Saoirse broke off her fight with Hurler as the girls crowded in beside her corner. It struck her how similar they were—all the same height, all a bit shorter than her. They had a 'look.' On the pitch, her size was a serious advantage, something she'd been immensely proud of. Now it made her stomach churn, like she wasn't a 'real' dancer.

Must not be that good if they care more about aesthetics than skill.

TRUE.

Orla, the older, imperious brood, was in a different ball gown today, this time a simple, shimmering silver with matching gloves. Her long pipe hung casually between two fingers.

"Kick out full legs for four, heel tape one. Then give me left boom-bat-bada with a big, high-volume ending on eight-and. Then take a roll, give me four clicks, heel tape two, and walk off wings out till the second eight," Orla commanded. "Muddy clicks are a twenty-five crunch penalty. This show will be perfect for Yule Night."

SLIP ME IN THE SHANNON. WHAT DID SHE SAY?

Both Saoirse and Little Hurler just shook their heads. They had no idea; none of them knew much of any dance jargon.

One of the girls from the proud trio stood at the front of the middle line, with the biggest smile Saoirse had ever seen, calling to the others, "Sporeshine Heads! Sporeshine Heads!"

The girls shook themselves into perfect posture, heads tilted slightly back, enormous smiles aimed high.

"Let them see your smile in the balcony," the girl said.

In an attempt to make some sense of what was going on, Saoirse decided she was the Leggy Leader.

"Audience is the mirror," Orla called.

There's no crime in watching.

IF THERE WERE, YOU'D HAVE ROLLED, 'NO.'

Saoirse found herself leaning forward out of the corner, trying to give her heart a good view. She didn't like these Leggy strumpets, what with their low morals and high hemlines, but how different could professional dance possibly be?

But the start never came. She realized everybody was looking at her.

"What?"

"Saoirse." Orla nodded to the group.

All her eagerness tumbled right out of Saoirse's chest, like the bottom had gotten ripped off Little Hurler's bag of happy sliotars. She pointed at herself. "Me?" she asked. Orla couldn't mean—not for her to join? Surely. Hadn't Wife Four talked to her about her injury?

When she didn't move, Orla's lip curled. "Hold."

Several of the strumpets sneered at her, all from Wife Four's group.

"Audience is the far wall," Orla said, and they snapped their faces forward, another call of 'Sporeshine Heads' resetting their smiles as the old brood swept her direction.

Saoirse quickly got to her feet.

"Glad you joined us," the woman said.

"Thank you, Madame."

"Get in line."

She tried to catch Four's eye. She couldn't dance. Not when she'd promised the gods. Not when her father's life and the county's continued existence relied on their favor. "I just want my lucky hurley."

Orla offered a hand. "Fine. Pay me the appropriate amount for your evening stay, and you can go. Ten bronze harps."

"Ten bronze harps!?"

Ladies and gentlemen, what a rip-off!

Hurler blew Orla a raspberry.

Several dancers shuffled their feet.

When Saoirse didn't move, Orla did, taking a predatory step into Saoirse's field of play. The old brood plucked her sleeve, rubbing the fabric between supple fingers after a menacing fashion, her deep violet eyes locked with hers.

"Stay or don't stay. It's your decision," she whispered. "But per the terms of our deal, if you don't participate, I get to keep your lucky hurley forever."

"No." Her words came out small. "Please," Saoirse whispered. "I'm Vi."

"I might have cared, but you're not even wearing your dress."

"But..." Saoirse glanced at the dress she'd spiked on the floor.

"A deal's a deal." Orla left her to start the warm-ups.

Saoirse braced herself on the wall. A queasy cold crept over her skin. She glanced at Wife Four, who did everything but look her way. Salm her!

WHAT ARE WE GOING TO DO? WE CAN'T DANCE!

I know.

A small foot stamped on the pitch in her heart made Saoirse look at Little Hurler, who still had her tu-tu on.

You're making it worse!

Her lucky hurley against dance? This was like the choice between dog meat and hospitality all over again. Her lucky hurley was given to her at birth by the gods. She'd sworn to uphold those same gods' ideals as the perfect Violet. She had to play with that hurley, but dancing was against the Violet teachings. Except this time, she had no clue which was worse. How she wished she could consult the Magic Eight Ball. Though it'd probably just say, 'Yes.'

Useless!

There wasn't much of a choice. Showing up here hadn't been enough. This—THIS—was how she paid for the taint of her last taboo. *Feck.*

Saoirse pushed off from the wall and took a spot at the back of a line. She stood behind another of the girls from the trio who had good energy. Spores, the girl really did just look like the spitting definition of 'a hater.' The one on crutches, with a large cast on her left leg and flabbier-than-normal arms, gave Saoirse a thumbs-up from near the mirror. Was she on her side? Or was she hoping she'd make a fool of herself as penance for the county, like everybody else?

Ow. Saoirse gripped her chest. Little Hurler had dashed across her collarbone and slammed a yellow card onto her heart—for negative self-talk. Grumpy little thing. The tiny her shook her stubby hands at her. Saoirse smiled.

Right, I'm sorry.

Saoirse slapped some energy into her cheeks. She couldn't lose to these girls! Not when her hurley was on the line!

She attempted to copy the other women's posture. Tall. Proud. Chest out, shoulders back. Spores, she was huge compared to these girls. Saoirse bent her knees a bit to try and fit their size, but her shoulders were still too broad. Tuatha Dé Danann, even the tall ones here were petite. Was she so far removed from being a dancer?

Focus. Hype yourself up.

Right. She had to try. This might be the only time she'd ever truly get to dance! *I will save the County Tyrconnell Hurling Club! I will score the most goals in the history of Pénis! And I will make them hard! (If I find the time) Let's fookin goooooo!*

A burning fire consumed her heart and soul. Her inner stadium roared to life. Satirical hyped on her loudshroom.

This is Saoirse Satirical back again. It looks like Little Hurler stoked a fire in our fight, girls!

Spirit Stadium chanted now. *'Saoirse. Saoirse. Saoirse. Saoirse!'*

We've all got this in us, us! Saoirse thought.

You're gods salm right, pardner. There's a sliotar in play, and it's called dance warm-ups. These sensual strumpets probably can't dance. I dare say they'd not even know how to handle balls!

'Shakey solos!' Spirit Stadium cried.

Saoirse bounced on the balls of her feet.

Little Hurler was ready. She was ready—her world on fire!

Orla counted in her flame. "Five, six, seven, eight!"

And the Daughters of Dagda doused it in an instant—not with a flow, but with a flood—They. Could. Dance!

The front row of women started in unison. They all knew what to do, leaping forward from the line.

Elegance. Grace. Poise. Posture. Expression. Perfection. These weren't little High Branch girls letting out energy—these were performers.

"Five, six, seven, eight."

To a dancer, they crossed the room in the most prestigious jig she'd ever seen. Every step matched for distance to their line mates, each jump the same height, every kick to the face, each slide, hip, shimmy, down to the very bounce of each curl in their hoe-tastic hair. They did not miss!

Gods! I'm screwed!

Little Hurler abandoned her tutu and ran for the lockers.

"Five, six, seven, eight!"

Hurler? Hurler!?

The third line. Perfection.

"Seven, eight."

The fourth. Perfection.

Ladies and gentlemen, I can't watch.

Saoirse stepped forward. Crowd colder than two bare sliotars in a snowstorm. She'd always known what was coming, but that was in the corner. Not near the front of the lines!—

"Five, six, seven, eight!"

—Orla expected her to dance!

Fear locked her legs.

Don't freeze!

"Six, seven, eight!"

Don't freeze!

"Six, seven, eight!"

Don't freeze!

"Six."

Someone pushed her in the back.

She took off!

...And it wasn't even her line!

Oh fuck. Oh gods.

She was already choking back tears.

Everybody was laughing.

No tears. She went for it. *No tears.* Do what they did. *No tears.*

She pulled her jacket as tight as she could—Hop—Each move a bit smaller than the one before—Hop, knee—Each step shorter than the last—Hop back...

...hop.

When she finished, Orla didn't even acknowledge that she'd passed her. A few girls doing crunches averted their eyes.

Gods. Oh gods... Saoirse slowed. *No tears.*

She stopped, staring at the wall—the door.

When Orla called out from behind her: "Again." Like nothing happened. "But this time with talent."

Tears.

Saoirse ran across the room to the far corner and shoved her way through the door, almost knocking a late-arriving Fiadh over as she broke into a run.

"Hey!" Fiadh shouted.

Dancing? Dancing!? Her whole life...! How she'd dreamed! To not be bound by Shamrock Violet. To be on the branch with the other girls. To jig. To leap.

To live.

"Do you need me to do your sporting braids?" Fiadh called.

These depraved freaks had given her that chance to dream, and the Shitty Forwards had taken it from her with their wicked taboo.

Saoirse kept running.

"Hey yadi-yada. Hey yadi-yada. Hey yadi-yada and a hoi-yoi-yoi.
"Mr. Magic Eight Ball, can I please be allowed to dance?"
"Saoirse, what are you doing in here?"

'No.'

Jobbery

Join the Jobbery! We've got all kinds of jobs: feed jobs, build jobs, even hand jobs, and more! That was the pitch when Saoirse was looking for what she could do to help in town during Little's School. Croaghgorm doesn't have many people, which means everybody helps.

When Saoirse turned ten, they went on a field trip all around the hollow, but nothing was particularly suited to her. A few weeks later, though, when spring came, and it was a good bit of drying out, what with the sun splitting the spores and all, the teacher took them all to the Jobbery. It was there that Saoirse fell in love with the art of Hand Jobbing.

Professional Hand-Jobbers can relax all kinds of muscles, back muscles, leg muscles; they work the bodies of the insects to help them feel relaxed, reset their skeletal structure if need be, and keep them healthy. Since the insects reacted particularly well to the golden dust that Saoirse can generate from her body, she'd finally found where she'd fit.

Female insects really don't seem to like her much, though; she's just never gotten the hang of how to massage them, I guess.

The First Twenty-Seven (Kickstarter)
Thank you,
Josh Hughes

Hurley Problems

"**I** am speed." Her hands rubbed the wood grain.

Nope.

Yeah, not this one.

Saoirse's hands moved to the next handle. "I am power." She gripped the leather.

Yikes.

Agreed.

Then to another new grip. "I am technique."

Little Hurler cringed in her chest.

Nope.

Saoirse spun another hurley between her fingers. "I am the Dancer—" Saoirse hauled off and drove the hurley into the dirt with all her strength. "The dancer!? THE DANCER!?"

Saoirse...

Satirical...

Her heart got between them to break up the fight.

Whoever pushed her in the back could die! Feck. She launched the hurley to the long line of equipment against the wall, where it shattered. The hurleys all sucked. What was the point of being equipment at Hazel Park if it was all trash! This would ruin her first day at trials.

I'm sorry, Twenty-Seven.

They aren't even that good.

An 'if that wasn't true' thunk resounded through her as Little Hurler face-planted to the pitch in dismay.

Are we still talking about the hurleys?

Of course, we're talking about the hurleys!!

Whoa.

With their perfect fucking legs and their tight little bas' and their oh I'm so good at kicking ash! Piece of shite! Saoirse seized another hurley off the rack and smashed it into the crete, where it splintered.

Her heart looked on apprehensively.

Twenty-Seven, it's okay. We didn't need them anyway. This way, we're still a good girl. There will be other groups to watch.

"I'm talking about hurleys!!!"

Right. I know you are.

She ran a hand through her hair. Her sporting braids got in the way. She shattered the rest of the splintered hurley on the wall by the first.

Several people gawked at her.

"Keep walking."

They did.

Deep breaths, me. Come on.

She ignored Satirical in favor of another hurley.

All they had were Cork-style 35 to 48s cause most of the team was feckin' huge. Her lucky hurley was a modified Cork/Tip hybrid—Tipp handle, round shaft, with a Cork bas she'd personally shaved thin to take weight off and enable faster flicks—and it was made from the Wave Ash only found in County Over. By comparison, these were all absurdly long, heavy, and bulky. The bas were enormous. Who could possibly need this much weight? The balance was completely wrong!

She held it in front of her, but it just didn't feel right. It wasn't her hurley.

You beat Wolves with limp noodles. You can do it again—with a real hurley, I mean.

Little Hurler seconded the motion.

It still wasn't right, but it was reason enough to breathe. *Tuatha Dé. If I knew it would be like this, I would never have stayed there.*

And still had the taints of three taboos? Satirical asked. *I'll admit you were right about that part.*

It's true she had needed to hunt the bad experiences necessary to remove the taints from her taboos, but the act left her without her lucky hurley. That awful morning... She'd narrowly avoided dancing, as far as she was concerned—

Saoirse.

—and she couldn't take another risk. If she didn't make the team, if her dad would remain imprisoned, all because she wanted to play fast and loose with the Shamrock Violet rules, she'd never live it down. In the six days she had left, she'd play perfect Shamrock Violet hurling, make the team, and save her world.

She grabbed the shortest hurley she could find, a 35 with a stupidly heavy Wexford-style bas. And gave it a quick rap on the back of both her heels—so awkward. She could barely hold it out at arm's length without feeling burn in her muscles. With so much weight, her solo style would be severely diminished, but it would have to do. She'd choke up on it and deal with the extra end sticking out. She was here—here at Hazel Park, the stadium of her dreams. She couldn't let this stop her.

Melak, the wolf goddess, watched the emergency trials with great interest from her spot atop the reverse falls, one paw dangling near the scoreboard. More hurlers than she could hope to count spread out across the pitch, warming up. Several used Spit on their hurleys, waxing them into the grass, or palmed their sacks of sliotars near the water spores. She'd like to join them, maybe help scrub their balls, and start some friendly banter to show them she was here to win, that she'd not meant anything by the song at carve downs, but after this morning, she was struggling to feel like her anymore.

If the Shitty Forwards never made that bet—*or if that Fiadh girl never challenged us!*—she wouldn't be in this mess.

Little Hurler shook Saoirse's sporting braids. The strumpet had offered to do them up for her.

Don't ask me to interpret how Fiadh's brain works, Saoirse said, understanding Little's gesture. *Getting hit is the price you pay to score.*

Hurler threw her arms out in indignation and knocked around sliotars around Spirit Stadium in anticipation of the day's events.

Saoirse twirled her replacement hurley when she caught Finley crossing the field to meet her. He looked even better today, probably because his wavy, deep blue hair complemented his custom training gear: blue with a white stripe.

"That hurley really matches you, cú." He joked, dropping his gear.

"Ha. Ha."

"See, you didn't hit the blow dryer." He winked.

So he had known! The hatch-snatcher.

"I didn't either," he said. "But I did leave all my flowers at home. Or did I?"

"Feck off."

Finley laughed. "Alright." He kicked her a sliotar from the side pocket of his bag. "Sorry about the hair."

"Thank you."

"Is that why you look ready to kill somebody?"

"You've no idea, cú."

She tried a few flicks with her stand-in hurley. She could do it, but spores if she wasn't after disliking the wood feel. It was hollow, the grip was wrong, and she didn't have time to tape a long grip.

"I've got some lighter ones."

"Really?"

"Yep. Here." Finley crouched and tugged a hurley from his sheath, a slender carrying case meant just for sticks. He set it aside. "And with it, here's my end of the deal." He stuck his hand back inside and whipped out his wood, a medium-sized stave wrapped in an interlocking weave of violet ribbons from end to end, each side sealed with the wax seal of Triple K.

The stave to get her out of her geas!

The hairs of her arms bristled at the implications. Now, if she did somehow manage to fix the team's hurl-ectile dysfunction before her father was incarcerated by PÉNIS, she'd be free.

"How?" She took it and watched as the mist for Finley's death pact formed into the triskele on the back of his palm, then burst with light, dissipating to nothingness.

"Family connections," he said, as if it were no big deal. "Since you can't read, I figure seeing the geas dissipate would be proof of its contents."

She nodded. It sure was. Solving Finley's mystery was still her second choice, but it was nice to have it in her back pocket. Saoirse stuffed the stave away in her own gear. "I'm not promising anything."

"I'd be impressed if you figured out the answer in five days anyway. Still, I had to try. Speaking of, did you find out anything?" he asked, handing her the hurley from his gear bag. Little Hurler practically melted in her chest at the touch of something they could actually play with.

Saoirse tested it, smacking her own palm, the backs of her heels, and swinging it along the grass. That wasn't quite her lucky hurley, but handling the sliotar from Finley's gear bag was done with comparative ease.

THAT'S BETTER, FOLKS.

Indeed. Saoirse scanned the pitch. Could so many men really be flaccid? After this morning, she was simply glad there was nothing naughty about being here—just good old-fashioned sports. Several men jerked each other in a circle nearby—vigorously, with alarming eye contact—fighting for possession of a sliotar, while many more slapped their balls around by River Eolas. "Nothing we didn't already know," she said, passing the ball to Finley.

"Who'd you ask?"

"Wife Four."

Finley popped a brow.

Was that so surprising a source? Wives might be little more than brain-dead pets, but they should still know their hurlers, right? "I asked her how to tell if men are flaccid. She got really upset."

"She got upset?" Finley took a few steps back and flicked a sliotar to her. "Women."

Saoirse soloed it absentmindedly. "Yeah. Figured she also hates terrible hurling."

Mr. Three-Torques-Rich smiled at that. "That's interesting."

"What is?" She passed him the ball.

He had an interesting solo style—he kept his hurley close to his chest. "Let me put my thoughts together during trials."

"Alright."

"But also, you should've told me you didn't know."

"I—" Saoirse flushed. "Players don't go flaccid in Croaghgorm, and we can't afford any Whiskeys anyhow."

"It's nothing to be embarrassed about."

She knew he was right about that, and yet she was. "I know some things. The basic mechanics of how a Whiskey works, the fallout from using one, and meta stuff like wrapped shafts, ogham, and things. I've just never gotten to see one up close."

"Look—you see everybody's hurleys?" Finley pointed with his hurley. She followed the line from the tip of his stick to a group of men striking their balls. "Well, look at the old team."

Saoirse did. Many of the old team had wrapped their sticks all the way down the handle and onto the bas, or had shafts with no ogham carving at all. She couldn't see a single Whiskey among them—at least not outwardly. Players hid their spells under the wraps, a way to keep the magic from prying eyes that could actually read. "They've got a ton either excessively wrapped or bare."

"That much grip would make sense if our team had any magic, right? Which we don't."

Saoirse sighed in new understanding. "They're embarrassed about that."

Finley nodded. "They don't want to be seen with Whiskey they can't use."

Which either meant not bringing the prized hurley they were fond of to practice cause it had magic on it, and that was embarrassing, or wrapping it so intensely nobody would be sure either way.

"That's terrible." Men who were self-conscious... her perfect image of the team slipped a little further down the Slieve League cliffs.

Finley rubbed at the side of his head in a way that made his bicep way too attractive. Man had those sleeper muscles. Pinch. Feck! Why did she pinch her injured thigh? They'd better go no-contact today.

Little Hurler replied with a thumbs down. She wanted to play.

"Keep an eye on the wrapped ones with me," Finley said. "If you see a man from the tryouts like him over there." He pointed with his hurley.

The man in question had a flagrant carving down his shaft.

"...wait till his wood becomes saturated with the mist. The letters will light up, and it'll start twitching—throbbing like it's ready to blow."

"Gotcha." Saoirse nodded. "I'll keep an eye out."

"Finley man Domhnaill and Saoirse Storm in *The Case of the Curious Whiskeys*. But don't forget to play, yeah?"

"That's one thing I'll never forget how to do."

He winked, and a whistle blew at midfield.

Feck them Daughters of Dagda. She'd bury their name on this field.

TYRCONNELL
FREE BALL
An assistant pucks a sliotar to the far side of the field. Get it and drive the ball into the falls. (The wolf puppies love it!)
HURLING CLUB · THE COUNTY TYRCONNELL
Finley
Group 12
Saoirse
TYRCONNELL

Free Ball

Being here risked her suspension. Not being here risked all of their lives. Time to get pumped.

Little Hurler pumped her pom-poms.

Will we see something special? Will we see a goal? Will we see hot men blow their loads—of magic? Stay tuned.

Tonight's coverage is sponsored by Fluppa Luppa Huppa Duppas—Ulster's most trusted gum for girls with godly goals!

I don't think I'm the only one excited here, folks.

She sure wasn't! Saoirse bounced in place, eager and drawing attention. *That's right, stare. You're about to get got by a girl!*

Spores, it was nice to be back where she belonged. On the pitch. She may only have six days to earn a spot, while the rest had two weeks, but she just knew she could do it. She'd make them pick her. She already was the best full-forward any of them had ever seen!

That's the attitude!

Despite the eyes, anticipation built in her breast. How long had she dreamed of being here, playing on this pitch, proving she deserved to be a Wolf? Now, in the strangest way, she had a chance.

The Spectators bottlenecked at her snack stands; a few early arrivals were already cheering from her stomach.

I sold extra tickets. It's a big day. They went for so much money!

Well, keep my stomach under control.

I will.

She hadn't gotten in much of a warm-up, but that was okay. She didn't need much in the way of stretching since she wouldn't dance.

WHAT?! Satirical shouted over her mind.

She and all the tryouts had gathered at the base of the bleachers at the whistle. Saoirse forced her way to the front of the crowd so she could see.

I'm sorry, what do you mean you're not dancing!?

I can't transgress.

But you're the Dancer. It doesn't count on the pitch. It's not dancing—it's hurling!

Doesn't matter.

My tickets... Hurler. Hurler, hit some sense into her.

Her heart was equally flummoxed.

It was too bad. She'd rather dance, but she didn't get rid of all her taboos just to come here and throw everything away. The gods would look after her. They'd lead her to freeing her father.

That's not... me! Are you sure you're not doing this because of this morning?

I told you I was talking about hurleys!

But you did a trick shot!

That's not even the same.

Tuatha Dé Danann...

Lorcan, the team captain, stood several rows up the stands, between twenty pretty wenches built like hurleys: slender, polished, and just waiting to be illegally curved. Seriously, one sneeze and they'd rewrite league rules. All the girls sat next to barrels filled with staves.

The obvious conclusion to draw was that this man was a flower hound, and she should kick him in the shins. The less obvious conclusion, of course, was that they were helping him track the different players.

They aren't the Daughters of Dagda, her mind whispered to her.

I'm aware of that.

Are you?

This had more to do with Lorcan—Lorcan the letdown. As much as she didn't like seeing him with other women, she liked those defeated eyes even less. They unnerved her. Had they been that way before she'd thrown, or only after?

I just hope it wasn't my fault. Though her antics at the carve downs likely didn't help. *Just give me a few days!* she thought, looking at his burly features. *I'll cure you with my hurling.*

What hurling? You're handicapping yourself.

You don't throw away a grizzly bearfly just because they've got some junk in their trunk.

Tell that to yourself!

Little Hurler sat in dismay. Several of the Spectators had gotten wind of Saoirse's intention to hold herself back, and the news wasn't going over well.

The captain got to his feet in the stands.

Around her, several hurlers shuffled with anticipation.

"Welcome," Lorcan said into a small black spore that made his voice come over the stadium's speaker mushrooms. "If you're here, it's because you impressed your cities; if you're here, it's because you believe in good hurling; if you're here, it's because you believe the gods will give us a second chance."

He let this linger. Furtive eyes turned to her.

You deserve that.

I know.

"If you're here," Lorcan continued, "it's because you want to make something happen that hasn't happened for Tyrconnell in some time. You want to win."

One of Lorcan's assistant wenches flashed the captain a dangerous smile, like she'd rolled a 'yes' on *The Violet Intercourse*—the strumpet!

Focus.

Yeah. Yeah.

Saoirse hit a little shimmy to reset her heart. Their presence didn't change what she had to do: score and score and score some more. She cast a quick glance for Finley, who gave her a wink that excited her Spectators.

"This first drill is simple," the captain said. "It's Free Ball."

"Yes!" many of them said together.

Saoirse pumped her fist.

LADIES AND GENTLEMEN, WE LOVE THIS DRILL! USUALLY...

Her Spectators cheered.

"Only with a bit of a twist," the captain continued.

A twist?

A murmur ran through the hurlers. Everybody knew Free Ball—it was an essential part of hurling. When a sliotar hit open space, it was anybody's ball. Free Ball helped a player drive their aggression, practice spatial awareness, and throw their body around. And if there was one thing she loved, it was throwing her body around. How could you twist something so simple?

"You'll split into twenty groups and play pitch-width. If you get the ball, drive it into the falls—the wolves love it." Saoirse turned to smile at the pack above the falls but found her view blocked by several players who had their heads and shoulders over hers. Spores, the pros were so tall. The exact opposite of that morning.

DON'T GO THINKING YOU'RE NOT SUPPOSED TO BE A HURLER NOW!

Never. Even if it was a touch disconcerting. She squeezed her hurley and was reminded she had one of Finley's; her hope sank a bit more.

"If you do, you move up to your left. If you are the furthest from the ball, down to your right. The twist is: the bottom four groups will be cut."

Feck yeah! Saoirse couldn't keep the smile off her face. That was a right proper challenge!

A TURN INDEED, FOLKS. THIS BROADCASTER, FOR ONE, HASN'T HEARD OF ANYTHING THIS RUTHLESS SINCE COUNTY LONGFORD HURLING EARNED ITS NAME, THE SLASHERS. MAYO'S NEVER BEEN THE SAME SINCE.

An outcry of indignation met this statement.

"I'm in from Inishtrahull!"

"It cost me life savings to get here!"

"What about goalkeepers!?"

Tuatha Dé. Complaints again? *Shout that you don't believe in yourselves louder, please?* Hurler nodded.

"The answer is simple," Lorcan growled. "Don't lose. Good luck."

The hair on the back of her neck bristled. A tingle raced through her arms. Free Ball!

Everybody broke for lines. Double-checking her braids to make sure her hair was locked down, Saoirse went toward the right.

She didn't need to join the scrum for the left side of the field. Why bother? If you needed to start there, that was like saying you couldn't make it up there with your skill. Which she certainly would—despite that morning, despite the jank hurley, despite not dancing. She was free of taboos. Today was all skill.

"Saoirse!" Sean, an assistant captain, called for her from the stands, then nodded to Lorcan, who was waiting near the safety bar.

He wants to talk to me? Just her and Aware Wolf alone. Little Hurler skipped a beat. Saoirse ran full-speed to the base of the stands where Lorcan was waiting for her.

The captain's brown hair spilled over his shoulders. He leered at her. "Last night we had to turn away another champion from Croaghgorm, some poor, injured girl named Kate."

Her whole inner stadium froze.

"You're not the Croaghgorm champion, are you?" Lorcan asked.

"No."

"I thought not."

"Am I kicked?"

"No. You'd have to live with your head under a rock not to have heard about the Dancer."

COME ON, THAT'S A SIGN!

"Right…"

"I'd have let you in regardless," Lorcan said. "I've lost for all of my career despite carrying the best stat line among all goalkeepers in Éire." He smashed a fist against the banister, and a sparkle of something flashed across his dead eyes. "I'm not so naive as to blame you for my failures."

DID YOU SEE THAT?

Yes. "I won't let you down!"

"Good girl. Now get out and hurl."

That happened. That just happened!

Her stadium cheered.

IS THE PART ABOUT YOU NOT DANCING RINGING A BELL?

Stop being such a worrywart. It's not like it was the only thing I could do. Saoirse ran back over to her spot in line.

I GIVE UP. IT'S YOUR NUMBER TWENTY-SEVEN AND MINE!

I won't freeze.

THE BEST FULL FORWARD IN ALL THE STAR!

A group of hurlers congregated in front of an assistant boy holding a hurley near a pile of sliotars. He'd puck a ball out for them all to fight over, and it'd be on.

"Well, well, the insulting girl." A man pulled up next to her. He had a blue headband and glowered at her through a deadpan expression: Ronan mac Eion. She knew him from his player stave. "I'm ready to see that awesome skill."

"Me too, cú." Finley joined her on the other side. "Won't say no to a friendly show."

"Then try not to blink."

"Ohohoho," Ronan smiled. "I do hope you're not all talk."

He flexed his hurley. It was wrapped pretty intensely. A Whiskey or just his own personal flavor? Spores, this added a whole different dimension to the game. She'd considered, in theory, how a Whiskey would change the pressure of a match, let alone a drill. Whiskeys couldn't be used in quick succession. After use, they gave a player heightened clarity, but then extreme fatigue—a double-edged sword. Using a Whiskey could net you an instant win, but you'd be on your ass for several minutes right after.

She'd never gotten to face one until that fateful game she'd sort of match-fixed. Now that she was potentially facing one head-on, it excited her.

How would her theories pan out? What did it feel like to get hit by magic? What did it really look like? How intense was the power? She had so many questions—and only one way to get answers.

JUST KEEP YOUR HEAD ABOVE THE HURLEY.

An early loss or two won't deter me. Little Hurler?

Her heart responded.

Saoirse focused on Little Hurler. She was there, standing at center field, hurley at the ready, helmet on.

The Spectators cheered. "Time to merge!"

Time to combine the embers of her magic with her will to win.

'*Dancing, fighting, making love—,*' said the Spectators.

Saoirse whispered, "Uilleann."

'*—That's her name.*'

The magic flowed. A warm fire burned in her breast. Little Hurler glowed bright white; hot fire filled Saoirse, fueling her. The water rippled around her. Her hair fluttered in non-existent wind. Saoirse clapped above her head, showering herself and her mystery partner in her special golden dust.

Her heart set; a warm crackle of energy danced about her skin.

Finley and Ronan cooed.

They were in group twelve. Saoirse and Finley pushed up on the line along with the other competitors—twenty groups, twenty players each. Each group had only a narrow strip of field on which to charge down a loose ball. This could get really brutal, really fast.

THE CAMOGIE CUNT OF CROAGHGORM MOUNTAIN!

She looked for Ronan. She wanted to keep track of his Whiskey. He was... back by the benches? Well, whatever. First to the sliotar. First on the team. She gripped her borrowed hurley.

SAOIRSE STORM!

Lorcan blew his whistle.

She leaped off the line—and the pack swallowed her whole.

The men on either side of her—including Finley—pulled no punches, and within an instant, she went face-first into the dirt, tumbling forward in a tangled mess of feet. How had she gone down so easily? "Shite."

Several more hit the dirt with her, tripping over her fallen body. She skidded along the grass, pulling up just in time to see those who hadn't fallen closing on the sliotar. "Spores!" This looked terrible! She needed to get back up. She pushed off the ground when somebody casually stepped over her head and shouted, "Whiskey!"

It was Ronan. His hurley quivered in his hands, twitching, throbbing, the magic ready to blow.

A Whiskey! Right up close! It was kinda weird looking. What would it do? Could he teleport? Was that why he was so far back?

"Gravacious Gale Cutter!" he roared.

In a blink, he zipped three times up the field like a fly—taking three wild angles tens of meters at a time before smashing into the pile surrounding the ball, knocking them over like it was nothing, and securing the sliotar with ease, which he drove hard into the falls.

A Whiskey! A real use of magic, up close and in person! Even down in the dirt, Saoirse couldn't help but tremble with awe. A thick white mist settled into the grass, then dissipated into the air.

She could smell it—salty, funky. But the twitching, and the glow, the heat?! She'd finally gotten to see a real Whiskey explosion! She'd never wanted to be so close to anything in her entire life. Now that she had, it was addictive. She had to earn her own!

Ronan staggered like a drunk at the far end of the field. He must have moved on from post-Whiskey clarity to fatigue. With something so powerful, she was surprised he wasn't a sleeper. But he kept his feet—and if she was right, he was likely feeling ashamed.

WHAT A CLIMAX—OF SKILL! THAT MAN'S GOING PLACES, FOLKS. IN THIS CASE, UP ONE GROUP.

"That's cheating!" shouted a man from inside the pile tangled with her feet.

Lorcan's voice came over the speaker mushrooms.

"I never said you couldn't use your Whiskeys. They're as much a part of the sport as the grass beneath your feet."

The annoyed man grumbled.

Saoirse didn't. An enormous smile stretched across her face. Endless magic? Hurling she'd never before seen? A whole new level of skill?

This drill had just gotten a lot more interesting.

Shitty Revenge

T his was amazing!

Her crowd roared! Hurler soared! Satirical could not stop the color from coming! Saoirse raced and pranced with the best of them—the cream of what Tyrconnell had to offer!

She was hurling.

And.

Losing!

SHE CAN'T KEEP THE SMILE OFF HER FECKIN' FACE, FOLKS! I'VE NEVER SEEN OUR GIRL SO HAPPY. TEN ROUNDS IN AND SHE HASN'T WON A SINGLE ONE, BUT KEEP YOUR HANDS GLUED TO YOUR POPPED SHOOMS AND FIZZY DRINKS! WE'RE NOT DONE YET!

On a knee, Little Hurler beamed.

The drill had been paused for water. Saoirse stepped off the line to get a drink.

Because of her trip in that first round, Saoirse had been the furthest from the ball, and nine straight losses later—three of which she'd been furthest away—she was down in group fifteen and starting to see the game inside the game.

Some of the other trials with Whiskeys had also let out their magic after Ronan, but they weren't exactly a rapid-fire thing. With one, a player could secure an almost sure-fire win, but the drawbacks of using one were so powerful that a player who poorly managed his magic would be almost guaranteed to be furthest from the ball the next round—or even rounds. She'd been a bit concerned that her lack of magic would hold her back. In some ways, it did, but even with Whiskeys, the way Lorcan set up this first day meant the hurling was still about stamina and raw skill.

THE ONLY PROBLEM, FOLKS, IS THAT OUR GIRL'S SKILLS ARE A TRANSGRES- SION—IN HER HEAD.

That was both true and not true. She was more than the Dancer.

Her heart protested that statement.

I can't, she said to Little Hurler. *We promised the gods. I'm going to be a Good Girl, the perfect Shamrock Violet*. If she didn't and the law declared her a Bad Girl, her father's sacrifice would mean nothing.

ARE YOU SURE YOU'RE NOT DOING THIS TO SPITE THE DAUGHTERS OF DAGDA?

Absolutely. She didn't care the least for those floozy strumpets.

Saoirse snatched a water spore and drained it.

If she could use her dancing skills, she'd keep up easily, maybe even win. She looked at Melak, who was watching the pitch from her precipice. What must she be thinking after Saoirse claimed she'd help restore Ulster hurling? Saoirse couldn't even blame this performance on taints. She'd gotten rid of all three of them last night, but that shouldn't be enough to stop her in Free Ball.

She stared down at her borrowed hurley. She didn't want to blame this. She knew it was wrong, but... spores, the balls were just out there for the taking!

YEAH, WELL, IF YOU DON'T FIND AN ANSWER SOON, IT WON'T MATTER HOW INNOCENT WE ARE.

Right.

Her heart scanned the pitch.

Ronan's stuck in group eleven. Whiskey fatigue. Finley's flown to group one. I bet the heroine of the hour feels bad about insinuating he bought his way in.

Yeah, despite her happiness, she looked pathetic. A little more time, and even her inner Spectators' cheers would wane.

Lorcan made it clear that falling asleep from mismanaging your Whiskey wouldn't stop you from moving down the groups. Since the bottom four groups were getting cut, she felt bad for the poor man on the bench by eighteen with a blanket and warm milk, but as the captain rightly pointed out, the drawbacks from using magic were part of the game.

She lined up for the next round, shoulder to shoulder with the other tryouts. Plenty of the men had been ground hurling really aggressively, swinging their hurleys as much to chop at the sliotar as other players' shins. It wasn't the kind of mix she liked to get herself into. Her skill was in playing the ball and using her body to gain positional advantage on the sliotar. It was shapers who played the man—tried to smash wrists and ankles and all. Tyrconnell wasn't a dirty team, which made their defense all the more impressive.

The whistle blew, and this time, she made a clean break off the line.

They jostled her, but she didn't go down. Saoirse shifted her hips to keep herself upright, using their weight to keep her in the running. Somebody else got there first.

Salm it!

No matter how hard she tried, she was almost always close to—if not actually—the furthest from the ball. This time was no different. If the man behind her hadn't tripped, she'd be down in sixteen.

There's no space!

YOU WERE BIG IN CAMOGIE.

Feck.

WHAT?

You didn't have to say it.

I DIDN'T MEAN FAT!

I know you didn't mean fat, cú.

Saoirse sprinted back to the sideline, noticing, for the fifth time in a row, that she was the only one running. Complaining off the field, lazy on—maybe they'd not be so sad if they played. Any kid in Croaghgorm would get kicked off the branch for acting like that. It made her sick. That, or maybe it was the Spectators in her stomach. Sat said she'd filled the stands; so many were eager to get tickets to 'The First Day of Trials,' it was a historic event. It was just a bunch of tests and drills, so far just the same drill over and over, but the Spectators were super fans. The tickets had apparently gone for a premium. Whatever that meant.

It'd be any moment now—she'd figure out the puzzle and win.

Big in camogie. Big for dance. Small for hurling. Cast a net on her. She'd realized it when she'd tried to wave to Melak. She didn't want to accept it. Even at her size, male hurlers all had a head and shoulders on her. Since throwing her size around at the back of the pitch won her more goals than she cared to admit, it was a problem. She wasn't exactly a giantess like Triple K, but her wide build made doing her dancing style easy. Her size cut space for her between the smaller women. Even if she was dancing, she couldn't do that here.

"Feck." Sweat dripping off her collarbone, a voice called to her from her right side, and she came face to face with the last man she wanted to see on this pitch—the Shitty Forward, Roudan.

The man who'd jeered her at the carve downs, his rat-like features and buck teeth on full display. "You're supposed to be first to the ball, not first to the sideline."

"Tell that to your hairline. It's been the furthest from the ball since before we started this drill."

Roudan smoothed down his short bangs, snarling. They grouped with the others for the next whistle, waiting on the stragglers.

Run. Feck. She urged the other hurlers, but nobody did. Hurling was something to take pride in—and if hurling was worth taking pride in, it was worth taking pride in the practice of it.

"Something tells me you're bound for group seventeen," Roudan jeered.

"Ten toes off my lucky number," she said.

Little Hurler threw him a rude gesture.

If anybody ought to be yelled at by their team about being an embarrassment, it was Roudan, not her—Tuatha Dé. But this was good. It was time to show Lorcan why she deserved to be full-forward instead of him.

All on the line.

Whistle.

Yes.

Quick with it, our girl's got another clean leap off the line and—

Pain shot through her skull. She screeched. Right off the jump, she was jerked back at the neck. "Ow!"

Foul!!!

Instinctively grabbing for her braid, Saoirse wailed with pain. It was like her braids were being ripped out of the back of her head.

Which they were. Through her watering vision, she spied Roudan. The Shitty Forward had a full fist of her red hair and a twisted smile. He hadn't even bothered to run. He just stood there, eyes on the play until—all in one motion—he threw her down and stepped closer to the ball.

Her Spectators bellowed their disapproval. Little Hurler called for the ref.

That was beyond illegal!

Eyes watering at the pain, Saoirse turned to the assistant boy who'd pucked out the sliotar.

"Saoirse—move down."

"You've got to be joking! Did you not see?!" Spirit Stadium threw incorporeal snacks in protest. Little Hurler was ready for some fisticuffs.

He shrugged. "The only rule is furthest from the ball."

Ah, but the ref doesn't call the foul! This is a rigged match, folks!

She jumped to her feet. "That's beyond unfair!"

Several of the other hurlers stared. Even Lorcan had turned from the stands.

"Did something stop you from getting to the ball?" Roudan sneered. "That's unfortunate. Too bad the ref didn't catch it." He nodded to Lorcan. "Or could it be you threw this match, too?"

In the stands, Aware Wolf wore a puzzled expression. Spores, she knew he couldn't be asked to watch the entire field, but that was uncalled for!

"That's what happened to the girl who cried púca," Roudan said.

Saoirse turned to face the rat. If he was going to play games, he'd win no prizes from her. Instead, she offered the classic phrase of good sportsmanship with as much sarcasm as she could muster. "May an evening star shine down upon you, Roudan."

He smiled. "May it be."

Saoirse snatched up her borrowed hurley and caught Melak's gaze. The look on the wolf goddess's face was plain: people cheat. Win anyway.

Shite.

Group sixteen. Her heart begged her to dance.

I can't.

IF YOU JUST START, YOU KNOW WE COULD GET OUT OF THIS SITUATION!

"Hi," said a haughty voice dripping with holier-than-thou insinuation.

She looked up. This group had *another* Shitty Forward—Michael, the weasel. There was no way.

Then another voice from group seventeen called her attention—false and peppy. "Hi there!" Seanan, with the squished-up face of a half-fae.

And it all fell into place. This was the payment for Roudan's perceived humiliation at carve downs, for taking Lorcan's side. The three of them were going to cheat to keep her pinned in the bottom four, in the groups where she would get cut from trials. They weren't playing to win. They were playing not to lose. And that was somehow funny.

Laughing, she lined up.

No wonder Tyrconnell had trouble scoring. The problem was—she wasn't sure how to beat them. Lorcan hadn't changed the drill and showed no intention of stopping. This could go all day. She had a badly beaten thigh from her loss at *Chastity!*—and had spent the first half of practice collecting new welts.

She'd played through pain before, but she'd been the big one. She wasn't tested on skill. She was being tested on pride.

Michael shunted her right in the thigh bruise with the butt end of his hurley. Saoirse crumpled to the ground, unable to stifle a shriek.

Whistle.

There was no way she'd get closest to the ball. If this kept up, she might actually lose everything, and on only the first day.

We're Still Here

Not here. This couldn't be happening to her—not here! Not on hallowed ground, not surrounded by the wolves, not at trials for the County Tyrconnell Hurling Club, not when her dad would soon be imprisoned, not when she'd already sacrificed so much—not here! Not when she'd been so good by her gods! Not after *Chastity!* Not after beating Melak! Not here!

And yet, it was.

Whistle. Tripped.

PLEASE DANCE.

Whistle. Slashed.

Spirit Stadium begged her.

Whistle. Clipped.

PLEASE PRANCE!

Whistle. "Saoirse, move down."

Nothing she did changed the outcome.

Whistle. Beat.

TWENTY-SEVEN, IT'S NOT AGAINST THE GODS.

Whistle. Bashed.

Little Hurler smashed an angry helmet into her heart.

Whistle. Bunted.

Spirit Stadium was in full chant. *'Dancer. Dancer. Dancer!'*

Whistle. "Saoirse, move down."

I can't! I have to be the perfect Violet. I can't dance!...here.

Wincing, bruised in more ways than she could count, Saoirse hobbled to group nineteen—nine-fucking-teen.

I wanna kill the Shitty Forwards.

Little Hurler sat on the bench in her heart, a pair of Spectators in tiny medi-druids robes wrapping her knee. Her heart couldn't even look at her.

Score? She wanted to score? She couldn't even find room on the pitch to run! Let alone play hurling. She'd been so naive.

Her game inside the game had entirely changed. It'd devolved into a war against one man every run. An Morrígan would be watching over her fights. The goddess must have been asking if she could out-muscle a rat, a weasel, or a púca—not to win, but just to be second to last. Why? Who knows.

And nobody was stepping in to help.

It was a laugh—a right laugh. She nursed her bruised elbow. They'd been at this for hours. The first day of trials could come to an end at any time. She had no idea what the plan was or how Lorcan's system worked.

I can't transgress. I won't transgress! If she complained, she was less. That couldn't be right. She didn't understand. Her gods wouldn't have spoken on the pitch, only for her to fail.

"Have fun walking home!" Roudan called from up in fifteen. He'd been playing to hold his spot—just in case she'd won out.

Roudan...

Free Ball shook out exactly how the Shitty Forwards had planned it. Michael and Seanan sat in group sixteen, while at the far end of the field, most of the original team and all the best trial prospects fought it out in the top groups. Lorcan's focus had remained on that end of the field all day. She couldn't blame him; he needed to pick the best team from the best players. His dumb, frumpy assistant wenches watched over the other groups, passing staves around as players moved up or down. Her stave had been in all the wrong hands.

Her heart nodded at that.

She was surrounded by short kings. *Tuatha Dé. I've got an inch or more on some of them.* No wonder they were in the bottom two groups. She smiled. What a joke. She was finally big again—and too beat down to do anything about it. She started laughing, small to herself, then bigger and bigger until she was just about fit to burst, and a soft hand tapped her on the shoulder. She had to believe it was right, had to believe that somehow, some ridiculous way, her piety was working for her—but this all was wrong!

"Sup, cú." The fish-like boy nursed a bruised cheek. "Fiachra," he tried a smile. It didn't go so hot. He looked like a salmon mid-sneeze.

"Saoirse."

A break was called for water. Saoirse collapsed on the spot. Feck a bench.

Fiachra got her a water spore; she swiped it and chugged.

The boy settled next to her and fixed her with a concerned expression. He was in full pads, including defensive mitts for his hands and shin guards, like a little princess. "You look like you can barely move, cú."

"I'm fine."

"Yeah, and I'm seven feet tall." Fiachra laughed.

He was full of energy. In group nineteen?

"Never thought they'd do something like this," he said. "A host of us have good skills and Whiskeys." He nodded to the other men in groups—'no hope' and 'beyond screwed.' "But they aren't good in Free Ball combat. They're tricky. Give us different kinds of leverage. I can't help wondering if kicking us out like this is normal for Lorcan. Maybe the reason the team is suffering is that it is too one-dimensional."

That was an interesting angle, but it sounded like loser talk to her. Men were supposed to power through adversity no matter what. Finding other ways around problems just meant you needed to hit the weight room. That's what her old coach would say. It made sense to her.

At least Fiachra'd been able to keep his head above the hurley and think. She'd expected to power through everything as she'd always done. Maybe there was something to him.

An assistant handed her a new water spore. She sipped it, wondering how much use she'd be trying to help Finley when she'd not be here tomorrow. Fiachra matched her drinking merrily despite being in the bottom groups. Did this idiot still have hope? How many more runs could they be getting in this late into the evening? He couldn't be hoping to win out, could he?

"Not sad about getting kicked?" she asked.

"Nope. All I can do is give it my all. If I don't have luck on my side this season, I'll just be back next year."

"Next year."

"I know you'll turn yourself in. And I know we'll win."

Win. She couldn't tell him the truth, of course—that she wouldn't have to turn herself in, that her father was taking the fall. That she had to make the team and save his life by winning the All-Éire. Then she really would end up in a dungeon, and with no way to avoid being one of *those women*, end up violated. That outcome seemed guaranteed. "I'm a Good Girl, cú."

"Yep." The boy tried another of his smiles, which was kind of endearing. He'd even managed to put a smile on Little Hurler's bruised face.

If this tiny stick boy wasn't giving up, she had to ask, "You say they've got good Whiskeys?"

"Sure do."

"I thought everybody on Tyrconnell was flaccid."

The mention got more than a few prying eyes. *Sensitive. Right.*

Fiachra dropped his voice. "They're bound to be."

"Really?"

"Whiskeys have to be hard to be used. No magic in a limp Whiskey." He drained his water, flushed terribly crimson, and mumbled something about getting back on the line.

She swirled her water spore, watching him go. It was certain at this point: the boys had lost their mojo. It seemed foolish to continue asking.

Stay in the game, self. Win.

She finished and tossed the water spore, then hobbled back to the line, wincing with each step. Facts were facts: she couldn't run anymore. She could barely walk, and when the whistle blew, and she inevitably fell into group twenty, she heard Lorcan's voice through the speaker mushrooms: "Last ball."

Strained cries called out around her, most everybody in the group simply fell on their butt. Last ball in the worst group—guaranteed not to make it. She wanted to join them. To wallow in wasted effort. To blame her gods, or her religious teachings, but you know what?

She was here.

You've been awfully quiet, she said to her spirit.

Little Hurler had her back turned. Satirical leaned back from the mic in her broadcast booth. Her inner stadium all but cleared out.

We're about to go down, she said. But you know, I don't recall being the kind of girl who won't put up her green and gold just because we lost a few games.

FECK. Satirical sniffled, coming back to the mic.

Little Hurler looked over her shoulder in tears.

WHEN WE PUT IT LIKE THAT, WHAT CAN YOU SAY? ON YOUR FEET, LADIES!

Her stadium rose, light shrooms held high.

We're coming to you live, here in Hazel Park! Here playing for the county, here for the wolves.

"Come on, Little Hurler."

HERE FOR OUR FATHER, HERE FOR OUR CITY, HERE FOR OUR PRIDE!

It's true she no longer knew what kind of hurler she was without dance.

Little Hurler staggered to her feet.

"Come on!"

WE'RE HERE!

That if she ever wanted to have a chance to play here again, she'd need to figure that out. Even the mushroom vendors in her lungs closed down.

Little Hurler wobbled to mid-pitch.

WE'RE ALWAYS HERE!

But she knew what kind of person she was—or at least wanted to be. So she lined up. Lined up with her heart on fire. Lined up with three other men who'd chosen smiles over sighs, effort over dreams. Lined up with Little Hurler.

"Hurley up for glory and pride!"

Her stadium alight.

WE ARE SAOIRSE STORM!

When the whistle blew, she ran as hard as she could. Hard to the sounds of laughing. Hard to nobody pushing, to no shoving, no shunts, no trips—hard—and when she finally won—

Little Hurler held her hurley to the sky.

WE NEVER DIE!

She lost.

And one day I'll make you proud. Dad, Aisling, Melak, everybody...

I'm so sorry.

Mist

Mist is pretty amazing stuff, folks. They call it the magic of Éire, the breath of the gods. I know that the Shamrock Blue claims it's the dying gasp of the Lia Fáil, whatever that means.

Druids recite that mist is what's responsible for the mushrooms' glowing. When a mushroom is saturated with mist, it will give off its brilliant color. When a player uses a Whiskey, mist will rush to the stave from close by, even if that means leaving the mushroom it was stored in. For this reason, there are usually a lot of mushrooms or mist-dense sources kept near hurling pitches to supply players with the magical energy they need to use their skills.

I learned that bit of info one day when Saoirse was busy at the jobbery and couldn't go see a famous druid passing through town. She wasn't interested anyway, which was too bad, because he was talking about the fancy hurling equipment they make in some of the underwater counties in Leinster, and it would have thrilled her. I'm still keeping it a secret from her. I can't wait to see her surprise!

Bruise Cream

S aoirse sat on a squishy brown mushroom cap, rolling a glass spore between her fingers—a small oblong shape with a hole in one end. She'd found an outdoor theater in the round, lined with brown fungi instead of seats. They called it the Ampi-sphinc-ter. The mushrooms angled down toward a hole that was somehow wider than she'd have expected.

Wonder what it'd be like to fall through.

Little Hurler kicked her heart.

"Ow."

YOU CAN'T LET ONE BAD MATCH GET YOU DOWN.

Sure thing.

ESPECIALLY WHEN IT'S YOUR OWN FAULT.

Saoirse hucked the glass spore through the hole, letting it fall to the ends of the Aurum. What was the point of being so pious if it was only going to cause her to fail? "The gods must be crazy."

Never transgress for absolutely any reason. The result? Disaster. "I will score, I will score, I will score and score some more." She sighed, sprawled across her cushion, and let her geas play on her hand.

Five days soon to be four. How was she supposed to make the team now?

If I'd gotten the chance to play full-forward, things would have been different.

THE FREE BALL CALL WAS FINE. YOU WERE SHITE.

No, I wasn't.

"Ow!" Saoirse grabbed her chest. Little Hurler had bunted her with the end of her hurley. "What was that for?"

A smug look was her response.

Feck off.

YOU COULD ALWAYS HELP THAT FINLEY BOY IN EARNEST.

Nah. She had even less of an idea how to solve the team's issues. They needed some PÉNIS therapy—that's what they needed. Feck it. She needed some PÉNIS therapy.

Saoirse adjusted the slightest bit and winced at her bruises. She'd picked this spot because it seemed the most out of view she could be while resting her battered body, staring up at the canopy—a place where she'd been hoping the vista would help calm her heart. It hadn't.

Orla still owes me my hurley.
WE'LL FIND HER.

She could hear Lorcan's deep growl reverberate in her head: *You've been cut.* She didn't wait for the official announcement. There wasn't much point waiting on all the men to get changed, only to be told words she didn't want to hear. "I'm such a fool." Or was she? The gods sometimes worked in strange ways. She'd never been truly pious. Maybe the reasons she was doubting now had more to do with the fact that she'd never lived a life like this before. If she believed in them, if she stayed the course, surely it would all work out. Right?

Clack. Clack. Clack.

The sound of important heels on the stairwell separating the sections of shroom cushions rang about the Ampi-sphinc-ter. "You really do show up in the most interesting of places." By the sound, Madame Orla stopped a few feet away.

Saoirse held her hand out without looking at the old brood. "Just give me my hurley." She couldn't look at her—not after she'd let her stay, definitely not after this morning, not after failing her gods.

Something hard hit Saoirse's hand. She caught it intuitively, but it wasn't her hurley. It was a small jar.

"What's this?" Saoirse unscrewed the lid.

Orla settled next to her in a prim lean, stunning in a lilac dress with matching long gloves, and joined her in admiring the forest. "You'd be amazed at how many bruises dancers get," she said. "Especially around the knees."

Saoirse popped the lid. Inside, she found a thick yellow paste with an odor so powerful it could have joined them at carve downs.

"It's a cream from the medi-druids in Munster," Orla explained. "They're the best."

"And they give you this stuff?"

"Tuatha Dé, no. I stole it from Fiadh. But she's got gobs. Tell a man you like something one time, he'll buy twenty of it for you the next day."

What was this all about? Was this part of her scouting for young talent that Wife Four talked about? Doubtful. The Madame saw her dance this morning. Saoirse was pathetic. What's worse—she wasn't sure she could accept. Not the medicine, not the offer, but it was hospitality freely given... she didn't need another taboo.

"Don't want it?" Orla asked.

Saoirse stared for a long time, searching for the right words. "I... I'm not sure what kind of hurler I am."

Orla nodded and took the spore back. "Don't worry. I know a way past 'hospitality freely given.'"

"Oh yeah?"

"A kindness forcefully applied."

Saoirse laughed despite herself, which made her wince in pain. The Madame removed her long gloves. Saoirse flipped onto her stomach on the cushions and didn't protest when the woman lifted the pelts on her back and went to work. The paste was freezing. Then it was hot. Sweet relief spread across her skin, sank into her muscles. This was amazing.

"Don't worry, I've blocked off the Sphinc," Orla said. "Nobody will disturb us."

"Thanks." She didn't want to be seen in a state of undress that would go against Shamrock Violet doctrine.

"I must say I'm impressed by you," Orla said, working her way down Saoirse's leg.

Saoirse sniffed. "What's there to be impressed about?"

The Madame massaged some cream into her lower back. "It's not every day you find somebody so dedicated to the gods. Your piety is impressive. It shows strength, dedication, determination."

She's proud of us?

Little Hurler tossed her helmet aside, her eyes—once watering—now glassy with admiration.

Saoirse hadn't thought of it that way. Maybe this had been a test? If there was still a way to make it.

"Flip," the old brood commanded.

Saoirse did as she was bidden and rolled onto her back. "How do you know how to do this?"

"PÉNIS therapy."

"You're versed?"

"I helped carve out a few of the stanzas with my own personal hand."

Aisling would get a kick out of that.

The Madame's hands worked her bruises—spores, it felt so nice. She had the perfect touch. Not too rough so as to hurt, not too light so as not to work Saoirse's muscles. She wondered if the old brood had experience giving hand jobs as well, perhaps she'd even given some instruction on physical PÉNIS therapy. Most of the sports medicine Aisling was interested in was the psychological aspect. Saoirse'd heard it all, memorized it all, even gone with her to a few medical recitations. Nearly every therapy module was an anagram based on the body: FACE, HANDS, TOES, and more. Surely a HANDS mental module would be better served with the addition of a physical massage to match.

"Enjoying yourself?"

"I didn't think I deserved this. I was worried my piety made it so I'd never get back on the field."

"You want to make the team, prove your innocence, and save the county?"

"Yes. I'm going to score. More than anybody in Tyrconnell's ever seen. More than anybody in Éire."

"From a dungeon?"

"I have a way." She winced as Madame pulled her pants down and found the walloping she'd taken from the sum's wooden spoon on her left thigh—a deep black welt in the center where she'd been shunted by Michael's hurley.

The old woman paused, two fingers in the bruise cream, a note of disbelief in her eyes.

"I, uh, got hit with a sliotar." She hoped she bought the lie. If Orla only liked her because of her religious dedication, knowing she'd been walloped by the sums probably wouldn't make the old brood very happy. She might even stop the massage.

But after a moment, the Madame continued.

Saoirse couldn't help whimpering, even though she was being gentle with it. When Orla finished, she wiped her hands on a rag she'd brought with her. Saoirse pulled her pants gingerly back over her thigh. "Thank you."

"You're welcome."

"Though it won't mean much if I can't get back into trials."

The old woman took a long drag from her thin pipe. Embers flashed in her eyes.

"Do you know a way to get me back into trials?" Saoirse swallowed—a hope developing inside her, a warmth she hadn't dared since speaking with her gods at Hazel Park.

Orla blew out her smoke. The gray trails twisted into a pair of twin serpents with ruby-red eyes. The snakes left the pipe to swirl about Saoirse's head, then examined her bruises.

Orla mulled over the coloring. "Just because you remind them of their issues doesn't give them the right." She fixed Saoirse with a stern gaze. "What do you think of the boys?"

"The team? I don't know now. I love that they don't give up, but—"

"But?"

"Ever since seeing them in person—at the carve downs, on the pitch—I thought they lost just because they didn't have magic. Now I think it's more that they're afraid of their own skin."

The snakes returned to the Madame's side.

"I think," Orla said, "you do know what kind of hurler you are, but you're asking the wrong question. Pros are different. They're bigger, faster, stronger."

"Yeah, that's the problem."

The Madame snapped her on the nose with her pipe.

"Ow."

"Instead of asking what kind of hurler you are, it's how can you be the kind of hurler they would make space for."

Saoirse laughed. "I don't need to make space. I just need the gods to let me play."

Orla indicated her bruises and raised a brow.

"The gods won't let me," Saoirse muttered.

The Madame's lips curled in a slight smile. She stood and retrieved something from the steps behind them.

"My hurley!" Saoirse leaped to her feet—which hadn't been her wisest decision. "Ah!" The cream didn't work that fast. She reached to snatch her lucky hurley, but Orla yoinked it away before Saoirse could grab it.

Little Hurler had a panic attack.

"Maybe," the woman wiggled it suggestively, "or maybe it's not. What do you think it is?"

"Wood." One of the snakes snapped at her. "Another deal."

"You're catching on quickly." Orla smiled.

She didn't want to, but—"I'm listening."

"I have the power to reinstate you in trials."

"Really?!"

"But you will owe me. No more fighting the dance outfits. You'll join hostess training the day after tomorrow, you'll ask your gods to let you dance, and you owe me one favor of my choosing at any time."

The power to reinstate her? That couldn't be! It meant the gods had been with her despite her doubts!

THAT OR THIS IS DUMB LUCK.

How could it be? The old brood herself said she liked her because she was pious. This all sounded too good to be true—except for the part about owing another favor—but for such a big gift, she supposed it was a fair due. "Is it a reasonable favor?" Saoirse asked.

"By whose standards?"

That was concerning.

"But I can't offer it to you unless you show me you're willing to play your style on the pitch." Orla held out a hand. "Púca Súcca!" and a Magic Eight Ball appeared in her palm.

"The voice of the gods."

"Ask them to let you dance, and we have a deal."

Dancing? You're going to actually dance again? Do it!

Hurler egged her on.

Saoirse grit her teeth. She didn't have room to negotiate. She couldn't give up on being the perfect Shamrock Violet, but it didn't seem like it mattered anyhow. The gods were rewarding her for her good behavior, and yet... her history with the Magic Eight Ball held her back. "I don't know. I don't have a very good record with these things. Can I ask them another way?"

Orla looked skeptical. "What way is that?"

"Is there a place I can pray?"

The small smile grew. "I'll show you a place."

Orla handed over her hurley. Saoirse gladly let her hand play along the fibers. Her soul was back. "You don't need to keep it?"

"No, but the deal won't go into effect until I hear back from these gods."

"Deadly, cú." They shook hands. Saoirse whispered, "And thank you."

"You're welcome."

She gave Orla a big hug, which seemed to surprise the skinny woman, who said, "Now, tell me more about these flaccid men."

Fiadh the Ferocious

Four Days Remain

T hanks to her agreement with the Madame, even though there was dance practice this morning, Saoirse got to skip to recover her bruises so long as she communed with her gods. She couldn't do another day on the pitch without dancing, and the old brood had given Saoirse just the kind of place to pray. In fact, it was the single most perfect little spot she'd ever been to dance.

Unfortunately, so far, Saoirse had spent the morning with her knees in the grass, eyes closed, stuck in her mind because Spirit Stadium just would not shut the feck up.

WELCOME TO SATIRICAL'S WHINE CAVE! Satirical called from the broadcast booth in her brain. *THE SEGMENT WHERE WE COMPLAIN LOUDER THAN THE KKK ABOUT WHAT HAPPENED IN THE FIRST HALF (OR JUST MY GENERAL LIFE PROBLEMS, LIKE THE FACT THAT I'VE HAD TO SELL MY MOST RECENT PRIZED RACING KELPIE!).*

You don't own racing kelpies.

I DO. I BET THE RANCH ON HIM, AND HE CAME IN LAST!

You've never even seen a kelpie. I've never seen a kelpie.

DON'T TELL ME WHAT I HAVE AND HAVEN'T DONE. YOU DON'T KNOW WHAT I GET UP TO IN MY OFF TIME.

You don't have any off time.

SPEAKING OF, I'D LIKE TO DISCUSS MY COMPENSATION PACKAGE.

You live in my head! Satirical was really off on one of her tangents. Why was it this way when she wanted to focus?

Her heart shrugged. Little Hurler was also getting annoyed. Hurler had been done stretching for some time now, eager to work off yesterday's trauma with some prayers and trick-shot practice. Alas, the Spectators filling the stands in her stomach were keen on the idea of a new broadcast segment, particularly when Satirical somehow found time to cover the outside of her booth with a wine motif.

OUR MEAT-HOST IS NON-COMMITTAL, FOLKS. SO LET'S SWITCH IT UP. HOW ABOUT THOSE SHITTY FECKIN' FORWARDS? TERRIBLE PEOPLE, AM I RIGHT? WHAT DO YOU THINK, LITTLE HURLER?

All eyes in Spirit Stadium turned to Little Hurler, who shrugged and posted up outside the broadcast booth window with a small micspore. She opened her mouth wide before whipping up a quick sign with an image of Saoirse's face with a red strike through it.

Saoirse rolled her eyes.

AGREED. THEY'RE ALMOST AS BAD AS THE GIRL PILOTING US AROUND THE AURUM. LADIES AND GENTLEMEN, SHE'S YOUR FAILURE, AND OURS—YOUR WORST FULL-FORWARD IN ALL THE STAR—YOUR GIRL WHO I TOLD WAS GOING TO GET IN TROUBLE FOR UNDERESTIMATING HER OPPONENTS: SAOIRSE DRIZZLE!

Saoirse Drizzle?

WELL, YOU'RE NOT EXACTLY A STORM RIGHT NOW, ARE YOU?

She supposed not. *Can I get some actual hype?*

No.

Satirical?

Little Hurler tapped the broadcast booth with her mic.

FINE. BUT ONLY 'CAUSE I LIKE YOU.

Thanks.

NOW, ABOUT THAT COMPENSATION—

Sat!

LADIES AND GENTLEMEN, PREPARE FOR, (IF YOU WANT TO), SEVERAL MINUTES OF SENSATIONAL SOUNDS; (POSSIBLY) A FEW MOMENTS OF MIND-BLOWING MOVES; THE OCCASIONAL BRILLIANCE OF BLASPHEMING—

Really?

SAOIRSE—THAT ONE GIRL WHO I WISH I DIDN'T KNOW SO MUCH—STORM!

Saoirse shook her head, then winced as a sharp pain from an overblown mic hit her eardrums. Little Hurler had dove into the broadcast booth to give Satirical what for.

"Ow."

DON'T LOOK AT ME.

Saoirse glowered inwardly at Little Hurler. The tiny her had escaped the booth and was trying—and failing—to noiselessly whistle her way out of Saoirse's inner sight, like she'd done nothing wrong.

Saoirse let her go. She'd decided this whole morning was supposed to be about calming herself down and creating inner quiet in her mind.

Which is going so well, she shot at her stadium.

SORRY.

She opened her eyes and pulled her mind free of her inner stadium.

Spores, this place was amazing. Saoirse sat inside a stone circle—a perfectly round, floating island that had gotten trapped in a knot of an Aurum Great Wood. Sheltered by rainbow-striped zipper shrooms, the real grass here was green because it sat at just the right spot for a tiny hole in the great canopy to let sunlight filter through the leaves.

She basked in the cold winter sun, admiring the way the light played off the river surrounding the island. Mist played tricks with water. A tributary of River Eolas cut through this section of the forest, flowing through the air, where it crossed paths with this circle, surrounding the small enclave in a moat of fresh, crystal-clear blue water and purple mist.

Fish slipped through the stream, nibbling at the droppings of nine hazel trees spaced perfectly about the circle before slipping off through the river.

She was there in the middle of it all, surrounded by rocks carved with the same strange 'fishhook' design.

IT REALLY IS SOMETHING.

An oasis trapped in a light dusting of winter's frost. Orla'd said it was called Beltany Circle. The Madame lent her her personal island ferry to sail here this morning. Saoirse didn't think she deserved so much help.

COME ON, YOU'RE TRYING.

I'm failing.

WHAT IS IT YOU SAY? WHAT IS IT SHE SAYS, LITTLE HURLER?

Hurler smacked herself in the noggin with her hurley and kicked a sliotar into her net. *GETTING HIT IS THE PRICE WE PAY TO SCORE.*

"You eejits." She sighed. "Time to pay, I guess."

Despite the cold, Saoirse took off her coat and top, folded them, set them to the side, and slipped out of her trousers. She had a sporting bodysuit underneath. She liked it because the light green color went well with her pale skin, and her red hair made it look like she was celebrating Yule Night early. Plus, she needed the flexibility.

A trick shot—a dance-infused pseudo-blasphemous bit of hurling. Doing this just to do it and not to spite the Magic Eight Ball struck her as strange, especially considering that the whole reason she was here was to curry favor with the gods.

She snatched her hurley. One at a time, Saoirse gave each leg a quick kick to her face, trapped them with her stick, and pulled them back to stretch her hamstrings in a standing split. She'd been enjoying the burn when a particularly annoying voice cut her anticipation at the knees.

"I don't like it when people use my secret spot," Fiadh said.

Saoirse dropped her other leg.

Fiadh stared at her, sipping from one of those annoyingly desirable water spores with the mouth logo on it. She'd dressed in all pink: stretchy dance pants, a puffy winter jacket, and matching kicks—a rolled mat and a weird-looking, bumpy cylinder pinned under one arm.

"I didn't know," Saoirse said.

"Yeah, I know you didn't know."

"Sorry."

"Move."

"Can't we share?"

At this, Fiadh dropped her mat and bumpy pink log, scooped up a hazel nut, and hurled it at her.

Saoirse dodged the frozen shot, temper flaring. "What's the big idea?"

"Oh. I'm sorry." Fiadh cupped her mouth with her now free hand and called in a flat voice, "Look out, dodge," then threw another nut at her.

Saoirse knocked it aside with her hurley. "Seriously, what is your problem?"

"My problem? Mine!? How did you get here anyway?"

"Orla wanted me to explain the flaccid men, and then—"

"That old fucking slag! She would saddle me with this shite job." Fiadh took a particularly angry sip from her spore.

WHAT DID WE DO?

I don't know.

But Hurler was sad. She'd really been looking forward to a round.

"Can I just do one?" Saoirse asked.

"One what?"

"A spore shower."

"What are they going to do? Magically pop 'cause you asked them to?" Fiadh waved a hand over the zipper mushrooms.

"Please."

"A please? A please." She hurled another nut. Saoirse let it sting her in the chest. "How about 'please don't match-fix our County away to Tyrone'?"

So that's what it's about. She should have known. "I didn't match-fix."

"Nobody believes that."

"Orla believes me."

"Does she?" Fiadh spat.

She did, right? Why else would she be helping her out, unless... was Orla trying to make her look guilty? Get her ensnared by the investigator to save Tyrconnell. That made so much sense. But without her, what hope did she have to get back on the field?

"The proof is all over your body," Fiadh waved her water spore at her. "I don't need to see the bruises to know why one of my creams is missing."

"I didn't take it."

"I know you didn't. I'm not stupid. You're like a harlot who just discovered the homeless—keen to help, but going about it all wrong."

She bit back her retort. "Please, just one spore shower. I'll be out of your hair. I'll go down to the pitch and play my best game. I'll get scoring and have a real chance to save the County."

"And the bruises?"

"I can't."

"They call you the Dancer. Try that."

How did she explain it was a transgression? That she was here for her gods?

Fiadh rolled her eyes. "Spores, you're useless. My answer is no."

"Then I challenge you to a Rite of Ritual Hurling."

"That's what I thought. Shamrock Violet to the core, aren't you?"

"Is it a deal?"

"Feck no. I hate the hag and her deals. No Rite of Ritual Hurling either. An offer. You can walk off at any point, and I won't stop you, but if you do what I want, I'll reward you."

I DON'T THINK WE HAVE MUCH CHOICE, TWENTY-SEVEN.

"What are the terms?"

"I'm assuming whatever you're doing uses your hurley?"

"Yes."

"Good. I'm going to throw these frozen hazel nuts at you—and rock spores and everything else—the entire time you do whatever you do. As long as you don't die, you can go."

"That's it?"

"And it had better be impressive."

Somebody needed to put this chick in a Gratitude Circle. "Bring it on."

LADY OF THE DANCE

The Tuatha Dé Danann love nothing more than good hurling. Can Saoirse pray to her gods by dancing a trick shot? Or with Fiadh feck it all up?

Fiadh

Saoirse

Spore Shower

S aoirse used one of the stones in the circle to give her a boost onto the zipper mushroom caps. She walked around the ring of rainbow-striped mushrooms, shaking her
dust free from her palms, liberally coating the fungi in gold.

Fiadh watched her with a dark expression, sipping casually from her water spore, hands
crossed over her puffy pink jacket.

THIS STRUMPET SURE LOVES TO MAKE US MAD.

We'll give her a show she won't soon forget.

There were a lot more mushrooms in this section of the forest than just those surrounding the little grove. What's more, they looked ready to blow. This spore shower
could be particularly intense.

"You might want to stay under the cover of the zipper mushrooms," Saoirse said,
hopping down to the grass.

"I might want to do whatever I feckin' please."

"Lethal."

"Shaper."

"Don't say I didn't warn you."

Fiadh flipped her blonde curls. "Like a hussy looking for a husband."

"What is that supposed to mean?"

"You think you know how to appraise the opposition, but you're always way under the
estimate."

HA! I KINDA LIKE THIS GIRL NOW.

Feck off, Sat.

"It doesn't matter if I underestimate my opponents when I'm this good." She made a
fist and immediately winced; the bruises were still sore.

"Oh. I believe you," Fiadh said, laying it on thick. "That's how you got all those
bruises—skill."

Saoirse grumbled.

"The only women with more undue confidence than you are four-year-old girls in
Tyrconnell named Lauren."

"Oh yeah?"

"They know they're gonna marry big."

"Nice."

"But they probably can't handle it."

Saoirse scowled.

"Just get this ridiculous shite underway," Fiadh said. "I want to hurt somebody, and it's not going to be me."

I've never seen a competitor better at getting under our girl's skin, folks. Satirical dropped her voice to a whisper as if she wasn't a voice inside her own head. *Seriously, though, are you okay?*

I thought you liked this girl.

She did have one good point.

Just let me play.

Give her a show, Superspore.

I will.

Saoirse popped her hurley to her hand with a deft heel click. Tuatha Dé Danann, was it ever nice to have her lucky hurley in her hands again. A sleek, well-balanced hurley with a rounded shaft, Tipp-style handle, and a wide Cork-style bas she'd shaved down for lighter, faster flicks. The bas wrung with the special wave-like grain pattern unique to the ash wood found exclusively in County Over.

Her hands squeezed the familiar grip. Croaghgorm's lifebound hurleys were special; they'd never split so long as the magic held—unless, of course, you shamed Shamrock Violet. After being put back together by Púca Súcca, she could tell it was as good as new, no matter what Triple K did. After everything, she'd give it a new grip and be sure to use Spit all over the shaft and bas.

Spit does have the best effect.

They're a good business. Here goes. Little Hurler, you ready?

They fist-bumped. Little Hurler grabbed her own hurley. It was time to merge—time to combine the embers of her magic with her will to win.

Dancing, fighting, making love—

Saoirse shouted, "Uilleann!"

—That's her name.

The magic flowed. A warm fire burned in her breast. Little Hurler glowed bright white. Hot fire filled Saoirse, fueling her. She reached up and clapped above her head, showering herself in her special golden dust.

Her heart set. A warm crackle of energy danced about her skin. Ready, she strode to the center of the stone circle, adjusted her light green bodysuit, and knelt in the grass.

"Yule is a few months off," Fiadh jeered.

Gods salm it. Saoirse chewed her tongue. *I should never have gotten this color.*

"You'd look better in blue, or black, or a whole host of—"

"I thought you said you'd throw hazel nuts."

"Oh, don't think I won't hurl insults too."

"Grand." *It's too bad we don't have music.* It was always the nice part of practicing, hiding above the Greensleeves in the forest.

Her heart nodded. Little Hurler, now wearing a black bodysuit—*really? Just because she said it?*—knelt in her own grove circle instead of the usual pitch. Was her heart betraying her for this strumpet!?

Music began to play...

"What?" Saoirse turned back toward Fiadh, who had opened a hidden compartment within the stalk of a zipper shroom, revealing a bizarre, complex-looking bit of gadgetry. A tall box with a rounded top and a see-through pane. Gears inside whirred and clicked, steam billowed from the sides, and music reverberated from a bloom of bronze dord horns.

"Do you mind if I use my Jukeitry?" Fiadh asked. "I usually like music when I go through my routine."

Do you think she knows?

About all the times we watched the dancers? No. How could she?

Fiadh rolled her eyes. "Not that I'd turn it off even if you asked me."

Nope.

Yeah, that's a no.

Saoirse subtly wiggled her heel to the music. An up-tempo beat—something she'd never had a chance to try dancing to before. The Greensleeves only ever pranced slowly and elegantly. This was full of grindy fiddles and hard drum beats. She wondered if this was the kind of music Four mentioned women banged heads to. The more it went on, she definitely found herself nodding more than anything else.

"Gifted to me by the King of Kildare." Fiadh slapped the gadget. "He could have done better."

Pretentious.

The rhythm worked its way up Saoirse's legs till her hips were bopping side to side as she knelt. "It's not what I'm used to."

"Too bad."

Let's go, Twenty-Seven. Take it back to the green.

With pleasure.

Saoirse focused on her golden dust, imagining her Whiskey—whatever it may be—and said a simple plea. "Please."

Danu, An Dagda, Manannán, An Morrigan—I wish to fly.

The 'please' was given.

The Great Aurum Forest echoed with a cacophony of dull thuds, thunks, pops, and thumps in every direction as the fungi reacted in a chain—one popping and letting out spores, then the next and the next—blessing their expansive grove with an indefinite amount of wonder.

Pollen, pop-spores, and puffballs shot out from mushrooms all across the forest, spores soaring high above. Swirling multicolored balls—yellow, blue, red, green, black—floated on lilac strands and hard greens, and more still that made noise: shrieks, screams, and blasts of amazing color—a special reaction only she could create with her golden dust—a spore shower.

Sliotars in the sky.

Saoirse seized her hurley.

...escaped from bitter youth...

For her gods, the Tuatha Dé Danann, she arose.

"Let's go."

For her gods, the Tuatha Dé Danann, she prayed—with hurling.

Poise. Grace. Essence. Back to the green. When her hurley hit her hand, she was one with the hazels themselves—one with the circle, one with the stones. Each lap of the river—her rhythm, every fish—the gods' percussion.

Percussion to her melody—ash wood and gold.

Uilleann.

Spores fell in concert around her. She pranced to Fiadh's new music, selecting spores from the shower and taking aim. She picked a stone with a symbol like a swirling 'fish-hook'—her goal.

Flick of the wrist—click. Ball on her stick. A twist. Saoirse soloed the spore up and down—up and down. Just her fingers, then her wrists, her lower arm, her shoulder to the full.

An energy crackled, crawled, contorted, controlled—a steady whap-whap-whap beneath her skin. Mist swirled around her ankles. A small puff of shimmering dust shook free with every hit, dazzling in the shroomlight. Every beat matched the rhythm of the star.

Forfeda.

She danced.

Spins, twirls, teases, jabs, and jigs. She could bounce it off the stones, bounce it off a shroom, and back again—the meadow her waxed floor, her hurley her heart's hard shoes. Bronze mastery. She pounced, jumped, ran, tucked, leaped, and spun—sending spores colliding midair in a dazzling spectacle of explosive combinations. Powers and powders. The deadly dance of exceptional skill.

A new spore fell.

Saoirse caught it on the tip, tapped it, caught it on the hilt, rolled the striped ball the length of the hurley, and back again. Caught it on her foot as she went into the splits. Let the spore roll the length of her legs. Flick of her ankle—back to her bas.

And when she shot—

"Boom."

Perfect corner every time. The spore shattered against the fishhook stone. Gods, that felt good. Finally playing hurling again, scoring after everything yesterday.

A frozen hazel zipped just past her back.

"You call that dancing?" Fiadh shouted. "Try using moves that actually match the music! Go to the ground!"

Another. She ducked.

"Be interpretive."

Another.

"React!"

Another.

"Grow!"

Saoirse pranced, dodging Fiadh's attacks, finding herself rolling more, adding slides on her knees, embracing moves she'd never thought to try.

"This is pathetic!"

Hazel.

"Give up!"

Hazel.

Saoirse leaped into a backflip. Diving, she rolled her hips back to the grass, plucked a sliotar, and scored.

"Give up!"

Hazel.

GOAL.

"Give up!"

Hazel.

GOAL!

"Give up!"

Hazel.

The nut caught her in the cheek, leaving a small cut—*GOAL!* Blood pooled on her fingertips as she touched the gash.

The last of the spores finished falling.

Fiadh stood by the gadget machine, shaking with rage—and something else.

For a response, Saoirse cocked her head and smiled. "How do you like that?"

But the strumpet spiked the rest of her hazels into the ground, irate. "I hate it!" Fiadh screamed—the music cut. "I hate you! I hate that you failed! I hate that you're going to go down there and fail again! I hate that I don't get why the hag is playing along!" She stomped a too-proud foot into the dirt.

"I'm not going to fail. I have the gods, see?" Saoirse indicated the circle.

"And what did they say?"

What did they say? She'd come to pray, only to end up challenged by Fiadh. "I was so busy dodging your stupid nuts I couldn't hear."

"How convenient for you. I'm sure that will be enough."

"What's your problem?"

"My problem?" Fiadh bellowed, throwing her water spore at her. "You say you want to help and then handicap yourself and hide behind your gods! Now you have to get the hag to put you back in—not so that you can actually do something, but so you can play pretend detective, because it's just so fun!"

She didn't have an answer to that.

"You're so selfish. That body, those skills, and you refuse to share them with the world!"

"It's my body, my choice."

"Maybe this has escaped your notice," Fiadh seethed, "because you're too busy failing on the first day for hatch-snatch reasons, but if the team dies, then there is no more Social Suicide, no more County Tyrconnell, no more Wolves. Everything I've worked for is gone—everything anybody worked for is gone—all because of you."

"I'm trying."

"Are you?" Fiadh pointed at her bruises.

"I'm not transgressing!"

"Not transgressing?"

"I'm not," Saoirse said.

"You don't know?"

"Don't know?"

"You don't know!"

"Don't know what?"

Fiadh wrenched back like a wild beast. "You don't know sex!!!"

Saoirse froze.

"You want the team to be hard, Saoirse?" Fiadh said, speaking slowly. "The only part of _The Violet Intercourse_—that is, intercourse—is sex!"

Saoirse shook with disbelief. "What do you think _The Violet Intercourse_ is!?"

Fiadh marched across the grass, kicking aside spores. "Okay, I'm going to put it in hurling terms so your empty little brain can handle it. Saoirse, when a man is palatable, and a woman is desperate, or feeling powerless, or particularly angry at her mom—" She started with elaborate hand gestures detailing what she meant. "The woman will commit a foul so the man can get a free puck on her goal—her vagina. The man's hurley will get hard, usually from seeing the woman naked or performing lewd actions, then he'll stick his hurley into her sex, thrusting all up in her guts until he busts his nut—his Whiskey—inside her net and scores a goal."

Saoirse went stiff.

ALERT. ALERT. ALL HANDS, BATTLE STATIONS—WE'RE UNDER A PANIC ATTACK. MAN THE HEART. SOOTHE THE SOUL.

She collapsed into the grass.

Fiadh merely picked up her things, waltzed past, kicked away the spores, shook out her mat, and tucked the bumpy pink cylinder under her thigh, then began rolling back and forth.

"Stay here while you have a panic attack, but keep quiet. I didn't fix your empty brain for you to ruin my morning."

It couldn't be. There was no way that was _The Violet Intercourse_! She was bound to it by death—a month-long ritual—with men who—no!

HER ARMS ARE SHAKING. WARM HER UP. PLEASE, FECK. PLEASE. HURLER, RUN OUR HEART ON MANUAL.

"Gods, feck Orla," Fiadh said. "You already messed up meditations. I'm not going to burn enough calories. I'm going to have to skip my double berry mushroom smoothie. I hate skipping that smoothie."

No. I refuse. I refuse!

Fiadh took a deep breath, staring into the fishhook-marked stone. "They say the Salmon of Knowledge sups from the nuts of nine hazels, but they won't come up this tributary. It's only ever trout." She sounded sad.

I refuse. I refuse. I refuse to believe!

Something bumped her leg—another jar of bruise cream. Fiadh had rolled it at her.

"I've known your hurling nickname since you first started playing." Fiadh shot her a desperate, pleading, nasty glance. "What a luxury it must be to claim your gods don't want you to dance."

Saoirse's Selfishness

Saoirse disembarked from Orla's sailing isle back to the hidden dormitory village at Social Suicide. Either Orla's sailing island captain had a terrible sense of when it was noon, or she'd just gotten lucky when they arrived early to take her off of Beltany Circle right after recovering from her spat with Fiadh.

She lied to me. She lied. Then sat there and stretched like it was no big deal. Satirical? Hurler?

Still not there... where had they gone? They were always there. She checked her head and her heart and found them drained. How long had she been out for? She couldn't even remember fainting.

You two better be okay.

The leaves that had been pulled and pinned from the branch above towered over her. For the first time, their height made her dizzy. She stumbled to the nearest wall and collapsed.

Why had Fiadh lied to her? Because she'd challenged her for a chance to use her favorite spot to pray? The strumpet had complained she was the reason her career would fall apart, that Saoirse was selfish, 'playing detective.' Detective of what? The Case of the Curious Whiskeys? She wasn't even helping Finley. Satirical might call her the 'Queen of Denial,' but even Saoirse knew that Fiadh hadn't been trying to help; she'd only been trying to tear her down—just like with the Wives, just like at the North Tree Hotel, or when she'd insulted the Shitty Forwards. Wouldn't anybody realize that the team lost twenty-six years in a row before she ever did?

No. Of course not. It didn't matter. None of the bad things happening to her mattered as long as she remained true to her gods. Being the perfect Shamrock Violet would work. She just had to trust it would all work out. Except... her deal with Orla. The old brood said she'd only help Saoirse return to the pitch if she'd heard the gods said so. And she hadn't heard shite.

Saoirse grabbed her things and headed for the dorms. She found Orla waiting for her. The old brood stood near the base of the steps, by the yellow mushroom stalk, and had on yet another gown, this time sky blue with matching gloves, made from a shimmering fabric she'd never seen before.

"Feeling better?" she asked.

"Oh. Uh... yes."

"And your gods?"

"They... said yes."

"You don't know, do you?"

"No."

Orla hummed. She extended her hand and, with a loud snap that could only mean Púca Súcca was present, the Magic Eight Ball returned to her hand. "If you want to return to trials with a stave bearing my message, you will ask your gods if you're allowed to dance."

The Magic Eight Ball—Shamrock Violet's secret tool for direct communion with the Tuatha Dé Danann. There were precious few Magic Eight Balls in the world; the fact that Madame had one was impressive. "The gods hate me," Saoirse said.

"You've been so pious."

That was true.

"Alright," Saoirse said with a start. "But I'm asking some other questions first."

"That's just fine." Orla offered her the ball.

Saoirse took it. She could feel the power in her hands—the warmth, the hope. Her people. Her Color. Her pride. She'd roll.

What was she going to ask? Maybe she should ask about what Fiadh told her? Her stomach twisted in knots. She couldn't do that. Besides, what that girl said was an obvious lie designed to get under her skin since she beat her at trick shots so badly that Fiadh surrendered. No. Saoirse had a better question.

"Hey yadi-yada, hey yadi-yada, hey yadi-yada and a hoi-yoi-yoi, abra-kadabra alakazam, come on gods mama needs a shazam! Was I kicked from trials?" She rolled.

Orla's eyes went wide.

They watched the black ball roll to a stop on the pavers at the base of the dorms. Saoirse picked it up with great caution. She couldn't read, but she'd memorized this terrifying symbol from years of it telling her she'd be a part of *The Violet Intercourse*.

"Yes."

"Well, I suppose it was bound to get that right." Now she knew for sure. She'd really been kicked. Going forward with the rest of this was the will of the gods.

"I suppose so," the Madame said. Her eyes flashed to the side. Saoirse heard scuttling, but saw nothing. Probably Púca Súcca. Trickster fae were notoriously difficult to track when they wanted to be.

"Alright." She grabbed it, went through the rigmarole, and asked again, "May I be allowed to dance on the pitch?"

Yes.

Yes? "Yes!"

Orla hummed, smiling at her, but Saoirse couldn't shake the feeling something was wrong.

"Will I be in *The Violet Intercourse*?"

Yes.

"Will I make the Wolves?"

Yes.

"Will I save Tyrconnell? "

Yes.

Saoirse got disconcerted. That was an awful lot of yes.

"What is it?" Orla asked.

Saoirse eyed the ball. Surely the Madame hadn't given her a fake. "Is... this Magic Eight Ball loaded?"

"Ask."

"Are you lying to me?" A new symbol—one she couldn't read. She held it up for Orla. The old brood leaned over her shoulder with an imperious glare. "No."

"No?" It wasn't loaded?

"Though if you doubt its authenticity, check the back."

Saoirse flipped the voice of the gods over in her hands. The éireconda eating its own tail was set with two violet gems for eyes. "This... is Triple K's own Ball!"

"I asked to borrow it."

That was it then. It was legit. If it wasn't for Fiadh's drain on her energy, she could have cried.

"Now," said Madame Orla, "Let's get to carving."

Claddagh

Éire is a pretty crazy place, and bursting with entertainment! You'll all be familiar with recitations, of course, but what I really want to see is the Claddagh! Hurler and I like to bet on sports, folks. She thinks I have a problem, but I've only lost my kelpie ranch two times! And I always managed to win it back. Kelpies are a kind of underwater racehorse. They might drown a person or two, but they're not all bad.

Anyhoo, I'm personally stoked 'cause the Merrow Grand Prix is in two days! Though I won't be betting on my horses—it's not that kind of race. There's this girl. You don't need the details.

Where was I? The Claddagh. A whole new form of entertainment to rival hurling, but sliotars does it ever tick off High King Bres! Male-female pairs bind their hearts together with a magical thread and use razor-tipped hard shoes to kill demons. It's like a partnered Feis for murder. If only we were allowed to dance... alas.

Check out this awesome image of Little Hurler I found floating around in Saoirse's subconscious! Isn't she cute?

Benchwarmer

I t was a well-crafted lie. The donors would pay her bail, so long as she turned herself in, and so long as she turned herself in, she'd get a chance to make the team. Saoirse herself had come up with it. Orla suggested adding a loophole so the team didn't get too mad at 'the donors' going over their heads like this. She might even call it the perfect lie—until she found herself yanked into the dirt in front of the team.

The hurlers at Hazel Park let her have it:

"That's cheatin'!"

"Fecking slag!"

"She's worse than me Wife!"

CAN'T SAY WE DIDN'T PREDICT THIS REACTION, FOLKS.

There was no other way.

I DON'T KNOW, HOW ABOUT ACTUALLY PLAYING YESTERDAY?

Little Hurler seconded the motion.

It was nice to have Satirical and Little Hurler back from their 'nap.' Saoirse tried to get back to her feet when something heavy caught her across the chest and flattened her into the dirt. Lorcan's boot. "Hey!" she struggled. Saoirse threw up her arms in defense. This was too much, but he put weight on it. She was pinned.

TWENTY-SEVEN!

Lorcan put up a hand and drowned the angry shouts. "It doesn't stop there," he said. "The stave demands we let her be present for the next three days—with no possibility of removal."

This made her look awful. She'd expected that, but what choice did she have?

"That's right," Lorcan continued. "She sold her soul to be a worthless *marketing stunt.*" He spat the last two words with savage accusation.

She sagged under the weight. Lorcan was taking the opportunity to anger the team—get some of the best hurling out of them. *It'll be worth it in the end, it will!*

"Never fear," Lorcan growled, spittle from his words speckling her face. "There's a loophole. She only has to be *present.* She'll be *benched* for the three days."

Hurler fell into hysterics.

"WHAT!?" she bellowed. *Not play? Not play!?*

RED CARD! GIVE HIM A RED CARD, REF! THIS IS BEYOND THE PALE!

Spirit Stadium groaned.

But the gods were supposed to be working in her favor! That's what the whole deal with Orla was all about!

Lorcan gnashed his teeth at her, then faced the hurling trials. "We simply thought you'd like to know what Tyrconnell thinks of you." He finished with a vicious snarl and tugged Saoirse off the pitch.

She hardly fought back before she was thrown onto a bench at the base of the bleachers.

He shook the stave in her face, its pink and black ribbons bobbing like threatening snakes. "How do you know her?" he growled.

"Who?"

"How? Did you sell your body? Sell your soul?"

"No, I just agreed to owe her a favor."

"There is no such thing with that woman as 'just a favor.'"

Saoirse swallowed.

"Maybe you had grand plans of trying out again after you served your sentence—after we fill the stands and come back from the shite you put us through—but so long as anybody here remains on the team, you can guarantee that this," he indicated the pitch, "will never happen for you again."

He rattled the bench so hard she squealed. Saoirse squeezed her lucky hurley with a grip so fierce that Satirical was beginning to worry she'd rip her skin off.

Lorcan prowled away.

Little Hurler spiked her helmet into the dirt like she'd just lost a championship and slammed herself onto a bench.

Benched and penalized, how can we win now?

Saoirse leaped from the bench and chased after the captain. "Wait," she cried. "Lorcan, wait!"

Aware Wolf turned halfway up the steps to glower at her through fierce yellow eyes.

"I promise I'm going to crush! Let me show you I'm worthwhile!"

"You wanna be throwing shapes that bad? You can do it from the bench." He turned, grumbling the rest of the way to his seat.

Saoirse returned to the benches and collapsed.

It was worth a try.

It was.

Her best-laid plans, four days left, and no chance at the field.

The chill trapped in Hazel Park crept through her game pelts. Thanks to the news, the rest of the hurlers returned to stroking their hurleys or playing with each other's balls with renewed vigor.

There's got to be a way to get your number twenty-seven and mine back on the field, folks!

Her stadium roared its approval. Many Saoirse Spectators had already loaded up on snacks in anticipation of a fantastic day full of great hurling. They didn't want their money to be wasted. She didn't want her life to be. She hadn't seen an investigator yet. Did that mean her father had succeeded in being found guilty? And she'd...

Come on, girls, brain power on three! One. Two. Three!

'*Brain power!*' Her stadium cheered.

Little Hurler hit a thinking pose.

What was she supposed to do? So far, she'd done everything by the gods, and they'd failed her at every turn.

A hurley tapped her calf. Finley, dashing as always, came to join her on the bench. He offered her a consoling smile.

"I broke your hurley," Saoirse said, thinking of how she'd shattered his borrowed hurley on a banister in the Carnal Carnival.

"Uh huh."

"I was going to borrow your Spit." She held her lucky hurley.

"Yep."

"You don't need to be here."

"Ah." Finley shrugged. "Too bad for you, I like people who made complete fools of themselves."

"Go feck yourself."

"I will, yeah."

She eyed him, then eyed Lorcan. The captain looked like he could kick Finley by association. "Finley."

He spared a glance for the captain and laughed.

Did he not care? "You're nuts. You could get cut!"

Finley placed a kind hand on her head. "No, Little Shroom, you're nuts." He fixed her with a terribly sincere expression. "Because you <u>never got cut</u>."

Spirit Stadium went silent. You could hear a proverbial spore drop. Little Hurler looked up from her thinking pose. Satirical had been left utterly speechless.

Saoirse forced herself to look into Finley's deep blue eyes. She could feel the tears welling up in hers. "You're lying." She'd rolled the Magic Eight Ball. She'd asked the gods. But the truth poured out of Finley's deep blues. "But I was in group twenty!"

"Yeah, and you won."

The gods toyed with her soul at the end of a hurley. "This is a big slip," she warned.

"He didn't cut the bottom forty," Finley indicated the field. "He cut like twenty. Anybody who had a working Whiskey could stay. Not every Whiskey is suited to Free Ball. The others had no Whiskey and no skills, or didn't even bother to put effort into the last rep—they're gone. Not to mention he dropped all the Shitty Forwards, cú."

"No."

"Yes."

Saoirse scanned the pitch—sure enough, she found Fiachra, the fish-eyed boy, but no Shitty Forwards. That only made her message worse. She'd signed her future over to Social Suicide to get back onto a field she'd never been kicked from—returned the next day to slap a big bas of disrespect right across Lorcan's face and everybody else besides.

Little Hurler spiked her hurley into the dirt. Her whole stadium cried.

"Tuatha Dé Danann! Great Goddess Danu, Manannán mac Lir!"

"Feck the gods you're praying to!" Finley rapped her on the forehead. "Everybody saw you getting cheated, ya eejit. The whole team was on your side. They don't blame you for their terrible seasons. It's like you thought you deserved to get kicked!"

Salm it. Gods salm it! If she hadn't run out of the stadium, she wouldn't be a feckin' marketing stunt! "I'm so stupid!"

"Yes."

Saoirse glowered at Finley. "You could've lied to make me feel better."

"That ain't my style, cú. What even happened? You hit your head or something?"

She told him about her deal with Orla. "That evil hag!" she finished.

"Let me guess. Did she have the Ball?"

"Well, yeah?"

"Saoirse, I need you to think really hard. Did she pull the Magic Eight Ball out of her pocket, or was it—"

"Púca Súcca!" Saoirse roared. They'd played her! Played her for a fool—maybe even from when she showed up with the bruise cream! Maybe... maybe even sooner than that. The Magic Eight Ball wasn't just loaded—it would show up with whatever the púca wanted it to say! Trickster fae.

Finley used a hand to crack his neck. "This is gonna cause some feckin' complications. The other donors will need to know. Tuatha Dé..."

"Complications?"

Finley gave her a meaningful stare and sighed. "It looks like I've got to be the bad guy."

"What are you talking about, cú?"

"Saoirse, do you know a man from your city, Cathal O'Brien?"

All of her snapped to Finley. "Dad?"

CHIEFY!

"What happened? Tell me!"

"He got arrested."

And a weight was released. Saoirse sank back into the bench with the biggest sigh of relief. She hadn't even realized how much the anxiety that her father might not get arrested had been weighing on her. *I can finally just play.*

STRANGE THAT THIS IS GOOD NEWS. Sadness tinged Satirical's voice.

Finley sighed, "For perjury, impeding an official investigation, and fraudulent hurling."

"WHAT?!" Saoirse sat bolt upright.

Finley fixed her with a meaningful gaze. "That was your way out, wasn't it?" He shook his head. After a moment, he hung his head. "Dad's always right."

"What do you mean by 'perjury'? What do you mean by 'impeding'? My father would never commit' fraudulent hurling'!"

"And yet he did. Apparently, he was trying to claim he'd gotten his hands on a loaded Magic Eight Ball and was using it to conspire to throw the match so some girls on the Camogie Cunts could get favorable rolls."

"Who would do such a thing?"

YEAH... WHO?

Saoirse leaned forward, resting her head on her lucky hurley. "Dad." She sobbed. "Dad, no."

"I'm sorry."

WE CAN ALWAYS WIN HIM WITH THE CHAMPION'S PORTION.

There won't be one. Satirical, don't you see? We're back to square one. She had to be found guilty of crimes she didn't commit. There was no way out of *The Violet Intercourse.* She'd gone out of her way to be one with the gods, and they'd ensured she'd be violated. Violated. VIOLATED!

If Fiadh was right? If that evil strumpet told the truth... Saoirse almost threw up.

"You know, for being a dirty cheat, you're a pretty good girl, Saoirse. I'm just rubbing your back." He announced ahead of placing a hand on her back and comforting her.

She couldn't believe it.

"Unfortunately," Finley said. "I don't think Aware Wolf cares much for the tricks of fae, and Orla will end your bloodline if you mess with Púca Súcca."

"I don't doubt that."

"Don't," he said. "But now you have to do something, or we won't be beating Tyrone."

"Can't I take a moment to rest?"

"Can you?"

Four days... Great Goddess Danu.

"My offer is still on the table. You might be bound for a dungeon, but at least you won't have to die."

She remembered. If she could figure out what was going wrong with the boys' magic and get their Whiskeys hard, Triple K was bound to release her from their geas.

Can we do it?

Her Spectators cheered, *'Yes, you can!'*

Little Hurler gave her a meager thumbs-up.

YOU CAN DO ANYTHING, TWENTY-SEVEN.

The sounds of hurling warm-ups: sliotars getting struck, ash getting clashed, cleared her mind. As long as she didn't focus on it, it wasn't real.

"What's the story with your sleuthing?" Finley asked.

Saoirse was grateful for the normal conversation instead of hysterics. "Fiachra agrees with you. And Orla flat-out admitted they are indeed all flaccid. And Fiadh..." her voice caught. Her mind flashed through everything she'd said.

"What about Fiadh?"

"Nothing. She tried to toy with me. Thought it was funny."

Three-Torques Rich shook his head. "It seems Dad was right."

"His secret conjecture?"

Finley shook his head. "Nah, just about the hurl-ectile dysfunction in general. He thought they were too tight-lipped at the sales pitch. Knew it was something. But ya can't catch a cow with half a bronze poker."

"At least now we know for sure. And you?"

"I did some more digging on the Wives. Tried to talk to the boys about their Laurens."

A question popped into Saoirse's head. "Why are they all called Lauren?"

He shrugged. "That's their names. Every man on Co Tyr has one. Quite the cosmic coincidence, but it's true. I even married one just to increase my chances. I'm not the only one, either."

"That's... that's absurd."

"Yep."

Somebody may as well have dropped a load of shock spores right in the center of her stadium. The whole crowd reeled back—totally stupefied. Stupid shite like this only ever happened in her dad's stories.

"Anyway," Finley continued, "none of them were too forthcoming about their Wives."

"They don't like talking about their pets?"

Finley snorted. "Nope."

She couldn't quite tell if he was joking or if his foxy features just laughed that way.

"Something's there," he said. "I don't know what it is, cú. Now we have to figure out why."

"Don't you mean how?" she asked, turning to watch the team warm up. The group nearby was polishing their tips.

"With any luck, they'll be the same thing. Besides, 'why' doesn't matter. What matters is fixing the problem."

"Don't you want to go deeper?"

Finley's face turned crimson. "I'm always game to go deeper, Saoirse. Right now, I want to win."

He was definitely holding something back now, but she was too upset to press him on it. "Whatever. You just focus on why. And I'll figure out how to make men hard."

"Deal."

They tapped hurleys.

Finley pulled a jar of Spit out of his gear bag and set it next to her.

"What's that for?"

"You are finding a way back on the field, ain't ya?" He tapped her calf with his hurley and jogged out to join the rest.

She watched him go, trying to put it all together. Her father: trapped in a PÉNIS dungeon for all the wrong reasons. Orla: played her for a fool. The gods: filthy liars. She'd followed their designs to a letter, and it got her what? Three cosmic bouts of bad luck, bound to stay in a whorehouse, nearly dancing without her hurley, nearly wearing dresses, beaten to a pulp, conned and banished from Hazel Park—the best field in all Éire. Salm, she was such a fool. But she couldn't bring herself to throw them away.

Her Color was her. Violet. Ownership and innocence.

Twenty-Seven.

Little Hurler had a hand on her heart.

It only made sense. She'd followed the gods' will, and they'd never deviated once from what they wanted her to do. They wanted her—for some insane reason—to be violated, to do *The Violet Intercourse*. If she thought about it from that angle, doing everything in their power for her to fail trials made sense. Of course, she'd play terribly, believe she was kicked, and do something rash. She had to be put in a position where fulfilling the geas was her only choice.

What do we do?

Saoirse looked to Lorcan and his twenty not-pretty assistants, all carving notches into the team staves. She'd spat in his eye; he'd sat her on the bench. Fair. She'd have done the same if they'd done it to her. But how could she prove she was a team player?

Not something Violet, that's for sure. So far, doing things by the Violet code of social etiquette had destroyed her. Perhaps—she rose with a start. *Oh... there was.*

Saoirse flushed with terrible, exciting heat. Even if she did this, it didn't mean Fiadh was right—necessarily.

I'M NOT LIKING WHAT WE'RE THINKING, FOLKS!

Come on, Sat. The closer you are to danger, the farther you are from harm.

Part of her couldn't bring herself to throw away the gods. She hadn't rolled the Magic Eight Ball, but if they were going to go out of their way to ensure she got violated, and being a good girl wasn't working—she could at least *pretend* to be bad.

A Marketing Stunt

S he'd had enough of going down. It was all up from here. Saoirse took the steps up the stadium pews with purpose—part to show Lorcan she meant business, part to show herself.

Violet preached that women should be confrontational. She knew the normal way it looked; it was a lot like how their Wives treated them, but if she wasn't going to be a good girl anymore, how would a bad girl do it? She'd have to say things like, 'You're handsome.'

CRINGE.

Or: *You're such a beast.*

Little Hurler twitched.

Or: *You're Aware Wolf, and that doesn't bother me!*

TWENTY-SEVEN, THERE'S A LIMIT TO HOW BAD WE CAN BE!

Then she'd attack him for a chance to get on the field. Her body flushed with heat. To be so lethal. She could be excommunicated!

Pretend. Pretend to be a bad girl. She wasn't really going against the Violet; she was only faking it. She paused partway up the steps, only to get slapped back to her senses by Little Hurler.

Sorry.

I CAN'T BELIEVE I ACTUALLY JUST WATCHED YOU FAN YOURSELF. I'M BEYOND CONCERNED NOW.

Right.

PLEASE TURN AROUND.

Right.

Saoirse continued her march up the steps to an all-out cheer dance from Little Hurler—green and gold poms pumping in her chest.

She, not her father, was bound for the PÉNIS dungeon. She could no longer make the team with her goals. She only had one way out of the geas—Finley's stave, and she couldn't do anything about the team's magic if she couldn't get back on the field. Sometimes, to score, a girl had to go for the big play. Sometimes, she had to do the baddest thing she could think of. Sometimes, she had to show the team her ankles.

Nooooooo!

Lorcan worked in the very center of the middle section, near the top of the pews. His wolf-like features creased in anger, chest hair bristling through the neckline of his open blue tunic. He might bite her head off, but if it got her back on the field, the risk was worth it. If it meant saving Tyrconnell, everything was on the table.

Spores, why did the captain have to be such an attractive man?

This isn't the right play!

It's the only play we've got.

Then, let's hear it for the strumpet with a surprise, the slag with a stroke of—hopefully genius—the—

I'm not a strumpet!

What? Satirical sounded annoyed. *Just calling it how it is.*

You are not! You know this is pretend!

Strumpet Storm!

At the top step, her stomach grew queasy. Little Hurler'd gotten her hands on a bag of popped spores to join the Spectators milling about in her gut, creating a sensation of unease.

Surrounded as ever by his twenty uppity wannabe assistant wenches who'd gone out of their way to all wear gold-on-top, green-on-bottom dresses, Lorcan steamed. The girls had apprehensive expressions—Saoirse didn't blame them. Aware Wolf's anger was intense. Her climbing the stairs likely made it worse.

Here goes something.

Saoirse strode the row. "Lorcan," she said, stopping a few paces away.

He growled something deep, dark, from the chest.

Gods, this was terrifying. "I'm—I mean I could, uh..."

Lorcan didn't look at her.

Great start, me. Could her own shame be committing sabotage, conspiracy, and match-fixing? This announcer, for one, hopes so.

Feck off.

Everything she could think of saying just sounded like a lame excuse. I'm under investigation. I had to follow my religious code. I didn't know the stave would say that.

The captain sat, his canines framed by a snarl. The assistant girls shot her disdainful looks. Her crowd still churned her gut, but Little Hurler leaned in with excitement. Saoirse held on to that ray of hope. There really was only one thing to say. She took a deep breath and told him, "I'm sorry."

A few of the tiny, uglier-the-closer-you-got assistant twits let out even tinier gasps. Lorcan didn't move. For a while, the only sounds were hurleys hitting sliotars. The pause lasted long enough to wonder if he was going to say anything. The tension strained her Spectators. The assistants shared her curiosity. Even Satirical held her breath.

Then finally he grumbled, "Go on," without taking his eyes off the field.

A point over the bar for Team Us! Unfortunately.

Some of her tension left her body. She could do this. She tucked a loose lock of her red hair behind her ear, stammering through her hope. "I thought... well... I thought that, you know, at the carve downs, I didn't accept the Shitty wager."

"I know what you have and haven't done."

"Right."

She cleared her throat. "Right. It's just..." The words escaped her in a rush. "What if I do a kind of similar thing?"

Lorcan threw his head back in exasperation.

Oh no, he's playing defense, salm it—whatever will we do.

"A sporting wager?" Lorcan barked cold, derisive laughs. "No."

"But—!"

"No!" He shot to his feet, towering over her.

She pulled back, but then she caught the look in his eyes. His eyes were empty—like the rage wasn't even his, not something he was feeling as much as an automatic response working him as a puppet. *Strange...*

"What terms are you doing this under, huh?" Lorcan jibed, brown hair spilling over his shoulders as he leered at her. "A gold coin for each goal? Gonna run an extra lap?" he snarled in mock tones.

"I—"

"Insulting as you've been to the team every moment you've been near them, it's not enough. Now you want concessions?"

That stung like a shunt to the ribs. She loved the team more than anything, but she knew Lorcan wouldn't believe her if she said it. Not right now. Actions spoke louder than words.

"I haven't meant to be insulting," Saoirse implored, still lost in the emptiness of his eyes.

"You sang 'The Humors of Whiskey' to a room full of men who can't use theirs."

She deflated. She'd never even thought-! Tuatha Dé Danann, no wonder the men became cagey at carve downs. Sure, a man shouldn't cave to being teased, but her actions were outright hostile. She was a fungal-fecked fool, a right hatch snatcher. How could she not have thought of something so obvious?

"Go back to the bench and get out of my sight."

Saoirse stood her ground. She still had her stunt to pull. If hard was... and skin did... Fiadh was lying. She had to be lying. But maybe—just maybe—there was some truth to what she'd been lying about.

"I told you to go." Lorcan's voice quaked with rage.

Getting hit was the price a player paid to score. Saoirse closed her eyes and leaned away. Sat shut her ears. Little Hurler and the Spectators were on the edge of their seats with glee.

"What if I show the team my ankles?"

A cacophony of clattering sounds tumbled down the bleachers like a spore shower. Carving knives and staves clacked to the wood below, followed by six shrieking women, five retracted heels, four hands to mouths, three hands to eyes, two more to ears, and a shocked "Tuatha Dé Danann" for good fun.

"Your ankles?" he asked.

Heat rushed to her face faster than a one-balled man with a stolen sliotar.

You've spent too much time at Social Suicide.

Saoirse had to fight to maintain eye contact.

Were Lorcan's ears pink? Gods, that was so cute. What was she thinking?

Ladies and gentlemen, the captain's throbbing with indecision. Seriously, look at that vein in his temple.

"Yes," Saoirse said much more confidently than she felt.

"How insulting."

"That's not a wager. That's an offer."

Shite—but he was right. "Um..." How could she make it a wager?

Lorcan seized her by the throat. "No is my answer. You think you can simply waltz in here, offer your body, and all will be forgiven? No. I don't want you on the field. I want you to suffer as you've made us suffer. I want you to sit on the bench till your ludicrously bought time is over and you're trapped in whatever deal that snake made for you."

"Please. Rite of Rit—"

He squeezed, cutting her off. "No. But since I'm an accommodating man, and I know you're Shamrock Violet, how about this? If you want to be on the field so badly, then you can really break your vows. And I'm only offering this because I know you won't do it. Every time you lose, you have to take something off."

An aghast "Hoo!" escaped the women behind her captain.

So much panic flooded her face, Little Hurler began fanning her with her hurley.

"E—every time?" Saoirse squeaked.

"Strip hurling." Lorcan's eyes darkened. He dropped her and was handed Madame Orla's message stave. "Says here," he waved the stave, "you have to stay for three days. Lose too much, and, well, I don't suppose the boys would be opposed to watching you play in the nip."

Tuatha Dé Danann!

IN THE NIP! DOWN IN HER DA'S DISAPPOINTMENT! MARKED BY HER MA'S MOR-TIFICATION! FECK HER MA'S MORTIFICATION—I'LL BE DOWN IN MINE!

Danu! Manannán! Dagda! Morrígan!

The call was so unfair her crowd was on their feet now, jeering and throwing things at the ref.

These stakes were far too high!

Little Hurler held her breath.

LADIES AND GENTLEMEN, THE SLIOTAR'S ON OUR HURLEY. TIME TO PLAY IT WIDE TO THE MISTS.

But he was giving her a chance.

Lorcan returned to his seat. "Get out of my sight. Worthless little stunt."

Saoirse took a deep breath. Following Violet doctrine made her lose. So there was really only one choice she could make.

"I accept."

Half-Time Entertainment

W addle. Thud. Waddle. Thud. Saoirse maneuvered her way across the wide space next to the Hazel Park snack stands, which were currently locked up behind bronze grates.

She would fix their magic. In order to do that, she'd have to get back on the team's good graces. After all she'd done, that started with a little bit of self-deprecating humor—for the boys.

LADIES AND GENTLEMEN, THIS IS THE ONLY PROPER WAY TO DO IT. SAOIRSE STICKWOMAN!

Spirit Stadium howled with laughter.

Saoirse could not bend her knees or elbows.

When she'd agreed to the deal, Lorcan tossed in an extra stipulation—she had to wear a frock. Wearing a dress: a pure transgression. Her terror at the prospect of actually breaking a Violet code prompted a few adjustments to her outfit to accommodate strip-hurling. Enough sets of winter furs layered on top of each other or stuffed up under her frock—and then, for some comedy effect, one of the wire 'fat suits' they did comedy hurling in at half-time. Today she'd be the team's half-time entertainment.

Her heart was all for the fat suit, but the hurling restrictions—not so much.

Don't worry, Hurler. I just need them to laugh. If she could earn even a bit of respect, maybe—maybe—she could help them. Even if she was terrified at the implications of her deal.

It was obvious her heart did not agree.

I JUST HOPE, FOR YOUR SAKE, THAT THIS GOES OVER WELL.

It's better than actually doing strip hurling.

You accepted!

Spores, the view from up here was so good: overlooking the field and the waterfalls of River Eolas that ran up the cliff face, bursting into soft mist at the northern lip of the field. No wonder Lorcan liked to sit up here.

She lumbered to a stop at the top of the steps and called across the seats, "Ready, Captain."

He turned. She knew at once she'd made a mistake.

Lorcan shook his long hair over his shoulders, tapping his temple like he was trying to calm himself down.

Saoirse sank into the stiff joints of her layers as the wenches shook their heads.

It was *a decent idea.*

Lorcan turned to the field.

"Attention," Lorcan said to a small black spore that caused his voice to come over the stadium speakers.

Several sharp coaches' whistles brought the trials to a slow stop mid-rep. Grand—she'd ruined practice.

"Saoirse Storm will be rejoining the trials," Lorcan explained. "We've made a sporting wager."

The whole pitch glowered at her.

Lorcan spoke the next in a mock too-happy tone. "Strip hurling."

Saoirse let her head fall as far as it could against her over-bundled furs, trying to bury her embarrassment in her chest.

When something magical happened. The unmistakable sound of laughter rang up the stands.

Saoirse perked up at once. Fiachra, the fish-faced boy from group nineteen, was smiling. He was the only one. His laughter died just as quickly.

Lorcan looked like he might kill the kid.

Shite, Satirical said, *amazed.*

Shite was right. *Thank you, Fiachra.* One wasn't everybody, but it was a start.

Lorcan pulled the black spore away from his face to speak to her privately. "Full-forward, right?"

Her heart skipped a beat. Saoirse snapped around—*as best she could, folks*—to face Lorcan. Her position? "Yes! Oh, yes! Of course! Full-forward, please!" she said. She'd do whatever it took.

He put up the black spore. "As a midfielder."

Foul! Her stadium roared.

This was something most of the stadium got a chuckle out of. They all knew she was a full-forward.

Lorcan lowered his cone to sneer at her. "If you'd just honored the agreement, you'd have gotten your position."

"I'm a terrible midfielder."

"I'm counting on it." He looked her up and down. "It's like you're playing not to lose instead of playing to win."

Satirical cried over the loud shroom in her mind, *swing for three, girl. Sock him. Feckin' shaper.*

With pleasure. "You absolute mother-feckin'—" Saoirse lined up a punch—"puss..." She swung—kinda—"spore—!" It backfired.

Saoirse spun on one foot, then toppled, flopping end over end all the way down the stadium steps like a mishandled half-time pretzel, where she slammed back-first into the safety railing a few feet above the field.

Oof.

Her Spectators pulled back with groans. She groaned. Thanks to her outfits, she didn't feel a thing.

Playing not to lose...

It's the same thing you said about the Shitty Forwards.

I realize, cú. I realize.

And then... laughs? Fiachra again—the fish-eyed boy thought her tumble was hilarious. He wasn't alone. Sean, Nolan, Finley—all three shook their heads with a touch of a bemused look and more than a few earnest chuckles. *Gods. Thank the gods.*

Thank yourself.

She sniffed. *Right.* She had the ball on her bas, and it was time to score—if she ever figured out how to get up.

Saoirse tried to "hurk" herself into an upright position when a woman's voice she didn't recognize sneered at her from below the banister. "Quite a first impression."

Saoirse let her head fall back to take in the upside-down appearance of a middle-aged woman.

"Miss Storm, I take it?" Tall, with sharp features, the woman's curves threatened the stitching of her brown pencil skirt and 'better-than-thou' white blouse. She had on black leggings underneath and adjusted her horn-rimmed lenses with just the tip of a carving knife. Her other hand held tight to a wound staviture—several staves bound together to form a long roll—feet comfortably lodged in heels that meant business.

Of course, she was pretty. With height like that, she'd have been a terror in Camogie.

The woman carved something on her first stave with the knife, her expression disapproving.

"Who are you?" Saoirse moaned, though she was sure she already knew.

The woman gave her a once-over through her lenses, offering only the smallest, most insincere smile. "Fanny Burns, PÉNIS Investigator."

Slang

I can't stop laughing, y'all. I can't. I'm recording this while Saoirse's busy getting into a reasonable number of outfits. I'm still mad at her, but Fanny?! Fanny is a slang term for a woman's private area—her special slit, her front butt! Hahahahahah! Fanny! Who would give their kid such a name? Fanny. Burns. Hahahahahah!

It's making me think of all my favorite slang. Slang like hatch snatcher, which is a reference to cattle raiders; or 'head above the hurley' for when you've got to keep your chin up; then there's 'slipping down the Slieve League.' That's a County Tyrconnell special—the Slieve League cliffs are a dangerously steep bunch of tumbles right down to the ocean. When something goes 'slipping off the Slieve League,' it's not coming back.

Feck. Fanny Burns! Ha!

Fanny Burns

They didn't send just any investigator; they sent *the* investigator. It hadn't taken long for Saoirse to figure out she was facing off against the very TIP of PÉNIS itself. Treasurer, President, and, in her case, Investigator: Fanny Burns.

Fanny put the I in PÉNIS. Saoirse would like nothing more right now than to put that eye out—not because this woman was out to put her in a dungeon forever, but for something much worse. Fanny was one of *those women*.

If she wasn't the top investigator, I'd say she has more cellulite in her legs than cells in her brain.

TOO RIGHT.

Little Hurler was doing everything in her power to stay sane.

Three of them stood under the protection of a hazel tree. Saoirse had an assistant girl peeling off some of her extra layers, paring down her overreaction to a point where she could actually play while Fanny pelted her with questions, answer after answer carved into the staviture.

Why did you care? What makes you think you won't go to a dungeon? Is there another person going to take the fall for you? Who else was involved? Why did you come down instead of staying? Surely you know this is pointless. Why are the donors sticking up for you? What dirt do you have on them? What's your relationship with Orla? Is she involved? Is she your fan? Are you going to work for her after this? You do know if you're convicted, there won't be any bail, so your stave is pointless.

"Dumb and ugly, Little Gale," Fanny said.

They just didn't stop coming, one snide remark after the other.

"Can you just shut up?" Saoirse asked.

"Annoyed, Little Gale?" Fanny indicated to her assistant, a disturbed-looking half-fae who carved on her staviture. The poor creature looked like a teenage boy covered in pimples and pustules, wearing a ragged, oversized three-piece suit with official PÉNIS paraphernalia. A strange rubber hat sat on his head, its tip inflated and deflated as the fae breathed—sometimes, the creature was mostly a mouth breather.

Gotta be a fear gorta right?

A MAN OF FAMINE? I GUESS SO?

"I've got to play, thanks," Saoirse said.

"Why? First, you're lucky I don't take you in right now for breaking your suspension. Second, your presence means nothing. Or is it..." Fanny came close. "You were hoping your chieftain would succeed at turning himself in, and now you're trapped playing a fake part?"

Saoirse froze.

"It was cute, really," Fanny said. "He made up a whole story about some secret loaded Magic Eight Ball, but when he went to get it, it wasn't there."

Little Hurler got shifty.

"It's almost like he thought I'd just believe him," Fanny sneered. "Guess your attempt to avoid responsibility failed spectacularly, huh? Shaking?"

"No, it's just hard to keep my balance in the wet leather." The spray from the falls had stuck her layers together. But yes, she was shaking—not that she'd tell the investigator.

"If you think this much of me is bad, just wait till I apply pressure. I'm going to ride your case till the climax."

The assistant got Saoirse's final piece free and tossed it into a pile near the wire fat suit. Saoirse tested her joints. They moved freely. She'd elected to keep five sets of clothing on over or under her frock. She'd be able to move and play now; with any luck, that would lead to fixing the team.

Wait—did Fanny say she <u>wasn't</u> going to take you in for breaking your suspension?

That was sus. She'd been so invested in finding an answer to Finley's proposition and escaping her geas that she'd forgotten all about her suspension. "I'm allowed to stay?" Saoirse asked.

"Oh sure," Fanny said. "I'm bound to figure things out faster with you here. With as poorly as you play on the field, I bet I'll book you for sabotage by the end of the day off it."

"Think I'm guilty of sabotage?"

"No, I think you're guilty of nothing at all."

The hairs on Saoirse's neck bristled. Nothing at all? If Fanny wasn't going to declare her a Bad Girl, the team wouldn't even get a second chance.

"That got a reaction, did it? How strange. You might even say it's enough to prove my conjecture. You're not guilty. You never were. You're just a good little girl larping at being a criminal."

She couldn't say 'not true'—that'd make her look even less guilty. "You sure?"

"The best part," Fanny jeered, coming to stand right next to her. Spores, this woman was even bigger than she was. Just as wide at the hips, just as broad at the shoulders—just a bit taller, probably even without the heels. "You're not even doing it to help the county or the team. You might say that, but you don't care about these men, not really. You're just here to escape *The Violet Intercourse*."

Her Spectators squirmed uneasily. "That's not true! I love the team."

"Humors of Whiskey, going over their heads, insults like these are more becoming of their Wives."

"I love the team!" Saoirse said, throwing her weight back into Fanny. "I love them more than you'll ever understand. You might work for PÉNIS, but you don't know shite about hurling. You didn't grow up addicted. You didn't create your own style. You don't understand what it's like to incorporate dance—to throw that away for the gods and—"

"Marketing stunt."

"Be quiet!"

"Why?"

"Because you're wrong!"

Several of the hurlers turned to watch the commotion.

"I'm never wrong, that's why I'm here."

Saoirse glowered at Fanny under the hazels. This woman. She had that look, the look of *those women*, their attitudes, their smirks, their anger. If Fanny were Violet, Saoirse already knew she'd never get picked by the Magic Eight Ball!

"Little Gale."

"Think you're hot stuff, old lady?"

"Old lady?" Fanny said, taken aback.

"One v one me. Right here, right now. No Rite. Just you, me. I win, you shut your mouth."

Fanny sneered. "Quaint." She flicked her carving knife, so it stuck in the dirt. Why did she even have one when her assistant did all the carving? Who knew?

I DON'T KNOW, SHE LOOKS LIKE SHE MEANS BUSINESS, TWENTY-SEVEN.

But Hurler and the Spectators drowned out her brain with war chants.

Fanny held her hand out, and another of her strange assistant creatures tossed her a hurley that had been wrapped tip to toe in a white bandage so the wood was impossible to see.

"Alright, Little Gale," Fanny said. "If you can put it in the falls at all, I'll eat my words."

"The falls?"

"I know, the goal is a bit small for me to defend. Try not to struggle putting it in."

OKAY. KICK HER BUTT, TWENTY-SEVEN.

"Bring it on."

Somebody tossed them a sliotar. Several hurlers turned to watch the matchup.

Saoirse stared Fanny down. She would not show this woman any good sportsmanship. She faced Fanny, who leaned casually on her hurley as if she couldn't be bothered to try. Did this hag want to make her Warp Spasm because she was about to!

The falls raced up the sheer cliff behind the investigator.

Another hurler counted them in. "Ready, set, hurl!"

"You're going down!" Saoirse ran up on the sliotar. She popped it into the air with a jab lift and spun to use her body to shield Fanny off the ball. Saoirse snatched it out of the air. She had four steps—she'd only need two—The world went black. Not black—Fanny was simply so fast...

She'd blocked out the sun.

HOLY FECK, FOLKS.

Saoirse stared up wide-eyed at the investigator. "That's impossible." She made a move and found herself bound inside Fanny's walls, pressed up against the investigators body. It was as if she were being swallowed. The investigator was so sticky, so grippy, like an éireconda coiled around prey. She'd never faced such defensive pressure!

"This is it?" Fanny mewled in her ear, her longer hurley toying with the sliotar from around Saoirse's behind. "This is Ulster's rookie camogie sensation? I'm still wearing heels."

I'VE NEVER SEEN OUR GIRLS O OUT-CLASSED, FOLKS.

The Spectators were deep in their seats, fear on their faces.

"Time, Little Gale. You see what a real storm is." Fanny crushed her with a shoulder. Saoirse went face-first into the dirt. "Whiskey!"

What? I already lost.

"Tulip Grip."

A pressure built up in her spine, as if she were being jerked backward. Saoirse flew off the ground, her head lodged in Fanny's grip.

What was that!?

Fanny sneered right in her face. "No matter what you do I'm going to be there when you climax. Now waddle on out there, Little Gale. I came all this way—I'm may as well indulge in your clown show," she said.

"I told you the fat suit was a joke."

"I was talking about your hurling."

7 ON 6

Most points in Hurling are scored by long drives over the bar, but Whiskey's add a new dimension: a lot more goals. Players need to be able to handle up close and personal play at a disadvantage.

Rún na Rince

I t was one thing to be investigated, quite another for that investigator to be a cheater! This was absurd! How could she, Saoirse Storm, get beaten by an old woman in a pencil skirt and heels?! How could anybody be that fast? Fanny walled her off before she'd even made a move, and that pressure—she'd never faced anything like it. The Investigator's defense was all-consuming.

You'd think we'd have heard of Fanny Burns before.

Yet there was no famous player that she knew of. Had she gone straight into working for PÉNIS?

Little Hurler was already itching to take another crack at Fanny, but she was interviewing other hurlers about Saoirse's presence at the trials. She was just lucky nobody decided to count that as a 'loss' for her deal with Lorcan.

Five layers. That was the magic number to wear under or over the frock—few enough that she could move, but not so few she had to worry about her wager. Hurler thumped her chest and took to the pitch in Spirit Stadium. The Spectators, eager to watch the day's proceedings with their 'Day-Two Trial' tickets, hunkered into the stands with renewed vigor now that she wasn't benched—zazzed at getting to see some hurling action, even if it was only a short spat. The real hurling could not come fast enough.

Several drills took place on both ends. She tested her lucky hurley on the back of her heel with a satisfying snap. Now that she was pretending to be a bad Shamrock Violet, she'd at least get to dance no matter what her gods had said. Saoirse fist-bumped her heart for hype. *We got this.*

Every strain of her being agreed. Little Hurler went hard at push-ups while the crowd chanted motivational slogans *like 'No shame, no gain!', foil the frock,'* and *'fist that Fanny!'.* Hurler kicked dirt at invisible referees. Revenge was on.

Her instructed line was near mid-pitch.

Sean rattled his dice spore when she arrived. His windswept blond hair was extra crazy under the floodlight mushrooms. "So, you're with us."

"Yes." Stupid dress. Saoirse kicked at the hemline. How was she supposed to run with her feet bound up like this? How had Fanny?

"It's seven on six," Sean said. "Midfielder puts it in play—no goals off the hop. We're practicing tight passes, zone work, then it's thirty seconds to score. The idea is to imitate the effects of a Whiskey by giving the offense an extra player."

Twenty-seven and three—she knew that number by heart—a pretty typical drill. Traditionally, most points in hurling were scored from much further out after being put over the bar for one point. Whiskeys changed that. Twenty-seven and three seconds should net any decent attacking team at least one point over the bar, but it sounded like they wanted to see goals.

She couldn't stop a huge smile. "Right." She made to join the line and added, "Thanks for laughing."

He grunted.

Saoirse tucked under the shelter of the hazel trees. Little Hurler cheered her on, holding her hurley over her head and mock-screaming like a barbarian that'd beaten back a banshee.

I will score. I will score. I will score and score some more. Sean could shuck her little seashell while sitting by the shore. She got a sudden flash of Fiadh and buried the thought, instead choosing to focus on Whiskeys—her one way out of her geas.

If their shafts were fully wrapped, there was a good chance of a Whiskey underneath. She could identify targets, but Fiachra, Finley, and Orla all thought everyone here was flaccid. That meant they all had magic; she just needed some way to suck it out of them—some way past their hurl-ectile dysfunction.

She shouldn't have to face a Whiskey if she lined out against the old team, which was a load off her mind, seeing as she still hadn't gotten a good chance to practice against one. Especially since her midfielding skills had never been very good—there wasn't much reason to play hurling if you weren't going to score, and the best a mid could hope for was a long try over the bar. One point for a one-point role. Boring. With a glaring flaw like that built right into the position, a goal from here was going to be a challenge.

"Finally deigning to join us?" asked an angry voice.

The half-back line was a few meters to her right. The men there eyed her with particularly angry snarls. She recognized a man in line—Seamus—a fantastic left half-back from their previous season. He stood with what she recognized as a dancer's perfect posture. His pink hair was shaved on the sides and pulled back into a tight ponytail—and he was maulding.

"Gonna speak?" he asked again, bullying his way into matching up with her. "I know some of the men here are excited to see you strip, but I just want to watch you burn."

"And yet you'll see neither."

Are we sure antagonizing him is a good play?

Just banter, cú.

"The Claddagh has rules for cheating stunts. They get put in the ring without their partners," he sneered. "I don't hate you. I merely hate those who think they are above the rules."

"I don't think I'm above rules," Saoirse replied, grateful, if a bit bemused by his reasoning.

"Actions speak louder than words," Seamus snarled.

The next players took the pitch. The line moved forward.

He continued, "I'm looking at a Vi that gambles when it suits her, shows skin when she thinks she can get away with it, and blackmails men to get her way. You're worse than my Wife. That's saying something."

Did he not like his Lauren? Why did they keep coming up?

"Saoirse, you're up," Sean called.

Saoirse twirled her lucky hurley. "The proof starts here," she whispered to herself, and jogged down the center pitch line, stumbling a bit and having to hold up her dress. So dumb.

At least they hadn't put her at goalkeeper. She'd have been in the nip before the day was out.

"You away with the fairies, stunt?" Seamus spat. He was five meters out, standing before her in a posture like he was ready to step dance.

Saoirse settled in by the sliotar. "An evening star shines down upon you, Seamus."

He sneered.

She tried again, firmer this time. "An evening star shines down upon you, Seamus."

Nothing. Little Hurler drew a line across her neck. Yeah. If he didn't want to show good sportsmanship, she'd make him pay for it. His hurley was wrapped, but since he was on the old team he shouldn't have a Whiskey.

A quick scan of the pitch—her side wrestled for position. They were playing the man: pairs fisting each other's hurleys, trying to force the other man to submit. She'd take it left. The fish-faced Fiachra had the deep corner.

The whistle blew.

Seamus bellowed, "Whiskey!!"

"What!?" Saoirse balked. How could he have a Whiskey? The old team was supposed to be flaccid!

But in an instant, Seamus's hurley lit up in his hands, violently throbbing and twitching. "Rún na Rince!" A white puff erupted from the tip of his hurley, and she could see the post-Whiskey clarity in his eyes. It was real!

Oh no.

"Oh yes!" Saoirse cheered. Her crowd roared in excitement. A full-geared Little Hurler stood ready in her heart. Saoirse's nostrils flared in excitement, her eyes wide. Her first real chance to fight a Whiskey! She leaned into the play.

Seamus started to jig—or maybe hornpipe. Either way, he tapped his feet so fast the field beneath his cleats became a blur.

What's he doing?

Who knows.

Saoirse made to play the sliotar with a clean swing, but Seamus's magic took effect. Her world rocked violently.

Little Hurler's eyes spun in dizzy circles.

Saoirse toppled to the ground, rolling this way and that against her will—the whole Spirit Stadium of Saoirse Spectators tumbling around her stomach as she tossed to and fro. It was as if she were lying on a water cap mushroom while her friends jumped on the sides.

Then it stopped.

Seamus casually popped the sliotar into the air, taking the round before it'd even begun. "Pathetic."

The magic ended almost as quickly as it started. Still woozy, Saoirse managed to stabilize herself. The world returned with jeers.

"Worthless stunt."

"Get off the field."

"You don't deserve to be here."

It was a good try, Twenty-Seven.

Was it? She'd been taken out instantly.

Little Hurler was still on her, but her eyes were a pair of dizzy, hypnotic swirls.

Seamus got innumerable high-fives.

Saoirse punched the grass. *Salm it.* Who could possibly play in those conditions? With the world twisting all around them? Spores, being a pro, was insane. Insanely fun.

"Well, Saoirse?" Lorcan shouted into the black spore that made his voice come over the speakers.

What now? She was trying to riddle out an answer. Couldn't he wait a second? But Lorcan wasn't the only one looking at her. In fact, the whole field had turned to stare.

"What?" she asked.

Lorcan growled. "Get off the pitch."

She—oh. Oh no... her sporting bet... "Fuck."

River Eolas became loud in her ears. Her hands wrung her hurley. Heat flushed her entire body. An intense awareness of where her skin touched her clothes bristled across her. She swore she could feel the grass through her boots.

She had to take something off.

Every eye in the stadium was on her. Every eye in Spirit Stadium turned to look away.

Her heart's Little Hurler had her hurley out, using the bas like a shield, as she crept sidelong for the exit, trying to sidestep out of the shame.

Tuatha Dé Danann.

Sure, the act of taking clothes off wasn't part of *The Violet Intercourse*, but showing skin was.

What if Fiadh was right? What if men liked looking at naked girls as much as she liked thinking about abs and flowers?

A jacket. That would be best. She'd worn all five over her frock anyway. Spores, this was embarrassing.

The field waited as she tossed her lucky hurley aside and pulled the laces loose at the neckline. The leather separated. She pulled it up over her head, and—

It got stuck.

Spores. It got stuck! The mixture of wet leather on wet leather locked her jacket in a tangled mess around her head. She fought, desperate to work it free, as she stumbled about the field harder than she'd done during Seamus's Whiskey.

What was worse, nobody laughed. She could feel their judgment through the indecent display. Her face could fry a mushroom. This was worse than just stripping.

"You know," she heard one say, "I always pictured strip hurling as much sexier."

Of all the things to say...

It took a few moments, but after a harder struggle with her jacket than a deer caught by an éireconda, she finally managed to spike it into the dirt—before immediately crossing her arms over her chest like they could see something despite the fact she still wore clothes. That was so invasive! How did the Daughters of Dagda do this?

They were all looking at her. *Gods, spare me.* But then... one raised his brow, another shook his head, several shared looks of 'not bad,' the corners of their mouths drawn down in begrudging admittance. Spores, the truth of it was obvious in their eyes: they'd not been excited at all. They just never believed she'd actually do it. Now that she had, they were impressed.

They'd wanted her to pay penance—an apology for all she'd put them through. Right?

She shared a look with Finley, who snuck her a quick thumbs-up and a little smile.

"Keep her honest, Sean," he called over the loud shroom.

The lackadaisical man rattled his dice. "Hear that?" he added to her.

"Yes, Captain."

Sean returned to running the drill.

For what seemed the first time all day, she smiled, managing to find the wherewithal to scoop up her hurley. Despite the news of her father, despite what she had to do, despite Fanny Burns.

The Spectators cheered.

She was back in it.

Sunshine Hurler

The team was starting to turn the corner on her. Who knew pretending to be a bad girl would work so well? And not just that—Seamus had his Whiskey!

Saoirse shared a look with Finley, who was also in the midfielder line. He got her meaning immediately. Their magic could be saved. She just had to find out how.

YOU GOT THIS, SUPERSPORE.

Salm right!

She caught Fanny's eye. The woman waved teasingly at her and made a big deal of pointing at her staviture, then giving Saoirse a big thumbs-up.

It took serious willpower to keep Little Hurler from jumping out of her chest and challenging that woman to a Rite of Ritual Hurling.

"Rún na Rince," Saoirse said. She gave Finley a high-five.

Finley beamed. "You're trying?"

"Yes."

He tapped her with his hurley. "Thank you."

"I want them to win," she said. "Let's figure out the Case of the Curious Whiskeys. Besides, I don't understand what I did, or how I did it, or even if it was me. I wanted to figure out if they could still use their mojo, but it still caught me by surprise. Now I'm not even sure I can handle his."

Finley rubbed the back of his neck, whispering over his shoulder without turning. "I think they still are. Flaccid, I mean."

"Then what did he do—pop a magic potion?"

Mr. Three Torques shot her a smile devious enough that even her Little Hurler pinched herself. "Nah, that's a Rage Boner."

"A Rage Boner?"

Seamus was still lording his win over the most hated player on the pitch among his fellows.

"Sounds terrifying. Is it like a Warp Spasm? My hair gave me one the other day."

Finley chuckled. "It's more like a Warp Spasm's little cousin. With raw emotion, a man can make his mojo go," he said. The line moved forward. "Regardless, they are pretty rare and pretty terrifying. A Rage Boner means a man can use his Whiskey repeatedly, with the regular drawbacks hitting much later—usually post-match."

"So, you mean I got him hard by being mad at me?"

"Yes."

Tuatha Dé, spore showers, and bear shite. The only real drawback to a Whiskey was the shame and fatigue that caused a player to collapse after. If they weren't present, it meant Rage Boners were big business. Maybe she could use this to the team's advantage? If they got angry enough for their match against Tyrconnell, it might be all they needed. "Shite."

"He'll be stroking his shaft all day. Be careful."

She smiled at that. She had only four days. She might be in the nip in front of men before she ever even did _The Violet Intercourse_.

I JUST HOPE IT'S NOT ENOUGH FOR SEXPLOSION.

You say that like I'm going to lose all my layers.

IF YOU KEEP PLAYING LIKE THAT, YOU WILL.

The line moved forward. Saoirse kept an eye on the seven-on-six, trying to pick up hints about midfield. Midfielders hung back so much—gross. Feckin' one-point role.

She eyed Fanny. The older woman was walking the sidelines near the defense with her assistant half-fae. Fanny swung a hurley, making lots of gestures like she was... giving pointers!? Now, who was committing sabotage? That woman was an Investigator, not a hurler! Just about everybody was hanging on her advice like it was pure bronze.

Her advice can't be that good.

PÉNIS SHOULD CHARGE HER WITH SABOTAGE.

Hurler nodded.

But Fanny caught her staring and came back up the field.

"Tuatha Dé Danann...." Saoirse groaned.

"Staring, Little Gale? You know if you need tips, I'll let you have some of my better ones, since you'll never be able to use them."

"I thought you said I'd be innocent."

"We both know you'll never return either way."

"What do you know about being Violet?"

"What is? It's my job for 300, Triple K. Besides, I need you free so I can track you with the donors."

Feckin Chastity!, really?

WHY IS SHE WILLINGLY TELLING YOU?

It did seem dumb. Did Fanny actually think she, Saoirse, was part of some big conspiracy? She was in for a rude awakening when she realized that it was just her. "Whatever." Saoirse turned back to Finley. "Any tips?"

"Tips?" Fanny asked.

Saoirse scowled at her.

The Rage Boner had been as much of a surprise for him, which calmed her nerves, but she didn't have a good way to counter Seamus's Whiskey, and she wasn't interested in going down a pair of pants.

"You could—" Finley began, but Fanny cut him off.

"Are you bad with Whiskeys, *too*, Little Gale?"

Saoirse took a deep breath and exhaled her frustration.

Fanny smirked. "Why are you even here?"

"Everybody has to learn sometime," Finley said.

The investigator waved him off. "Here's a real tip. If you're always offloading the heavy thought to others, you'll not be able to figure out an answer during a match."

"Won't we have pre-match recitations?" she asked, more to Finley than Fanny.

"We will, but a lot of players get new Whiskeys frequently in the pros or change them out for games."

Each hurley could only have one. She supposed it was extremely rare to have only one hurley, as she did. "Spores." When money wasn't a factor, magic got a lot easier to come by.

"So it's good to have a sense of how to tackle them in your back pocket," Finley agreed.

"I'd like to worry about that when I have more than four days left on my life, thanks."

"You think you're going to get all four?" Fanny asked. "I'll be seeing to the donors faster than that."

"For your information, Fanny, I care a lot about the team. I'll do whatever it takes to make sure they succeed."

"So, you admit you're innocent."

"I admit nothing." Saoirse kicked at the hemline of her stupid frock. The salm thing was an ankle trap. Just like her life. *Gods, I hate this.*

Finley took off with the whistle. Saoirse looked across to the half-back line. Seamus smirked at her, shaking his stupid pink ponytail. He was making sure they'd match up all day.

She'd at least not get caught off guard this time. Unfortunately, it looked like she'd have to make a sacrifice just to learn how to play. She'd better learn fast. If she was going to make the team, she couldn't struggle to deal with a constant of professional hurling. Whether she learned fast or not, she was not about to spend any of that time hurling in an unsociable state.

Right, Little Hurler?

Little Hurler shrugged. All Little Hurler wanted to do was play hurling. Her state probably didn't factor into the equation.

Finley's group scored, and her group barely bothered getting on the field to play. One fail, and they already didn't believe in her that much? *Tuatha Dé...*

"Ready to burn, little stunt?"

"I've got hurley insurance."

"Too bad you didn't buy it for the county." Seamus cocked his head back with a snide, shite-eating grin and his perfect dancer posture—except this time, his face fell.

Saoirse had matched it—a dancer's posture, tall, proud.

She had no idea what she was doing, but she smiled at the spooked look on his face. She was, after all, the Dancer.

WE'RE DANCING AGAIN?! YES!

"Spooked, cú?"

Sean blew the whistle.

No Whiskey?

Her crowd roared.

Feck yeah!

For some reason, Seamus fell back. Saoirse got a clear puck-out to her right front corner. It was a pretty poor pass. She never claimed to be a midfielder. The man bobbled it, and the ball rolled free back up the field. She had a line. *Free ball.* She was not making the first day's mistake again!

Saoirse hiked up her dress with both hands and went full bore, laying it all on the line for a chance to win the open ball—ready for any Whiskeys. But they didn't come. Competing ash clashed about the sliotar, knocking it airborne. She moved with her usual grace, slipping through the cracks, snatched it with an open palm, spun, and broke loose with the ball. She tossed it to her hurley. She could do it! She could solo!

SAOIRSE STORM, THE MOST MID MIDFIELDER IN ALL THE STAR!

"Rún na Rince!"

Spores! Not now!

The world began to rock. She had to shoot, but she caught the hem of her fecking dress! She fell forward in a tumble, closed her eyes against the confusion, trusted in herself—but the Whiskey had done just enough. Her aim was thrown off. Her shot sailed well wide. It hit the post. The clang reverberated across the pitch. Saoirse slid on her back to a halt.

She missed a shot? That didn't happen!

Seamus towered over her. "I told you I'd break you, stunt."

"Try harder then." Saoirse rubbed her temple—her heart seeing stars.

"*Sunshine Hurler.*" He chewed on the words.

Something inside Saoirse broke. She leaped to her feet and socked Seamus across the jaw. Yelps and shouts broke out across the pitch. She was quickly pulled off the half-back, who was holding his face in pretend shock.

"A fighting Shamrock Violet!" Seamus cried in mock defense.

"Fuck you!"

Her stadium bellowed, throwing incorporeal cheese, mushrooms, and at least one small giraffefly plushie out of the stands.

"Saoirse, calma," yelled a voice, arms bracing her from behind. "Saoirse." Sean dragged her back.

"Feckin' amadán!" she shouted. The nearby trials stood stunned, as if struck by a shock spore.

"Tuatha Dé," Sean muttered, wrenching her all the way to the bank of the Eolas on the other side of the pitch, where he threw her to the ground. "What's gotten into you?"

"He called me a *sunshine hurler*, Sean!" It was supposed to mean 'fair weather hurler,' but in Tyrconnell, it meant blood traitor, but it was so much worse.

He sighed. It almost sounded understanding. "So?" Sean ran a hand through his permanently windswept blond locks.

"So?" she repeated. "That's—"

"That's banter!" He tapped his dice spore against his forehead. "Do you really think you're not gonna hear worse on the pitch?"

Saoirse dropped her protest. Of course, she would.

"You gotta keep that under control. Go too hard, and it'll be a card, ya?"

Her crowd still didn't agree with the call.

"I—" She tore her gaze away. But Sean was right.

Fanny Burns arrived with her staviture out. "Fighting—another taboo! Slip me in the Shannon, Little Gale, the gods are just letting you do whatever you want now? Or was that also pretend?"

Saoirse said nothing. Something was carved on Fanny's stave. "Feck you, too."

"Hostile. Did I do something?" Fanny asked, the question dripping with implications.

"You're here to investigate me. Stop fecking with my team."

She smiled. "I think you're doing a fine job of that on your own." She carved, she cackled, she walked away.

Was she really not going to book her? Maybe she wasn't lying about the donors. It's like she thought Saoirse was part of some grand conspiracy. Saoirse punched the dirt. "I'm sorry."

Sean helped her to her feet. "At least you gave him what for. Unfortunately, that was still a loss."

She sighed. She'd almost wished she could take off the frock. She had pants on.

I DON'T LIKE WHERE THIS IS GOING.

"Sean?"

"Yeah?"

"I am trying."

Sean tapped his nose against his dice spore like he was considering something. "Everybody's Whiskey has a weakness," he said. "Sometimes it's in the body. Sometimes it's in the mind. Ride it, and you'll get Seamus off—his game—without any repercussions."

"In the body versus the mind?" Well, her body sure was having a time falling over itself. "Can't you give me more than that?"

"Nope," Sean said. "I wanna see you in the nip, as it were."

Saoirse's mouth fell open. "Sean! I'm not a loose-ankled strumpet!"

All she got back was a wink.

THIS IS EXACTLY WHAT I WAS AFRAID OF, LITTLE HURLER.

But Hurler had flushed bright red.

Am I the only one not crazy?

"Would you count me rolling up my frock as payment for the loss?" Saoirse asked.

"Pick a number between one and twenty-seven."

"That's easy—twenty-seven."

Sean rattled his dice spore; the dice tumbled free, and they both stared at them.

Saoirse smiled. "Do you have clothespins?" She'd might not have beaten Seamus' magic, but at least she was only down, not out.

Ulster Hurling

ULSTER IS ONE OF FOUR MAJOR PROVINCES, ASIDE FROM LEINSTER, WHO ARE PRETTY COOL; MUNSTER, WHO ARE WEIRD PEOPLE (THEY'RE WRONG IN THE HEAD, I'M TELLING YA); AND THAT ONE OTHER COUNTY WHO ACTUALLY THINK THEY'RE GOOD AT HURLING. WHAT ARE THEY CALLED AGAIN? CUNT-OG? CLOWN-OFF? WHERE BAD HURLERS GO TO DIE? SOMETHING LIKE THAT. WHO CARES.

ANYHOO, WE'RE AIMING FOR ULSTER INTER-COUNTY! THAT'S THE PROS. THE TOP TEAM IN EVERY COUNTY PLAYS ONLY THE TOP TEAM IN EVERY OTHER. IN ULSTER, WE'VE GOT TYRCONNELL (OBVIOUSLY), ANTRIM, ARMAGH, CAVAN, DERRY, DOWN, FERMANAGH, MONAGHAN, AND THE FREAKS IN TYRONE.

ANTRIM AND DOWN ARE THE REAL DEAL—THE TWO WHO CAN CONSISTENTLY STICK IT TO THE BIG THREE: CORK (MUNSTER), TIPPERARY (MUNSTER), AND KILKENNY (LEINSTER), AKA THE REBELS, PREMIER, AND THE MARBLEOUS.

AT LEAST REBELS IS A COOL NAME; PREMIER ISN'T EVEN A PHYSICAL THING, AND KILKENNY? THEY NAMED THEMSELVES AFTER THE MARBLE QUARRY IN THEIR COUNTY, EVEN THOUGH IT'S ACTUALLY LIMESTONE. DUMB-DUMBS.

Slapping Frogs
Three Days Remain

Their magic was still somewhere locked inside, and Saoirse only had three days left to find it. She'd spent the night going over everything she knew about Whiskeys. No matter how she looked at it, she didn't know enough. Facts were facts—with so little time left, she'd have to throw her caution to the winds and take risks. Finley said the secret lay with Social Suicide; the dancers here would know a thing or two about how to get men hard, if, that is, Finley's father's conjecture had been right. That in itself presented another problem: when she was on the pitch, she had to battle against her favorite team; now, here in the dance hall, she'd have to battle their Wives.

Saoirse half-heartedly stretched at the back of the dance hall, trying to decide who to ask and how to go about it. The topic was sensitive enough that everybody talked about it in whispers, and she couldn't alert Four or Bob or any of their cronies to her cause.

The dangerous pair of Wives stretched in their clique on the other side of the floor. It was almost freeing to know she was bound for a dungeon, knowing that all she could do was give her all to get out of her geas before the rest of her life was taken from her—almost. At least she'd not been in the nip. Once she'd bound the frock up with pins so she could actually run, the rest of the trials had gone reasonably well. She'd only gone down one and a half sets of clothes, and she'd also fielded a few relatively poor sliotars.

Whiskeys were in the body or in the mind. She recognized Sean wasn't pulling her leg; he'd told her straight up, but she didn't understand them as well as he did—he wasn't a very good teacher. She wasn't sure what she'd done to spook Seamus that second round, either.

Too many mysteries.

Too little time. At least you don't have to do anything rash at dance.

Except dance.

Don't remind me.

As per her deal with Madame Orla, Saoirse wore one of the hot pink Social Suicide floor-length step-dance dresses. It had a long pink cape on the back with black ogham she was told read 'Social Suicide'; she wore matching soft shoes—no hard shoes today—and was thankful for the long sleeves and full front panel, combined with her bodysuit, nobody could see anything.

Saoirse watched a few warm up beneath a large banner of their logo. The gap was so obvious. She was a hurler who pretended trick shots were something more special than they were—and in more ways than one. She might be in a dress, but she didn't belong.

They remind me of the Shitty Forwards, Saoirse said, staring at Wife Four and Wife Bob.

YOU SHOULD HAVE STOOD UP FOR YOURSELF.

A tutu in her heart told her what Hurler thought she should have done.

Huh.

WHAT IS IT?

Pretending not to listen to Violet teachings had been fruitful on the field. A small smile crossed her lips. Why should it be any different at dance?

Saoirse strode toward the group of three girls she remembered from her first day—the ones she'd thought had great energy.

They stood in a circle near the front, toward the middle of the mirror. She remembered the tallest of the trio leading all the other dancers during warm-ups with her calls of 'sporeshine heads.' The woman with longer-than-average arms stretched them out deep behind her back as if to show off her wingspan. Though Saoirse got the distinct impression she was showing off her wings' span.

Talk about putting two over the bar, folks.

Gods, they were huge. Probably why she was Leggy Leader.

"Sup, cú." Saoirse caught her attention.

"Hello," said Leggy Leader.

The other two turned to face her as well. An innocent-looking girl with puffy, freckled cheeks, buck teeth, and a pair of slightly flabbier arms—though that might have been the crutches—smiled at her. The other, well, there still really was no other physical way to describe her... she just looked like a hater. She scowled.

Leggy Two and Hater Leggy?

SEEMS GOOD TO ME.

"Can I help you?" Leggy Leader asked.

"I was wondering if you saw who pushed me."

"Sorry," she said. "I wasn't watching. I was doing crunches in solidarity with the girl who muddied her taps."

"Salm."

"Sorry," said Leggy Two. "Wish I'd seen."

"It was Bob," Hater Leggy said flatly.

Saoirse looked from Hater to Wife Bob. "Thanks."

"What are you—?" Leader began, but Saoirse was already slipping between dancer legs like they were sins in the Shannon.

Four and Bob were in their group of seven again—the one in question, Wife Bob, was in white leggings, a teal shirt with a picture of a dog, her shiny black bob cut complementing her gleeful sneer.

Saoirse stopped, towering over Bob in her frog pose.

"What are you doing here?" Four asked.

"We heard you were cut," Bob added. "Or did you lie to Orla for extra time indoors?"

They giggled.

"I'm not cut," Saoirse said. "And thank you for the advice, by the way."

"Oh, was it helpful?" Four lied through her teeth.

"Very."

Her crowd roared: *'For Tyrconnell!'*

Saoirse bent and slapped Bob as hard as she could across the face, knocking her worthless ass right out of its frog pose.

Everyone froze, stupefied, as if stunned by a shock spore.

She was finally back on a field where she was the big one. "Don't ever push me again," Saoirse said.

With that, Saoirse headed back to the mirror, thanked the trio, then put herself back in the corner next to her lucky hurley, where she spent the next several minutes eye-sparring with Wife Four. The only sound: the open, naked laugh of Hater Leggy.

Spores, but it always felt good to be bad.

PRETEND.

Pretend to be bad.

The Leggy Trio

T uatha Dé Danann. Why did the players keep Laurens as pets when they were so awful?

PERFECT VIOLET? HELLO?

Satirical had not gotten over the slap.

I still am one. If she'd been good on the pitch while dancing, she could be good off the pitch and still put up a fight. She'd definitely overcorrected when the Magic Eight Ball put her back in *The Violet Intercourse*.

YOU CAN'T MEAN YOU'RE GOING TO DANCE? THAT WAS ONLY OKAY BECAUSE YOU WERE HURLING.

I'll watch. I'm only pretending to be bad, remember?

DO YOU?

Little Hurler flopped onto her backside in a huff. She'd gotten back in her tutu and all.

I can't. Not without my hurley.

Her heart pointed to her hurling gear, stashed at their feet next to the dance bags and oversized water spores.

What would I look like dancing with that?

TOO RIGHT, Satirical said, *BUT IT ONLY HURT HER HEART WORSE.*

I'm sorry.

Hurler was upset, but she couldn't deal with her right now. Leggy Two was crutching her way. "I'm not saying sorry," Saoirse said as the girl reached her corner.

"Don't worry!" Two chimed in a merry voice. "Nobody likes them."

"Really?"

Leggy Leader and Hater Leggy were currently talking with the Wives. The pair of unfairly legged individuals were currently apologizing to Wife Bob—half-apologizing. Leggy Leader was making an attempt, but Hater Leggy was not helping.

With one last "I didn't tell her to slap you" from Leader and a "but you feckin' deserved it" from Hater, the pair left the Wives and joined them in the corner.

YOU ARE IN TROUBLE.

Grand.

All eyes were on her now. She supposed it couldn't be helped. She had just smacked one of them into the dirt—er—wax.

Little Hurler grabbed her stick defensively as they were surrounded.

"If she says sorry," Hater said with a spiteful flip of her hair, "I'm walking away."

"Stop the lights." Leader cleared her throat and faced Saoirse. "Ahem. As the designated head liaison of the Daughters of Dagda—"

"It's nice to meet you!" Two leaped in front of the others and hugged her violently. Saoirse was taken aback.

"Two." Leader stamped a foot.

But Hater cut in as well with a sneer. "You've got to cut Leader off quick, or she never shuts up. So boring."

"It's not boring," Leader said with a posh accent. "It's following proper procedure."

What?

I'm as lost as you are.

"Saoirse," Leggy Leader said, "we wanted to say hello."

"Hello?" Saoirse asked.

"We didn't get a chance to meet you owing to... never mind. It's nice to meet you." She took both her hands in hers, which were joined by the happy hands of Leggy Two.

"Yeah!" chimed Two.

"Whatever," Hater said with a hair-flip, eye-roll combo so lethal that Saoirse actually ducked to avoid being hit by it.

"We wanted to meet you the first day," Leader said, "but we had things to take care of, and then you got into a group with the Wives, and the warm-ups..."

"Shut up, Leader," Hater said.

The girl shut her mouth with a snap.

Two leaned over, whispering, "She always says too much."

"Right." What did they want? Why were they over here? If they weren't going to reprimand her for smacking Wife Bob, then there must be some other reason, right?

The trio backed off the wall. For one scary moment, Saoirse thought they were going to bust out a Wife-esque poetry routine, but then they stopped and started stretching.

"Aren't you going to leave?" Saoirse asked.

"Why?" Hater gave her a begrudgingly impressed look. "I've been waiting years for somebody to slap that frog. I'm not about to walk away from the one girl that actually did."

"Indeedy!" said Two.

Hold the porridge, people. Do we have teammates?

Saoirse couldn't believe it either.

Little Hurler practically dove into her stretches, waving out her chest at each of the girls. It was only too bad they couldn't see her.

"Anyway," said Leggy Leader, "we're not really sure how or why you're here, but welcome to the Daughters of Dagda."

"Thanks?"

"We hope you won't run away again." Two smiled.

"It's easy to learn in pieces," Leggy Leader added. "So if you stay back, you can practice in place. Watch us, watch the mirror, and Leggy Two has agreed to help teach you step-dance."

Are these... decent strumpets!? Was there such a thing? Impossible, right? "I'd like that," Saoirse said, registering something for the first time. "Did you just call her Leggy Two?"

"Sure." Leader winked. "We're all kind of leggy here. It's a part of the uniform—height, hamstrings, and total delu-lu-lusion."

"And that's just in warm-ups!" Two said.

Saoirse snorted.

"So, I'm Leader, this is Two, Hater," she pointed at Hater Leggy, "Four," she pointed to Wife Four, "and Leggy Bob." She pointed to Wife Bob. "I'll introduce the rest later."

Saoirse's mouth fell open.

What kind of cosmic coincidence was that?!

She'd picked their nicknames at complete random and gotten every single one right?! "Let me guess—that's Leggy Wiggle?" Saoirse pointed to the one with 'distinguishable legs.'

A few eavesdropping dancers, including Wiggle, snorted.

"More like Leggy Jiggle," Hater said, "but no."

"That's Sinead," Leader said with her heavy posh accent. "She doesn't have a nickname since everybody can tell her apart."

Two put a hand to her mouth to shield her whisper. "She's the only one with different legs."

This time, Two had to duck a Hater eye roll.

"I don't think anybody's looking at her legs," Hater said.

Leader rapped Hater on the forehead. "That's not very proper."

The other girl scowled. "Rebel skank."

"Premier slag."

"The fuck do you know about straw?"

Leader and Hater both grabbed fistfuls of each other's hair and started fighting. Two just laughed.

Saoirse fell into the corner, in complete disbelief. She was on the branch a quarter mile down from her secret spot. She was with the dancers, and they didn't hate her.

She'd broken yet another Violet rule, and somehow it had gotten her friends.

Confidence

I KNOW WHAT THAT LEADER GIRL SAID, BUT YOU'RE NOT PLANNING TO DANCE, ARE YOU?

What? No. Just watch.

THEN WHY ARE YOU STRETCHING?

Um.

"We were wondering," Two asked, stretching like she was trying to compete with Leader's wings' span, "what's your Color?"

"Violet, cú."

"Ooooooh." They said in unison.

They weren't alone; the whole room went 'Ooooooh.'

Saoirse rubbed the brim of her nose. She'd not realized so many of the other dancers were listening in on the conversation.

"That explains so much," said Hater.

How could it? Did her Color really mean so much to them?

"Well," Leader smiled, casually pulling one leg up behind her ear and leaning to the side like it was the most normal thing in the world, "we're glad you came. I know you didn't have a great start, but we believe in you. Anybody who doesn't quit on themselves is right by the Daughters of Dagda."

"Except Two," Hater said.

"Hey!"

Saoirse couldn't help but smile. *Shockingly supportive strumpets.*

I MUST AGREE, I FIND MYSELF AT ODDS WITH MY PRECONCEPTIONS.

Most of the room seemed keen on their own conversations again. She'd have to watch out for their propensity to snoop. She'd already made her decision to ask the trio about flaccid men. If everybody was listening and it was too sensitive a topic for their ears... well, it might be best to just section one off on her own. But who? Was Two the kind of girl you asked about getting men hard? Something told Saoirse she wasn't the right girl. And she didn't want to risk their new friendship. But there were only three days left. She'd have to lead into it, and she did have a question. "Where do I get one of the tall water spores?"

"A Your Maw?" Two asked, excited. "Oh, we have 'em shipped in. We've got a ton in storage. You can pick one if you like."

"Shipped in?" Saoirse asked.

"From Armagh to Yours," said Two through her very pronounced buck teeth. "That's the slogan."

"They're named after the family in Emain Macha that owns the factory," Leader said. "My family knows them. Of course, their slogan doesn't apply to me—I've got a mouth, not a maw."

"Bitch, have you seen your teeth?" Hater sassed.

Saoirse laughed. Leader's teeth were perfect.

"I'll do that then," Saoirse said. *Yay. I get a Your Maw.* She didn't know why it made her so happy; it just did.

Hurler pumped a fist. She had a Your Maw of her own, and the Spectators were bum-rushing a new stall that'd opened in her lungs: a souvenir Your Maw stand.

THIS IS CUTE AND ALL, BUT THIS BROADCASTER, FOR ONE, WONDERS IF SHE'S GOING TO MAKE OUR PRETEND BAD GIRLING WORTH ANYTHING.

It's a sensitive topic.

WHISKEYS!

Perhaps Satirical was right; now did seem as good a time as any. "Um... do you know anything about Whiskeys?"

"What, for like, hurling?" Two asked.

Leader placed a dainty hand to her chest. "I have been very well educated in this regard."

"Shut up, Leader, and stretch yer arms," Hater said.

Leader stuck her tongue out at Hater Leggy.

Saoirse raised a brow at the pair of them.

"Hater's just salty," Two explained. "It seems to be a Tipp thing to ask people what they know about straw. One day, Leader actually gave her a full druidic recitation on the stuff."

"Leave it off," Hater huffed.

Saoirse and Two giggled.

"What do you want to know about Whiskeys?" Leader asked.

None of them had balked at her so far, but she'd not gotten to the big hit. "I was... uh..." Orla banned her from mentioning trials, which hadn't been a problem when she hadn't intended to ask the Leggies about getting hurlers hard. Now she needed hurling information; this was an issue. "Playing in the park the other day, and got to face my first Whiskey. He did this dance thing, and I didn't know what to do. I don't want a straight answer," she said, thinking of Fanny's advice. "I'd like to figure it out myself. I don't want to be dead weight." She was feeling like enough of some already.

"That's stupid!" Hater laughed.

"I, for one, can't believe I'm saying this," Leader shook out her shimmering locks, "but I agree with Hater."

Hater sneered at her. "Did those words spoil your food, Slut?"

The top Leggy flipped her hair through Hater's face, and they were back at it.

Two leaned forward as if to say something, then almost fell. Saoirse caught her. "Where are your crutches?"

"Hater!" Two cried.

"What?"

"I need those!" said Two.

"Yeah, I know," Hater laughed, and shoved the end of the stolen crutch into Leader's stomach, her other hand busy with a fistful of her hair.

"Look," Leader said, her poise faltering under the strain of battling Hater Leggy while trying to speak, "if somebody has the answer and it's all you need, why not ask for it?"

"I'm not helpless," Saoirse said.

"Asking for help and being helpless are different things. You got help coming back here, didn't you? And you took that help, didn't you?"

That's an astute assessment.

The two women finally broke apart with some help from Two.

"Saoirse," Leader said, "the Daughters of Dagda are here to help, not hinder."

"It's our creed!" said Two.

"Sorry," Saoirse said.

"There's no need for the sorry," Hater said.

This was still so strange—finding women so willing to help her. After her first day at dance class, she'd thought... It didn't matter what she'd thought. She was in their dance hall after all.

"What was the Whiskey called? Names often give them away," Leader asked.

"Rún na—"

Leader slapped a hand over Saoirse's mouth, stopping her from speaking.

"TDD! I was right!" Two squealed in a tiny voice.

"Great goddess, Danu!" Leader said.

Hater looked over the rest of the dancers. "They're not listening."

"Thank the gods." Leader let out an enormous sigh. "Saoirse, Wife Four is Seamus's Wife!"

His Wife!? Had he said she was worse than his Wife and meant Four? Four was awful! Why was it every time a Whiskey was involved, their wives were too? There had to be a connection.

Leader pulled her hand away.

Wife Four's group was indeed in an intense conversation and not paying attention. Saoirse still thought somebody needed to put their whole group in a Sisterhood Healing session with a particularly intense Gratitude Circle.

WE NEVER CONSIDERED WHOSE WIFE WAS WHOSE!

"I knew you were doing trials!" Two cheered. "We heard about what happened in your last game of the season. It's awful."

"I don't know what you're talking about," Saoirse said. She didn't want to lose her place to stay.

"Oh, please." Two bapped her on the arm. "We might not be from Tyrconnell, but all the men here never shut up about Saoirse Storm!"

They didn't?

"Then you show up," Two continued, "and disappear every day conveniently right after practice to climb on top of a wolf that goes racing off towards Ballybofey."

"You'd have to be as dumb as Leader not to put the two together," Hater agreed.

That made so much sense.

"Isn't your county going under?" Leader asked.

"Unless I'm found guilty, yeah."

"I mean, even if you are... the Wolves." Hater made a face.

Had no magic and no hope of winning without it in their redemption match. "Which is why I need to learn as much about Whiskeys as I can."

Leader nodded. "You're practically a Daughter of Dagda yourself."

"Thanks. That means a lot."

"Let's put it like this," Leader whispered.

They all shot Wife Four a quick glance—safe.

Leader continued, "Did you know Seamus competes in the Claddagh with his Wife during the off-season?"

"He competes in the Claddagh!?"

TALK ABOUT TWO STUNNING REVELATIONS BACK TO BACK, FOLKS!

He'd mentioned the name, but she didn't realize he competed. She didn't know what was more shocking—the fact she'd met somebody who actually fought demons with Éirish step-dance, or the fact he'd do it with a Wife he says he dislikes. No wonder they were both so... hardcore.

"Just so," Two chimed. "They're good."

"Not top by any marks, but quite respectable," Leader said.

"What does that have to do with his Whiskey?" Saoirse asked.

"Whiskeys make sense. They operate on confidence," Leader explained. "What a player can and can't do, who they are on and off the pitch, has a great deal to do with what their Whiskey(s) can be and how they work."

Confidence? Confidence! They operated based on confidence?

SLIP ME IN THE SHANNON AND CALL ME A SIN, DID YOU HEAR THAT, FOLKS?

The men don't have any confidence! She'd seen it at the carve downs, then more on the pitch—not to mention all the things she'd done only served to cut them at the knees. Shite. "So because he's a dancer, he dances?"

"Something like that," Leader said.

Saoirse reeled at the new information. Their Wives belittled them publicly. If that was normal behavior, could their Wives be a root cause?

THAT'S GUESSING.

I know I'm reaching here. We'll have to get evidence.

It wouldn't matter anyway.

WE JUST HAVE TO GET THEIR CONFIDENCE BACK.

That's true, but she wanted to go deeper. She'd told Finley so.

"Think about it," Leader said. "I've got to do rounds."

"I'll join," Hater said.

The pair started jawing at each other:

"Of course you will," Leader rolled her eyes.

"Rebels can't lead."

"The only thing Premier about you is how well you hold down third place."

And they were off.

Saoirse bit the end of her thumb. She'd leaped out of the water one time. Was she a salmon? She did eat a lot of salmon, on and off the pitch.

"Don't worry about them—they're always slagging each other." Two leaned next to her, sipping from her Your Maw.

"You know what, Two? You're alright," Saoirse said.

"You're alright yourself."

"Girls!" Orla's familiar claps tolled the hall. The day began in stride.

Saoirse stayed in the corner while Leader explained the situation to Madame Orla. To her great relief, everything worked out all right. Maybe today wouldn't be so bad after all.

"Ready?" Leggy Two asked as the others spread across the sleek red floor. Salm it. She liked this girl's energy.

NO DANCING!

"Actually, one second, Two." Saoirse grabbed a sliotar from her things. "Okay."

I SUPPOSE THAT COUNTS...

Relax a little, Sat. So far, every time I've pretended not to be Violet, things have worked out for me. Now we've got some answers to our questions on Whiskeys.

BUT NOTHING ABOUT WHAT TO DO ABOUT THAT.

Saoirse rejoined Two. That was true, but for the first time in her life, she was using dance as an excuse to hold a sliotar and not the other way around.

"Basic step," Two showed despite her cast. "Hop. Hop knee. Hop back."

Saoirse followed.

They danced.

She sucked.

But if she could run on the last ball in group twenty, then she could dare the dangers of dance with the Daughters of Dagda.

Primadonna

"Five, six, seven, eight."

After some much-needed fun, Saoirse stretched along the back wall with Leggy Two, and it didn't seem so bad to look at herself in the mirror anymore.

It became much more palatable to join the Daughters of Dagda after Two explained that they weren't actually strumpets. They might show a bit more skin than a Violet girl, but unlike the House strippers, the Leggies danced an entirely separate show loved the land over by women and girls of all ages. They even turned off the nude shroom lights and cleaned out the Carnal Carnival during their performance.

Something else had her worried: a plan for the boys' confidence, and more urgently, an answer for her impending strip hurling later that night. It was nice enough to know Whiskeys worked on confidence; perhaps their lack of confidence was why they couldn't get hard, but she had no way to be certain about that without information. She still thought they needed some good therapy—maybe a CALF module, or a FORE-ARM—she kicked herself for not paying more attention when helping Aisling. What she was sure of was that if she was in the nip before dealing with Seamus's Whiskey, it wouldn't matter; she'd be too ashamed to face them.

At least things are finally looking up.

Say that for yourself, I still don't like the pretending-to-be-bad schtick. What happens when what you have to pretend to do is too much?

It won't come to that.

Today was apparently a pretty important day. Today, the Daughters of Dagda auditioned for Fiadh's show.

To keep the atmosphere light-hearted before the rude, curly-haired nudist finally deigned to make her appearance—apparently she always ran late—the girls decided to work on their 'Stiff Spearman's Fall,' a famous part of their show in which they all fell backward, locking into one another in a coordinated wave. Not only did they ask her to join, they even let her take the front—and it was awesome—but with time becoming a factor, she was back on the wall with Two.

"Reach. Reach," Leggy Two was saying. Saoirse had her feet pressed against the Leggy's legs, which were in full splits, her hands on her lucky hurley as the wholesome, freckled girl pulled back, working Saoirse's spine. Spores, these women were so flexible. It made her feel like a hunk of dried clay.

"Nice." Two slowly let the hurley travel back toward Saoirse; her spine rolled up to a sitting position. Two did all that in the splits, with a cast on one leg—unbelievable.

The Wives eyed her with disgust. She didn't care. Having to strip for losing to Seamus was more embarrassing. Saoirse was more concerned that he apparently hated his Wife.

Little Hurler nodded.

She and Two stood. Two continued her instruction.

"This," Two said, "is perfect step-dance posture. Remember it. It's, like, super-mega crucial."

"You know, Two, you said the three of you weren't from Tyrconnell. Where could you possibly be from?"

"Kilkenny."

"You're from Leinster!?"

"What can I say? I'm a Marbleous menace!" she cheered.

Kilkenny's team, the Marbleous, might be the best team in Éire. That didn't change the fact that she was from halfway across Éire! "You came all this way from Leinster just to dance?"

"Obviously! There is no higher honor for a dancer than to dance with the Daughters of Dagda. We're the best. Thousands of girls from all over Éire come every year for our trials. Everybody is so good."

That first day here made so much more sense. She'd thought all of them looked the same—same height, same build. She'd thought they had a look because they were brats, but the Daughters of Dagda didn't have a look because they prioritized it; they had a look because they were so impressive that they could afford to.

"Spores," she said, watching the women warm up with even more respect. "I didn't know you were hiding something like that."

"Silly Saoirse. There's more to people than meets the eye." Two booped her on the nose.

Saoirse admired herself in the mirror. A dancer's dress, a dancer's poise—about the only thing she was missing was the trademark curls. *More to me than meets the eye?*

"Sorry you can't try out for her show, cú," Saoirse said, watching the other dancers warm up.

"Oh, I never do. Fiadh's show is not my cup of tea," Two assured her. "There's a lot to it, and her final move? The 'Social Suicide'? No thanks. I'm just happy to be useful in some way while I'm injured."

"She named it after the House?"

"It's a cowfly-and-egg situation."

"Huh."

Her lucky hurley sat in the corner. Things were better when it was around.

Hurley or no hurley, you've got to get past the Whiskey. I don't want to be bound to your stupid wager with Lorcan.

Mr. Claddagh's mojo. "Confidence," she mumbled to herself.

"Hmm?" Two asked.

"Nothing." Saoirse paused. She had a perfect chance right now to talk to Two alone. None of the other dancers were within earshot. Leader was talking to a pair by the mirror. Hater was already sweating from her warm-up. If she kept the topic off of flaccid men directly, she might discover a thing or two from Two.

Ha, two-Two.

Not funny.

Tell that to Little Hurler.

Her heart was rolling with it.

"This guy I know has a Rage Boner," Saoirse tried, hoping the hurling language would disguise her real question.

"Mmhmm." Two flushed bright pink, but didn't explode.

Nice. "I think it's got something to do with his... little hurley complex."

"TDD!" Two squeaked.

"So, I'm going to pay extra close attention to how you girls move today. I think I've got to use my body." When she'd struck the dancer's pose, facing down Seamus, she'd totally gotten in his head. "Two?"

Her friend had turned purple.

"Two, breathe!"

Little Hurler (with some physical assistance from Saoirse) slapped Two in the cheek. She started breathing. "You good?"

"That," Two managed, her voice high-pitched, "that... sounds like it might do something."

Alright. Good news. "I'm hoping that if I go fast enough, I can defeat his boner."

Two turned purple again... And then she fainted.

You can't say I didn't try.

I WISH YOU HADN'T.

What's wrong?

I DON'T KNOW ABOUT ALL THIS BAD BEHAVIOR, PRETEND OR NOT.

The gods didn't do anything for me when I was a good girl; now that I'm pretending to be bad, I'm back on the field, and I've learned a ton about Whiskeys. It's all an act, Sat. I'm not actually a strumpet.

I GUESS THERE'S NOTHING WRONG, BUT LET'S DRAW THE LINE HERE. I DON'T WANT TO SEE YOU DANCING FULL OUT.

Well...

WHAT?

I was thinking of drawing the line at showing skin.

YOU CAN'T BE SERIOUS!

I didn't dance against the Shitty Forwards because I was mad at the Daughters of Dagda.

I KNEW IT.

Seamus's Whiskey is dance, straight up. I don't think I can play pro if I don't.

SO, YOU'RE STILL THE BEST FULL-FORWARD IN ALL THE STAR, AND WE SAY FECK OFF TO THE TUATHA DÉ DANANN?

Just a bit.

I DON'T KNOW.

Little Hurler tried to encourage Satirical with a glass of wine.

Fine. She heard the glass set near the microphone. *BUT NO SKIN! AND YOU HAVE TO HOLD THE SLIOTAR.*

You know, drinking is a Violet transgression.

DON'T ARGUE PAST THE CLOSE.

"Phew." Two'd come back around.

"How are you feeling?" Saoirse asked.

"Better. That was quite the conversation. Ready to dance?"

"You sure you don't need a break, cú?"

"Positive. Help me up."

It was easy getting Two back into a standing position on her crutches. She was so light. Together, they practiced along with the dance.

As the Daughters let off their mark, Leggy Two helped keep Saoirse in line with useful whispers about which part she could focus on. Saoirse kept pushing higher and higher in her jumps—watching, listening, jumping, watching—gods, this was a lot to handle—

"Whop!" She came down awkwardly. The world started to wobble. Leggy Two caught her.

"Careful! We don't need another injured girl."

"Sorry."

Saoirse tested her foot. Completely fine. It was lucky she hadn't rolled anything.

Wild. Coming down had almost been like... Seamus's Whiskey. "Huh."

"What is it?" Two asked.

"No, it's just... I feel like I almost figured something out."

"What?" Two had turned pink again.

Saoirse shook her head. "I don't know."

"Oh, I hate that feeling. I hope you figure it out soon."

Bang!

The doors to the studio had flown open and smacked against the wall. A curly-haired blonde strumpet slunk her sultry ass across the room—Fiadh. She paused midway, stopping the elongated sip from her hot-pink Your Maw, and ogled them all. "Did I say stop?"

"Tuatha Dé," Saoirse and Two said at the same time. The pair giggled.

"Gods." Leggy Two hissed. "The Hoe overflows in that... girl."

Saoirse popped a brow. "The Hoe?"

"Need something?" Fiadh shot.

Spores, Fiadh was so bossy. Somebody needed to stand up to her for girls like Two. "Yeah," Saoirse jibed, "you forgot a sock in your hair."

The strumpet's free hand flew to her curls.

"Made ya look."

The Daughters of Dagda snickered with laughter.

Fiadh's face turned a slight shade of red. She snapped, and the giggles subsided. "Funny jab," said Fiadh. "From a girl on the sidelines."

"I'm staying out of your way."

Fiadh scoffed. "Either join the dance or don't indulge it. Half-measures only make you fall."

Goddess Danu, this girl was just such a—*ugh*! She wanted a rival? She'd get one!

Leggy Two patted her shoulder. "Good luck in there."

Saoirse snatched a sliotar and stormed over to the warm-up lines. Did this strumpet really think she wouldn't rise to the occasion?

"Not going to crash out?" Fiadh asked.

"Absolutely not."

Fiadh popped a brow.

Wife Bob chimed in from behind. "Only Sluts deal in absolutes."

"Like how absolutely abysmal your haircut is?" Fiadh asked.

Four stepped in. "You're such a bitch, Fiadh."

Fiadh set her things down by the mirror, then stepped in front with a clap, as if nothing had happened. As awful as she was, Saoirse admired her thick skin.

"I know most of you don't participate in Fiadh Nights," Fiadh said.

They were named after herself? Spores.

The strumpet clucked her tongue. "That's your poor choice, not mine. That doesn't mean you stop learning the crucial skills I'd like to see come across in your dancing. But, just throwing it out there for the new girls, being my backup pays better than your lead role."

Whoa. Saoirse was taken aback.

THE OPPOSITION HAS DEEP POCKETS FOR EXCELLENT PLAYERS; SOUNDS LIKE AN EXPENSIVE WAY TO WIN.

Several Leggies bristled at this comment, but it didn't stop them from primping themselves to their best. She was starting to feel seriously outclassed at more than just dancing.

"Right," Fiadh said. "Simple combo. If you can't keep up, step up till you can."

Fiadh clapped herself in and proceeded to steal the light from the spores. It was as if the world were a raised platform, and the sun a spotlight for her every move. Saoirse didn't even take in the combo—she was too busy being mesmerized.

When Fiadh stopped, both she and Little Hurler blinked themselves back to reality. That had to be a trick of the light. It had to. This woman, of all women, could not be—

RIGHT?

—*Good.*

"Let's see it," Fiadh said with a hair flip.

Leggy Two mimed 'keep it low' from the side.

Good point. Saoirse wasn't here to make the show—just to prove to this sensual... thing—

NICE ONE.

Thanks, me.

—that she wasn't afraid to dance.

She watched till it was her turn, squeezed her sliotar, and sort of walked the combination with rhythm, which earned high marks from the Daughters of Dagda but a scoff from Miss Primadonna.

"TDD. You call that in the show?" Fiadh laughed.

In the show? Saoirse eyed her hurley. That was being in the show like this girl knew anything about performing for a stadium of men, all chanting your name.

Little Hurler nodded.

Saoirse went again, adding a bit of oomph. Probably too much 'oomph,' too little 'bit.' She couldn't take her eyes off her hurley.

"What are you looking at?" Fiadh stopped the runs to confront her. "Hmm?"

"Huh? Me?" Saoirse pointed at herself.

"Yeah. You. You keep looking over there."

Saoirse rubbed the bridge of her nose. "My lucky hurley."

The source of all things annoying crossed her arms, looking from Saoirse to the hurley to Saoirse. "Well, grab it."

"What?"

"Grab. It."

She looked to her new friends for some support. They all shrugged as if to say, guess you should.

"Right." Saoirse jogged across the room, all eyes on her. Her early arriving Trial Day Spectators sat upright—everybody intrigued. Why would Fiadh want her to get her hurley? Saoirse popped it to her hands with a deft heel flick, dropped her sliotar, and jogged back to the lines.

Fiadh addressed the group.

"On my nights, it's important to keep men's minds on one thing and one thing only. To that end, when you're on my stage, you need to remember this: when you're in my show, you're dancing so your teammates can score."

BOOM, WHERE DAD KEEPS THE STRAWBERRY MUFFINS, FOLKS.

A hurley clattered to the floor in her heart.

"What's with the doofy smile?" Fiadh asked.

Saoirse tried to hide it away, but couldn't. "I'm in the show, cú."

"Oh, so now your gods want you to dance?" Fiadh struck her with appraising eyes.

This girl! Saoirse skipped to the head of the line. Everybody cleared out of her way.

"No." The gods had never said they wanted her to dance; she'd just chosen anyway.

AT LEAST YOU'RE FINALLY NOT DENYING THAT.

Fiadh tried to count her in, but she didn't move.

"You okay?" Two chimed.

"Saoirse?" Leader asked.

"Frozen eejit," said Hater.

She closed her eyes, imagining Seamus standing in his perfect posture, his pink ponytail, imagining the strange, tumbling, woozy world of Rún na Rince.

Here goes. Little Hurler, you ready?

They fist-bumped. Little Hurler adjusted her tutu. It was time to merge. Time to combine the embers of her magic with her will to dance.

DANCING, FIGHTING, MAKING LOVE—

Saoirse shouted, "Uilleann!"

—THAT'S HER NAME.

The magic flowed. A warm fire burned in her breast. Little Hurler began to glow, bright white. Hot fire filled Saoirse, fueled her. Saoirse reached up and clapped above her head, showering herself in her special golden dust.

The women oohed with awe.

She hit a dancer's perfect posture, with her arms out to hold her hurley.

Let's dance.

Majesty. Clarity. Purpose.

Escaped out of her crowd.

This was no different from a spore shower.

Elegance. Grace. Poise.

Hurling *was* dance, especially when it felt like it.

Her hurley, her hard shoes.

Ash wood and gold.

Half-measures make you fall.

"Five, six, seven, eight."

Ruining the Rince

Hazel Park was cold this morning. But her heart was on fire. It was time to handle a Whiskey. Seamus stood across from her. He held his Whiskey high and cried, "Rún na Rince!"

Saoirse struck the same posture she'd used that morning in Fiadh's challenge.

Five, six, seven, eight.

Mist coalesced in Seamus's hurley. It glowed, throbbing with power before it blew. White mist erupted from the end, the dancer's pink ponytail flapping in the fallout of the power.

As she expected, nothing happened.

The world did not tilt.

His Whiskey wasn't in the body at all. It was completely mental. Fiadh's statement came to mind:

Join the dance or don't indulge it.
Half-measures only make you fall.

Fiadh's words had the answer, and today she was present in her body. Mentally, she'd joined the dance, which meant Seamus's Whiskey wouldn't work.

Seamus still jigged as if the illusions his magic affected on her sight were occurring.

Saoirse smirked. Today, she wasn't the one who looked like a fool. "Asking me to dance, are you?"

He paused just before lunging at the sliotar—his eyes wide.

"I accept."

She might not be nearly as good as he was—certainly not from midfield—but she'd learned something this morning dancing with an injured Daughter of Dagda. Even up against the pros, she could play.

Saoirse did the simple jig from that morning, and instead of going wonky, the world remained steady.

Hop—roll the sliotar.

Hop knee—flick it up.

Hop back.

And pass. So our teammates can score.

The sliotar sailed to Fiachra, the fish-faced boy playing corner-forward. Seamus shouted something primal, his Whiskey completely nullified.

Spores, folks. She's done it! We've not seen a Whiskey fail this hard since 322, when County Clare ran into the famous Awful Offaly Isosceles! Try saying that three times fast.

She'd gotten off the line and into the game!

"Saoirse!" Finley cheered behind her as she rushed toward the ball, which went sailing over her head and out of bounds.

She heard Finley groan.

But who feckin' cared!?

Little Hurler leaped for joy.

Her stadium roared.

She let out a cheer!

It's a win in my book, folks!

She'd beaten her first Whiskey!

Saoirse whooped with a little jump and turned to face Seamus. "Hey!" He didn't look. "Hey!"

"What?" he snapped.

Saoirse raised her hurley. "An evening star shines upon you."

He clucked his tongue and begrudgingly lifted his hurley slightly off the dirt. "May it be."

For a moment, her heart touched the clouds—till she caught something from the corner of her eye.

Seamus's hurley wasn't glowing.

Oh no. No. No. No!

The man fell forward and hit the grass, out cold.

She'd won, and in doing so, made him go limp.

Feck.

THE MERROW GRAND PRIX

DEEP WEXFORD – ISEAL

Demanded

*G*AME, SET, AND MATCH... KIND OF. A WIN TO SAOIRSE, BUT THIS ANNOUNCER, FOR ONE, ISN'T SURE SHE SHOULDN'T HAVE THROWN THE MATCH. WHAT DO YOU THINK, LITTLE H?

Little Hurler was down, sprawled across the pitch with a straw to a tasty-looking smoothie stuck in her limp mouth.

Who said she could get a post-practice smoothie without them? Rude.

In lieu of something to do while waiting on the showers, Saoirse rolled a large barrel full of sliotars to the twenty-seven-meter mark and took it upon herself to practice her shot. She'd lost the other half of her second set of clothes today, which put her down to only three sets remaining, and no guarantees she'd get to play full-forward—but who cared? She'd won! Finally, she'd won. Well, kinda.

Her ploy worked. She'd crushed Seamus's Rage Boner, but his Whiskey remained flaccid the rest of the day.

YOU KNOW, Satirical said, *SINCE PRACTICE HAS WOUND DOWN, WOULD YOU MIND IF HURLER AND I GO TO THE RACES?*

At the mention of the races, the mini-Saoirse ceased her slurping to jerk her head ever so slightly toward her.

The races? Is this like when you go listen to recitations without me?

YOU SEEMED UPSET WHEN YOU LEARNED ABOUT IT LAST TIME.

She still didn't believe her alter-ego did things without her, but she didn't see how it could hurt.

Betting on the kelpies again?

OH NO, THIS IS THE MERROW GRAND PRIX. IT'S MUCH MORE EXCITING.

Her heart was pleading now, though the sprawled-out Little Hurler seemed totally tuckered.

Saoirse let out a reserved sigh. *Fine.*

And instantly, her heart leaped for joy, racing off to the locker rooms to get changed.

LADIES AND GENTLEMEN, TONIGHT'S GONNA BE A PARTY! THANKS.

Sure?

JUST PROMISE ME YOU WON'T DO ANYTHING TOO DUMB WHILE I'M GONE.

Me?

I KNOW YOU. ONE GOAL AND YOU GO FOR MORE. I DON'T WANT THIS CRAZY STUNT GOING TO YOUR HEAD. WITHOUT ME, YOU'LL START DOING SOMETHING REALLY CRAZY, LIKE WALKING AROUND WITH YOUR BACK OUT.

Heat flushed her face. Saoirse thought her hair bristled so much at that it might have gone back through the blow-dryer. *I would never do something so bad!*

Just checking. Get some rest, Twenty-Seven.

The Merrow Grand Prix? What was she really agreeing to? But a chill cut through her a moment later. She suddenly felt as if her brain and half her heart were missing, like there was a cavity where her 'her-ness' should be.

Saoirse clutched at her chest. *Satirical? Little Hurler?*

Nothing. Weird. It's not like they really had lives of their own... Saoirse shook her head. She was just tired from the day's events—and a little jealous she couldn't hit the showers. They were still occupied by the last of the dwindling men.

Saoirse pulled herself another sliotar from the pile and loosed a lovely shot. "Boom. Top left, where dad keeps the bear jerky."

She plucked another.

Do you think I did the right thing with Seamus?

Silence.

Right. Spores, not having Satirical was weird. She was definitely overthinking this. Saoirse loosed another shot and reset her head. They'd be back. It was just the races. She'd have to do her own thinking.

So, Seamus's rage boner. She'd killed it. The only man from the old team who'd gotten hard since she'd been here—and losing to a girl made him flaccid.

Maybe it was a good thing. Fanny would be more convinced she was guilty, but if things remained like this, the second chance against County Tyrone wouldn't matter. Sure, if Fiadh was right, hard had something to do with *The Violet Intercourse*—not that she had any leads in that direction—then there was what she'd learned from yesterday about them working differently in the body and in the mind. In her conversation with Wife Four, the brunette mentioned not blaming her for her husband's problems—that made it sound like it had something to do with their Wives. Seamus mentioned his yesterday, too. There was nothing connecting it all together. There had to be more to getting hard than she'd been led to believe.

"Bam, bottom right. And the sliotar goes slipping down the Slieve League, folks," she said, mimicking Satirical, watching the sliotar roll into River Eolas and be carried up the cliff.

She pulled on another sliotar, cutting it off the ground. Orla's words came back to her: *be the kind of player worth making space for.* Would that get their mojo moving?

Leader said it was about confidence. The team certainly didn't have any. A rage boner was based on anger. That made them unstable. She pulled another ball. It seemed like it all came back to a player's emotions. Was that the glue If only she could see into a player's psyche like Aisling did. It's not like she was a therapist.

"Boom—"

"Nice shot," Lorcan growled beside her.

Saoirse spun.

The captain had snuck up on her. The hair on his powerful, vein-cracked forearms bristled in the winter chill, and he carried a strange package wrapped in green oak-leaf snippings and twine in his arms. He eyed her with a curious expression.

"To whatever it is, no," she said. She wanted to help him—she didn't know how—and after 'the frock,' she wasn't about to make any more deals with Lorcan feckin' Maguire.

"Can't wiggle out of this one, I'm afraid."

"Wanna bet?"

Lorcan's eyes darkened. "Bet?"

"Tuatha Dé. I meant it as a turn of phrase." She said, pulling another sliotar. Then she spun back around to face him—right as he seized her wrist. She squealed in fright. The force in his grip scared her, but then he blinked in surprise, as if he'd not expected her to face him—or at least not squeal.

For more heartbeats than she ought to have dared, she stared into his yellow eyes, past the semi-braided hair spilling around his face with perfect sheen. It was still there—the emptiness in the back of his eyes. For the second time with Aware Wolf, she got the feeling that Lorcan's aggressive behavior was a response. It wasn't the man inside.

"Yes?" she asked, her voice breathless, her throat still working through the shock.

It took a moment, but he thrust his package into her chest. "Here."

Instinctively, she took it with both hands. Stiff and awkward, he let her go.

She wiggled his package. It seemed... flimsy? "What is it?"

"It's a dress."

At this, Saoirse put her foot down. She was not letting him get away with this again. She wouldn't let him bully her into doing something she didn't want just because he was six-foot-nine. "Go swim the Shannon."

"Put it on."

"No."

"Just do it."

"In case you haven't noticed, me and dresses—"

He lunged forward and seized her by the throat. She jumped in fright—her heart raced around the pitch a few times—but this was different. Lorcan thumbed her cheek, fierce yet gentle, like he'd wanted to tip her chin but hadn't known how to do it. Part of her knew she shouldn't let him treat her like this, that if he wasn't Aware Wolf, if he wasn't six-foot-nine, he wouldn't get away with it—but he'd read her like a stave, and she so desperately wanted to help.

"It'll cover every part of you I desire," he snarled. "Put it on. I'm taking you to the place I used to take my Wife."

☘ Satirical Story Time ☘

The races! Races...

Little Black Danger

S aoirse thanked the gods for Aisling, showers, and Aisling in precisely that order, in the showers she'd found her answer, Lorcan needed PÉNIS therapy, and what's more? She'd give him some.

"Ow!" she said.

But it looked like being a therapist might be harder than she'd thought. She'd never worn heels, and Lorcan was still angry.

"Keep up," he growled, yanking her arm, forcing her to practically jog two paces to every one of his.

She stumbled after him, one arm clutching his bicep for support, the other holding down her dignity by the hemline as she half-clacked, half-skidded along the wide thoroughfare at the top of the bleachers, passing the pitch on one side, closed snack vendors locked behind bronze grates on the other.

He yanked her.

For An Dagda's sake! He needed PÉNIS therapy more than she thought. Not to mention, he'd coerced her into a sexplosive dress! Satirical would never let her live this down. *Why me?*

Saoirse clutched at the tight fabric. A stupid little black danger with a hem so far from the floor it may as well have been waving goodbye. It came with no sleeves, and the designer had forgotten to put a back in it! It might have been okay, had the assistant wenches not 'accidentally' taken her clothes for 'cleaning' while she'd showered, leaving her no pelts or wraps to put over or under it. For feck's sake, she almost had her knees out! *Half her calves were showing*... oh, she was basically naked.

To distract herself from the terminal embarrassment—and hopefully add some hype to her upcoming whatever Lorcan had in mind—Saoirse forced herself to mentally recite the five big things the Medical Druids Association of Éire recommended for handling hurlers' emotions, which she memorized from the 'So Your Men Are Sad, and You Want to Work for PÉNIS' recitation Aisling schlepped her to in Donegal:

> 1. Make Them Comfortable - When a player feels at ease around you, they're more willing to open up about what they think and feel. Put the player in a calm state of mind by addressing them in a setting where they are most comfortable.

> 2. Massage Their Ego - Most men will see therapy as admitting they are worthless,

and hurling players take great pride in their appearance as major figureheads in town. Be sure to assuage these fears. Lubricate their emotions liberally, massage their ego.

3. Maintain Eye Contact - Men are used to being cut off by their significant others (all of whom will swear to the grave this isn't the case), meaning a player may not be used to letting out their deep, complex web of thoughts and emotions. Eye contact signifies that you are listening and that you care.

4. Handle Their Bawls - Be aware that in the process of fixing a player's emotional baggage, you might see things you don't want to or put yourself in dangerous places you don't want to be. Crying, outbursts, threats, physical violence, or other dangerous situations are hazards (sometimes even perks!) of the job. Protect yourself, and be prepared—handle their bawls.

5. Let Them Unload - A player may have been carrying around problems pent up inside them for longer than you could imagine. Let your heart be the vessel they can release inside of. Don't keep up your walls—let them unload.

Saoirse smiled as she finished her recitation, feeling much better now she'd given words to her anxiety. But she was frightfully worried. She'd never actually given anybody therapy before. Despite knowing a lot of the basics from talking with Aisling, her hands were sweating. What if she couldn't make him comfortable? What if she didn't massage his ego properly? And maintaining eye contact with a beast? Spores. She wasn't so sure. Especially not when she kept getting forced into these strumpet behaviors. Not that she had a choice. She'd started winning by pretending to be a bad girl—an immoral Shamrock Violet: drinking, gambling, dresses—great goddess Danu, this dress—and even... dare she dream it... dancing! Without hurling equipment! Oh, the thought was so risqué! But she couldn't stop winning now.

Lorcan's anger still bit at the air around her. She made her choice—this was her chance. She could fix him.

They reached the end of the walk, where a large railing separated the stands from the roof of the home team's lockers. Lorcan threw the gate open and forced her through, staying to close it behind them.

Saoirse paused. This was where he brought his Wife? The lockers? Spores. He needed more therapy than she thought. Then again, since Wives were little more than pets—with seriously weird personalities—they might enjoy being up here.

River Eolas raced up the cliff face in front of her, lit by the stadium floodlight shrooms. Slips of pink and purple mist spiraled off the water, disappearing into the night air.

She shot him a curious glance. It struck her just how many times she'd been sitting on the precipice jutting out from the top of the falls, staring down at the stadium, and never considered looking through the windows at the one man bullying her now—the man she'd been most keen to see. Now she was down here, now she could see the emptiness in his eyes; she wished she'd started looking sooner.

Saoirse threaded her hand back through his arm when he came close again and squeezed his bicep—as much as she could squeeze. He'd dressed up in classy trousers, clean boots, and a daring black tunic with a red rose embroidered on the collar. His long brown hair spilled over his shoulders, braids highlighting the sharp, angular beard, and his yellow eyes. If he wasn't gorgeous enough already, he hadn't needed to put on the scent—poisonous masculinity and cinnamon shrooms. Tír na nÓg in a bottle. Salm him. He'd probably picked that smell on purpose.

Naughty thoughts floated across her mind: her and Aisling's version of _The Violet Intercourse_, back when she'd been convinced it meant going to the Carnal Carnival. Still hard to believe that was a real place, but she could imagine doing the Hurling Hearts game with him, the pair of them participating in inter-city underwater basket weaving, or maybe even—dare she think it?—picking flowers! A rush of heat filled her cheeks faster than a one-balled man with a stolen sliotar. This is why Shamrock Violet called excommunication 'exiled in shame!' Pinch. Maybe the Magic Eight Ball rolled yes while she was gone. Double pinch! She could get pregnant! Triple pinch! She really didn't want to get pregnant. Wait—was that what he was hoping for? To have her become pregnant and unable to play, then the donors couldn't force him to keep her?

She glanced at Lorcan again. He hadn't brought flowers, but—

There was a rose on his lapel!

A cold clamminess crawled across her skin. She and Little Hurler really needed to have that talk about men who were six-foot-nine, because Lorcan was a big fat liar. And she was letting him get away with it—again.

She could still run...

Then the waterfall split open.

Saoirse's mouth did the same. "Tuatha Dé Danann!"

Small walls protruded through the reverse falls, connecting with the top of the lockers, pushing aside the water, and revealing a winding set of stone steps leading up the inside of the cliff. All that time watching games, she never could have imagined—a secret passage!

That was too cool.

"You didn't think I wanted to show you the top of the locker room, did you?"

This feckin' hatch snatcher.

Lorcan smirked and led her through the parting to the shroom-lit steps.

The river closed behind.

Saoirse yelped. There went her chance to run.

"Problem?" Lorcan growled.

She shook her head, even though her insides screamed, yes!

She was cut off from the exit, trapped on a date with danger himself—with a man she could murder if she wasn't careful. What if this was _The Violet Intercourse_ after all? What if Lorcan's pain had truly become too much? What if he was going to sexplode near her, then his Wife came back for revenge and killed her!? The stress of this whole situation was killing her.

She'd be the next damsel in her favorite satire. She could hear it now—CSI: Enniskillen - The Girl Who Hurled Too Much! (A Ballybofey Special).

An angsty underling would ask, '_Where did you find the body?_'

Answered by a worn-out detective with a squeaky voice: '_Floating down the river, see?_' '_Down the river._'

'_Last we know, she was trying to make men hard, see?_'

'_That'll do it. It's always those kinds of girls who meet with a sticky end._'

That was a lot less fun without Satirical for the other voices.

She snapped back to reality when her captain yanked her arm, forcing her up the steps. She was barely prepared for the evening, much less his therapy session, but nothing could have prepared her for a statement somehow worse than anything else she could have imagined.

"I'm taking you to meet with the donors."

Dangerous Donors

T he donors!?

An empty gap where she'd expected Satirical's useful input rang in her mind. And the hole in her heart? Little Hurler wasn't there. The salm races. She was about to be tossed to the lionflies—and entirely alone!

The lightshrooms lit the secret passageway. She was trapped on the other side of the waterfall with Lorcan. There was no backing out now.

Saoirse stared up at the towering figure looming over her. Lorcan wanted to discover the truth about the stave Madame Orla had given him—the stave that undercut his authority. Except the donors didn't put her back into trials; Madame Orla had. Even if the old brood was a donor herself, neither of them accounted for this! How much did the other donors know about their ploy? And worse, how was she supposed to give Aware Wolf PÉNIS therapy when tonight he was her enemy? She needed an answer, and quick, before more than her back got exposed.

"That's not a problem, is it?" he asked.

"Nope..."

"Good."

Shite.

He seized her wrist, dragging her up the steps. Saoirse stumbled after him, praying her arms didn't look nearly as flabby as Leggy Two's in this sleeveless slagwear for sassy strumpets! Tuatha Dé Danann, if she ever got the chance to get back at Lorcan, then so help him—!

But all thoughts of revenge evaporated, and her breath hitched as they crested the rise to a new vista. "Wow."

A long hall stretched before them with a towering ceiling cut right out of the stone behind the falls. Lit by chihulooshroomdeliers and lined with sleek wooden tables, arches to the right gave wide views of the racing water. To the left, a long bar served women in dresses that made hers seem plain. Down the center, a dance floor of glazed tiles turned its nose up at her before a stage boasting several live musicians. High-class and stunning.

Her free hand at war with the decrease in her dress's yard count, she managed to find her breath again. This was where he brought his Wife? *Lucky pet.*

Number One: make him comfortable. "This place is amazing, Lorcan."

"It's called the Den," Lorcan growled.

Did he just smile? That was a smile, right? Gods, it was impossible to tell if her therapy was working.

"The Den?" She eyed the bar, unsure where to go first, but that decision was made for her. Lorcan wasted no time escorting her by force through the standing tables.

She managed fewer stumbles, but everyone had their eyes on her. Saoirse pointedly avoided the hate being hand-passed her direction, some of it shot with the effort of sending it a tens-of-ten yards, hoping to leave mental welts. The women here were more hostile than the county's defensive line.

It wasn't difficult to tell where they were going. Lorcan made no deviations. They were headed to a table near the dance floor where three absurdly important-looking people were staring at them. A hurley of a man who wore a contented smile and had a jovial air; a fat, angry little fellow who looked like an overgrown bronze sliotar; and a wispy old woman in a red dress, she couldn't get a read on: The donors.

When they arrived, Aware Wolf thrust her into the table. She slammed against it with her rib cage. "Ow."

"Don't bruise our merchandise," mewled the voice of the old woman.

"Good evening," Lorcan said.

Saoirse followed suit, catching herself halfway between a bow and a curtsy as she wobbled on one heel.

The woman scrutinized her with a cold gaze. None of the three seemed to like her. They could take their pick of reasons.

Lorcan indicated the first. "Ernán. Banba." The fat man. Lorcan bowed again. "And of course, Fódla." The wisp of a woman let Lorcan kiss her hand.

"And this must be Saoirse," Ernán, the hurley of a man, said with a jovial stride.

"Hi." Spores, she felt exposed in more ways than one without Satirical or Hurler.

"Hi? Ha!" Ernán barked. "It's good to meet the faces in front of my money." He placed a hand on his chest. "Owner and operator of Ernán's Iron. Get it while it's hot, eh? Except don't actually—waiting for it to cool is much wiser." He winked.

"What's iron?" she asked, trying to calm down a bit.

"A metal for a new age. Big money in Tyrone, I'm telling you," he said.

Before she could press him, the fat one held out a hand.

"Banba of Banba's Balls," he said in a squeaky voice.

Saoirse had to stifle her laughter.

"Finest..." he trailed off.

"Sorry," Saoirse flushed.

"Provider of sliotars in Ulster," Ernán finished for him.

Had she heard right? Was his name Banba? She missed that from freaking out.

His face grew deeper in shade, waiting for Saoirse to hold back her laughter. "Something funny?" he squeaked.

"Isn't Banba a woman's name?" Saoirse asked.

"You!" His voice shot up to a shrill before turning to the others. "I demand she not play!"

"Come now, Banba," Ernán was also laughing. "I like her spunk. When's the last time we'd a player with some of that, huh?"

Lorcan grumbled. Saoirse caught it but didn't react. How was she supposed to battle the donors and keep Lorcan comfortable? She'd never be able to move on to Step Two: massage his ego if he kept catching disrespect.

"I don't care," said Banba. "I'm not paying to be insulted."

"You're not paying her at all—yet." Ernán thumped him on the shoulder in a move that was clearly not appreciated.

She felt the heat of eyes on the back of her neck. On the fact that Lorcan still had not moved his hand, which sat in a precarious position. Maybe he was more comfortable than she thought? Saoirse shuffled her feet. The woman, Fódla, hadn't stopped staring at her. She didn't know what to say or do.

Finally, Fódla extended a hand. "I've heard you are quite the stunt."

Both she and Lorcan bristled at these words.

"I—" Saoirse began, but Fódla cut her off in an instant.

"It's why we're all ever so glad we put our weight behind you."

Saoirse stared at her, mouth agog. She wasn't the only one. Lorcan looked like he'd been stunned by a shock spore. His hand slipped away.

Fódla stared back at her with knowing eyes.

Was she... covering for her and Orla?

"You are?" Lorcan asked in disbelief.

"She is?" Saoirse said it like a question, then quickly recovered. "She is." Why?

Ernán had the answer. "Well, come now. Look at the size of her breasts."

Instinctively, Saoirse covered herself.

"Yes, see? A pair of pelt piggies that fine—"

Pelt piggies!?

"Men will fill seats just to watch them jiggle. Spores do we need to fill seats... I take it she's performing adequately?"

What kind of reason was that!? And how could he be so frank to her face about it! Fiadh laughed inside her head.

"She's terrible."

Saoirse held a hand to shield her eyes from Lorcan's wrathful gaze. "I... haven't gotten to play my position yet," she said in a small voice.

Her captain's aura bubbled over in rage.

Oh, bad choice of words, me! Where was Satirical to tell her that would have been stupid?

"Interesting," Ernán addressed Lorcan. "Why?"

"Because I said so." He marched off in the direction of the bar, leaving her alone.

What was she supposed to do? This was usually the point in a conversation when she'd get some snappy quips or Hurler would play with some part of her anatomy, which led to her having ideas. Instead, she'd failed Step One. Lorcan was most definitely not comfortable. Was there something in PÉNIS therapy for dealing with abrasive players?

"Don't mind him," Fódla said.

Saoirse whipped back to the donors. "Sorry."

"But do mind us," she said. "I don't know what Orla's got going on in her head, and we most certainly will not be paying any kind of bail."

"Fanny was just here," Banba squeaked. "Accosting us about this and that. Thanks to your antics, she thinks we're all in on some grand conspiracy!"

Grand. Now, even the people who'd sided with her were dealing with Fanny Burns.

"And such a strange topic," Fódla said. "Magic Eight Balls, our knowledge of Shamrock Violet's ludicrous teachings, some strange ritual I've never heard of."

"She is their lead investigator," Ernán cautioned. "Though it sounds strange to say it, I am excited for you to be found guilty. Don't mess it up."

That seemed like her cue. Saoirse curtsied and almost fell over in her heels, and scuttled away. They weren't on her side—not really; they only stuck it to Lorcan to keep her on the field so Fanny would have an easier time arresting her. Spores, that made good sense, but it felt awful. It was one thing to remind herself, quite another to hear it out loud.

Aware Wolf leaned over the bar, a mess of angry frustration. Why was her first patient so difficult? Nobody ever mentioned how hard it was to make a man comfortable enough to receive his PÉNIS therapy. But what she'd learned from the Daughters of Dagda was that it was all about confidence. Something was eating her captain's mind; she just had to figure out what.

As she crossed the long walk to the bar, she found herself glad for Satirical's absence. If she'd seen her in this dress—the exposed back, half her calves out—she'd not be hearing the end of how big a strumpet she was. She probably wouldn't be giving anybody any therapy, but if she could feel confident enough to be here pretending to be dressed as a—sexplosive danger fire!!! Her nostrils flared. Then he could feel confident, too.

She reached the bar. Lorcan didn't look at her.

"I'm sure they have water," he growled.

"I—" She flushed. "I'd not say no to something hard."

"Is that so?" He grabbed her wrist. Lorcan leaned over her, his long hair tickling her bare shoulder as he whispered in her ear, "Then how about we have sex right here?"

Heat rushed to her face—so hot her freckles turned to fry pans. She tried to leap away, but Aware Wolf's grip was too strong. "Never!"

"I'm only teasing," he said, reeling her in so she'd stop fighting.

"You better be."

"Maybe."

"Oh!" She punched him with her free hand. Feckin' arrogant piece of absolute shite! "How could you say that? And in front of so many people?" wasn't that what Fiadh? What Fiadh-? NO. No. It had to be something else...

Grunt.

A man of many words. Saoirse recovered from the surprise and held to the bar counter as Lorcan, ever pretending to be a gentleman, placed an order for her. Salm, that scent. Poisonous masculinity and cinnamon shrooms were too good a combo. Her captain cut a statuesque, imposing figure hovering over the bar. She wondered if she shouldn't just say feck it to the whole comfortable bit and skip straight to massaging his ego anyway. It's not like she knew what she was doing, but the Druids expressed that messing up steps could have catastrophic consequences for a player's mental health. She could doom all of Tyrconnell if she didn't play this moment right.

"I bet you're the best drinker on the team," she tried.

Lorcan grunted.

Okay... "And nobody could down whiskey like you."

Grunt.

Yeah. She should have left PENIS therapy to Aisling.

Saoirse looked up and down the counter. Several other men ordered drinks for their partners.

"Team's looking good."

Grunt.

"I appreciate you bringing me?"

Grunt.

Oh come on! How was she supposed to salvage this after failing two steps? If the donors hadn't said all that... If, as Leader said, flaccid Whiskeys were a sign of low confidence, it would explain his dead eyes...

Screw what Finley said. The answer had to be deeper!

Saoirse leaned across the bar, admiring all the bottles behind the glass casing, the colorful steam puffing from various contraptions along the back wall, gadgetry for mixing drinks. They really did think of everything.

If only they could think up a way to loosen men up and make therapy slide along faster. Something to make him less abrasive. What was that part of the recitation!? Oh, she should have paid better attention!

"You're talkative," she tried.

"Right back at ya, cú."

There were modules for different parts of a therapy session. She remembered some advanced ones. HEEL, FINGER, NAIL. None of those were useful, and she definitely wasn't advanced. What were the beginner ones? Shite.

She took the moment to look around while Lorcan grumbled at the bartender to hurry on her drink. She'd not expected to collect another vista, but this place was phenomenal. It even had—"A LIVE BARD!?" she shouted, and was immediately tackled by a shoulder of embarrassment. She planted her face in the counter to ignore murmurs from the crowd. Salm it. She looked like a fool!

"What was that?" he snarled.

"Sorry," She hid her happiness. "I've never seen a bard. Croaghgorm only had a set of Wicklow pipes, a few bronze dord horns, and some drums..." She snuck a glance under her arm at the stage at the far end of the venue.

The courtly man in a pompous hat winked at her when he followed the outburst. Lorcan seized her by the neck and forced her to face him instead.

"Always the skinny minstrel boys." Aware Wolf glowered toward the stage.

Grand. She's just made him even angrier. Wait? Did he just flex his hairy pecs on purpose? She wasn't knocking it.

The bartender slid her a red-looking drink. She sipped it.

"Oh. Strawberry!" She sipped again. "This is good."

"Keep screaming at bard boys, and you won't get any more."

She froze, staring up at the yellow eyes, framed by her captain's unfairly perfect shoulder-length brown hair.

Was Lorcan jealous? He couldn't be. He hated her. She was the stunt, the girl who'd refused the bet, A terrible midfielder, not to mention he'd only brought her here to expose her for her lies. Right? The place where he brought his Wife...

No. She was building everything up in her head. How could he see her as a woman when she couldn't even see herself that way? The back of her dress was open! Saoirse spun round and slammed herself against the bar. "You're a great teammate, cú." She said flatly and punched his arm.

All of a sudden, the drink didn't taste so good.

In her... MOUTH! That was it! That was the module for dealing with abrasive players, and she'd only found it by being bad! *Pretending. Pretending* to drink alcohol. That she would keep drinking... yep.

Saoirse got the biggest smile.

Take that, Satirical. With her her MOUTH, she had a chance.

BANBA'S BALLS

FAMOUS PRODUCER OF
ULSTER SLIOTARS

NOBODY HAS BETTER BALLS THAN
BANBA

Using Her MOUTH

MOUTH! That's it!

Saoirse took another sip and felt a surge of excitement. That's what they'd said! In the 'Talking with Team Members' subsection of the 'So Your Men Are Sad, and You Want to Work for PÉNIS' recitation. If a member is particularly dry and abrasive, causing difficulty or pain to either party, massaging their ego might not be enough; you may need to use your MOUTH! Minimize, Open, Uplift, Touch, and Hype! You'll never hear a player moan (about their problems), giving you a chance to 'Handle Their Bawls' if their emotions aren't fully lubricated!

With a snap, Saoirse snuggled up to Lorcan's powerful arm, trying not to focus on the embroidered rose on his lapel, or his powerful beard, and the enchanting way it caught the light of the shroomdeliers. She could do this! She could lubricate him! She could get this member—of her team—moist!

"You know," she spoke softly, "bards have nothing on hurling boys." *Minimize negative emotions.*

Lorcan shook his head.

Open the conversation. "What do they have that you don't?" She added a playful shoulder nudge and, like with the leafboard cutout at the Warm Pools, missed, making the nudge basically all breast. *Whoops.* Hopefully, he wouldn't mind.

"Nothing." Lorcan lowered his eyes at the performer.

"Right." *Uplift positive emotions.* "Not everybody can be Aware Wolf." *Touch on their strengths.* "The single best goalkeeper in professional hurling. You maintain a ten-point spread, and that's despite playing for the worst scoring team on the star."

She put a hand on his forearm. Hot to the touch, she could feel the hairs bristling as if rising to meet her words. Did he never hear kind words or something?

Hype the finish!

She put a delicate hand on his heart, which came with perks—namely, his massive chest. "You're captain, coach, and keeper. No bard boy's got anything on a man like you." She let the words hang, wondering if she was actually supposed to put her mouth on him; somehow, licking his shoulder felt like undercutting the moment, even if she had a strange compulsion to bite him.

A deep, cavernous hum thrummed from the core of her captain's being.

Spores. Was he... purring? That was way too attractive! A warmth built in her vagina, like her lips were yearning, reaching for the alpha of their pack—*bark, bark, woof, woof, howl.*

When he looked at her next, she swore there was a glint of light in his eyes. Her heart raced. Had she done it? Saoirse traced his face. That definitely was the hint of a smile, right? Was he upset or not? Why did he have to keep her guessing?

Suddenly, the wispy donor, Fódla, cut between her and her captain. "Do you dance?"

Shite, she was right there with his therapy! "Not really."

"Wonderful," Fódla smiled. "This fantastic bard is about to begin a round of songs." She seized Saoirse by the wrist. "And don't think for a second, Lorcan Maguire, that I'm not fully aware of the games you play on or off the pitch."

Saoirse didn't have the foggiest what that meant, but Fódla yanked her away before Saoirse could protest. They knocked through shoulders and backs and elbows. Saoirse felt a hand let go and spun into a table before ricocheting to the dance floor.

Saoirse spared a glance for Lorcan and couldn't hide her smile. It was working!

"Come," the donor said.

Saoirse tore her eyes from the happy wolf. Her captain seemed lighter somehow, definitely less angry; he'd not unloaded yet, she'd not even handled his bawls, but Tuatha Dé Danann, she might just be GOATED at using her MOUTH!

A huge smile stretched across Saoirse's face. She couldn't help it. It'd been nothing but wins since yesterday morning. Her head spun in a tizzy as Fódla led her to the floor. The bard and his musicians struck up their first tune—something up-tempo and fun. Also, men who could sing! Ah! To die for. She could not stop herself from squealing.

Fódla let her watch for a bit before striking up a very simple jig. "I'm aware you can do this much."

She must have heard from Orla. Saoirse watched a few repetitions, then joined—eager to really be dancing... in public... in a dress with no back... after drinking... with Lorcan nearby... and no sliotar in her hands... Oh, great goddess Danu. She could not tell Sat!

"Chin up," Fódla said.

The bard sang a happy tune; musicians behind him tapped along: the uilleann pipe player pumping the bag beneath his elbow, another on the fiddle, bowing strings.

She and Fódla faced each other, one hand holding their dresses up to dance, the other locked together as they twirled in their simple step. Saoirse focused on each foot. Her heels made this impossible! Hop. Hop knee. Hop back. She kept it small. Spores, she wished she knew the names of moves or any technical jargon—she'd have to ask Two.

"Do you like hurling?" Fódla asked, her red dress exposing her bare ankles.

Saoirse tried not to think about her own exposed foot joints. "Oh yes."

"County Tyrconnell, of course?"

"Yes."

"From Croaghgorm?"

"Yes, ma'am." They took a few spins. Saoirse followed the older woman's gaze.

To the side, a wide cut in the rock wall showed—but it wasn't possible—"the pitch!" Sure enough, a small section of stadium pews, which she had not noticed before, lined the side of the venue behind a dip in the floor. Somehow, some way, she could see through the reverse falls! Spores. To watch a match from here...

"It costs a lot to outfit a player, you know. Gear, travel, salary expenses... with declining ticket revenues, we can't afford to make mistakes this season. If there is a season."

"Don't worry. I can score."

"Can you? From what I understand, you left the first day after throwing a hissy fit. You also failed to showcase any team culture fit at carve downs, and in your last match against Tyrone Camogie, you seized up at the line and lost it all for your team and the county."

She knew about that? Saoirse's feet stumbled.

"Oh yes, I know about that. I know quite a lot more than you think—your propensity to freeze. Your unwillingness to play your style," Fódla's voice dripped with insinuation. "Your unquenched desire to get yourself involved in dangerous games."

It was fairly obvious what she meant by that—strip hurling. The bard was not helping. "I don't. I'm not bad. I'm just pretending."

They spun. This woman knew way too much. Saoirse started to lose her jig step, small beads of sweat formed on her temple—and not from the strain of the dance.

"But I also know more," Fódla said. "Your Éire-wide record-setting rookie season—I know what you can do when unleashed." She smiled. No—sneered. A wicked, cold grin. "Aisling," said the wispy woman.

Saoirse's heart skipped a step. She wobbled on her wavering dignity—or no, that was just her heels. "What? What did you say?"

"Aisling," she said again, plain as could be.

Was this woman threatening her friend? Saoirse stopped dancing.

Fódla stopped as well. "It's a donor's job to keep track of just where their money is going. One thing can be said for seasons like this—they are cheap. Orla must see something in you, or she'd not have stuck her neck out."

That implied Orla was on their side. What was going on?

They were face-to-face. The woman toyed with the stitching on Saoirse's neckline. "If you don't deliver, we know which branch to cut down, and when to do it."

A shiver shot up her spine.

"Welcome to professional sports," Fódla said. "There's more to you than just games now."

In a snap, the old woman returned to her wispy self. "Good luck in trials. I never thought I'd live to see the day a Violet willingly danced." She laughed all the way across the hall.

Shite!

Her friends! Her people! Aisling! It was one thing to think that if she didn't turn herself in—she'd ensnare her dad—another thing to think about how this woman would cut them all down. A crushing wave of nausea rocked the strawberry in her gut.

She kept the panic down, and a warm hand cupped her back. Lorcan. Thank the gods. She could use some kindness after that, and she got exactly what she wanted.

Lorcan looked at her with his eyes firmly dead. "We need to talk."

Her smile returned. If she didn't think she'd break a leg, she'd do a heel click! She'd used her MOUTH. She'd seen the light in his eyes—which means it could come back—and now, after the breather with a dangerous donor, Lorcan was ready for Step Four. "I'd love to talk."

She would get to Handle his Bawls!

Handling Aware Wolf's Bawls

Her captain looked like death warmed over. Saoirse tried to match his energy so she wouldn't ruin his moment, but she was so excited! How would he bawl? Was he a sappy man or a swinger? No matter how he came at her, she'd take it. That was the price you paid to save County Tyrconnell and Aware Wolf!

He had escorted her to a patio terrace that extended into the reverse falls. The water ran up in a thin veil around them, leaving an almost see-through wall of water flecked with slips of salmon-pink wisps of mist.

"Sit." It was a demand, not that she could have fought it, as Lorcan thrust her with one powerful arm into a chair of corrugated bronze and set a steaming goblet of something on the matching table next to her.

The velvet curtains to the terrace pulled closed behind them. Lorcan walked to the water.

Pretending to be flustered, Saoirse took the chance to adjust her dress. She'd almost forgotten how much of her calves were showing, and quickly tucked them under the chair like a pair of newborn cows hiding behind their mother.

Come on, Lorcan, bawl for me. Hurler would have been digging this if she were here.

He looked regal, standing on the clay pavers, the shiny buckled shoes, the outfit.

She tried to read his movements, his expressions, unsure what he was about to whine about. The Medical Druids Association of Éire said in their recitations that you had to be prepared for just about anything—that a lot of players had to work through the surface to get what mattered. She could remember how many times she'd been talking to Aisling for minutes on end, only to finally get to the meat of what was important ages in. Would he be the same?

"It's never a woman's fault what happens to her, only her man's," Lorcan grumbled into the water. "Drink. While it's still warm."

He'd said it without looking at her. The smell of eel tea tickled her nose. Delicious, but she couldn't. This was too exciting!

"All of them seem convinced that this was a plan all along." Lorcan let his hand play in the water, carving a small slice into the veil, revealing the world beyond—mists swirling, lifting ever upward. "That they were behind you one hundred percent. I just don't see it. Going over my head to put you back in trials? Why? You weren't even removed."

So, it was about the donors first. It had just happened; she supposed that made sense.

"I don't know." She'd never bothered to figure out why Orla helped her. After meeting the donors, she was even more confused. "Lorcan…"

"I'm not angry," he said. "I just want to understand."

He turned, and she met a void.

Stillness. Dead yellow eyes.

Framed against the water like that, Saoirse was struck by a sudden overwhelming sense of her situation. It all poured into her—a raging river of emotion: fear for her friend, fear for her life, and fear for the wolves. What she had to do, what was to become of her life. She found herself sinking into that river, slipping behind a rock, grappling for purchase, and it crumbling at the lightest touch of her fingers.

At any moment, she'd be ripped from the small refuge of her safety and flung into the turbulence with nothing to guide her.

She caught herself in that sliver between panic and peril by seizing the tea, suddenly realizing she'd forgotten to breathe, and sucking in reality to bridge the gap, narrowly escaping being banjaxed to the bone.

Lorcan was still there, staring at her, but his eyes… his eyes were wrong.

For years, she'd admired the team and this man above all of them because no matter how hard they tried, they still lost, and they never let that stop them from trying. Lorcan's eyes… they were… wounded. Yes. Wounded. That's where she was—surrounded by wounded wolves.

Lorcan was supposed to be her rock in that river, a shield—the man she'd always admired—and if he crumbled, there was no hope. She really couldn't mess this up.

"Are you alright?" he growled, a note of sincerity buried in his voice.

It took a few breaths, but she managed to steady herself. When she'd been excited about her therapy working, she'd not expected that.

"Yes."

Step four: Be aware that in the process of fixing a player's emotional baggage, you might see things you don't want to or put yourself in dangerous places you don't want to be. Crying, outbursts, threats, physical violence, or other dangerous situations are hazards (sometimes even perks!) of the job. Protect yourself, and be prepared.

She might get yelled at, lampooned, harangued… she might get hit.

So what? She fixed Lorcan with some firm eye contact—one of the men she loved.

That's what happened when you played hurling in dangerous corners. If there was one thing she knew from years of playing offense, getting hit was the price you paid to score.

"I'm fine. You were saying?"

He took a moment, but continued. "Did you know the whole team went to watch you play Tyrone Camogie?" he asked, snarling with anger.

Saoirse shook her head.

"When I saw you at that match, it was as if there was a string between the sliotar and your hurley," Lorcan said. "Like you could never lose it. That dance of golden dust. The radiant beauty. Where is that?"

Radiant beauty? This wasn't about her. It was about him. Spores, handling bawls was a tricky endeavor. They were soft things, delicate and sensitive—one wrong move here and she could make everything worse.

She decided on the truth. "I need space."

"Space?" Lorcan squeezed the banister so hard it cracked.

"I've never used my style against opponents so big, or with so much skill or magic. I'm not used to it."

"So, it's our fault?"

"I'm not saying that."

"Yes, you are!" He slammed his fist on the rail.

Saoirse squirmed. Lorcan might hit her.

"Nothing to say?" he asked.

The donors, PÉNIS, Shamrock Violet—she needed space. On and off the field. Part of her always thought that hiding behind Lorcan, he'd protect her. Now she was back here, she could see cracks in his crumbling façade—and wanted desperately to pick at them with her fingers. What if the rock crumbled and left her with nothing? Just a hollow husk of a rotten spore? But, what if there was something more, a soul trapped inside?

"I let you back on the field. Is that not enough?" Lorcan asked.

Saoirse squeezed the bronze wiring of her chair, feeling it push a pattern into her palm. She didn't know what to do, what to say.

"I..." The truth was, she didn't know how to bring that side of her out in different positions. Midfielder felt foreign. He'd just say that was an excuse. Other players worked just fine without space. She didn't want to blame him, but...

"I don't know," she mumbled.

"You don't know?" He dropped his voice low. "The girl we saw at that match? Does she exist?"

Saoirse picked at the table. Perhaps it was better to pick at this than him. She wasn't even sure she could answer. She'd been so confident coming out here to handle his bawls. Now the gap in her knowledge was showing. This wasn't as exciting anymore.

If she were put at full-forward, she wasn't sure. She'd lost her identity as a hurler that day of Free Ball. No matter what Madame Orla said, she was feeling less and less like a woman. This dress wasn't helping.

But that didn't mean there wasn't a way to help him.

"I—no, that's not right." She shouldn't start with 'I.' Therapy wasn't about her. It was about him. This was a chance to pick at his cracks. It was dangerous. She—Tyrconnell—might end up with a broken rock. But she didn't want to see a man she loved go on living like this with a hole where his soul should be.

Was that selfish? Maybe, but that was the secret to every strike. Every goal was. She could choose to pass. She just never wanted to do anything other than score.

Saoirse braced herself. She didn't know enough about PÉNIS therapy to make the right move here. All she had was love and the truth. Staring into the void, facing down Lorcan's balled fist, she had to hope that would be enough—if not for her sake, then for his.

Deep breath in. Deep breath out. "Why don't you run?" she asked.

Lorcan grumbled, as if he'd expected a change in topic. "We don't need to."

"Says the last-place team in Éire for twenty-six years?"

Some of the crack crumbled into the river.

Lorcan's nostrils flared. He kicked off the banister.

"So that's what this is about? Guaranteed practice time for you to ridicule us more?"

"I'm only trying to understand."

"Understand what? Why are we lazy?"

"No."

"Why don't we all have hands of gold?" He fluttered his hands through the air.

Saoirse licked her lips despite herself.

"Say it," Lorcan sneered, prowling dangerously close across the patio. "Say it. Say what you really want to know."

No matter what happened, she was ready for it. She wanted this. She would never hold it against him. "I want to know why you're all flaccid, cú."

Aware Wolf howled with rage, smashing her unappreciated drink off the table across the floor. She could hear patrons gasping beyond the curtain. Nobody peeked—not on the almighty Lorcan Maguire, who placed a hand on each of her armrests, leaning till they were nose to nose, his voice a terrifying hush.

"No one's flaccid," he growled.

Denial. Just like with Wife Four. Saoirse didn't shy away. She faced full-forward. "Yes, you are."

"No, we aren't!" he roared, slamming a fist against the table.

She squealed and shielded her eyes.

"We are a good team that works hard and is just unlucky."

She could feel his breath now—sense his teeth.

"You're lazy cowards."

In an instant, Lorcan seized her, thrusting her back to the reverse falls, one massive hand tight around her throat. She felt the water rush up her back, picking up her red hair, chilling her to the bone. She didn't scream. She couldn't, looking down at those eyes. It was like watching the last of a great man's grip on life seep through the cracks in his soul.

There was no going back now. Either the rock crumbled and the river took her—and all of County Tyrconnell—to eternity, or there could be a prize inside.

"Everybody is lazy," she hissed, hanging on to his hand for dear life. "Nobody runs. Maybe the reason you're all lacking in confidence is that you insist your failures are out of your control. You dwell on losing—not winning. Saying that you don't need to change, when I won't see you take the first step!"

Lorcan huffed, but he didn't squeeze, just pushed her further into the reverse falls. More of his stone crumbled away.

"You spread that to the trials already!" she continued through choked gasps. "They're losing Whiskeys just being around your energy. You're the captain, and you walk every where."—thinking of Seamus, she threw caution to the wind—"No wonder your Wives dislike you. You don't even try!"

That had done it.

With a guttural shriek, Lorcan pulled her off the falls and threw her across the stones. Saoirse rolled, scraping against pavers. *Please. Please work!* She winced against the pain in her palm, but it was nothing like a welt from one of the sums—the bruises from the Shitty Forwards. Nothing about this was unearned. She knew the pain she'd put him through was far worse than a few scrapes. Slips of mist swirled through the cracks as she nursed her neck—and locked eyes with...

"You're an evil stunt. I should never have vouched for you." Lorcan let the words hang, then threw aside the curtain and headed back into the Den.

Such drama. The big smile returned. *So much drama, Mr. Lorcan Maguire.*

"Are you okay?" To her surprise, the first person on the scene was Fódla.

"Yeah," she said, and found herself laughing. "Yeah, I'm fine."

"You're smiling?" Ernán, quick to the scene, helped her to stand.

She looked toward the Den, then back to the unlikely pair. "Actually, I need your help."

The woman looked intrigued. "Help you?" she asked, definite confusion in her voice.

Saoirse brushed herself off and pulled herself into a step-dancer's proud posture.

"How much did that old brood tell you?"

The old woman balked. "You didn't just say that about Orla!"

Oh, but she did. She'd handled his bawls with a bit of pure luck. The light had returned to Lorcan's eyes along with all of his fight.

Aware Wolf deserved her all.

BLACK
MYCELIUM

POISONOUS MASCULINITY
AND CINNAMON SHROOMS

THE SECOND BITE KILLS

Letting Lorcan Unload

The nice thing about doing PÉNIS therapy, Saoirse figured, was that at least it was wholesome. Nothing like the depraved nonsense Fiadh'd gone on about. Just her and her teammate, going back and forth until she got him to unload, and after seeing that glint in the back of Lorcan's eye, she knew it was all about to be on her BREASTS.

When Fódla finished dusting her off, and Saoirse's scrapes had been thoroughly fussed over by Banba, Ernán took her through a blow dryer, ensuring her hair did not overstay its welcome—she was still annoyed about last time. Then together they returned to their standing table, where she watched the bard while Fódla did *her* dirty work.

The wicked woman might have scared Saoirse half to death, and she was certain she'd meant that threat, but they had a common purpose; neither wanted the county to lose their hurling club.

Saoirse tapped her foot to the music. She really liked the bard's floppy cap, his amazing voice; it seemed impossible not to be happy. Somehow, despite it all, her first attempt at therapy was going well, or at least as well as she knew how to judge. Hopefully, she wasn't swinging wide for the mists. Now, she needed to find out how deep the scar was. Lorcan reacted to one thing more than all the others. Same as Seamus, the Shitty Forwards, and likely the rest. She wasn't stupid. There was something off with their Wives.

"So, it's you?" A portly woman in a mauve dress joined their table with a look of disgust etched in every line of her face.

Saoirse looked back, but it appeared the donors had left her standing, admiring the bard alone.

"Not with his Wife. Tut-tut," the woman mused.

"It's a team-building exercise."

"Oh, I'm sure there will be plenty of exercise," she said.

"Yeah?" Was that really so shocking? "It's a dance hall."

The woman sipped her drink, never once dropping Saoirse's gaze, before she simply left.

What was that all about? Lorcan said he used to bring his Wife here; now he'd brought her instead. Surely going out with a member of your team wasn't always a big deal? Even if she wanted it to be.

Lorcan arrived at her table, still angry. "Raudan's Wife," he said.

"His Wife?"

"Don't worry. I've stopped harder shots with my little toe."

Saoirse followed Raudan's Wife as she swept across the dance floor for a group under a green-and-gold chihulooshroomdelabra. At least she'd not asked her name; she didn't need another of the pitiful creatures' strange introductions.

"Dance," he said. It wasn't a question.

"No." She declined his offered hand. Even though this was her idea, she wanted to say yes. She caught Fódla's expression. The woman rolled her eyes at Saoirse's audacity. But Saoirse couldn't just say yes right after Lorcan had thrown her. She needed him to open up. It'd be easier if he'd let down more walls. Aisling taught her that one.

"Unfortunately," he said, "the donors insist we put on a good show. They're trying to bring in more money."

Her gaze met his. He didn't even attempt a smile, but it was still there—the light. A tiny glint, but a glint she could cling to nonetheless, like seeing the first sign of a buried chaun's golden treasure.

"Fine. I'll do it for the team." She drained her new strawberry wine. It felt weird being the manipulative girl, but, spores, if this wasn't the least of the lengths she had gone through for the team so far.

She offered an arm, and he took her whole soul, sweeping her onto the floor with a powerful hand that warmed her to the core. She caught herself leaning into the pressure before stopping herself. She wasn't going through all this effort just for him to die in a sexplosion. They were dancing under dangling rock spores. One misstep, he'd be dead, even if more and more her fears about such a thing occurring seemed absurd.

"This one is for the lovers," the bard crooned.

Music swayed across the glazed tiles.

The bard sang:

"You've got me in a spiral of emotions..."

Saoirse tried to force her feet into a jig position, but Lorcan stopped her with a foot, taking one hand in his, and placing the other around her waist.

"Pick up your dress."

"Is that a command?"

He scowled.

She giggled and gripped the dress. "Fine. But only because it's you."

Lorcan perked up like he'd gone from Aware Wolf to Alert Puppy, unsure if he was being offered a trap or a bone.

That did something for him? She flushed. And her offer? It was kind of both, if she was honest.

Hiding her face while she snuffled like a bull getting ready to charge, she scooped up her loose fabric and... revealed her knees! *May the Morrígan watch over my battles*, both with her hemline and Lorcan's plight.

They spun once. She ignored the crowd. If Fanny showed up now, she might not book her for being a Bad Girl, legally speaking, but they could certainly book her for being a bad one, Violet-speaking. How hard a sin would this be to slip in the Shannon?

"You alright?" he asked, his tone somehow more regal than she'd heard before.

"Yes." She pulled back to face him.

"Good."

The first signs of the real him. The dream she'd imagined all those years, staring at the mural in the Warm Pools. Who cared if her knees were showing? She couldn't bring herself to care about much of anything other than the man right in front of her. If she helped him, she'd save the club, and if all it took was letting him unload on her BREASTS—that was easy.

Their shadows swayed in the light of the chihulooshroomdeliers, the lingering strawberry wine tantalizing her tongue. In their spin, Saoirse realized Aisling might have been on to something; giving PÉNIS therapy was pretty fun.

"Making me hot. Making me cold..."

But she would not let him unload on her FACE—that was an advanced module meant for girls like Aisling. Focus fully, Accept without judgment, Celebrate their boldness, and Encourage elaboration. It was all focused on the other and fairly assertive.

BREASTS, however, focused, in part, on the self. The Medical Druids stated it was the more nurturing approach, cushioning the players' emotions in a soft, squishy receptivity.

Smooth bronze dord horns crooned their curl before the judgment of the well-heeled. Lorcan wasn't even looking at her—he was glowering at the bard. It was time for the first step. Saoirse stepped closer, pressing her body into his, holding him close.

B - Breathe with them: match pace until they're steady. She knew he was looking at her now. She held to him, matching his breath, slowing his pace, and waiting for him to speak first.

"Marriage," Lorcan grumbled after a third spin, "is when one man and one woman, a husband and Wife, decide they are going to be each other's one and only partner for the rest of their lives."

Her heart skipped a beat in her chest. *No.* He pulled back. Had he felt her honest reaction? "I see." She'd not expected that. What awful news. The one and only? "Not pets?"

"No." He actually laughed. "I know it's a foreign concept to Shamrock Violets."

She nodded, but her head was reeling. She was here, dancing with him at the place where he usually brought his Wife! Wasn't this evil!? She was stabbing the woman in the back. How could he? How could she?

She almost pulled away, but his disarming scent—toxic masculinity and cinnamon shrooms—pulled her back in. If the problem was their Wives, as she'd concluded, then being here was the right thing to do. His Wife should have handled him better.

Though she couldn't say for sure.

R - Reframe the problem: twist the bad into a possible good. "You must *Intercourse* all the time, cú." Why was that her response!? Spores. She didn't even have a free hand to pinch herself with.

"Not as much as I'd like." The jaded tone had crept back in.

Did the lack of *Intercoursing* annoy him? It would annoy her. If she were Lorcan's Wife, they would *Intercourse* all the time! There were so many fun things to do—go to Cook Street, see fun plays and shows—but she couldn't say that. The next step was: *E - Engage Gently: small prompts, no heavy questions.* So she settled on, "That's too bad."

They spun slowly for a while. She hoped he didn't notice her clammy hands or how one strap had fallen over her shoulder. More than once, she caught herself leaning too close, yearning too hard. *I want to score and score some more. To have my flowers picked by Lorcan. It wouldn't be a bore.*

"Finding the words I don't know how to say..."

"You're right," he growled.

"What?"

"You are right. The team's all flaccid."

A jolt raced up her open back. Confirmation straight from Aware Wolf's mouth?! Finley had been dead on the money! They had hurl-ectile dysfunction! Could it be connected to their Wives? Were they the cause of their lack of confidence, as she'd postulated after her conversation with the Leggy Trio?

Don't jump to conclusions, she told herself. Saoirse took a deep breath. *A - Affirm progress, tease out any resistance.* "It's fine."

"No." He shook his head. "I thought about what you said about how our energy is rubbing off on the new hurlers. I'm not convinced. But I am convinced that you are trying to help. Or you wouldn't be looking in the first place."

Was he trying? She dropped her dress to rest her other hand on his arm. He pulled her in so her head lay on his chest. A flush of cold terror ripped through her for a moment, but Lorcan wouldn't try to sexplode himself—not when he'd taken such a step.

S - Stay steady: keep a good rhythm, don't pull away mid-flow.

"I'm grateful," he said. "I don't know how to fix the boys, but nobody on the team starts that way. Most can carry a Whiskey through their first loss. But—"

"It's okay," she said. *T - Take it on the chest: slow down as emotions soften.* Saoirse stopped dancing, turned her full focus to his yellow eyes. The ones with the light inside—the little glint of hope had grown larger. "You can tell me."

"That's when—" he paused to look around. "It's when—"

"Let it out. I'm not going to judge you. I've got you right here." She took the hand she had in his and placed it on her heart. "You can let me have it. Everything pent up inside you. I'll take it on my chest."

Lorcan's eyes went wide, staring at his hand, squeezing her heart like he couldn't believe a woman would care.

Gossiping whispers cut their moment; her captain quickly restarted the dance. Saoirse caught the bright, flushed face of a shocked-looking Fódla; a dainty hand of disbelief.

"That's when they attack," Lorcan growled.

"They attack?"

"Our Wives."

Now they were getting somewhere!

"That first loss is the trigger," he snarled. "Women don't want to be married to losers, so their home life becomes unbearable, their peace destroyed. Then the next week their heads are wrecked; it's easier to lose again. And the cycle repeats. A cycle of shame that destroys their spirit."

Those salm Wives! Saoirse's nostrils flared. The embers of competitive drive roared to life—a blazing inferno in her chest. They weren't pitiable; they were evil. The way Four and Bob treated her in dance practice made sense, too. A girl who wanted to help the husbands they were actively destroying? Her presence would bring balance to their husbands' psyches. To keep their home life in their favor, Saoirse's meddling was untenable.

Lorcan's pain, Seamus losing his Rage Boner when he'd failed to stop her, their anger at her at trials—in their eyes, she'd been acting just like their Wives! She'd brought their home to the field with them. If she didn't fix this, it wouldn't just be wrong by the County Tyrconnell Hurling Club—it'd be wrong by the men who made it great.

She squeezed the captain's arm and returned her head to his chest. Time for her finishing move. *S - Suck out the rest: ensure the player's been fully cleansed of the pent-up negative emotion.* "Thank you."

"Thank you?"

"For giving me back my heroes." Her team was still trying. They were just more beaten down than she'd thought.

"Heroes?" Lorcan huffed and stopped dancing.

"Captain?"

He was glowering at the bard again. "I've got something else I need to figure out first."

He let her hands drop—along with her heart—just when it was getting good. It must have been all he was willing to do for the donors. But... Lorcan wasn't heading for the exit. He was heading for the stage!

In a few strides, Aware Wolf took the floor from the bard, who looked from Lorcan to Saoirse—then grew the biggest smile.

What was going on?

"Enough of this," Lorcan snarled. "I think we need at least one round of the star's very best song, don't you?"

Saoirse looked around. The whole of the hall had turned to admire Lorcan with quizzical looks.

To them, they faced a strange man, but when she faced him, she met his soul, in heartbeats.

Hello.

Heartbeats and yellow eyes, passed and locked with hers, intertwined and a whirling dance up the pitch, slipping together between the mists into the falls, racing to be released in the spray at the height of River Eolas.

She caught herself in that sliver between a moment and eternity later by seizing her own, suddenly realizing she'd forgotten to breathe, and sucking in reality to bridge the gap.

Women eyed her with a mixture of jealousy and scorn. She didn't care about that. For the first time, their river of hate was breaking around her, and she wasn't behind a crumbling rock. She lay in the shade of a powerful, glowing golden shield. Her captain sang in a voice so deep it could nuzzle the under-trees. He'd not lied—he picked the very best song.

"Come guess me this riddle, what beats pipe and fiddle..."

The Humors of Whiskey.

Tuatha Dé, was she glad she'd picked open that crack.

Satirical Story Time

Satirical Slinger

Yeeee-haw! Get along and ride 'em, cowgirl! I have no idea what that means, but I know I like saying it! It's all here inside Saoirse's subconscious. Why and how? I have no idea.

I gotta say, I used to hate when Saoirse went all 'Saoirse Noir' on me. We've only ever seen one noir recitation, folks. She just got super invested in the dark ambiance, and I think she has a complex around red thanks to Tyrone.

My misgivings all changed a few months back, however, when I found a few cool motifs all mashed up inside her brain. Now even I can join in her fancy-pants role-playing by being somebody equally hard-nosed. I'm a girl from out west, where the fields are dry, and the cows are a-plenty. Tumbleweeds symbolize the emotional desolation of my heart.

I dub this alter ego Satirical Slinger.

I think Hurler should get her own alter ego too, but she's too into the soulful music she can make with the dord-ophone. I get it. If I couldn't talk, I'd get really into music, too.

How to Make Men Hard

Two Days Remain

S aoirse's stomach pews were packed, the Spectator's snacks purchased, Your Maws out. Little Hurler had on all her Spirit Stadium merch. Today they played an away game. A promise made from her heart's Little Hurler to the stands...

THAT'S RIGHT, FOLKS. TODAY, COME SWARM OR STORM, THIS HUSSY IS LEARN-ING HOW TO MAKE MEN HARD! WE'RE ASKING THE LEGGIES, Satirical satirized sarcastically. *BECAUSE MY PIOLOT'S A FECKIN' SLAG.*

Hey!

WHAT? I LOST THE RANCH, AM I NOT ALLOWED TO BE MAD?

You don't have a ranch, and I can't believe you.

YOU WERE A HUSSY! A STRUMPET! YOU WORE A DRESS WITH NO BACK AND DANCED!

I had no choice.

THERE'S ALWAYS A CHOICE.

You had a choice of horse, too.

THE GIRL I PICKED IS AWESOME.

She came in dead last. Nobody else bet on her.

SHE NEEDED SOMEONE TO. SHE'S A GOOD EGG, AND SHE'S FAST, YOU'LL SEE.

I'm ignoring you.

Little Hurler's big head bobbled back and forth for the argument, though Little Hurler had been taking her side since last night. Satirical needed to get over her goody two-shoes about Saoirse's choice to wear a dress and give Lorcan some very much needed PENIS therapy when she wasn't even there!

WE DESERVED A BREAK AFTER SAVING YOU FROM YOUR PANIC ATTACK!

Thank you. Now stop attacking me, or I might just have another one.

I DON'T SEE WHAT'S <u>PRETEND</u> ABOUT ACTUALLY DOING SOMETHING.

Whatever.

An angry spike of some unknown object came over the loudspore in her brain.

Satirical could be pissed, for all Saoirse cared. With the fix to Lorcan last night, she was winning!

Leaning on a banister, Saoirse leaped and clicked her heels. She couldn't contain herself. PENIS therapy! Lorcan! Spores! She'd learned so much, she'd had so much fun! What kind of therapy would the other team members need? She didn't think HEAD, SHOULDERS, KNEES, or TOES applied, especially when it was recommended to do KNEES and TOES twice, with at least a week in between. She'd been racking her brain all night.

She and the Daughters of Dagda were in a practice ballroom today, a bare space set aside by the dorms. The staff used it to design setups for large-scale events. A pitch worth of unused space. They congregated around a banister overlooking a faux greeting area. The section around her hosted a nest of set dining tables. She hadn't a clue what they could be practicing with silverware and tablecloths. Two said only very few of the Daughters of Dagda doubled as strippers, and somehow she didn't think strippers would dance atop tables.

"Rún na Rince. Rún na Rince." Saoirse repeated the term to herself in a soft rhythm as she practiced the ankle dip maneuver called "rocks" done by the Daughters of Dagda, one hand holding to the banister. It was much easier singing the little ditty to herself than counting numbers, and even more so now that she knew this was all an illusion. She'd almost broken her ankles twice trying to follow the Greensleeves.

Four, Bob, and their cronies gathered at the far end of their little setup. Their Wives weren't necessarily evil, she'd decided. Women lacking enough brain cells to do their funky pose routine probably weren't destroying their husband on purpose, but they were part of a spiral of shame that was causing their hurl-ectile dysfunction. A medical issue, Saoirse only had two days left to find the answer for. When she did, Finley's deal with Triple K would get her out of her geas. She'd join her dad in a dungeon, but she'd save Tyrconnell.

Her heart snickered, drawing the ire of Satirical, as the Leggy Trio of Leader, Two, and Hater made their way in from the cold and waved up at her from the greeting area.

"Good morning," Leader said.

"Sup, cú." Saoirse smiled.

The three swept up the steps beside the practice entry, joining her by the sets of silver table settings. As per usual, Leader took the moment as an excuse to flex her privileges and looked past her for the Wives.

"Where were you last night?" Leader asked.

"Yeah, Silly Saoirse," said Two. "We were hoping to dance."

"Oh." The three girls leaned in, and Saoirse told them all about her night with Lorcan at the Den.

"Spores," Two said. "I've always wanted to go dancing there."

"I can't believe he needed therapy," Hater scoffed.

Saoirse bit back her retort. To be fair, she'd thought similarly not all that long ago. "All that aside," she said. "I've got a question I'm hoping you can answer for me. Girl to girl. I need help."

Several nearby ears pricked up at this. She'd been hoping for that; these dancers could not stay away from gossip, and maybe it would work in her favor if she played a little bigger this time up the pitch.

"Sure." Leader fixed her with an attentive stare.

Two, leaning on her crutches, shook out her flabbier arms and did the same.

Hater—well—she hated.

A deep breath was necessary. *Spores,* just asking this made her feel less like a woman, but she had to help. "Actually... this might be a weird question, but I'm playing with—I mean—I'm with a man."

At this, *all* the Leggies turned toward the conversation in unison. "Uh huh." They said, eyes wide with excitement.

"And..."

"Yeah?" they asked, pressing closer together.

Saoirse passed some side-eye to Hurler. Yep, city women were strange.

SPEAK FOR YOURSELF.

"Well…" Saoirse flushed. She couldn't throw the game at the goal line. She couldn't tell them about the trials because of her deal with Orla. The topic was sensitive. If Fiadh was right..? No, she couldn't be. "He… can't get his Whiskey hard…"

"HE CAN'T GET HARD?!"

The effect was bedlam. You'd have thought the world ended. Hands went to breasts, gasps were inhaled in shock, gasps were exhaled in shock, and even Hater Leggy looked as if she might actually cry.

"NO!" they all cried. Followed by a smattering of "You poor things," and "It's not your faults," and "Don't blame yourself, girls," and even a few poignant whimpers.

Tuatha Dé… Saoirse rubbed her temple in annoyance and sat down at a table. She picked at a piece of silverware and waited till the Leggies recovered.

Leader nibbled the end of her slender painted nails in horror and sat across from her. "Not being allowed to dance is one thing, but to experience such a tragedy—"

"And at your age!" Two agreed. "Cast a net on her! You really are a poor thing."

Leader took both Saoirse's hands in hers across the tablecloth.

Spores. She'd spent most of her life around men who weren't hard—what gives? This wasn't quite the overreaction she'd expected, but she supposed that was hurling for you. It really *was* just that important.

She never knew the Leggies cared about quality hurling. Two placed a calming hand on Leader's shoulder, pulling a chair to join them at the table.

"Just know, first and foremost, it's nothing you did," Leader said.

"Yeah, I—"

"Nothing!" The Leggies all shouted in agreement.

"Okay?"

"If he's having trouble getting his, uh… *Whiskey* hard," she insisted, "That's on him. He's overthinking. Not present in his body."

"Not present in his body?" Like the body-mind split Sean talked about?

There were hums and nods at this.

What Leader said aligned with what she already explained about confidence.

It's got to be my own lack of shame that lets me have golden hands.

SHE'S DEFINITELY LACKING IN SHAME, FOLKS. I CAN ATTEST TO THAT.

All the Leggies in the hall packed in around their table, faces red, but eager for more tea. *I should have come to them sooner.* To be fair, she didn't know the Daughters of Dagda would be so knowledgeable about hurling. "Is there anything I can do?"

"I'm sorry, Silly Saoirse," Two said. "It's on him."

On him? "But I need them to get hard."

"THEM?!"

Saoirse face-palmed.

The Leggies burst out in an uproar. Slags rushed about like wingless giraffeflies, several river-danced in a frantic display, Little Hurler climbed a bronze banister, others yelled and shrieked, each girl trying their own way to brush off the secondhand embarrassment.

What exactly is so bad about making men hard? This topic might be too sensitive. *Tuatha Dé!*

YOU'D THINK EVERYBODY WOULD WANT TO HELP TYRCONNELL WIN.

They are from other counties. Saoirse sighed. This couldn't be about what Fiadh said. It couldn't. Heat fizzled across her face as she waited for the women to calm down.

Eventually, they did, and a crimson Leggy Leader held her gaze across the table.

"Well," she said, her voice high-pitched. "Who are we to judge?"

The dancers agreed.

"If she wants to marry two men—"

"Pft. I don't want to marry them."

"NOT MARRY?!"

"Tuatha Dé Danann!" Saoirse buried her head in her hands as the panic ensued again, but she cracked open her fingers. Through the slit, she saw several hoes leap the banister,

Little Hurler go streaking up the path, more do backflips, and at least three who jigged up against the wall like they'd put themselves in time-out.

This was going nowhere. This was a ridiculous amount of overreacting for just bad hurling!

Hater had gone bright red and was telling Leggy Leader in barely hushed whispers, "I'll judge all I want. I will. I swear on Danu's soggy wet britches. There might be more Hoe in this girl's little toe than all of Fiadh's curls!"

When one of them loaded themselves onto a practice jump shroom and took off into the ceiling, Saoirse puffed in indignation. She just wanted her teammates to get their mojo back. It wasn't that big a deal. *Feckin' strumpets...*

Finally, Leader held up a hand to silence the crowd as the missing Leggies launched themselves back over the banister.

"If she needs *them*"—her voice cracked on the word—"to be hard, we are here to help, not hinder. That's the creed of the Daughters of Dagda, after all."

Agreeable murmurs met this statement.

Saoirse huffed in exasperation. At least they were still willing to help.

"Brace yourselves!" called Two. The dancers gripped banister, flowers, pots, silverware, chairs, or any other object they could get their hands on. One hid under a tablecloth.

Little Hurler wanted to join.

Deep breath in. Deep breath out.

YOU SURE YOU'RE STILL ONLY PRETENDING TO BE BAD?

The question nagged at her gut. Was she? She had to be right. She couldn't step away from the Violet, from her father, from Asiling, from Croaghgorm, but she had to know if she didn't, and Fodla made good on her threat. Saoirse went for it, "I got one hard from a Rage Boner."

Wood creaked, bronze squeaked, but the Leggies remained calm.

"But he lost it when I beat him in hurling."

There was a visible relaxing. "Oh," Leader said. "We're talking about hurling."

There _were_ two kinds of hard?!

WHAT A TWIST, FOLKS!

"Losing to a girl will make most men soft," Two admitted, flattening out the table weave which had gotten disheveled.

"It will?"

Hater, Leader, and Two all agreed, "Absolutely."

Absolutely? So it was guaranteed then.

That was awful news. How was she supposed to keep her clothes on during the drills if winning was going to destroy their chances against Tyrone? Or maybe? Two different hards... hadn't Finley mentioned something about his father thinking that very thing? "Shite."

"You okay?" Two almost looked scared to ask.

"Yes. I just need a bit more information."

OF COURSE YOU DO.

The women nodded.

Saoirse sighed. "Right, well... some of them—"

"SOME?!"

"Oh, Tuatha Dé Danann!" Saoirse threw up her hands in indignation as the explosion of coping mechanisms flared off another time. Though her annoyance didn't stop her from furiously flushing and mumbling, "Only one or two, maybe..."

"We've measured her Hoe, ma'am—it's off the charts!"

"Now I see why she wants to work here."

"We must bring her to the light before

"She's consumed by the Sexy side of the Hoe."

Saoirse reprised, rubbing her temple. Hater Leggy high-fived her. Seriously, what was all this about? Why were they freaking out? What did she not understand?

FIADH SAID...

I know what she said. It was a lie.
Queen of Denial.
Leader, hair now a frizzy mess, had a white-knuckled grip on the table. Most of the women had returned from their outbursts in similar states of distress.

Leader squeaked through her question. "What about *some*?"

"I need some way to get them... *sturdy* once more. And keep them *rigid*... at least until the... *game* is over."

"THE GAME?!"

"No!" Saoirse threw out her hands. "No. No. No."

Their panic attack calmed down. Finally, some of their pent-up anxiety seemed to deflate. A sense of rationality came over the poorly dressed, bare-ankled strumpets.

"Any ideas?" she asked.

"Glue?" suggested one.

"I've heard of this one mushroom..." offered another.

But it was Hater who came in clutch. "Have you tried fondling their sliotars?" she asked.

"Their sliotars? Like their balls?" Saoirse blinked. What a curious suggestion. She'd never considered that men might like having their balls fondled. Though handling Lorcan's bawls last night worked wonders. Were the two somehow related?

"Yes, their balls. Their liaroidí," Hater said.

"There are like ten twenty-sevens of them in the stadium," Saoirse murmured, ignoring the alarmed look this statement painted across Leader's face.

A sassy voice she didn't want to hear entered the conversation. "What's this about fondling balls?"

The whole group turned. Fiadh—as always—had arrived late.

Saoirse picked her way through her word choice, keenly aware of the women around her. "I need a way to make a... *single individual* retain a... state of... increased... rate of... stiffness?"

Fiadh popped a brow. "I see you've finally learned it's a woman's job to make men hard."

"HARD!!!"

Fiadh snapped. And all was quiet.

"Yes?" Saoirse hoped Fiadh got her head nods that this was about hurling and *not* whatever was triggering the Leggies. She showed that she did.

"Then yes, fondle their balls."

Good.

And she's done it! A victory on the match. Knowledge acquired! Mission complete! Unfortunately...

Do you want to satisfy Finley's geas or not?

Satirical did not have an answer.

"They've got performance anxiety," Fiadh explained before adding in a lyrical recitation:

"Whether it's hurling or erectile, the same thing rings true:
"A man ashamed will stay lame till his confidence renews.

"That's a stanza from the medi-druid's poem on practical medicine for men. I don't know why they bothered to study it, though, when they could have just asked me."

I don't know if we should trust her.

Part of her wanted to remain convinced Fiadh didn't know a thing about getting men hard, but she'd had the stanza, and nobody told her off.

She is kinda the queen thrumblebee.

Yeah, but... Little Hurler eyed Fiadh with contemplation.

"Something on your mind?" Fiadh pressed.

Saoirse stopped her pondering to answer. "It's just that it's awful. I couldn't imagine how bad it must feel to have your game suck because you think you don't deserve it. I know I wouldn't like it if that happened to me."

"Now you know. Try not to get the Leggies acting up again. It'll make being here even more annoying."

A clap caught their attention—Madame Orla.

It was time for practice.

Stableboy

Had she really fallen so far from Shamrock Violet? She didn't have time to ponder the thought. Saoirse squeezed into the huddle of dancers forming around Orla—only, despite her years of knocking opposing players into the bark, she was utterly incapable of breaking past the Leggies' defensive line.

What in the Shannon is going on, folks?

"Two?" she asked, but Two, despite her broken leg, had already climbed a chair.

"Okay," Saoirse said to herself. What could possibly warrant a chair? Curious, she did the same—and immediately understood. Between the tables, his visage glimmering off every piece of silverware, lit by every chandelier, the source of the excitement gleamed back at them.

Orla was not alone. She was standing with a vista.

"Ladies," the old brood said, indicating her guest. "Meet Stableboy. He's one of our stable boys."

Salm! Gods salm!

Great googally moogally, that boy is juicy!

Little Hurler disappeared behind enormous heart-shaped peepers before collapsing into a puddle of drool.

Saoirse went weak at the knees. She stole one of Two's crutches for support. Tuatha Dé Danann! He wasn't one of their stable boys—he was *the* stable boy. The literal physical definition of the term. Tuatha Dé Danann, Tuatha Dé Danann, Tuatha Dé... They made men like this? Since when? Feck! Was staying a night in the stables on the approved list of *The Violet Intercourse* activities? Because she could do a lot of the Carnival activities with that! Over and over and over again! She wondered which of the events he'd like to do most: Petting éirecondas? Or maybe rolling in hay? Picking flowers?!

Spores, what was she saying? She was for the County Tyrconnell Hurling Club and the club only! Through and through.

Unless they dissolve, folks!

Shut up, me!

Stableboy cracked a cocky smile. "Ladies," his voice was soft and assured, no extra manly bravado, just Stable and stable. Then he whinnied, brayed, and shook his mane.

Holy feckin' shite. Saoirse melted into a sudden heat.

A gurgling noise slipped out of some girl. Two fell off her chair; it made Little Hurler faint, but nobody said anything. They were all probably holding back the same.

"Right," Orla said, ignoring their reactions. "Down to business. You will not recover the costs incurred from your time with the Daughters of Dagda—veterans know this all too well. Or you might be looking to stay during the off-season. Whatever the reason, we offer the chance to work in the House."

Ah, that's what this was about—being a sensual, ankle-baring strumpet. No, thank you.

HURLER AND I SAW WHAT YOU WORE WITH THAT LORCAN BOY WHILE WE WERE AT THE RACES.

I know Lorcan.

FROM A MURAL.

Sure, look.

"You don't have to be a stripper. We always need staff. Receive orders," Madame continued, "flirt with customers, serve beer, run the gambling tables, or other services—and yes, if you're bold enough, there is always the option of working the VIP floors or offering lap dances."

"Lap dance?" Saoirse whispered to Two.

"It's optional," she hissed from the floor, eyes fixed on Stableboy through the other dancer's legs.

This didn't count as cheating on Lorcan, right? Or Finley? Nolan? Sean? Oh... looking wasn't illegal.

THIS IS THE WRONG WAY TO GO ABOUT THINGS.

Get off the sporebox. You had the same reaction.

REACTION AND ACTION ARE DIFFERENT THINGS.

"As with hurling," Orla was saying, "it is important to drill every aspect of our sport so that it all goes smoothly on game night."

Absolutely.

"Today, we serve. I'll break you into groups, practice on each other, and we'll pass Stableboy around."

Pass him around!? Tuatha Dé!

MID-WINTER'S NIGHT COMES EARLY, FOLKS.

See? Hypocrite.

I'M JUST YOUR ALTER-EGO.

"Fiadh, Leggy Bob, Leggy Two, Saoirse. Take that table," Orla pointed.

Glad to catch her name, Saoirse hopped down from the chair and joined Two, who'd recovered from her spill.

"Most of the girls come to practice every year just to see Stableboy," Two explained while the rest of the girls were sorted. "Everybody works, but only about half are so bold as to work the House and mostly as bartenders."

"That's fine," Saoirse said. "After that experience, I think I found Tyrconnell's new defensive line."

"Really?"

"Yeah. Pick a few of you, then put Stableboy behind the other team's net."

Two giggled. Together, they shuffled off with the others for their table, following behind Fiadh—her perfect-as-always blond curls bouncing with every sultry step—and Wife Bob, her perpetually angry face softened by Stableboy.

To a woman, they'd worn the all-important Éirish step-dance dresses Social Suicide seemed famous for—though Saoirse noted Leggy Two and Wife Bob had theirs pinned considerably higher than usual. No guesses as to why. And she wasn't even about to start on Fiadh, who had her feckin' thighs out!

She really is top strumpet.

I don't think that's a good thing.

Little Hurler didn't seem to mind. She was waving out her heart at Fiadh as merrily as if she were greeting Two.

Not to mention, Saoirse had been wrong about Fiadh. The girl had the answer—spores—the medical druid's entire verse for flaccid Whiskeys—and she'd never known.

WHAT ARE YOU DOING?

"Fiadh," Saoirse asked as they got to their dining table.

The strumpet turned with an effortless toss of her hair. "Yes?"

It was a shame she was so pretty, but she just had to ask. "Is there anything else I can do? Other than fondling balls, I mean?"

Fiadh pondered her for a moment. Saoirse did her best to make herself look desperate—which, to be fair, she was. "It's my last protected day at trials."

"Oh, I've heard about your wager with Lorcan."

Saoirse went wide-eyed.

"You must think nothing of me," Fiadh said. "No, I didn't tell anybody."

"Sorry."

"Tell you what," Fiadh flipped her hair. "Impress me."

"Really?"

"Do a good job today, and I'll give you another trade secret."

Trade secret? What, did she make men hard for a living or something? How ridiculous. Well, whatever. Saoirse nodded. "I won't miss, cú."

"Don't," she said. "If you don't do a good job, I'm going to have to. The more your charade unfolds, the more it looks like Lord Man Domhnaill—Finley's father," she added, "was right."

Finley's father? Fiadh knew his conjecture? Finley hadn't even told her what his father was on about!

Orla arrived at their table.

Saoirse bristled. She wasn't the only one. Only Fiadh didn't seem to care.

Stableboy.

How could Fiadh stand so confidently like that? And Tuatha Dé... Wife Bob's face. Saoirse suppressed a snicker.

"I don't see much point in saving the best for last," Orla spoke exclusively to Fiadh. "Not when so many will be looking to you for help."

"TDD." Fiadh rolled her eyes.

"But first," Orla addressed the rest of the room with another clap, "for the new girls—some knowledge. For the veterans, a refresher. I bring Stableboy for a reason."

That piqued Saoirse's interest.

"We serve many kinds of clientèle. While the rabble take up most of the floors, VIP and the upper balconies are for men of a more provocative nature. Kings, lords, foreign barons, sporting stars, top bard idols, cattle ranchers, fae with real money, and the land's best satirists—men who are used to getting whatever they please, and from whoever they set their pleases upon."

That sounded terrifying.

"When they get drunk," Orla added, "their real beasts come out."

"Beasts?" Saoirse asked.

"The bruises." Two shuddered.

"Bruises from what?"

"Just sit back and watch a master at work," Fiadh said. The strumpet with bare thighs whipped her hair dangerously. "You might finally learn something for once."

Saoirse grit her teeth. Why was Fiadh always so... *aaah!* But maybe she'd do that famous move Two mentioned—the Social Suicide.

Stableboy sat at the table—oh feck, could he sit.

Fiadh seized a large clay pitcher from a nearby tray and sauntered up to Stableboy. The way she moved—it'd be graceful if it wasn't so... her. She threw her leg up on the table.

"Welcome to Social Suicide," she said, playfully slapping his hand away before seizing his clay and filling it with liquid. "What's a handsome guy like you doing at this table?" she asked in a voice so sweet, Saoirse was surprised it belonged to the same person. Then she let her foot drag playfully along Stableboy's thigh. "Ten harps. You chase me up the stairs?"

Stableboy smiled. His teeth were so bright they actually dulled the silver.

"Good," Orla clapped.

Saoirse did as well, though she didn't know why that was good. All she'd done was pour a drink and kick him. Definitely no special move.

Fiadh pranced back to their table.

"Now, what did she do well?" the Madame asked.

"Her lean," chimed a voice.

"Her expressions."

"She poured the drink?" Saoirse asked.

Orla moved on.

Well, she'd like to be poured a drink.

"She used her body line," said one.

The feck was a body line?

"Wonderful," Orla said.

Wait—those answers were wonderful? Yeah, she was lost.

THAT'S PROBABLY A GOOD THING.

Stop being such a prat.

I LOST THE RANCH.

Whatever.

"...give a wolf a taste, then cut them off," Orla said. "It's the oldest trick in the book. Next."

Wife Bob immediately entered the fray. Salm, what was wrong with her? She was married! Saoirse understood what that meant now. Doing dancing shows for girls was one thing, but this? Saoirse's nostrils flared.

DIDN'T STOP YOU.

That's different, and you know it.

She tried to pay attention to everything Wife Bob was doing, despite the fact that Wife Bob was stabbing her teammate in the back. Was it wrong to want her to—

Bob bubbled the pitcher. In that moment, a 'seemingly drunk' Stableboy hauled off and punched her in the thigh.

Wife Bob let out a screech, holding her leg, and she went down hard in pain.

"Whoa!" Saoirse shouted.

She wasn't the only one.

"Free puck, cú! That's a foul!" Saoirse said. Even if Bob deserved it, that came out of nowhere!

Orla smiled down at Saoirse. A terrifying smile. She whispered, "This is why you don't break my deals." Then stood up and faced the girls at large. "It is indeed a foul. But here's the unfortunate truth." She took a long drag on her pipe. "By now, you'll know just how much money you can make working the floor, and Social Suicide takes a cut. We have guards—the only armed men allowed on the premises, save for a King's security guarda—but that won't always stop what might happen.

"And if you're up in VIP, well... we probably won't stop anything that might happen. Drunk men are unpredictable and dangerous."

Saoirse swallowed. "You mean you're not going to ref the sport?" she asked.

"We're not here to outscore our opponents. We're here to get paid while they think they're scoring on us."

"That's awful."

"Dodge the bruises, and it won't be. Now, groups."

Saoirse shook, her skin clammy, watching Wife Bob roll on the floor, Leggy Leader tending to her. A completely lawless pitch! She'd never have thought being a whore could be more dangerous than hurling!

"Alright, back to your groups, start practicing." Orla clapped, and they broke off. Maybe Satirical had a right to be concerned.

You're salm right I do!
"Well," Fiadh handed her the water pitcher, "impress me."
"Wait. What?" Their table had Stableboy!
Don't do it. Don't go.
Her heart was thumping out of control, but... Little Hurler wasn't scared. She was nervous but bouncing up and down, ready to perform.
Saoirse gripped the handle firmly.
Sorry, Satirical. I'm with my heart on this one. Every time I've pretended to be bad, life's gotten better. And she needed Fiadh's knowledge.
Leggy Two made an encouraging gesture. "You got this."
Pompoms pounded against her chest.
Saoirse nodded, trying to stuff away how attractive and dangerous—and dangerously attractive, and attractively dangerous—Stableboy was and focus on what mattered. Scoring. She'd dodged plenty of tackles in her time, but that'd been on the field, not in a dress. Actually... she couldn't even say that anymore. Was this really something women did? Did it matter if Shamrock Violet considered her a good woman if she ended up in a PÉNIS dungeon? Why was it every time she wanted to grow, her femininity slipped down the Slieve League? She didn't need a Magic Eight Ball to know her outlook here wasn't so good.
Saoirse walked to the table—
And froze.
And number twenty-seven does it again. Frozen stiff. Does this count as a goal line? Would this count as a win?
It went against everything she'd been taught.
"Come on, Saoirse!" Leggy Two cheered. "You got this! Are you a woman or aren't you?"
Thank you, Two. Saoirse threw her leg up to the table. "Welcome to—AAAH!" With a wail like a banshee, Saoirse missed the table and landed hard on her bum. "Ow."
Stableboy was quick to help her, as was Two, both laughing.
"Nice try," he said.
He spoke to me! An Dagda, Good God, thank you. Thank you, gods.
Why must I share this head with you?
"I'd have thought you," Two said, "of all people, had more coordination than that." She pulled her to her feet and handed her a towel for the spilled water.
Saoirse dabbed at it while Wife Four screeched with laughter near a still-pained Bob.
"Pathetic," Fiadh said, dismissing the Wives.
"At least I tried."
"I didn't make a deal for trying."
"Shaper."
"The only one throwing shapes out here is you."
After massaging her butt, the rest of the practice went somewhat better than her initial go, likely because Stableboy moved to another table after ripping off half of Two's skirt. Saoirse'd almost died of embarrassment on her friend's behalf. That was definitely worse than the laughter she'd endured for her missed leg swing. She'd never make that mistake again.
Again? Why did she say again? There never would be an 'again.'
A friendly hand tapped her on the shoulder. Hater?
"See you tonight?" Hater asked.
"Sure." But first, she had one last question. "Hater?"
The usually spiteful Leggy spun back around.
"What's a lap dance?"
In response, Hater shouted, "Stableboy!" Stableboy left his table, much to the chagrin of the other group.
Hater paused to look back at Saoirse. "This."
First Stableboy sat down. Then Hater... sat... down...

"Great gods!" Saoirse could not keep her thoughts inside. "Oh... my—Tuatha Dé... spores. Feck! Wow... yikes! You. Really? TDD...!"

WHORE.

For a reason Saoirse couldn't pinpoint, Satirical's comment made her upset. She took over Satirical's commentary duties.

That's it, folks! A perfect ten on the pelvic pirouette—she's out of her seat and into the history books!

Little Hurler laughed her heart out.

Saoirse thanked her friend and headed to the trials, excited to put her new knowledge to the test, but a bit put off. She had more in common with her heart now than with her head, but one thing she could agree with Satirical on was that she would never be doing *that.*

Fuzzy Cuffs

*A*ND WE'RE BACK ON THE PITCH AT HAZEL PARK! WHERE DEBAUCHERY GOES TO DIE. THANK THE GODS, FOLKS.

She and Hurler blew raspberries at Satirical's broadcast booth for that. Saoirse still hadn't gotten over that comment about Hater. Lap dances weren't—okay, they were—but it was Hater... and well, it just wasn't very nice.

Everything seemed more crisp than usual: the water, the field, the air. It was a dry, clear day, with the sun splitting the spores. A small rainbow crested the span from the top of the reverse falls to just behind the far goal—where Fanny stood. The investigator was back in her tight business attire, with her puss-ridden assistant fae, talking to Lorcan. He looked livid. Two sights she didn't want to see, but she'd have to deal with that later. She had to fondle balls!

Fist-bumping her heart for hype, she and Hurler waved across the pitch and jogged to the man with the plan. "Finley!"

He smiled, dressed in yet another new, colorful, striped set of training gear—teal today. Spores, to be rich.

"You seem happy," she said.

"Not as much as you," he said. They tapped hurleys.

"I've got something to test!" And she told him about her conversation with the Daughters of Dagda and Hater's surprise revelation. "Fondle their balls!"

Finley paused for a moment with a slight smile. "I suppose that would make most men hard."

"Really?" If Finley agreed, that basically confirmed it. "How did you not think of it then?"

"Well, uh..." He got shifty. He was hiding something again. "I always thought hard and hard were different things."

"There *are* two hards?"

Finley flushed. "I'm actually not sure anymore."

What did that mean?

He smiled. "Let's just give it a shot."

"Saoirse and Finley in The Fondling of the Balls."

"Ha!"

But her excitement was stolen away. Fanny Burns crossed the pitch in their direction, flanked by the strange fae in a three-piece suit and an inflatable helmet—and worse, she was smiling.

"Little Gale," she said, producing a pair of pink fuzzy cuffs from her cleavage. "You're under arrest."

"What?!" Saoirse said, yanking her hands away just before they were snatched by Fanny. Finley got between them.

"I can put you away too, Man Domhnaill."

"What happened to letting me play?" Saoirse squeaked, intensely aware of the assistant next to the investigator. The fae had a strange hurley over his shoulder. A chain had been threaded through a hole in the bas and was hung with two intense, smoking, blue balls.

Fanny cocked a hip in her pencil skirt, adjusting her horn-rimmed glasses with the tip of her carving knife. "I wanted to follow up on your stave with the donors, but I have all the evidence I need."

"I'm a Bad Girl."

"That will be determined at trial."

"When?"

"Tomorrow. This matter is to be expedited as fast as possible, but it seems fairly obvious to me you're going to be declared a Good Girl."

No.

"What do you want, Fanny?" Finley asked. "We're busy."

Fanny sneered at them both. "I always love facing full-forwards, full of themselves and full pieces of shite, little girlies trying to score on goals under my nose, and always shocked when I body them to the outside line."

Saoirse stepped face-to-face with the arrogant investigator. "Don't be surprised when I cut to the inside and score."

Fanny stabbed her in the stomach with the end of her staviture. "Nobody slips inside this Fanny."

"I will."

"And yet you can't. You are under arrest."

Finley snatched Fanny's cuff hand.

"Going to fight the law, Little Domhnaill?"

"When it comes to the law, it's never much of a fight." He said. "I challenge you to a Rite of Ritual Hurling."

I WASN'T EXPECTING THAT TURN.

Her Spectators spluttered with due excitement.

He was going to fight Fanny for her? Saoirse eyed Finley with appreciation.

Fanny looked flabbergasted. She looked from Finley to Saoirse. Shite, didn't she think she was working with the donors? She said so herself, and Finley was one!

"Master Man Domhnaill?" Fanny asked.

"What can I say?" Saoirse said. "Never underestimate cattle."

Finley didn't even blink. He played right along. "Aggressive repatriation."

Spores. That business jargon.

Fanny pulled back. Had she taken the bait?

IT WAS PRETTY EGREGIOUS BAIT.

"What's in the sliotars for four hundred, Triple K?" Fanny said, but she traded her cuffs for her hurley. "Alright, little lordling. Name your terms."

Little lordling?

I'M MORE ANNOYED SHE CONSTANTLY TEASES US ABOUT CHASTITY!.

"I win, and you can't arrest Saoirse until she enacts her plan."

AT MOST, THAT'S ONLY A FEW MINUTES!

Fanny doesn't know that yet.

WELL, COME UP WITH SOMETHING THEN!

Hurler thinking pose.

"Sideline cuts," Saoirse said. "Skill only, no Whiskeys."

"It's not your choice, Little Gale. It's mine."

"You're only trying to dodge because you know you can't do it." Saoirse jabbed her.

Fanny cocked an arrogant hip. "Fine, but Whiskeys *are* allowed."

"Fine," Finley said.

Saoirse balked. If Fanny's Whiskey worked the way she though tit did, Finley was doomed!

"Don't worry, Little Shroom," Finley stared down Fanny Burns. "This is going to be easy."

Fondling Balls

E asy? Saoirse sat on the team bench watching Finley square off against Fanny. The Rite of Ritual Hurling was the exact reason PÉNIS purposefully sought out powerful hurlers. Fanny was in the TIP of PÉNIS, and he thought it was going to be easy?

YOU THOUGHT THE EXACT SAME THING.

Yes, but I'm me!

Word got around fast this time, and the trials ground to an excited halt. Finley was going to take on the best investigator in the world; it hadn't taken long for an arch to form facing the action.

"How should we judge it?" Finley asked. "Distance feels unfair?"

"Oh, I'm fine with distance, Little Domhnaill."

Saoirse's stomach twisted in knots. *I'm so used to Tyrconnell not getting points.*

FINLEY'S NEW, LIKE YOU, AND HE'S GOOD. I'VE BEEN WATCHING.

It was nice to have Sat not angry for a bit.

He did finish in the top cut of hurlers in Free Ball. But Fanny had insisted on allowing Whiskeys. Did Finley even know about Tulip Grip? Fanny's powerful magic had sucked Saoirse right into her palm—and against gravity! If she could use it on sliotars.

DISTANCE WAS A TRAP, FOLKS!

The Spectators bit their nails. Little Hurler had a death grip on her hurley. Saoirse joined her. Nobody wanted to get arrested. Yet.

"I'll go first," Finley smiled.

Murmurs ripped through the crowd. Saoirse checked behind her, where the angry Lorcan glowered down at the proceedings with his 'definitely less cool than a carnival pop' girls carved away. What happened between last night and today to make him so mad? If Finley didn't win, she may well never find out.

SPEAKING OF WHICH, YOU NEED TO FIND A WAY TO BUY US TIME! IT'S THE WHOLE REASON HE CHALLENGED HER. WE CAN'T RELY ON THE IDEA THAT FINLEY'S GOING TO BEAT AN INVESTIGATOR. IF SHE WINS, IT'S A COIN FLIP ON WHETHER SHE LETS YOU RUN AROUND FOR PRETENDING TO BE PART OF A CONSPIRACY WITH HIS FAMILY.

One free slip to you, Sat. You're right.

OF COURSE, I'M RIGHT.

But what?

Finley swaggered up to a sliotar; he and Fanny were going for points over the bar off sideline cuts. Since the goal was distance, they'd started at midfield.

"Come on, Finley."

Melak watched with intense interest from the cliff, and more than a few sporting wagers were shaken on.

He swung.

With a clean snap, Finley cut the sliotar off the grass, really pullin' on it. This wasn't just going over the bar; this could go over the bar even if he hit it from the other side of the field!

"Whiskey!" Fanny cried.

Of course.

IT WAS TOO GOOD TO BE TRUE!

"Tulip Grip!" Fanny held her hand out to the sailing sliotar, it stopped mid-flight and soared backward, sucked straight into the investigator's outstretched palm.

Groans for lost bets rang through the crowd.

She turned to see Lorcan hit a 'not bad' face.

She wished she could say the same.

"Looks like you missed," Fanny said.

"Don't count your cowflies." Finley smiled. "You've still got to make yours."

Fanny, her hurley was so strange, wrapped tip-to-toe in a large white bandage. She'd never seen anybody wrap their hurley like that.

As far as Hurler was concerned, it was salm cool.

Fanny, still in heels and a pencil skirt, the arrogance, stepped up to a sliotar. And she stepped up wrong. Saoirse narrowed her eyes, taking in every bit of the investigator. Why was she tense like that? It was a tiny thing, maybe barely noticeable unless you were really looking, but her muscles were all wrong, not relaxed at all. Was she feeling the pressure? The I of PENIS shouldn't be worried about a little Rite, surely?

I KNOW WHAT YOU MEAN, TWENTY-SEVEN.

It couldn't be. You don't think... not that Fanny is bad at side-line cuts?

I DON'T THINK A WOMAN COULD MAKE IT UP SO HIGH IN THE LAW AND BE BAD AT HURLING.

Fanny took a deep breath. And swung. It certainly didn't have as much power as Finley's, but it was sailing true. She looked to Finley. It was a one-round rite...

"Whiskey!" He cried.

Wait! "What?"

Several others got excited as well. Finley's hurley twitched. It was glowing white! He had a way to win!

"Trickster in the Táin!"

What did that do? Did it confuse the sliotar? Send it wide? No, it—

Made him smack Fanny hard on her butt.

"Master Man Domhnaill!"

"Sorry, but it is my whiskey," he said. He held his palm to the ball exactly as Fanny had done and cried, "Tulip Grip!"

The ball stopped just short of the bar and was sucked back into Finley's palm.

Holy feck, cú. He can steal Whiskeys!

Finley shook as if he had gone weak.

"Don't fall asleep!" Saoirse shouted. That whiskey was so powerful, but Finley had to go more than one round!

"Don't worry about me, worry about you," he said.

Shite. She still didn't have a plan!

I think he's faking the fatigue.

MAYBE THAT'S WHY FANNY LOOKED OFF? SHE'D JUST USED HER MAGIC.

Maybe. But it didn't feel like it.

Finley went again. This time, Fanny didn't use her magic; all Whiskeys needed a recharge time. Finley was easily over the bar.

Several cheers met this result.

And... Fanny did it again. *She looks so uncomfortable!*

She'd changed her grip. Why was she choking up on her hurley? *It's like she's afraid to swing. Her muscles are all wrong. Can she not put the sliotar out there?*

Fanny swung...

And it was short!

FINLEY WINS.

Saoirse cheered. Her spectators bellowed their approval, more than half the trials lost bets, and Lorcan shouted into his black spore, which made his voice carry over the stadium and reach the mushrooms. "Back to trials."

She was saved!

Finley and Fanny both made their way to her.

"Finley!" She hugged him.

"Told you it was nothing."

Fanny was miffed, but there was nothing she could do; she had to wait to arrest Saoirse now.

Saoirse stuck her tongue out at the investigator, who scowled.

"What are you two up to?" Fanny asked.

"Don't tell her," said Saoirse.

The devious legendary warrior shrugged. "We can't stop her joining."

"Salm."

He turned to the investigator. "Saoirse here thinks she's found a way to make men hard."

Fanny flushed. "In Tyrconnell?"

"I'm going to fondle their balls."

Fanny turned crimson.

"Still want to come?" Finley asked.

"Yes. I think I shall."

Saoirse narrowed her eyes at the investigator, but it wouldn't matter. "Whatever. Thanks, cú."

"Anytime, Little Shroom."

The spray from the river misted the north side of Hazel Park. She figured it was best to avoid it. She wasn't all that interested in palming cold sliotars. Today was her last protected day—the last day of her strip hurling, too. If this didn't work, she'd have to spend the day losing for fear of killing the team's mojo by beating them as a girl. She'd be off the field and maybe in less than she came in. But if it did—spores, if it did—she had a plan.

DO WE HAVE A PLAN?

Nope. Just some manifesting.

THAT I UNDERSTAND.

Finley snatched up a pair of sliotars and put them into a small carrying pouch, one hanging a bit lower than the other, then held them at his waist, casting anxious looks around at the men warming up nearby. He nodded. "Let's try them." A group laughed, practicing their soloing by keeping their balls up while thrusting their sticks through moist hoops, damp from last night's rain. "Look at them in a coy manner, while you fondle these balls."

"Gotcha." She smiled.

"Why did I agree to come again?" Fanny shook her head.

"You can leave," she spat at Fanny. "Saoirse Storm and Finley Man Domhnaill in the Stroking of the Sliotars."

Finley snorted with laughter. It was a pretty funny name. She made her best coy face and started to rub them suggestively.

The hurleys, the group of men was holding, began to fill with mist, the ogham on their shafts steadily storing up light.

"It's working!" she squeaked. "It's working! I can do this, cú!"

Storm's got one hand in the bag and two in the heart of the game, folks!

Finley could not stop laughing. Eager, she switched to milking the balls like cow udders.

"I haven't felt this seen since my wedding night!"

"Cú, my hurley hasn't glowed since Junior League!"

"This is... glorious."

Every moment made her energy rise. "Who knew men liked having their equipment fondled? Their sliotars stroked? Their balls bobbled?"

"Little Gale..." Fanny pinched the brim of her nose.

But after a while, the light in the shafts began to fade. In a desperate attempt to salvage the situation, Saoirse squeezed the sliotars—but it seemed to have the opposite effect, as the rest of the light drained completely. The men cringed.

"Spores! It was working."

She turned back to the pair of them. Why were they looking at each other like that? Finley was wide-eyed, looking from Fanny to the men in shock. Fanny seemed equally floored.

"It can't be," Finley said.

"It's impossible," Fanny agreed.

"Did you see that? I almost had it!"

He quickly seized her shoulders. "Saoirse," Finley said. "Don't hate me, but I think it might be a false trail."

"False trail? You're not lying to me, are you? Didn't you see?"

He shared another glance with Fanny, who shrugged. "Don't look at me. I'm here to investigate, not educate."

"It's just not proper..." Finley said. "My dad. Spores. Men I know—they can get hard right away, whenever their Whiskey requires it. Fondling balls might be a step in the right direction, but it won't get them all the way. Besides, what are you going to do? Run around the pitch all game, fondling balls and fisting hurleys?"

His dad's conjecture. Was that what he was hiding? Fiadh mentioned she knew about it, but she had to take anything Fiadh said with a grain of salt. Though even that seemed less and less true. Still, he was right. She couldn't play like that. "I was really confident for a moment there."

Finley smiled, resting comforting hands on her shoulders, his ball sack dangling across her chest.

"So, we keep going," he said. "We find something similar to playing with their equipment."

"Right."

"You can't give up after coming this far."

"You might be that Fiadh girl's one true rival," Fanny nodded.

Her? A rival to Fiadh in balls? "I'd never aim so low."

Says the girl who considers herself her rival.

"You'll figure it out. I know you will. Something tells me you're the only one on the team who can do this. I believe in you."

"Thanks, Finley. I will. I promise. I will get this whole team hard if it's the last thing I do!"

Fanny snorted so hard she started coughing. "Was that your whole plan, then?"

"Nope."

"It didn't work, not how I was hoping, but I had a backup."

"Why are you doing this?" Fanny asked. "Why go to such lengths for a team you can't ever play for?"

She sighed. "I just want to know I've at least left here having made a difference. Knowing that I did it. That I did all I could to save the County Tyrconnell Hurling Club."

"They won't thank you."

"Maybe not. I can fondle all the balls in the world, but it'll only go so far. Their Wives have them in a downward spiral."

"That won't get them to make you space," Fanny chuckled.

"I know that. I am not asking them to. I am making space for them. It's too bad Wives aren't easy to replace, cú." Lorcan said a man's Wife was his one partner for life.

"*You* make space for *them*?" Fanny made to carve something.

And it clicked. "Finley," Saoirse smiled. "You know how I wanted to go deeper."

"Yes."

Saoirse did her best impression of his devious smile.

"Slip me in the Shannon," he said.

"—but I need you to recommend it. The team still hates my guts."

"Alright, cú."

WHATEVER IT IS, COUNT ME OUT.

Saoirse bit her lip. *Don't worry, Sat, you're going to love this.*

OUR GIRL'S GOING FOR A GOAL! AGAINST MY BETTER JUDGMENT.

Little Hurler thumped her chest.

Her crowd roared.

Finley clearly understood. He cracked one of his own devious smiles.

"What?" Saoirse asked.

Finley smirked. "It's Fiadh Night."

High Society

As with every place, Tyrconnell's high society is comprised of thieves who are too rich to actually pay for their crimes. See, folks, the number one way to have money is to have cattle. Never underestimate cattle. In fact, it's a matter of great Ulster pride that one of our kings has the single best bull in all of existence, Donn Cúailnge! It makes those losers over there in Province "Bad and Should Feel Bad" go right green with it, and I'm not talking about the Shamrock sect.

It's a fact of Éirish life that if you have cows, you either stole them or they're about to be stolen from you in a táin: a cattle raid.

Bands of a county's, kingdom's, or crazy lads group's best men band together to rush off and steal the cow flies of another king or county. But there's one kind of cattle raider nobody likes—the kind that plays dirty, the dishonorable kind—those that steal the eggs of cowflies before they're born. We call them 'hatch-snatchers,' and everywhere in Éire they are prosecuted to the full extent of the law.

Bear-Back Riding

T here was one place that had a group of women with all the answers; one place with a group of women big enough to replace a whole team's Wives; one place that could boost confidence; and tonight, entry was free. Saoirse found a way to solve the team's problems and, to Satirical's great pleasure, remove herself from the equation entirely. Social Suicide!

RIVAL NIGHT.

FREEDOM STORM VS. THE WILD LOVER OF STRANGERS.

SAOIRSE VS. FIADH.

STRAP INTO YOUR SEATS, SPECTATORS, TONIGHT'S GOING TO BE WILD!

Fiadh couldn't be that impressive.

I DON'T KNOW, I'VE NEVER SOLD SO MANY TICKETS FOR A NON-HURLING EVENT. AND I DON'T KNOW WHAT TO MAKE OF THAT INFORMATION.

Saoirse pulled on her freshly cleaned furs. Spores, it was nice to be in a regular outfit after that practice. It turned out Lorcan had gotten into a row with his Wife after their adventure the previous night and been left maulding. He'd put her at half-back, and she'd just barely escaped with her clothes on. She was smart enough to forgive him. Did that make them a better match? Would he ever see her that way?

THOSE ARE DANGEROUS THOUGHTS.

It wouldn't be so bad. I could be like an extra Wife on the team. Like, a side Wife? Wife part-time? Adjunct pet? There when you needed her, hurling when you didn't. At the very least, she came to agree with Aisling. Every team should have a woman dedicated to PÉNIS therapy.

WHAT HAPPENED TO SCORING?

It'll be Aisling. I'll put in a good word. Just you wait, boys. Tonight you'll all be hard!

She stepped out of the locker rooms onto the paved walkway surrounding Hazel Park. Baby floodlight shrooms, long black-stemmed fungi with brilliant light at the tip, curled over the walk, highlighting the path of pavers lined by flower boxes. In the distance, she could see a bronze statue of Melak pawing a sliotar.

CRISP NIGHT.

I'd say. Borrowing a move from Leggy Leader, Saoirse stretched her arms out like she was trying to score two over the bar and cracked her back. *Showers really are amazing, cú.*

I still can't believe you handed over your possible innocence in the match-fixing scandal to that strumpet's performance.

I handed over the fight against Fanny to Finley, and look how that turned out. Back me up. She owed Finley for that.

Little Hurler lazed inside her heart in a towel, soaking up the residual shower steam.

No. Let's just turn ourselves in now. If you're right, we've already won. Now we just need to be found guilty.

I need to make sure it works. She could do this.

Why do I let you solo me like this?

Would you rather do this or The Violet Intercourse*?*

Fine, I'll go, but if you so much as take five steps without resetting the count, I'm headed to the horse races.

Fine.

Fine.

Fine.

Fine.

Fine. When Satirical didn't respond, she added—*and double fine.*

Her mind sighed. *I suppose you'll be wanting an intro then?*

She wanted her friend to stop fighting her, but then Satirical should know that she could read her thoughts. *I'd appreciate it.*

Alright. Sat took a deep breath and started the evening off properly. *It's time for the next match. Rival Night. Saoirse versus Fiadh. You know it, I know it, we all know it. This is gonna be one for the ages, folks!*

At the call, Little Hurler hustled out of the heart in full gear, a ball gown like the well-heeled wore at the Den but with added cabaret accouterments, and cleated hard shoes, hurley at the ready.

Saoirse fist-bumped her heart for hype, but Little Hurler was disappointed in Saoirse's choice of clothes. She'd worn dresses now and wanted to again, but tonight she wanted to be comfortable, and heels were way too hard to handle. The last thing she needed was to be on edge with Fanny prowling around.

Saoirse started her walk around the stadium toward the Melak statue; it was the signal that she was ready to get picked up by her ride. Maybe Fiadh could do it. Maybe she could get them hard.

"You know," Finley's smooth voice carried through the chill, "I was beginning to think you'd died in there."

"Finley!" Saoirse turned. "Whoa."

Until Stableboy, she'd never really thought of people as vistas, but that was beginning to change. Mr. Three-Torques-Rich had gotten dressed up, wearing a classy blue tunic, angle-cut, and looking sharp.

And Finley joins the night's line-up, folks. It's a dynamic duo.

"No dress?" Finley chided her.

"Ha. Ha. Why are you here?"

He shrugged. "Somebody had to wait."

"Had to?"

"Oh, don't think I'm opposed. Just figured I'd ride you."

"Excuse me?" She shoved down the image of Fiadh in the spore shower.

Finley smirked, and a moment later, her question was answered with the loud, powerful flapping of insect wings—

Fump-fump-fump.

—and a black bearfly, which landed on the brick path like a fat, hairy god.

Little G. It is just a regular insect.

"Meet Ewe." Finley bleated like a sheep.

Saoirse tried to hide her embarrassment at the misunderstanding by walking around the fly. Much smaller than the grizzlies she was used to but no less impressive, the hairy creature had huge paws, a black snout with a furled proboscis, six wings, and bulbous red eyes of tiny crystal-like lenses. Why would Finley have one here?

"My ride."

"My ride..." The realization struck her.

YOU SAID WE WOULDN'T BE DOING THE VIOLET INTERCOURSE!

Tuatha Dé! Of all things, a bear-back ride! Feck what Fiadh had said. Aisling swore this would be the one to get a girl pregnant! Feck.

DON'T DO IT. OUR CAREERS!

She pressed down the fright. This must have been the bearfly he'd mentioned during the Carnal Carnival. Finley had taken her through, and they'd turned out fine. She and Lorcan danced at the Den, which was also okay. No sexplosion. Come to think, wouldn't men be just as cautious about sexplosion as she was? Surely a man like Finley didn't go around seeking death? She walked around front to stall for time, giving the fly a golden hand job. "Where did you get one?"

"I liberated it," Finley smirked. "From Drumboe Castle."

"You stole it!?" Saoirse shouted, both surprised and impressed. The bear fly let off a low toot when she unfurled its proboscis to fully erect, scattering her golden dust on the wind.

"Need I remind you, my family made most of its wealth from the successful repatriation of foreign cattle." He came to the front of the fly, and it clicked.

"Táins! You're a thief! You run táins—cattle raids!"

"We prefer aggressive entrepreneurs," he said, offering a hand.

Saoirse eyed it with apprehension. This man was a thief. Quite possibly a literal hatch-snatcher! But... he'd also saved her life. "You're not going to steal from me, are you?"

To this, Finley reached out and caught her chin, tilting her face to meet his. Spores, but her thighs could seriously stop doing that!

Something unreadable flickered in his eyes. "I'll take anything I think is valuable."

Saoirse swallowed—hard. Oh no. Bear-back rides were definitely where you got pregnant! There was always a chance it wouldn't happen to her. Her heartbeat stuttered. Little Hurler dove under the bench. Dare she risk it? Dare she pretend this hard to be bad? It's not like it was against Violet codes. She thought she'd gotten over her now childish-seeming misgivings with Aisling.

I TOLD YOU IT WAS DANGEROUS.

"Come on," he said. "I want to ride Ewe."

And, in that moment, she knew it was because she had gotten over them.

Finley seized her around the waist and lifted her. She sat side-saddle, brushing her hair behind one ear in the hopes of cooling down.

"Want to get off?" he asked and swung around beside her. He seemed to have something hard in his pocket, which was strangely comforting.

She shook her head. "I want to ride Ewe."

Finley smirked. "I want to ride Ewe, too."

She clung to Mr. Three Torques as Finley kicked, far too busy praying to her gods that the Magic Eight Ball had started rolling—outlook not so good.

Fiadh Night

S pores! Flying through the sky! On a fly! With a fly guy! She'd never been so high!

Ewe zipped and bobbed between branches, and she found herself pushing her hips back into Finley's. Rich-Rich had one hand on the reins, one bracing her waist. She could feel the knife in his pocket and tried to adjust for his pleasure, subtly wiggling back and forth, till he moaned in her ear. She stopped. She didn't want him to be uncomfortable!

"This is amazing!" she screamed over the wind, as the lights of Social Suicide crystallized in the distance.

"I'm glad you like it, cú."

Her heart had on big goggles and a floppy cap, waving in the wind. Even Satirical had to dump her grump and agree that—*THIS WAS ONE FOR THE AGES, FOLKS!*

When it finally came to an end after a few laps around the hive, Saoirse screamed, "Whoooooo!" and Ewe touched down on the Jobbery grounds at the back of the hive.

Now she understood why the elders made this activity a part of *The Violet Intercourse*.

She doubled over, panting, Finley laughing in her ear, one arm bracing her waist as he lay over her. Her heart was hot in the face, still darting around somewhere in the shroomlight high above them.

It was a moment before Saoirse slid from the saddle. Little Hurler only snapped out of the clouds and back to the ground a few moments after she did. Saoirse stumbled forward, away from the bear fly. "That was the best ride of my life."

I DON'T DOUBT IT, AS IT WAS BASICALLY A LAP DANCE.

Stop the lights. Saoirse shook her head—but not the implication. Now Hurler was seriously red. A lap dance!? She was a pretend bad girl!

Finley laughed. "First-time flier, huh?"

"I'm not pregnant, am I?"

"What?"

"Aisling swore it was bear-back rides."

"Ah, Violets." Finley snickered. "I have no idea what you're talking about with bearflies, but I can promise you that didn't get you pregnant."

"You sure?"

"I am certain."

"Thank the gods." Saoirse collapsed against a nearby post. What a relief, because she *had* to do that again.

Men in Social Suicide's bright pink uniform hustled this way and that, caring for more people in more fanciful dress than she'd ever imagined. Nearly every square meter had someone on a mount the likes of which she'd never seen.

"Fiadh Night," Finley said, knowingly.

"She can't really be that amazing."

"Jealous?"

"Maybe of her special move. I want to add it to my dance repertoire so I can use it on the field. The Social Suicide. Two said the name was a real cowfly-and-egg situation."

Finley handed Ewe off to the stable hands, then, instead of taking her to the House, paused to look around.

"What's up?" Saoirse joined him in the yard.

"Want you to meet somebody." Finley cupped his hands around his mouth and began shouting over the din. "Oi, moron!"

Moron? What was he up to?

"Moron!" he shouted again.

She needn't ask twice. A moment later, to her horror, Stableboy came running out of the hay with a doofy grin on his perfect feckin' face and leaped into Finley's arms with a huge hug.

Oh no. They were gay.

"Brother!" he shouted.

Oh no. They were brothers.

Tuatha Dé, what an unfair family.

"Crazy night?" Finley asked.

"It's got its perks," Stableboy laughed. "Here for Fiadh?"

"No, I'm here for her," Finley said.

Stableboy followed Finley's gesture to her. Saoirse could tell his brain was trying to put two and two together. Did he recognize her from that morning? She desperately hoped he wouldn't. But to be safe, she attempted every conceivable not-obvious gesture to indicate he should shut the feck up.

After a while, Stableboy nodded. "She's got huge tits, bro."

Oh no. He was a himbo! How could one man constantly get so much more attractive?

PUT HIM ON THE TEAM!

Satirical?

I DIDN'T SAY SHITE.

Finley put an arm around her shoulders. "Saoirse, meet Stableboy."

"That can't be his real name."

"It is."

"Holy feck!!"

THAT'S SO DUMB.

"This," Finley explained, "is my little brother." He pulled Stableboy over to meet her and paused. "He's fourteen."

Oh no!

KEEP HIM OFF THE TEAM! KEEP HIM OFF THE TEAM!

Her heart went down in a dizzy tizzy.

"Four—fourteen?" she squeaked. There was way too much wrong with that.

"Only joking, he's twenty," Finley cracked up again.

Her Little Hurler put up fists. Her stadium cried, *'Foul!'* but the refs didn't make the call.

Saoirse shook her head. "He's got to get back to work, is what he is," she said, praying to all the gods he didn't recognize her.

Stableboy mock-pouted. "She's mean, cú."

Finley shook his head. "Indeed."

"Feck you both."

Finley and Stableboy said their goodbyes. When Saoirse's Spectators went absolutely nuts, they were on the top rail of the stands in her stomach, looking behind her and jabbing her like mad.

What? Saoirse turned. Her heart cratered. "Finley, we've got a problem."

Finley turned, Stableboy—who hadn't left yet—also followed where she was pointing. "It's the Wives!"

There, climbing the last stairs from the Jobbery to Social Suicide, were Wife Prime, The Fun Wife, Wife the Third, Wife Four, Wife Bob, and a host of other women she could only assume were the rest of the team's Laurens.

"Social Suicide is a big place," Finley said. "They might be here just to gamble and have a good time."

"Do you believe that?" Saoirse asked.

"Not in the slightest," he said.

Saoirse shook her head. "Neither do I."

"What do we do? If they show up when their husbands are about to get hard, everything is ruined!"

Satirical knocked on her temple. *I've got an idea*, she said.

What?

Distract them!

How am I supposed to do that? If they see me, that's even worse!

With Stableboy!

Genius! "Stableboy?"

"Yes, butt-plant girl?"

That got Finley's attention.

Saoirse flushed furiously, but pointed after the Wives, who'd disappeared around the corner. "Go fetch."

His features darkened in a dangerously attractive and attractively dangerous manner. "On it."

Satirical came back in. *Oh, excitement on the pitch! The way-too-attractive-to-the-point-it-should-be-illegal brothers are hugging now. Stableboy's headed to the field. This is a wild Rival Night, folks.*

Saoirse shook her head the whole time. *You're getting into this.*

No, I'm not. Satirical sounded indignant.

Hmm.

"I know he's ugly," Finley smirked. "But you don't have to stare."

"As if. I'm just checking out the stables."

"Sure." Finley smiled. He turned her a new direction.

"Aren't we headed to the House, cú?"

"We are, but our entrance is this way." Finley placed a hand on the small of her back as Lorcan had done. She let him guide her to an elaborate bronze gate set up at the edge of the Jobbery yard. The gate sectioned off the rest of the commotion from... nothing? The other side was just the edge of the yard and a steep drop she wasn't keen on taking.

"Don't worry," he said. "Just because my Wife's here doesn't mean we're about to jump."

Saoirse flushed, but Little Hurler smiled as foxy as Finley himself.

He chuckled.

"What, cú?" she asked, punching him playfully on the arm.

"You're excited."

"Well, yeah. It's an important night."

"Not that." He smiled. "Last time you and I were together, we walked the Carnal Carnival. If I recall, you practically had three—" he held up three fingers. "—three conniption fits!"

Heat flushed her cheeks. "Go swim the Shannon."

"Ha!"

As they approached the gate, a young man in a slick black uniform with pink lettering leaped into action, prying it open. Together, she and Finley stepped to the other side. Finley slipped him a tin piece, and the usher boy closed the gate behind them.

Saoirse marveled. She'd never seen a real tin piece before.

"How much is that?"

"In twenty-sevens?" he joked, then added, with her annoyed pout, "It's about two months' wages for him. Come, let's go up."

Go up? She was going down! Two months' wages! Her stomach twisted. He could drop money just like that? Three-torques-rich—and giving it freely to those in need. He might be a thief, but he wasn't a bad guy. If she had to pick between him and Lorcan...

She'd take both!

Feck off, Satirical.

Just stating facts.

And we don't need those right now.

Finley pulled her closer. She inhaled his scent. "Honeysuckles."

"Knew you'd like that."

Spores, he was so dastardly. "Are we waiting on something?"

As if the world was waiting for that very question, there was a sudden rumbling, cracking sound. Saoirse squealed, leaping into Finley's arms as their portion of grass and flowers broke itself free of the tether to the stable yard and began floating upward as if carried on a soft breeze. Slips of purple mist streaked by in strips and spirals to nowhere.

He smiled. "That."

"Tuatha Dé, shroom showers, and bear shite!" She held tight to Finley as she watched the people in the stable yard grow steadily smaller—the isle rising higher and higher up the side of the hive. "You could have warned me!"

"Where's the fun in that? Besides, I thought you liked vistas."

The audacity! But her fingers insisted on digging deeper into his chest. She did like the view.

Tonight, the grounds were a different beast. One she'd been too busy enjoying the wind on the back of the bear ride to notice. Pink. Everything was pink. The carvings decorating the outside of the House glowed with it. The three shamrock gardens surrounding the base, the Carnal Carnival, and the walk to the House. It wasn't hard to figure out Fiadh's favorite color.

The hive itself 'breathed,' growing and shrinking as the wind swept through its open pores. Tonight there was a thunderstorm, though you'd never know it where they stood. Above them—high, high above them—hung massive thatched roofs suspended by enormous rope cables. The roofs distributed incoming rainwater away from the hive, where the water became three massive waterfalls: one green, one white, and one orange, each falling in front of one of the three two-mile-tall Aurum Great Woods from which the hive was suspended. The water of the white waterfall was split at the base by a large awning jutting out above the entrance to the North Tree Hotel. The thick scent of rain filled her chest.

She appraised the falls, where massive neon stencils of an evocative woman in the nude were colored pink and donning spills of blonde curls.

Alright, she'd hand it to her. Fiadh Night was something else.

Snaked

S omething struck Saoirse at the sight of the falls. Earlier that evening, she'd been dealing with Fanny Burns. Yes, it was Finley who finished Fanny off with his lovely stick, but the juxtaposition between the two women, Fanny and Fiadh, reminded her of something Melak had said. She wouldn't get her Whiskey until she put herself out there. Fanny couldn't even put a sliotar out there. Fiadh—well, it looked like she had problems being anywhere else. Could she be as bold as Fiadh? Her dance must really be something special. She may even have a True Whiskey of her own.

OF COURSE YOU CAN.

Hurler gave her two big thumbs-up.

She smiled. Even if she was bound for a dungeon—a Whiskey. Salm it. She'd like one.

Finley held her close. He must have sensed she was satisfied with her view of the grounds, because he started to speak as their isle continued to drift lazily upward. "My brother is under fosterage here with Madame Orla," Finley explained.

"Fosterage?"

"It's something noble and well-to-do families do. Let each other raise their kids. Goes back to the Tuatha Dé Danann. So, I only get to see him when I come to visit. I've seen him often during trials."

"That's fascinating. Don't you miss him?"

"I do, but every time I come, it's fun to catch up. He always fills me in on the best stories. Though I've not heard about butt-slam girl."

Saoirse flushed. "You can't dangle 'best stories' in front of me like that and not expect me to be interested."

"I should have known, Miss CSI: Enniskillen."

Saoirse beamed at him, glad he'd moved on.

"The barkskeeper here," Finley said, "likes to tell a story about Queen Maeve. Her husband, King Ailill, rode in on his prized bull to meet up with his friend, who'd arrived on his equally majestic cow, Donn Cúailnge."

"What did Queen Maeve ride?"

"Most of her kingdom," Finley laughed.

"What does that look like?"

Finley flushed over his dashing blue tunic. "That's a bit more difficult to explain."

She smiled as the island came to a rest, connecting to a wooden deck boasting boxes of brilliant flowers sheltered in miniature greenhouses against the winter chill. With, of course, obscene fungal gardens of nude women. This morning, she learned that several Leggies worked the House. What if a Leggy recognized her? What if they recognized Finley?

"Apparently, Maeve was green with it when she saw Daire's bull. Everyone knows it's the only thing Ailill has on her fortune. Though that's debatable, I think Maeve's got a better reputation after brute-forcing her True Whiskey during a live match."

"She is so cool." It's the reason Saoirse held Maeve in her heart as her idol. She'd like to earn her own True Whiskey. They were extremely rare, and nobody knew how to do it till it happened.

"That she is."

"Bet you'd like to steal those cows, cú."

"Not in this lifetime," he said. "The last thing our family wants is to fight the entire province of Connacht or Ulster. We're comfortable, but that's a whole different territory."

They crossed the decking, and a pair of usher boys pried open a set of large oak doors.

Anticipation built in her breast. Anticipation built in Little Hurler. Feck it, anticipation was the name of the game, the stadium, and Satirical's broadcast segment, as she waited for the doors to open.

And open they did.

"Tuatha Dé Danann," Saoirse slipped from Finley's arm to rush into Social Suicide and, more importantly, the vista.

Rival Night. This away game, this stadium was some kind of special.

Hazel Park, Social Suicide, Center Pitch Line, Ballybofey from the Precipice, and the zipper-spore shower from when she was a kid. One of them was going to have to go from her top five, because this evening she'd stepped inside the House at Social Suicide, and it was impossible not to think it'd been handcrafted by the gods.

Twenty-seven stories of pure bronze.

Saoirse threw herself against a banister to look out on the hall. She and Finley were about three-quarters of the way up the hive.

Pillars layered with carvings of kelpies and púcas dancing held each floor. Bronze banisters and balconies dripping silver, chihulooshroomdeliers, piccashroomdelabras, and endless streams of plush red Donegal carpets pulled the eye to what everyone was here to see: a stage, right there in the center of it all, lined with gold.

"Really something, huh?" Finley said as he joined her on the banister.

She wanted to drink this in. A place that'd turned from a terror to a delight. A reward for her eyes, the gods had given her for helping fix the team. "Yes."

It was impossible to take all the House in, not from one angle, not from one sitting. The majesty on display was a different beast.

"Here, let me help you." Finley took time to direct her gaze, showing the things she'd never have known, helping her make sense of all the wonder this one building contained.

On the lower levels, men and women danced together to the fanciful music that she'd heard "singing" out from the palace the first night she'd arrived. A bit above the dancers, dining levels were split by how much you wanted to spend; lavish meals the likes she'd never seen sat on every table, then on to the gambling sections and up to where they were in a special VIP level.

They were like two baby thrumblebees in a spore shower of glory.

"It's so full," Saoirse said.

"It's always packed on Fiadh Night," Finley said.

"Always?"

"But it'd be more packed for me."

"What a save."

Despite her worry about being seen by Leggies, she really liked meandering the VIP hall with Finley. He went slow—unlike Lorcan's brute-force march—though walking with either felt like showing off. Finley might not be his brother, but he was still gorgeous.

Pretty in that way she knew she was supposed to say she didn't find attractive because it made men upset—but she knew for a fact the Leggies in here working the floor would be miffed. She wondered if his Wife would be too. Was it wrong that she liked both of those outcomes?

Saoirse spent a minute marveling at how the bronze decorations looked fuller with people in their reflections before Finley steered her to a set of spiraling steps.

They climbed up one more set to the next level before stepping out onto the plush red carpets. This particular floor was rung by the kinds of fancy dining tables she'd seen that morning when she'd learned hosting.

It was all so much. She didn't know how to begin to show her gratitude. So she simply grabbed his arm and turned him to meet her. That wavy blue hair, the matching eyes—his weren't dead with just a pinprick of light, like Lorcan's had been. Finley had plenty of prick to hold on to. So she grabbed onto it, that glint of his, with her eyes, and spoke softly and meaningfully. "Thanks for letting me ride Ewe."

Finley flushed.

When a familiar voice called out, "Saoirse!" Madame Orla swept toward them.

Instantly, Saoirse pulled away. Finley's face had gone a deep crimson; based on the heat rushing through her body, she wasn't sure if she didn't match it.

"There you are." Madame Orla—snakes on full display—in a purple sequined gown rushed to greet her. "What's going on?" Her gaze shot between them.

Finley cleared his throat. "Madame Orla," he said, and bowed.

"Master Finley."

She knew him? Orla, this feckin' clam-jammer! Of course she did—the fosterage and the donors—duh. Saoirse tried to force herself out of her funk. If she hadn't shown up right then, she could have kissed Finley. She might have been about to get her little seashell shucked!

Are you trying to kill us?

Nothing else in my headcanon of <u>The Violet Intercourse</u> *has!*

Well, something tells me a good shucking is particularly dangerous!

"Saoirse?" Orla snapped her fingers.

"What, old brood?"

Finley went stiff and elbowed her in the side. "You can't say that!"

Orla whipped up a hand to silence him. "Saoirse. It's a spore shower in a whirlwind out there! The entire group of hurling trials showed up on top of two kings, with full entourages—not to mention a separate milieu of the biggest and best. On a Fiadh Night!" The Madame looked frazzled.

"They all made it?" Saoirse exchanged a look with Finley.

"Fanny wasn't lying!" Orla exclaimed.

Saoirse bit her lip. "I thought it would help them get hard."

"Saoirse..." The stress-stricken Madame pinched the bridge of her nose. "It will, but—"

"Really?" Saoirse asked. "Then why didn't you tell me about it before!?"

"Hard and hard—" Orla said.

But Finley cut in. "Actually."

"Master Finley, I—" but she cut off at the look on his face. "No."

"Yes," he assured her.

Saoirse was totally lost. This had to be more of the cryptic language around Finley's father's conjecture.

"But they're in their twenties!" Orla said.

"And this morning their sliotars were fondled," Finley explained.

"Yeah!" Saoirse jumped in, grateful to understand what was going on in their conversation, miming that morning's discovery. "I was like this with Finley's balls."

He put up a hand and clarified. "Actual sliotars."

"And—" Saoirse said, but she was cut off.

"Great goddess Danu!" Orla exclaimed. "We never thought! We insisted it couldn't be! They are too young!"

"She thought, Wives for a night," Finley said.

"I've heard enough," Orla turned back to her.

This had to be about Finley's secret information, but it sounded like she'd hit the nail on the head.

"Saoirse," said the old brood, "I didn't account for such a large influx of people."

"On a Fiadh Night?" Finley asked, as if that didn't seem likely.

Orla promptly stabbed him in the ribs with her pipe. "I didn't," she said flatly.

"I mean..." Finley's eyes grew wide. "Saoirse! It is a Fiadh Night!" He turned and grabbed Saoirse by the shoulders. "Saoirse!"

What were they hiding from her now? The pair of Finley and Orla shared a look. Oh no. No, no, no. Orla couldn't be about to do what Saoirse thought she was going to do.

"I'm sorry," Orla said. "But I'm pulling that favor I asked you. You're working a table."

She was!

THAT'S IT. IF WE DO THIS, WE'RE BAD GIRLS FOR LIFE.

Spores! Spores! Spores! What do I do? What do we do?

WE SHOULD NEVER HAVE COME HERE IN THE FIRST PLACE! I TOLD YOU.

This was awful.

Finley cut in. "Might I inquire?"

"Worry not, Master Finley." Orla winked. "They're around there."

Excitement creased his smile; he settled it down before he petted her hair. "Don't worry, Little Shroom, it's just one table, and I'll still be here. Scream, and I'll come running. I promise."

Saoirse placed a small hand on his elbow. "Thank you."

All the excitement of seeing her best-laid plans come to fruition had been zapped away. The prospect of serving a table while her teammates were in the building was not a pleasant one, let alone when there was still the matter of their Wives. What if the team saw her? This would be worse than the frock she'd been wearing at practice! A dancer passed by with her skirt considerably higher than usual.

It would be *much* worse than practice.

So much for putting yourself out there.

Little Hurler wanted to run and hide.

Orla escorted her toward the servants' steps.

Saoirse reluctantly followed. She'd just been snaked.

ERNAN'S IRON

A METAL FOR A NEW AGE

A Treacherous Table

The old brood could kill herself and die. Nothing that woman did in life would *EVER* prepare her for the sins Saoirse would set for her to slip in the Shannon!

Saoirse stared out the threshold between life and degeneracy at the ONE TABLE she had to go be a feckin' hostess for... it sat the TEAM CAPTAINS!!!

Her nostrils flared. Satirical cringed. Little Hurler thought it was hilarious.

Lorcan, Nolan, Sean, and Finley! Her Spectators were on the edge of their seats.

Was this even possible?!

"I can do this. I can do this. I can do this." Saoirse gripped her silver tray.

Stepping out after half, 'cause she's feckin' crazy, it's Saoirse!

"I can't do this."

Good.

One foot down, Saoirse changed her mind and flattened herself against the yellow wall of the servants' steps. Strumpets buzzed up and down them like flies.

She would kill Madame Orla!

Or would she? How many ways had she dreamed of doing *The Violet Intercourse* activities with the team members? She'd even done some with Lorcan and Finley, and now she was getting to serve them Whiskey! In a dress!

Nope! Nope! Nope!

You shouldn't do this. Fanny's here, and think of the Wives. If you make this play and miss the table like this morning, we all end up in a dungeon for the rest of our lives! This could be sabotage charges—and without the match-fixing, the county needs you to give them a second chance! Satirical said.

But Saoirse was distracted by Little Hurler dancing in her heart, full booty shake, ready for action. Why did her heart always want to go where her head thought was dangerous?

She didn't have to go out there. As long as Fiadh's dance worked, the boys would be hard—even Orla thought it'd work now—she'd be freed from her death pact thanks to Finley's stave. She'd go to a dungeon without being violated. Without being turned into one of *those women*. She couldn't do this. And not her after being in this dress!

Orla'd given it to her. A Social Suicide Éirish step-dance style solo dress. Except black as the dominant color with pink frills—the mark of a girl working VIP. It had a daring cape off both shoulders, with ogham for Social Suicide. Belled-out pleats in the front, matching hard shoes, and pink poodle socks. There'd been no time to do her hair in curls, and worse... the world could see her knees!

THEY'LL SEE MORE THAN THAT IF YOU'RE NOT CAREFUL.

She 'soloed' another sneaky peek around the edge of the archway.

Roll. Lean off the wall. Peek. *Yup. I'm fecked. Roll.* Lean back on the wall. Freak. *Nope. Why?*

Her skull throbbed, nerves playing rock-water-spore with the idea of actually doing this. But how was she supposed to walk up to that table with any shred of dignity left in her soul?

What do I do?

YOU GET YOUR BUTT BACK DOWN THE STAIRS BEFORE YOU TAKE THIS SLIPPERY SLOPE TO STRUMPET CITY.

But the team.

Feck the team, Saoirse. <u>The Violet Intercourse</u> *starts tomorrow at midnight. If you don't go to PÉNIS before, then even if the boys do get hard, they won't get a second chance. And you'll... we'll...*

Saoirse hugged her silver tray to her chest.

A daring Little Hurler broke out the pom-poms, an encouraging grin on her oversized face. She'd swapped into her own Social Suicide step-dance dress but kept the fanciful burlesque accouterments.

Yes, she'd promised she'd get the team new Wives for a night. She just never dreamed one of them would be her! She'd never had that nightmare either.

I COULD BE A WIFE PART-TIME, Satirical mocked her. *AN ADJUNCT PET.*

She peeked around the corner one more time, scanning the floor, when something else caught her eye. The donors were here—and talking to Fanny Burns! Of course, the investigator would be here and accosting the donors again. Her ploy with Finley earlier would have sent her on the rounds. What if she came to sabotage her attempt to fix the team? The investigator only promised to wait to arrest her.

WHAT DO WE DO?

We find out what they're talking about.

Little nodded.

THIS IS A BAD IDEA.

And challenge her to a Rite of Ritual Hurling if we have to.

YOU CAN'T BEAT THE INVESTIGATOR, YOU ALREADY KNOW THAT!

I have to try.

A psych-up song. That's what she needed—Saoirse hummed softly—an absolute stadium banger.

She's the Celtic Tiger!
In the pub every night.
Rising up to the drinking of her rival.
He's a clúrachán, and he's down half a pint
And he's watching as she takes him on!
Celtic Tiger.

Let's do this.

Let's not.

"One. Two."

FINE. AND STEPPING OUT AFTER HALF, IT'S SAOIRSE!

"Two..."

STEPPING OUT, ANY TIME NOW...

"Two..."

Taking to the pitch, Rival Night and all...

"Two..."

THANK THE GODS SHE'S GROWN A BRAIN, FOLKS.

Saoirse almost stopped, but her heart cheered her forward. Saoirse popped through the arch—***Finley twitched!!!*** "Tuatha Dé Danann!" Saoirse immediately dove for the ground on the other side. Shite! Had he recognized her? Had he seen?

HAD HE EVEN TURNED ALL THE WAY AROUND, FOLKS?

Shite, shite, shite! Great gods, that had been close! Finley *almost* turned her way! He definitely at least moved.

She tucked behind a small potted tree. She'd been so confident after singing Celtic Tiger, but she couldn't do this. They couldn't see her until the last second. That was the 'rule of the reveal' that she'd just made up.

YOU SHOULD REMAIN ON THE BENCH.

I should hire new color commentary.

The tables at VIP were really spaced out. The donors' table was dressed in a fancy black tablecloth and golden dinnerware, but it was a ways away, with only one large ugly púca statue to hide behind.

A trickster fae. How fitting.

BETTER THAN ANOTHER NAKED MUSHROOM GIRL.

She'd like to hear what Fanny was up to before challenging her. They could see her if she went now. She'd have to wait for a good moment.

Hiding behind her tray, Saoirse watched as girls zipped up and down the aisle in various states of undress, trying to plan her maneuver with a distraction.

Let them make space so I can score.

Her head spun when one woman jogged past with her skirt halfway up her thighs! Tuatha Dé Danann.

Wait, her own skirt was halfway up her thighs! Tuatha Dé Danann!

I SEE ULSTER, I SEE MUNSTER, I SEE RIGHT UP HER UNDER—

Satirical!

JUST SAYING. THAT'S GOING TO BE US AT THIS RATE.

It already is.

AN DAGDA, THE GOOD GOD, FORGIVE US SAOIRSE'S SINS, AS SHE FORGIVES THOSE SHE PUTS AGAINST US!

Really?

CAST A NET ON ME. AT LEAST ONE OF US IS TRYING TO ENSURE WE DON'T DROWN WHEN WE HAVE TO SWIM THE SHANNON!

With a half-stand-squat maneuver, leaning against the wall, Saoirse worked her dress over her knees and down her calves so her legs were pinned to her chest—thankful for whatever absurdly stretchy material the side panels were made from. The result was probably something like a particularly fat, ugly, giant leprechaun, but she didn't care.

She kept a keen eye on Fanny.

Despite the overwhelming atmosphere, her instructions had been simple:

- Get their orders—Well, she'd skipped that part.

- Go to the bar—Not likely.

- Get the drinks

- Do what they'd practiced this morning.

- Do not engage in a lap dance.

SHE'S ADDED THAT LAST RULE HERSELF, FOLKS.

No shite.

All of which seemed so much easier when she thought the table would be full of strangers.

The captains kept glancing toward the servant's portal. Spores. She was making them wait—the mark of a terrible hostess.

Sorry, boys.

At that moment, one of the Leggies—the one they called Sinead, because everybody could tell she had "different legs"—sauntered up the middle walk with more swagger in her hips than a full-back with a twelve-point average.

It was the distraction Saoirse needed.

Pom-poms pushed her to go, go, go! Still crunched up, dress pinning her legs to her chest like a veggie sack of shame, Saoirse weeble-wobbled her way down the wall, tray held between her and the open floor like a shield.

Fanny and the donors didn't look Saoirse's way; they were distracted by the just... spores... the fattest ass on the planet.

IT IS KINDA ABSURD.

Thanks, Sinead.

With a final huff, she managed to plant herself behind the púca statue. It wasn't exactly her best solo, but she was in scoring position. Unfortunately, her arrival marked Fanny's departure.

Shite!

The back of the investigator's head caught in the shroomdeliers. Saoirse counted her lucky sliotars she'd headed past the bar and away from the team. She wouldn't have to challenge her to a Rite of Ritual Hurling.

"Saoirse?" asked the jovial voice of Ernán, the thin hurley-like donor.

Her stomach dropped straight through her good intentions.

"That is you!"

Saoirse waddled off the wall and the rest of the way to the table. "Sup, cú."

"What are you doing down there? Pretending to be a púca?" He laughed and slapped his knee.

"No," Saoirse admitted.

Banba peeked out from behind him, caught sight of her, and promptly retreated.

"Must be a new crazy dance, then." He slapped his knee again. "It's chance we should be meeting, but I'll take the opportunity to tell you something."

She eyed him over the tray.

"There's been a vote tonight. Just now, in fact. We, donors, have decided that if the County Tyrconnell Hurling Club does not prove it has adequate players tomorrow night, we won't even bother with the PÉNIS investigation. We'll just fold."

"WHAT?!"

"I'm sorry," Ernán said. "I know you're working hard to prove your innocence. But it's been agreed. Besides, this way, even if you are a Bad Girl," he leered at her for a beat as if trying to see if she'd break, "you'll get off for free."

"No..."

"It's true."

"But the team is about to get hard!" she spluttered.

Ernán turned bright red. "Well," he cleared his throat, "be that as it may... gracious child. I am sorry. I just figured you'd like to know."

And just like that, he turned back to Banba and resumed his conversation, leaving Saoirse stranded—heart hollow, spirits bruised. Her confidence had just taken a penalty-worthy blow, and yet the ref offered no red card.

By tomorrow?

NO. STOP. DON'T EVEN THINK ABOUT IT. PÉNIS DUNGEON, REMEMBER?

She let her head thunk back against the wall. Little Hurler put a hand on her heart. A warm touch that helped some. Satirical was off the mark this time. She hadn't yet come to understand.

Saoirse peered through a gap in the tables to her captains. Look at those happy faces. They'd brought their hurleys and were sword-fighting with their wood, smacking each other and laughing. They had no idea.

Hurler looked at her with pleading eyes.

WHAT DO YOU MEAN? WHAT DON'T I UNDERSTAND?

In one fell swoop, the world had given her an escape route. If she got the team's magic back, then sabotaged the trials tomorrow, not only would she be free, declared a Good Girl, she'd be free of her geas. It would only cost her and everyone else their entire way of life.

Fiadh Nic Gallchobhair

N o girl could make this choice. No girl was strong enough to cast aside her whole society, to throw away her Color, her friends, her family, her pride. If Saoirse made that choice, she would be free and alive.

Saoirse sat on the floor, leaning against the bar, reeling from the news. The hive seemed darker now. Strumpets pranced up and down the floor, waiting tables in their black step-dance dresses with pink frills, pink poodle socks casting shadows; the dancing púcas and the kelpies carved on the columns between the floors looked like they'd decided to rest for the night; across the way she saw Sinead giving the bard from the Den a lap dance; she didn't even have the strength to be aghast. This was the worst news she'd gotten since her father had been arrested. If Tyrconnell collapsed, the only way to win his freedom would be by winning the All-Éire as part of Tyrone. If she even dared wear the white and red, she knew her father—he'd commit suicide, and so would she.

WHICH ARE YOU GOING TO CHOOSE?

Her choice had been so much easier when she thought she was guaranteed to die.

The unmistakable voice of Leggy Two shouted, "Wow!"

Saoirse perked up but stayed crouched. Was Two working the bar? "Leggy Two!" she hissed and popped up to peek just over the counter. It was Two.

But Two, who was busy with some other girls, pointed excitedly at the special premier seating surrounding the golden stage. "Fianna! Look!"

Two men in green armor and green capes embroidered with a large insignia of a deer took their seats. With them: two dark-skinned men in large white masks covering their mouths.

"Foreigners," Two explained to the other girls.

They should go back where they came from.

"Gross," a girl said. "I hate pretending foreigners shouldn't die."

Saoirse agreed.

"They really do have to wear them," she heard Two say, probably talking about the strange masks.

One of the other servers squealed. "Ooh. Kingsmen!"

Another group of men in formal attire, like Finley's, filled a row near the Fianna.

Tuatha Dé, shroom showers, and bear shite. The king's own guard is here?

FIADH'S OVERCOMPENSATING.

Saoirse shrugged. What *did* Fiadh have to do to draw a crowd like this?

"Hey, Silly Saoirse. Whatcha doing down there?"

She looked up to the innocent buck-toothed face of her new friend. "Hey, Two."

Two glanced toward the hurling table. "The boys ain't looking. You can stand."

"You knew?"

"It's my job," she said. "What's got you rattled? You know, beyond the obvious?"

Queasy knots filled her stomach. "I'd rather not say. Where's Hater?"

Two pointed to the top of the House, way up on the twenty-seventh floor. Little Hurler's eyes had turned into tiny hearts. She followed her heart's intention to the stage.

A series of small floating islands stuck with bronze poles hovered at various levels above the stage, and on those poles, women soared—dancing and spinning in lewd combinations of elegance and grace—and, thighs be salmed! They were in lingerie!

"Great Goddess Danu," she said.

She peeked over the tray. Being that high up was brave, but being in those clothes? Performing like this on the twenty-seventh floor with nothing but skill and a small lace panel between a girl and two different kinds of eternity. She squinted up at the highest pole in amazement and realized she knew those arms!

Tuatha Dé Danann! She gawked. "It's Hater!"

The leggy Daughter of Dagda dazzled under a series of chandeliers that dripped diamonds and daring. Light spilled across her legs; glitter shimmered in her cleavage. She was beyond alluring.

AND A DOWN BAD STRUMPET!

Hater's every spin was a yellow card. Her every twirl was an open goal—An Dagda. There was being sensual, then there was being a pole—A poler? Polarizer? Polacious skankacious? No, that'd be the Druidic term.

A hoe.

Little Hurler snickered.

See, there's no way you could do anything like that. Let's just get out of here.

In that moment, she realized Satirical was wrong—wrongish. She could do this. She wasn't like Hater, but compared to *that*, all she had to do was serve some drinks, and no matter what conclusion Saoirse came to, in both futures, the boys *had* to be hard.

Saoirse shook both her and her heart out of their trance and tore her gaze away from Hater's upside-down stripper splits—*so not the drama.*

"Beautiful, huh?" Two asked; she'd been watching her watch Hater.

"Yes." She found herself admitting. "Leader?"

"So doesn't work the House; her father's rich enough to pay the room and board costs. Now, buzz." It was a demand. "Buzz." Two held out her arms. "You can't go over there like this. You need a buzz."

Saoirse rolled her eyes, smiling, but offered her hands and let Two buzz her.

The quirky dancer began shaking violently, vibrating with good vibes, passing that frequency to her. With a smile, Saoirse joined the shaking, laughing till her smile was honest.

"Thankfully," Two said, "they all just want one thing."

"What?"

"Whiskey." They both giggled at the implication, though she had the distinct impression they were laughing for subtly different reasons. Two loaded her tray with four Waterford crystal goblets.

Saoirse took a deep breath. Everything would be fine as long as she didn't miss the table.

AGAIN.

Feck off, Satirical.

A laughing Little Hurler reset her head. It had been kind of funny. She didn't even want to imagine what kind of penalty Orla would tack on to the play if she repeated the mistake. A free puck for Social Suicide? Benched? Or beat like Wife Bob?

"Hey," Two said. "Tipp or Kill."

"What?"

"It's a little saying, Hater, and I made up," Two said. "Make sure they tip, or I'll have to crutch over there and kill them."

"Oh." Saoirse picked up the silver tray of drinks. "I thought it would be for something like Tipperary and Kilkenny."

"This ain't hurling." Two winked.

"No. I guess it's not." *I can do this.*

Her 'pitch' was set: a carpeted aisle that separated two rows of tables, those on the lower inside track up against a bronze safety rail, and a similar circle against the outside of the hive raised halfway to the ceiling. Tiny mushrooms set into the floor helped light the way in the darkness. The boys' table was on the lower inside track.

Thanks to Little's school, she checked both ways before stepping into the aisle. This whole ordeal seemed oddly similar to launching off a jump shroom, and she wasn't interested in being taken out by a rogue fly—or, in their case, a stripper.

Then it happened. All the lights winked out in the hive. The music stopped—

It was Fiadh time.

Men cheered like they'd lost their minds.

The goblets rattled. Spores she was shaking with it. The lights came back on. Then pulsed again.

"Saoirse," Two hissed.

Saoirse hustled back to the bar and set her tray down. Unable to tear her eyes from the stage, she found herself more excited than she'd been in ages. Fiadh Night. Rival Night. The best dancer in Social Suicide, queen thrumblebee of Rath Hoe! Right here, right now, she'd find out if her plan paid off—if she was right.

The lights pulsed on and off again to alert the crowd.

"Get on the box," Two said.

She gave Two just enough attention to see where she was pointing and climbed atop an oak Whiskey barrel to an eruption of sound.

Come on, Fiadh!

Little Hurler pressed vision-enhancing lenses to her face.

The Spectators jumped up and down with hope.

The House lights shut completely, and spotlights flicked on—beams crisscrossing over the stage to intense music. A magnified voice spoke to the crowd:

"Are you ready?!"

The crowd screamed.

"Are you ready?!"

Again, screamed.

Saoirse couldn't help being drawn in by the music. The dazzling lights. She had a perfect view. For feck's sake, she was getting more hyped than for the Tyrconnell hurling team!

"You've been waiting."

The voice rumbled around the arena.

"You've been wanting. Now be willing."

All around the hive, men grabbed coins and held them to the banisters.

"It's time to Rock the Rainbow!"

A hissing sound, almost drowned by the music, caught her attention. Magic rainbows of mist arced from every banister in the building down to large cauldrons that surrounded the stage. Was this Fiadh's Whiskey or something else? The rainbows solidified. Men whooped and let free their coins of copper, tin, and bronze; they rolled down the banisters, onto the rainbows, and into the pots below.

Saoirse bit her lip. This was how far the gap was between her and Fiadh? Fiadh hadn't even taken the stage and was already making money? Ridiculous.

The spotlights went out. The hive darkened once more—black save the tiny emergency lightshrooms lining the walkways as the music changed to something strange.

Thump-thump.

Not jig music like she'd been practicing to, or the up-tempo fiddling they played on men's and women's dance nights. No. This was... a beat—pounding, hard, heavy on big drum hits, with fanciful bronze dord horns, and the vocals of one nasty bard.

Spectators shook it in Spirit Stadium. It was nothing like Saoirse had ever heard before, even at Beltany Circle. It must have been music special to the House—House Music. The Leggies who qualified for Fiadh's show pranced across the stage in lingerie. Saoirse flushed terribly but tried counting the beats as she'd practiced with Leggy Two. One, thump, three, thump. One, thump, three, thump-thump. Drum hits on two and four. How could anybody step-dance to this?

The music cut.

Drum roll.

She leaned in. She wasn't the only one. The woman next to her leaned forward, as did the rest of the crowd.

The Leggies danced off the stage.

Lightshrooms flooded the stage with an array of dazzling colors. They panned the hype. The voice returned:

> "She's fighting spores by daylight.
> Finding love by moonlight.
> Always dancing through the night.
> She's the one you've been waiting 'fair'.
> She's Fiadh Nic Gallchobhair!"

The array of lights fell out to five spotlights at center stage. Was Fiadh going to dance as a shadow? No. She was going to come out of the feckin' ground!

Fiadh rose to the stage through a black square! A black feckin' square, cú!

Saoirse's nostrils flared in alarm. Her rival was in some kind of dress!

An Éirish step-dance solo dress, sure, but only in the most kindly sense—ornamental with intricate designs. Pink. Sequined. The dress belled out in flat pleats in the front, a cape off one shoulder. Painfully beautiful on her. It didn't show her arms, it didn't show her cleavage, but what it did show were her entire legs! That wasn't a taste. That was a whole-ass feast! And her hair! A voluminous spill of perfect, tight, blond curls—with a crown. Spores! There was being a strumpet; then there was being just plain pretentious!

The music paused.

For a second, the star was silent.

A universe waiting for her taps to begin.

And boy, was that pause milked.

Men, eager. The bar women fanned themselves, Hurler hanging onto her collarbone like she might slip—the Fianna in their green and gold capes, the foreigners with their bug eyes and wild white mouths, the Kingsmen, and all the rest, pulled in by the gravity of the goddess of beauty. Till a single man broke the silence with a squeak.

Fiadh whipped her head to the sound, "Hmph," And tapped her toe. The clack from her hard shoes reverberated through the House. Fiadh led them with her feet.

Tap. Tap. Tap.

Clap.

Fiadh's quick taps were answered by a single loud response from the building.

> The bard sang, "Dancing in the green. Uhn."

Tap. Tap. Tap.

> "I said Fiadh is a queen. Uhn!"

Tap. Tap. Clap.

> "Dancing in the green."

Saoirse felt it in her chest.

> "I say bow and scrape ya knees."

She started clapping with the rest.

> "I said dancing in the green. Please!"

Tap. Pause. Tap!

Fiadh froze.

One hard shoe pointed to the stage. "Hmph." Her soft scoff nonetheless carried the entire building. "Boys."

Silence.

"Music!" Fiadh snapped.

"Give it up for Fee, she's a dancing machine!"

The song exploded back to full sound.

Thump. Thump. Thump-thump!

Saoirse tried to understand, but Fiadh didn't break into step dance as she'd expected. Instead, she walked—no, she didn't walk. She demanded the stage move under her hard shoes as she strumpeted around the circle, caressing men with her feet, flirting with more than just danger.

Spores, sex appeal wasn't something Fiadh had. It was something Fiadh was. She was unfair. There wasn't a rivalry. There wasn't even a fight. Just when Saoirse thought she couldn't get any better—

The goddess began to dance.

Thump-thump.

Hip, bump. Tap, slump. Sultry, sexy, jig-step slay. Slide, dip. Boys hit-hit. Click—heel. Click—knee. Tap. Sashay.

Tuatha Dé, shroom showers, and absolute Sluts! Fiadh pranced in combinations of sexy, modern, and step-dance styles in one.

Saoirse forced her eyes off the woman she'd branded a rival in what was obviously very undue hubris. Behind her, all around, and across the stage, no eye in the place was anywhere but on Fiadh. Even the other dancers stared, enraptured by the seductive skinful display the curly blond-haired strumpet used to dominate not only the stage but the crowd as well. How was she not afraid of the attention?

Saoirse tried following the moves.

Just as she thought she'd caught on, the cadence changed.

Thump-thump.

Breasts, jumps, jiggles, pumps—put Éirish step-dance in her play. Clicks. Kicks. Body—stiff, broken up with sexy legs.

She added real step dance. Perfection! Exquisite, exceptional leaps! She could jump to the gods' blessed sky! Saoirse couldn't help but wonder if they'd hidden tiny jump shrooms in the stage or if Fiadh could just do that.

Kicks to her face! Her feckin' face, cú! Fine. She gave. The score is, was, and always had been Saoirse nil-nil, Fiadh infinity. Her embarrassment at posing as a terrible hostess washed away in the music and epic bard vocals. Saoirse grooved—she couldn't help it—caught between being mesmerized by Fiadh and realizing that she, Saoirse, really did belong in the corner.

The black square appeared on the stage once more, and a bronze spinning pole grew from the center. Saoirse shook her head. The coins just didn't stop falling. She was too good.

Fiadh leaned. She teased the pole. And her dance elevated once again.

Rump. Pump. Whip. Dump. Drop it low and bring it slow. High kicks. Silver clicks. Fiadh worked her nasty show.

Backs could bend like that? Gods, the men in the front row could see right up her dress! That better be a skort. This was unbelievable!

"Fiadh! Fiadh! Fiadh!" they cheered, chanting her name. Fiadh changed to a slow stride to center stage. Her pole disappeared. She stopped dead center. The music dropped to a slow build, drums only, and she turned her back to Saoirse's section of the crowd. The men roared.

Something was coming.

The stage spun slowly as if to show off a living doll. Fiadh took one hand and slipped it up her skirt to her hip with a sly smile, then paused. Saoirse put a hand in front of her face—deathly embarrassed. She cracked a finger to keep watching. Fiadh slipped her other hand to her waist and added a faux face of shock, like, 'Did I do that?'

Saoirse could see it, but she couldn't believe it. This woman was insane!
The strumpet hooked her thumbs around the waistband of her panties.
This could not be happening.
The crowd choked on their anticipation.
This could not be happening!
The drums cut.
What kind of woman!?
Bent at the waist.
No way!
And commit Social Suicide.
One moment—and Fiadh Nic Gallchobhair stole every man in the building.
The 'Wild Lover of Strangers.'
Saoirse could never compete.

Hostess with the Mostest

The opposition scores, and scores, and scores again! So much for Saoirse vs. Fiadh! This is as one-sided as watching the Rebels play County Dúlamán's U12 camogie.

Fiadh's got one fine Whiskey, folks! And by Whiskey, this announcer means she's got the poom-poom of power, the razzled pizzazler of pretty gazzazlers, the dazzled razzler of zazzled mazzlers—that is to say, she's got one wet vagina, folks. And it's got sequins!

That it did.

This show is sponsored by viewers like you. Seriously, I don't think that strumpet would do it without the coins.

So that was a Social Suicide? Saoirse huffed as Fiadh let all pretense drop—along with everything else—and began dancing in nothing but socks and hard shoes.

Talk about giving it socks.

Proper deadly.

Her traitorous Little Hurler tried to tuck her pom-poms behind her back.

You can cheer if you want to.

Saoirse leaned against the wall. She wouldn't.

I guess that means Faidh told you the tr—

SHUT THE FUCK UP, SATIRICAL!

Who'd have thought such a woman as Fiadh could exist?—a girl comfortable being naked in front of an audience. She'd had trouble taking off a jacket when she was wearing five layers, and not just physically. She may never get over prancing in front of all the hurlers like a baby deer. Yet here was a girl who didn't give a damn what her Color or anybody else thought of her.

Fiadh wasn't just *a* stripper. She was *the* stripper.

Coin after coin rolled down into the cauldrons below.

Lorcan, Finley, Sean, and Nolan all had their eyes glued to the treasure at the end of the rainbows. And—Great gods!

THEY WERE HARD!!!

The hurleys they'd been sword-fighting with just before the show—their game hurleys—glowed, twitching and trembling with bright white magical power! They were fit to blow! Ready to explode with excitement! Pop off for pride! Their mojo was maxed! Their flaccid flow fixed!!

Take that, donors! It'd worked!!!

Saoirse made the Shamrock, whispering a prayer to her gods, and her backup gods, and any rogue deities willing to stabilize a tray of beer. Thank you! Still standing on the oak barrel, Saoirse exhaled, falling back against the wall.

ARE YOU GONNA GO PLAY HOSTESS WITH THE MOST-EST?

Was she? She was. Fiadh was impressive, but watching her show, seeing what it really meant to 'commit Social Suicide,' it wasn't the girl Saoirse wanted to be. She loved the team. She loved Tyrconnell, even if it meant a slow death in a dungeon.

BETTER MAKE IT COUNT WHILE WE'RE STILL OUTSIDE, THEN.

All she had to do now was walk over and celebrate with them. She could handle that. Saoirse hopped off the barrel and grabbed her silver tray of drinks, but her feet remained firmly planted. This would be so much easier if she weren't in this revealing dress. Heels together. Toes apart. Shoulders back. Chest tall. Saoirse squeezed her silver serving tray and counted herself in. "Five, six, seven, eight."

"Hello, Saoirse-tron," a sinister voice mewled beside her.

Saoirse jerked in a panic, barely keeping the drinks up before, coming face to face with Wife Prime.

Shite!

Not just Prime, but The Fun Wife, The Third, Wife Four, Wife Bob, and more. She'd forgotten about the Wives!

"Two?" Saoirse squeaked, but Two was nowhere to be seen.

"Prepare for headaches." Prime seized her by the hair.

Saoirse moaned in pain.

"'Cause we'll give you some," said the Fun Wife, with a punch to the gut.

"You can't fight us," The Third said, stepping on her foot.

Wife Four sneered. "What are you, dumb?"

Saoirse reeled from her attack, coughing, holding her ribs.

"Our husbands can't get hard without our permission," said Prime.

"You can't bake your sourdough up in our kitchens!" Wife Bob slapped her.

"Prime."

"The Fun Wife."

"We won't even play hurling," said Wife Four.

The Third added, "You'll just catch your death."

"You couldn't beat one Wife," The Fun Wife said.

Then they all spoke together: "And we've brought the rest!"

They grabbed for her. Saoirse screamed. They wrenched her off the wall.

"Ladies?" Prime asked. "Let's say hi to our husbands."

Please no.

Saoirse was marched down the bar, then across the aisle.

Danu, An Dagda, Manannán, An Morrígan, please. No.

Give her defenders. Give her a hurley. Give her any table but those filled with those she loved.

The Wives cackled.

The boys' elated faces didn't help.

Finley spotted her first. His jaw dropped to the table. He elbowed Nolan. Nolan spun Sean. Sean slapped Lorcan.

They all stared.

She deserved this...

The Wives halted at the base of the table. Saoirse couldn't bring herself to look.

"Say the line," Prime sneered.

"Say it," echoed the Wives.

Saoirse opened her mouth. "W-we-welcome to Social Suicide!"

The Wives collectively threw her up on the table, where she sent it, herself, and everything else crashing to the ground.

Twenty-Seven!

Lorcan got drenched. Sean leaped in time but fell over in his chair, crashing into another hostess. Nolan got most of the table. Only Finley made it out in time.

For a moment that lasted a lifetime, the entire Hive was silent, save for the derisive laughter of the Wives.

And then—Saoirse saw it. Her captain's hurleys went dun.

Everybody stared now. Saoirse wanted to curl into a ball, to hide, to cry. There was no way out now—not from her geas, not from her time in the dungeons. She'd be sentenced both as a girl and a Violet. She'd be violated, *violated, VIOLATED!* And all for naught.

Twenty-Seven!

The Wives simply would not stop laughing.

"Finley?" If ever she needed her friend, it was now.

He glanced at her, then looked away.

The bottom fell right out of Spirit Stadium; the Spectators cried.

"My Wife was right," he said. "You are just a stunt."

A sharp stab through her chest. Betrayed.

Stay down, Twenty-Seven!

No. I can still save it. The spilled drinks. The shattered table. She could... she could... give Lorcan a lap dance. "That would help, right? Haha."

No! Me don't!

Saoirse crossed the distance, barely aware of her aching feet, of her soaked clothes. Other women gave them. They said men liked them.

"What are you doing?" Lorcan growled. "Don't."

She turned her back to him and placed a hand on each knee. The Wives howled with laughter.

"I said, don't!" he bellowed—then threw her. Not just off him, but into a pile of passersby. They toppled to the ground.

You deserve this.

You should never have stepped outside.

You should've listened to the Magic Eight Ball.

An usher rushed—not to help her, but to help the others she'd crashed into to their feet. Saoirse offered a stream of frantic apologies. This couldn't possibly get worse. The team? Her gods!

"What was that?" asked a wizened, balding man whose robes shimmered like they were made of actual gold. "A bark troll?"

"Do not blame the girl, Mac Da Thó," came an oily voice. Another man rose slowly to his feet, brushing himself off. His hair was long and greasy, his skin sallow, his robes more black and slick than a kelpie mane. "She was thrown."

Mac Da Thó eyed the table. "Of course. County Tyrconnell hurlers. I'd be drunk and angry too if I was that terrible." He popped the collar of his robes. "My apologies, girl."

Saoirse locked eyes with the greasy man.

He stared at her intently, like he could cut through her with a glance. Then, with a flick of his wrist, he turned to escort the man called Mac Da Thó. "Come, let's not let terrible sportsmen ruin our night. Tell me more of this lovely pig of yours, and the wonderful feast you're thinking of having."

"I never said anything about a feast, Bricriu."

Saoirse waited until the pair slipped out of earshot before hustling for the exit.

But she was seized by Lorcan. "Why?" he asked. Pain colored his voice, strain trapped in his yellow eyes.

Her mouth went dry.

The wounded wolf had returned, crumbled rock reforming around her shield. "No. Your required time ends tonight. As of this moment, you're removed from trials!"

Something cracked inside her soul.

"Little Gale?" Fanny sneered behind her, her hands twirling a pair of fuzzy pink cuffs. "Looks like your plan is up."

"Thanks for the tip, Fanny," said Prime.

She met her captain's pained expression, horrified as the spark of light died in Lorcan's eyes.

"I guess I don't need to ride you to your climax. I'm closing your case early. Saoirse Storm, you are hereby under arrest."

She heard the chink of chains—and she ran.

The Violet Intercourse

S aoirse left the House, sprinted through the fung-tanical gardens, and right through the Carnal Carnival. It wasn't until she got to the garden outside the North Tree Hotel, where she'd sat with Finley what seemed an age ago, that she slowed to walk. The flower box was still missing from where he'd pulled it off the window. *Finley...*

At the entrance, Saoirse turned for a sweeping pathway carved into the trunk. It sloped upward, and she had a hunch where it ended. It's not like she knew any better place to hide, so she climbed. The path turned back and forth on itself. From what she could gather, it seemed to be meant for the gardeners who took care of the fungi that backlit the waterfall. She could see how different effects were made by placing large caps over different colors. This fat, bright pink mushroom was probably part of the massive naked Fiadh's thigh.

The image of Fiadh facing forward, thrusting her hips out, hands flat against her pelvis like she had something to showcase, had been worth the climb—all because Saoirse had spied a stupid bench, and it was exactly what she needed: a pagoda right inside the lips of the giant Fiadh's vagina. A fanny in which to await her arrest by another one.

She took a seat on a fanciful bench.

Hurler joined her, uprooting a goal-net from her pitch and flipping it on its side so she could lie in the net like a hammock and stare out her chest with her.

From here, she could see the Pink and Brown Districts near the House, the Red Light District, and... and...

The tears came, and she couldn't stop them. She choked on what she'd never wanted to admit.

Fiadh hadn't lied. She was right.

She was... Saoirse was... going to get gang raped.

Twenty-Seven...

Saoirse slipped from the bench, burying her face in the seat, banging it with her fist. She'd tried. Spores, she'd tried. The positivity, the insistence she'd like it—! She wasn't going to make it! She wasn't going to fulfill the geas! And she was too afraid to die!

"AAAAAAAAAAAAAAAAAAAAAAAAAARGH!"

"AAAAAAAAAAAAAAAAAAAAAAAAAAAAAAAAAAAAAAAAAAAAAAAAAAH!"

The Violet Intercourse? Triple K bound little girls to a death pact to get raped. Raped and raped and raped!

She slammed her fists into the bench over and over again.

That woman—the one who'd been crying, the one who'd been *violated*—she hadn't been taken to the Library of Lived Experience. They hadn't put her in a Gratitude Circle, hadn't had her say her truth, hadn't had her say 'thank you for holding me to account.'

They'd held her to account. Triple K had held her to account.

That woman had been killed.

Queen of denial? Of course she was the queen of fucking denial—fuck Satirical. It wasn't her body. She wasn't the one going through with this. She wasn't the one with one more day. She wasn't the one who had to keep up a fake brave face. She wasn't the one about to be taken and claimed!

For the first time in an age, the geas—the death pact—coalesced into a trickle on the back of her hand. All she'd had to do was get them hard, get the magic working, and Triple K was bound to remove her geas—but with her hostess fiasco and the Wives... there was no magic. There was none. No proof.

Little Hurler sobbed in her heart, squeezing it as if she could hug the pain out of the truth out of reality. Move them to a new star where they weren't in this shite.

"You really made me crutch all the way up here, huh?" said a cheery voice.

"Two..." Saoirse turned to see her friend.

Two threw her crutches on the back of the bench and aggressively hopped around, slamming into her and pulling her into a hug. "Hater, move your ass!"

Moments later, Hater came sprinting into view, took one look at her, "Saoirse," and threw her arms around her.

"What's going on?" asked Two.

Saoirse flexed her geas hand.

Neither of them said anything. They didn't have to.

Olives and Cheese

I *always knew it was true. If I didn't, I wouldn't have crashed out.*

THEN WHY ACT LIKE THAT THE WHOLE TIME?
What would you have me do? Sit there in self-loathing? Cry? Worry? None of that would have helped us solve our geas. Problems only get bigger if you focus on them, Sat.
NOW?
It doesn't matter. My one chance to fix the team is passed. I made a deal with Fanny. I'm getting booked for sabotage without the match-fixing. It's done.
YOU AND I BOTH KNOW IT'S NOT DONE. OR IS THIS SOME MORE 'DEFINITELY NOT AVOIDING THE PROBLEM' NONSENSE?

Saoirse sat in the middle of the bench with her knees pulled to her chest. Two hards. One for hurling, one for sex—everything PÉNIS-related just 'extended' the joke.

"I still can't believe it," Leader said. "I mean to say, erectile dysfunction? They are all in their twenties."

"You know, Saoirse," Hater said, "if you step back from the Violet for a second, it is kind of funny you ended up trying to fix the magic on the one team where hard and hard were the same thing."

It didn't feel funny.

"Cheese?" Two offered her a platter full of little cubes and spreadable kinds. Leader brought it with her from the kitchens.

The waterfall gushed past their vagina.

Hurler, in the fetal position, rocked in her hammock. The Spectators were not even excited for the cheese—they'd been down in the dumps. Tonight was supposed to be fun, Rival Night; now it was like she'd not just lost the match, but the season.

"Don't worry," Leader said, "Orla is following all the appropriate blocking procedures. Fanny will be forced to submit soon."

"Why?"

Leader popped some cheese into her mouth. "Beats me. She seems to think you've found some answer."

Some answer indeed.

Hater huffed with faux shock. "A Rebel poshlette speaking with her mouth full?" she asked, and got a "Suck these olives, Premier," in response—and an olive to the face.

Saoirse stared absently at Social Suicide.

Two asked again, "Cheese?"

She took one.

The Leggy Trio, engaged in idle prattle—lots of "did you see her tonights?" and "that lipsticks," and "not in her color wheels."

I offered to do strip hurling, and I've fondled their balls, and gave Lorcan PÉNIS therapy! I should never have been in those situations.

AND YET YOU ALWAYS FOUND A WAY.

She didn't have an answer for Satirical. She didn't want to think about the fact that it could be true, but... well, what if it was?

YOU'VE ALWAYS BEEN MORE INTO THE VIOLET INTERCOURSE *THAN MOST WOMEN. FOR FECK'S SAKE, YOU HAVE A WHOLE SONG AND DANCE NUMBER CALLED 'I WANT TO SCORE.'*

That churned her stomach. She took another piece of cheese.

"You know," Two said, joining her on the bench, "they had to change the name of it from charcuterie board to the Girls' Dinner Cheese Platter on the menu. It's basically the only thing any of the Leggies order from the kitchens. Though we have to get ours with triple extra olives 'cause Hater is a fiend."

"They're delicious!" she shouted from on top of Leader.

"I've never had an olive. Are they also a dick joke?"

"No, it's just an olive," said Two.

Saoirse took one of the small green spores from the platter and tried it out. The pungent taste stuck to the roof of her mouth. It was... alright. Saoirse grabbed another piece of cheese, but no olive this time. She'd alternate between cheese and cheese with olive. The taste was good, but she didn't want too much of it.

"Sorry, we ran out of crackers," Leader puffed, getting to her feet. "Hater's on a carb spree and snuck two crackers to every one cheese while she thought I wasn't looking."

"I did not!"

Saoirse finally let her knees fall away from her chest, back to the bark. The other two forced their way onto the bench.

"Why are your eejit hips so wide, Rebel? We need a bigger bench."

"Púca Súcca!" Two called. Nothing. "It was worth a shot."

"Get on top, bitch," Hater said, ripping Two off the bench and sliding underneath.

Two flopped back on her lap, turning to Saoirse. "Cheese?"

She went for three. Hater forced an olive into her fist for good measure. And all was well for a moment—when a cacophony of scuffling feet drowned out her happy.

Marching, if you could call it that, soldiers shuffled their way out of the North Tree Hotel entrance below them and toward Social Suicide. She could see them go through cracks in the top of the Carnal Carnival.

"What in the Shannon?" Saoirse craned her neck to see, but both Hater and Leader jerked her back. Two slid quickly into position on her lap to block her from view.

Block after block of soldiers in a three-by-nine columns marched down the silver sinew—blue business suit uniforms adorned with large PÉNIS logos, pointed rubber hats inflating and deflating as they went. They were more of Fanny's assistant fae!

"Simps," Hater said.

"Fear tart!" Two snapped back.

Saoirse looked on.

The simps—*FEAR TART*—began a war chant, "Condom! Co-ON-dom!"

Skinny. Pimpled. Sallow skin.

"I thought they were fear gorta," Saoirse said—zombified men of famine.

"No." Two shook with rage on her crutches. "Not fear gorta. Fear an bhfuil tart air—a man who has great thirst on him. Fear tart for short."

"You mean these fae are suffering from dehydration?" Saoirse asked.

"A different kind of thirst," Leader said.

"Yeah," Hater nodded. "Simps."

"They're not simps!" Two snapped. "They're fear tart. Men of Thirst."

"Sounds like simps to me," Hater said.

"These would be the kind of fae Fanny would attract to do her dirty work," Leader hissed. "There must be a thousand of them."

"Spores, they're on the other branches—look!" Two pointed.

More three-by-nine blocks marched down every length of silver sinew toward Social Suicide.

"So much for Orla blocking Fanny. She's going to be so miffed PÉNIS sent this many enforcers into her castle."

LOOK AT THOSE TERRIFYING WEAPONS.

They were just like the hurley Fanny's assistant fae carried on the field. Each of the simps had a long flail over one shoulder, a pair of glowing sliotars dangling from the ends—one slightly lower than the other.

"What are those?" Saoirse asked.

"Blue Balls," Two quivered. "Just thinking about getting hit in the chest is painful. Do you know how much crutches chafe your nipple? And don't get me started on the face. If they unload on you there—"

"I'd die!" Leader's expression went grey.

"Is it so bad?" Saoirse asked.

Hater shrugged. "Not really."

"Not really!?" Two shrieked. "The smell will paralyze you where you stand! You'll be completely exposed!"

Saoirse nodded. "Simps."

"Fear tart!" Two stamped her good foot. "Don't even get me started on the sky-blue stains of shame!"

"That's a nightmare," Saoirse said—and not just because Fiadh once said she'd look better in blue.

WHAT ARE WE GOING TO DO? WE'RE TRAPPED.

The team isn't even hard anymore.

They only had one shot to impress the donors, and that was tomorrow night. If she turned herself in now and the team failed, not only would she be bound to a dungeon for years, it wouldn't even mean anything.

She could have walked away. She didn't have to serve the drinks. She didn't have to accept Finley's offer. She could have pressed when he snickered. Spores, she didn't have to stay at Social Suicide. Sure, she'd have had one more taint of one more taboo, but there wasn't anything wrong with staying at the Puritan.

But she realized something else, too.

I like it.

LIKE WHAT?

I like it. I like it when they look at me. I like being taboo.

Finally putting words to it was a relief.

AT LEAST YOU ACCEPT YOU'RE A HOE.

Satirical, what even is being a hoe to you?

LIKING BOYS.

You mean this entire time you were giving me a hard time, it was for that?

ONLY HOES LIKE BOYS.

I'm not a hoe. I'm not Fiadh. I'm not going to dance around naked in front of every man on the star.

A PRINCIPLED HOE.

I just don't think it's so wrong.

"Saoirse, we've got a place for you to hide," Leader said.

Saoirse smiled.

"You're smiling? After all this?" Hater asked.

"Silly Saoirse," said Two. "What is it?"

"It's just it's kind of stupid. Everything I've been doing for the team has been one big dick joke."

Hater put a meaningful hand on her shoulder.

Two did the same on the other side.

Leader took both Saoirse's hands in hers.

Together, "Saoirse," they said, "Welcome to sports."

Art

What are you looking at? Just because I put it on my manifestation board doesn't mean it means anything. I just happen to like the artistry of dance, okay? It's something Saoirse and I share. It's not like I thought Hater looked like anything or didn't look like anything or did anything or anything.

How about you keep your nose on your own manifestation board? I bet you don't even have a manifestation board. You don't, do you? Loser.

There's a knock at the window.

Who? Little Hurler, were you spying on me? I told you to stay away from my broadcast booth! (feck, feck feck!)

Yeah, and stay out! Ye feckin'...

A window snaps shut.

Shite!

Something Bad
Half a Day Remains

W hat would it feel like to be in a PÉNIS dungeon? It would feel like this.

She'd get up every day to the chirping of some alarm gadgetry in her cell; There'd be no windows, just walls; She'd have just enough time to wash up and eat before they hauled her off, and she spent all day doing something pointless, slaving away in the local building, making nothing just to walk the hour back to her prison and do it all again. Trapped in a cage with the rest of the men who'd done life wrong.

That was a PÉNIS dungeon. The cell probably wouldn't be much different than the safe room she was locked in now. A windowless dorm room built into the back of the Social Suicide jobbery, it had a small wardrobe on the door-side wall, a bed, and a wash basin. It was meant for temporary use, a place for women who'd managed to ensnare the unwanted attention of a particularly eager customer. The smell of wet fur seeped through the wood.

It's like being back in the grizzly bearfly exclosure.
Kinda.

A pile of 'good luck' sat mounted on her bed. Some time in the night, one of the Leggies had dropped off a care package. She had tape, Spit, sliotars, breakfast, her lucky hurley, a brand-new sheath, a blue Your Maw, and a whole jar of olives. It was only too bad that all she had was this stained dress. It didn't exactly scream 'raid the stadium.' She wasn't even sure she should. What if she showed up and made things worse? Caused another scene that made the boys lose their magic? What if just the sight of her caused them to? If they even *had* gotten their magic back.

She didn't even know how or what to do with Fanny. The investigator made no sense. Saoirse still hadn't been able to piece together why she threw that Rite of Ritual Hurling against Finley. It's like she'd let her try to get the team hard—but why? She'd also insisted Saoirse was innocent. It was almost like she didn't want to arrest her.

Somebody rapped on the door.

Saoirse froze. She held her breath. Nobody was supposed to know she was in here except Hater, Leader, Two, and Stableboy. What if it was Fanny? What if she never even got to make up her mind?

"Saoirse?" Lorcan's deep growl asked through the doorway. "It's me. You don't have to open the door."

He sounded sad. Should she answer? What if this was a trap? She crept to the doorway and leaned against the frame.

"I get it if you think it's a trap. That's fine. I'm—" He paused. "I just want to say I'm sorry. I'm sorry I threw you at the Den. I'm sorry I let my temper get the better of me and hurt you. If that's why you did what you did at Social Suicide, I understand."

No! He was blaming himself? She'd goaded him at the Den on purpose!

"At least you figured out what was happening, too late. You won't know this, but tonight is the team's last night. After the fiasco, the Wives attacked—as you might remember I said."

She pressed her fingertips to the frame, desperate to see him, to touch him, but knowing this could all be a bad mistake.

"Everybody lost their magic again. They're so beat down, nothing helps. If we can't put on a worthwhile show at trials, the donors are pulling all funding. You'll be free. There won't be a county to come after you for your crimes—though even if you did commit them, I'd love to know why. I'm sure you had a reason."

Saoirse bit her tongue. Salm it, how she wanted to speak now—to tell him how it would be. How it was. She waited. For more words. For something. Anything.

Nothing came. Lorcan McGuire had gone.

Feck.

THAT HURT.

Hurler just stared at the walls.

She couldn't go. She couldn't. Not in this dress, not in this mess. Saoirse returned to her bed when—

Bang!

The door to her room suddenly burst open. Saoirse squealed and leaped for the corner, gripping her hurley to her chest, not ready for whatever was coming—but nobody came in.

She peeked around the small wardrobe.

The door to her room squeaked closed.

On the back hung a scream.

Saoirse raced for the door, squealing. Clothes!

Tight black Leggy leggings, high-waisted, with a teal stripe up the side, a compression sleeve, she pulled up her right arm, and her first-ever sports bra—a bright teal triskele above the belly button. For once in her life, she wouldn't have to crush her chest with a sports wrap just to play. Orla had picked her out a brand-new hurling fit—one that had the best of both a dancer's world and sport.

PUT IT ON!

Satirical? You're into this.

WHAT? NO!

Waving a hurley—Little Hurler caught her attention. Saoirse closed her eyes and focused intensely. She manifested herself in her inner world. Saoirse was in Spirit Stadium, down on the pitch at the base of the stands. Little Hurler sprinted up to the broadcast booth and pulled the window open, directing Saoirse to look inside. She focused and was at the top of the steps with Hurler. She peeked through the window.

There, on the wall in the empty room, was a manifestation board full of all kinds of little icons. Including, among other things, wine, a girl in a funky hat, and—

Spores. Is that a pole dancer!?

I JUST APPRECIATE THE ARTISTRY, OKAY?

It looks like you appreciate Hater.

FECK OFF. IT'S AN ELEGANT FORM OF DANCE.

Saoirse smiled and returned to the safe room. "Okay, Satirical, I'll put it on."
YOU'RE A RIGHT HATCH-SNATCHER. YOU KNOW THAT, HURLER?
Her heart laughed.
And maybe when this is all over, we can discuss that compensation package.
WHOOO! THANKS, HURLER.
Her heart held her hurley to salute.
TRAITOR.
Now it was time to fight these pants. They weren't a fight at all. In fact, she couldn't remember ever being this comfortable; even though her midriff was exposed, she didn't care.
She popped her lucky hurley to her hand with a deft heel click and pulled out a sliotar from her pile of good luck.
She didn't have a clue how she'd 'defeat' Fanny and save the team, but she had her hope, her heart, and her lucky hurley.
"Let's go."
...Or out of her black cloud...
Bad. Girl. Dancing. When her hurley hit her hand, she was one with the challenge itself. One with the effort. One with the stride. The House—her rhythm. The Daughters—the gods' percussion.
Percussion to her melody—ash wood and gold.
Uilleann. Forfeda.
She danced.
A mix of hop and heel, tap and knee, with the rolling floor elements she'd learned with Fiadh.
She dropped the sliotar to her bas and paused.
YOU'VE LOST YOUR CITY, YOUR SECT, YOUR INNOCENCE.
Yep.
YOU'RE A FUGITIVE, YOU'RE DYING TONIGHT, AND THE TEAM WON'T FORGIVE YOU.
Yep.
YOU'RE NOT ASKING FOR HELP, AND YOU'RE ALL OUT OF PLANS.
Yep.
HAVE I LEFT ANYTHING OUT?
"No, that about sums it up," Saoirse stretched out her wings' span, dropping the sliotar. It bounced.
SO WHAT ARE YOU GONNA DO?
And when she shot—
She faced the door.
BOOM. TOP LEFT, WHERE DAD KEPT THE SUGAR SPORES.
"Something bad."
Perfect corner every time.

PÉNIS

These feckers better watch it—I'm about to be the biggest sin they'll ever have to slip in the Shannon! They called themselves PÉNIS for being virile and strong?! Well, I'll show them virile and strong. I'm going to lasso those penile punchers and wrangle 'em to the ground!

Hurler, you ready?

Little Hurler dons a headband—green, white, and orange. She's ready to take the stage.

I'm charging ten times the usual price for this match, folks. I've double-ordered everything for the snack stands and swept the stomach. We're going to take PÉNIS, and we're going to show them we mean business! Gods, salm it! Slip me in the Shannon with these fecking puns! They're ruining my feckin' broadcast!

Little Hurler holds up a tooth-picket sign showing an éireconda popsicle with a strike through it.

Salm right. Down with PÉNIS! I do declare! Spores, stupid jokes are everywhere.

Little Gale

Mere Hours Remain

"They're called the Greensleeves, Saoirse."
"I like them, Chiefy."

"Move your leg like this.
"Not quite like that—like this."

"I hate it! I hate it! I hate it! I hate it!"
"Saoirse..."
"I'm never going to drop the ball again!"

Saoirse plucked herself a sliotar from a pile set aside by the base of the Melak statue. Hazel Park, Ballybofey—the home of the Wolves; The home of the County Tyrconnell Hurling Club; The home of her last-ditch attempt. Little Hurler strapped up a new piece of gear with each bounce of the sliotar: boots, tape, hurley, jersey, then steepled her fingers in concentration. Finally, her heart, her mind, and her spirit were thinking the same thing: score.

Fanny Burns, PÉNIS investigator, stood blocking the entryway to the stadium, flanked by an insane amount of fear tart. Fanny didn't move. Their Rite of Ritual Hurling was agreed to. It was up to Saoirse to start.

Their pitch was the stadium walk, a long stretch of pavers lined by garden boxes about knee-high, with honeysuckles wrapped around a low chain fence. Spirit Stadium had sold out and was at full attention. Each Spectator at the edge of her seat for the match of her lifetime: Saoirse Storm vs. Fanny Burns. She didn't even want to know what Satirical charged the tiny gremlins to get in here today.

IT GOT ME BACK MY RANCH.

Saoirse let the sliotar roll down her hurley, up her arm, her neck, and onto her head, where she balanced it, eyes closed, on the bridge of her nose.

Serene. Fearless. Grace. She said she'd do something bad; there wasn't much more than strip hurling. If she won, Fanny let her into Hazel Park, let her try one last time to save the county, and declared her a Bad Girl. If Fanny won, Saoirse would be arrested and, in all likelihood, declared a Good Girl. The county would go under, the team would come to an end, and she would either be violated or die.

Saoirse took a deep breath in and exhaled.

You're smiling.

Of course. All I have to do is win. Satirical, announce me in.

You got it!

Little Hurler clapped her taped hands.

Ladies and gentlemen! We're here!

'*We're still here!*' the Spectators cheered.

On your feet.

They rose.

On your feet for the challenge of our lives!

'*We're here!*' they cried.

On your feet for the match-up you paid several kelpies' worth of money for.

'*We're here!*' Her Spectators lost their salm minds.

On your feet for her, for our girl, for your number twenty-seven and mine—the best full-forward in all the star! Saoirse Storm!!!

If she wasn't here after having her blood pumped! *Nice call.*

Night of the final day, a few hours remain. Kick her butt, Superspore!

Time to put on a show.

"You're never getting into the stadium, Little Gale."

Saoirse let the ball fall from her nose, popped it into the air with her chest, then spiked it into the pavers with a brutal swing of her hurley, sending it soaring high above her. "You're never going to stop me!"

Little Hurler?

Her heart responded.

Let's set the tone!

Saoirse set her lucky hurley behind her. The great theater of her emotions. Little Hurler was there, in the lockers, hurley at the ready, helmet on. Her heart nodded. It was time to merge. Time to combine the embers of her magic with her will to win.

Dancing, fighting, making love—

Saoirse shouted, "UILLEANN!!!"

—That's her name.

The magic flowed. A warm fire burned in her breast. Little Hurler began to glow bright white; hot fire filled Saoirse, fueling her. Flower petals whipped around her. Her hair fluttered in non-existent wind. Saoirse reached up and clapped above her head, showering herself in her special golden dust.

Her heart set, a warm crackle of energy danced about her skin: 'Hurling Sense.' With a deft heel kick, Saoirse kicked her lucky hurley to her hands, rapped it once on the back of each foot, held it out to point at Fanny, catching the sliotar she'd sent high, cradling it on the bas.

Spectators screamed.

That's an amazing challenge set down by Saoirse! Fanny's gonna be shaking in her boots!

Heels more like. The hubris of this woman, Fanny, dressed in a button-down blouse, a pencil skirt, and heels. "I suppose I have to make this fair," Fanny said with a knowing smile.

What does she mean, folks?

The answer was quick; a moment later, Fanny had lost the blouse and skirt.

State of this woman! She's copying our fit!

Saoirse's nostrils flared. The investigator had chosen the exact same clothes as her! She had a striped sports bra and leggings, except with Darragh knots instead of triskeles!

Her Spectators threw incorporeal shroom sacks out of her stomach. '*Boo, Fanny!*'

At least Saoirse's leggings' stripe was teal; Fanny's was turquoise.

OUR COLOR IS CLEARLY SUPERIOR!

"Is that it?" Fanny laughed. One of the simps—*FEAR TART*—near the stadium handed Fanny her hurley. It was still wrapped from handle to toe in a white bandage. "I suppose I shouldn't have expected much of a show from you."

Fanny's going to answer?! Nobody answers! This feckin' shaper!

It got her Spectators going.

Saoirse popped the sliotar to her hand and crossed her arms. *This show-off.*

Fanny gripped a loose tail of the wrap concealing her hurley and snapped it hard above her. The knot ripped, the bandage slipped. Fanny's hurley unraveled, traveling higher and higher till, with a snap, it popped free, spinning like a propeller, continuing to soar higher—

LIKE IT'S ON A STRAIGHT SHOT TO THE STARS!

"Strumpet in the schoolyard." Fanny adjusted her horn-rimmed glasses nonchalantly and whipped the wrap out to the side like a deadly ribbon before going into a twirl. "It's time you see how big the world is." The ribbon wrapped around her in a dazzling flow, swirling around her in a cone, then rising above the investigator to a point.

A LASSO OF JUSTICE!

With a flick of her wrist, Fanny's cloth snapped back down to her arm, binding itself to her wrist just as her hurley landed with ease in her outstretched hand.

Spirit Stadium cheered.

Satirical calmed down from her call, speaking as if whispering so the Spectators couldn't hear. *OH FECK, TWENTY-SEVEN.*

Nah, we got this. "You call that a pre-hurling psyche out? Pathetic."

Fanny smirked.

Now Saoirse saw it, Fanny's hurley was so strange. It didn't look like it'd been taken from the right part of the tree at all. It was covered with knots, a flagrant ogham carved down to the base for her Whiskey. The way she held it... spores. It's like an extension of herself.

"I can still make the goal bigger," Fanny indicated the large hallway behind her, leading into the stadium. "Last time we faced off, you couldn't even hit a waterfall."

Several of the ornery half-fae were trapped inside the hallway leading to the stadium by a strip of waist-high, see-through film, all of them wheezing sporadic calls for "Leeeeegs."

A different kind of thirst, indeed. Fanny seemed to have full control over the simps.

FEAR TART!

"I think you'll do just fine," Saoirse smiled.

To a tiny woman, her Spectators wore the county colors, gold and green—all in for the Wolves. They shoveled fistfuls of shroom nachos covered with olives and cheese into their greedy faces. Little Hurler rapped the walls of her heart. She was inside the lockers and ready.

A subtle shift above the stadium caught her attention. Melak, the Wolf of Enniskillen, Living Goddess over Ulster, but a shadow in the distance where she lay above River Eolas, had shifted her gaze from the stadium to their match, her pink eyes narrowed into dangerous slits.

Saoirse checked her sports bra, where she'd pinned a funky black spore Fanny said would capture her confession. She wouldn't be confessing to shite.

Saoirse pulled herself a new sliotar, undaunted.

What even was magic?

LADIES AND GENTLEMEN!

Spirit Stadium roared.

Was it when you beat the odds?

Little Hurler was in the back of the tunnel, bouncing on the balls of her feet.

Or when you went the distance?

BOYS AND GIRLS!

When you saved your world?

Her Spectators rose to their feet.
Or did it come just from showing—fearless, proud, and strong?
LIFT YOUR VOICE AND SING THIS:
"Ready to get out and hurl?" Fanny sassed.
Saoirse merely raised her hurley. "An evening star shines down upon you."
A delighted, focused woman met the same. "May it be."
She would beat those odds, she would go the distance—even if that meant that jail was right where she belonged.
YOU'LL NEVER BEAT MY GIRL, BITCH!

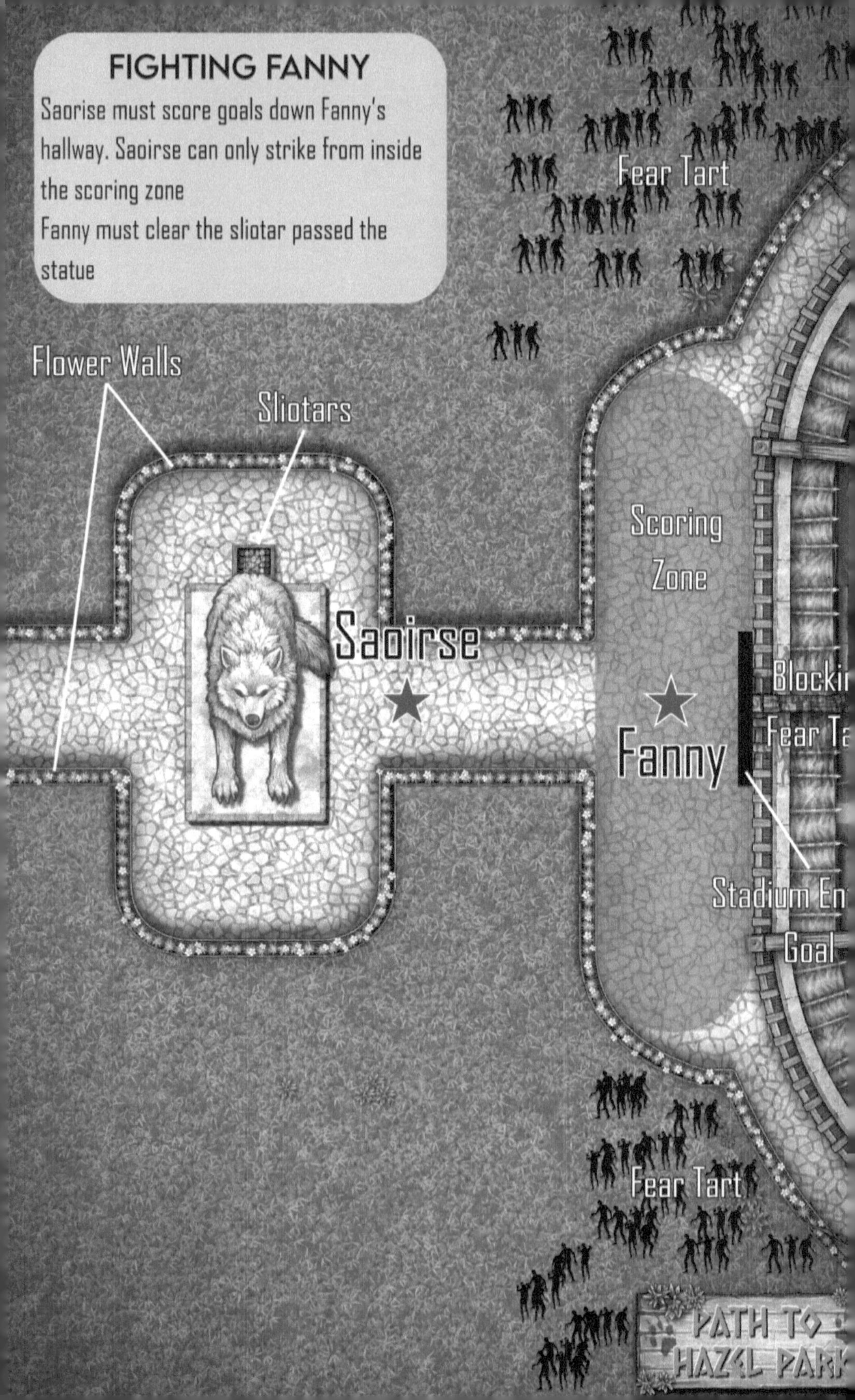

FIGHTING FANNY
Saorise must score goals down Fanny's hallway. Saoirse can only strike from inside the scoring zone
Fanny must clear the sliotar passed the statue
Flower Walls
Sliotars
Fear Tart
Saoirse
Scoring Zone
Fanny
Blockin
Fear Ta
Stadium En
Goal
Fear Tart
PATH TO
HAZEL PARK

Fanny Pressure

Two Hours Remain

J ust because last time she'd gotten whooped once doesn't mean she would again.

Satirical?
Two hours!
She had this. Easy.
Get her!
Her heart roared.

Saoirse jab-lifted a sliotar off the pavers and ran full-boar for the investigator. Fanny came up to meet her, blacking her off at the end of the path.

"Taste dirt!" Saoirse crashed shoulder-first into Fanny's chest—and was swallowed whole. "What?!"

"Poor thing."

Spores! Saoirse shielded the sliotar with her body, toying with it on the pavers, and tried to force Fanny back with brute strength, but still, Fanny didn't budge. Only Saoirse did, her shoulder seeming to slowly get further and further enveloped by Fanny's presence.

Her boots scraped the walk. *What's going on?*

"Comfy?" Fanny crooned.

Salm. She was. Usually, a defender stood like a wall, ready to be knocked down or break to a strong shoulder, but it was just like last time, Fanny's walls were unlike anything Saoirse had ever experienced. The investigator enveloped her, welcoming Saoirse in, absorbing the blow like a spongy cushion letting the force reverberate through her body.

Warmth. Depth. Desire. The harder Saoirse fought against Fanny's walls—the left, to the right—the harder she wiggled, the more Fanny sucked her in, disabling her skill.

She felt weak; her mind slipped; her grip on the sliotar slowed.

Hypnotic swirls spun Hurler's eyes.

"Ow!" Her heart was struck in the head by a nacho. In that brief moment of presence, she raced back up the path.

"You pulled out?" Fanny stayed back.

Saoirse growled.

"You know what they say, Good Girls don't score!"

Salm, Fanny was just like one of *those women*! The jaded older ladies mad at *The Violet Intercourse*. She could understand those girls now, but Fanny? "Jilted by your lover? Now you work for PÉNIS?" she tried.

The investigator didn't react.

Feck, she could trash-talk all she wanted, but that wouldn't get her into the stadium.

Little Hurler reset herself. Being inside Fanny's influence took a lot out of her. She was beyond the point of thinking the investigator was a lesser player for the heels. Saoirse needed an edge, but they were the same body type, broad in the shoulders and wide in the hips, except that the investigator was taller, her stance strong and low.

"All size and no skill," Fanny said. "Must suck to have it taken away."

If I can't bust my way through, I'll go around. Take me away, Little Hurler! Saoirse let her heart guide her. Her heart swapped her hurley for glowing batons.

Right. Saoirse flicked the sliotar to a solo and ran right.

Spin left.

She did, pushing Fanny further back down the path.

Spin right.

Again, she followed Hurler's guide, pushing her deeper.

"Don't think I don't see what you're doing, getting space won't help you!"

"I don't need it."

Spin. Saoirse heeded her heart and ran straight at the low garden boxes.

"I knew you'd leap!"

She did. Fanny followed suit—except Fanny hadn't accounted for the Dancer.

With a deft flick of her lucky hurley, Saoirse sent the sliotar off the pavers, off the flower box, and behind her. One foot on the box, Saoirse leaped into a backflip, leaving Fanny headed in the wrong direction into the grass.

Saoirse floated above the sliotar upside down and swung. "Boom."

The sliotar sailed over the heads of the wrapping-trapped simps—*FEAR TART!*—and into the back of the—

"Whiskey! Tulip Grip!"

"NO!"

Right on the goal line, the sliotar was sucked backward into Fanny's palm.

The Spectators booed. Saoirse landed in a heroic one-kneed pose on the pavers, but without the added effect of a goal. "Shite."

"Cast a net on me, Little Gale. That was unbelievably impressive," said Fanny. "But not impressive enough." The investigator flipped the sliotar to her feet. Saoirse launched herself over the wall to block the clear, but Fanny's casual strike merely rolled the sliotar back to the pile at the base of the statue.

"Whoops," Fanny smirked at her. "I wonder if you've got enough time to play like this?"

The clash of the ash echoed out of Hazel Park.

"Only a few precious hours and your county will be done forever."

"I won't let that happen," Saoirse said, but retreated back to the pile of sliotars all the same.

TWENTY-SEVEN IS COMPLETELY ROUTED! THERE'S A REASON FANNY PUTS THE I IN PENIS! Satirical lowered her voice, *WHAT DO WE DO?!*

Saoirse eyed Fanny's hurley.

TWENTY-SEVEN?

She did the same against Finley. She didn't clear the ball.

I REMEMBER, BUT WE AGREED THAT WAS TO INVESTIGATE THE CONNECTION BETWEEN YOU AND THE DONORS.

I don't think it was. Saoirse smiled. Little Hurler agreed. The investigator had a weakness: Fanny's exclusive focus was on defense. And she knew just how to pull it apart.

YOU MEAN SHE'LL NEVER CLEAR THE SLIOTAR?
I doubt it.
THEN HER DEAL IS TO LOSE?!
Or stall for time. She wouldn't find out without another try. Saoirse pulled herself a new sliotar fromt he base of the statue. *Fanny's Whiskey, is it in the body or the mind?*

"Try not to break an ankle, old lady." This time, Saoirse leaped straight into the grass, soloing the ball with ease.

"Old?!" Fanny leaped the walls surrounding the goal zone and hustled out to meet her up high. How confident could one woman be in her ability to limit space? When she'd had Saoirse trapped between the garden boxes, that was one thing—but out in the open field?

SHE'S PLAYED RIGHT INTO OUR GIRL'S HANDS!
The Spectators bellowed, *'Saoirse!'*

"I'm only forty, you tramp!" Fanny was quick on her backside, riding Saoirse no matter where she went. That was fine, she'd let the investigator think she'd swallowed her up.

The way her body pressed into hers—it was so overwhelming. Every twitch of her muscle, every pulse of breath, Saoirse could feel her own pulse surge through her. The Spectators kept her honest with some nachos to the heart.

OUR GIRL'S SLOWING DOWN, FOLKS.
"A few quick pumps," Fanny jeered. "That's all you're good for."
YOU'D BETTER EXECUTE THE PLAN BEFORE IT'S ALL OVER.

Fanny's body control was so immense. It had to be the source of her Whiskey, and she hadn't been able to handle the Dancer. She'd beat this old lady's body with her own!

Spore shower. She was back at Beltany Circle, dancing with Fiadh. She'd use the new ground moves she'd tried while dancing to the head-banger music—go low where Fanny's walls couldn't contain her. Saoirse tapped the sliotar left and skidded on her knees, turning round for a quick jab-lift and sprint—only—

Fanny was sliding right along with her!
The investigator sneered. "Cute, but no-no."
"What!?"
WHO IS THIS DEFENDER?

She tried again, this time going into a backward salmon leap, rolling her body along the grass. The sliotar traveled the length of her legs, as if she were doing a trick shot. When it got to her foot, she kicked it back to her bas and—

Fanny was there again!
THIS ANCIENT BROOD IS MATCHING OUR SUPERSPORE MOVE FOR MOVE!
The Spectators were tweakin'.
"No-no."
Saoirse wallowed.

"All-Central County Tyrconnell Trick Shot Champion?" Fanny leaned over her. "Did you really think you were the first girl to add dance moves?"

Her stomach churned. Hurler was rattled.

TAKE THE LINE! In the moment of Fanny's gloating, Satirical screamed. Saoirse whipped around her.

"Whiskey!" Fanny said. "Tulip Grip!"
Tuatha Dé, she's unbelievable.

Just like the day she'd agreed to strip hurling with Lorcan, Fanny's magic yanked Saoirse into her. She slammed into Fanny's body with force that the other woman didn't seem to feel, one arm bracing Saoirse against her as her tummy—the investigator's lower abdomen—quaked, convulsing with the residual effects of using her magic power.

"I control the pitch. Why do you think they called it my No-No Zone?"

I've heard that before!
I KNOW!
Little Hurler did an anxious flip.
But where?

"The good thing about having a knotty hurley," said Fanny, waggling her hurley with just the tip glowing white, "is I can use my Whiskey over and over and over again."

At the cost of making it particularly brittle! No wonder the investigator wouldn't clear the sliotar! She was afraid her hurley would break!

Saoirse smirked at the trash talk. She couldn't help it. "Suck me all you want, Fanny, but your Tulip Grip won't be enough to keep me off the goal line."

"I'm counting on it."

OUR GIRL'S INSIDE FANNY'S REALM—WHAT WILL SHE DO TO BREAK FREE?

"Now go ahead and put one in the net, would you? I'm getting a little hot."

Fanny hunkered down. Saoirse did the same, facing her. As she'd thought, despite all that, Fanny hadn't cleared the ball.

Saoirse scooped the sliotar with a jab lift. Fanny could say her magic was endless, all she wanted, but all Whiskeys had a fatiguing time. If her's didn't she'd have used it the second time against Finley!

SHE TAKES OFF!
Saoirse dashed through the grass.
Spirit Stadium leaped to their feet. *'Saoirse!'*
Hurler worked triple time.

Shoulder to shoulder, Saoirse and Fanny ran the field for the goal box. Saoirse used Fanny's fatigue to her advantage. She leaped over the boxes. Fanny overcompensated to keep up. Saoirse casually spiked the sliotar back between her legs, snatching it with a spin, taking off the other direction and leaving Fanny in the dust. One strike—Saoirse drilled her shot straight through—

"Whiskey!"
"You have got to be kidding me!"
"Tulip Grip!"

Fanny's knotty hurley was unstoppable. The sliotar, one inch from scoring, soaring over the head of the simps, slowed to a stop, then flew backward into Fanny's palm. Fanny laughed—a full-on belly laugh.

WHAT'S GOTTEN INTO HER?

"You still don't get it, do you?" Fanny came to meet her. "You're proving my point. You could have scored in that match."

Shite.

"Here you are, all the pressure in the world, and you aren't holding back at all. You are a Good Girl. And without a Whiskey, you can't beat me. You made a mistake, Little Gale. I can keep you here all night. I'm not trying to prove you're guilty or innocent. I don't care if I declare you a Good Girl or a Bad Girl, I'm just trying to get to the bottom of your case—whatever that bottom may be. Whenever I bother to beat you, if I bother at all, we both know what's waiting for you: *The Violet Intercourse*."

Saoirse went pale.

"Ah, you see now, don't you?" Fanny said. "You never conspired, you never sabotaged, or match-fixed. You are just a selfish, worthless little trollop who didn't want to commit to the rite!"

SHE'S ALMOST RIGHT.
I can't.
YOUR TRUTH IS—

"No matter what you do from here on out, you're going to be declared a Good Girl, because you and I both know when I clear this ball, you won't be a bad one."

"That's not true!" She had at least one card to play!

"Spore in the storm," Fanny sneered. "Only the guilty trip."

Spores that came right out of one of Triple K's sermons.

The woman took two steps—just two—and, in less time than Saoirse could blink, she was left falling backward, Fanny behind her, ready to clear the sliotar.

What?

How did that happen?

"Okay, Little Gale, prove me wrong," Fanny raised her hurley for a cut, "show me just how bad you are."

Saoirse lunged, her hand outstretched. She couldn't do it. "No!"

Clack!

The clash of the ash.

The sliotar tumbled but a few feet. Two hurleys and a crutch had blocked Fanny's cut.

"On your feet, Superspore." Three different kinds of arms stretched toward her, offering hope in the form of three new hurleys—and the biggest, gods-salmed smiles she'd ever seen.

"Stupid Leggies," Saoirse said.

Leader smiled. "We figured you could use a few more girls with hurls."

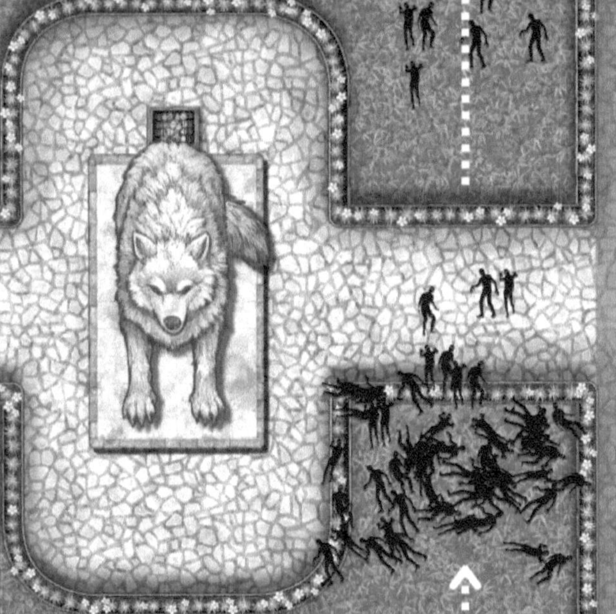

LEGGY LEGGING
With the Leggies arrival the simps (fear tart!) have been unleashed by Fanny Burns. How can the girls hope to score on the investigator now?
Hater
Fear Tart
Scoring Zone
Fanny
Hater's Track
Saoirse
Leader
Two

Blocki
Fear Ta
Stadium En
Goal

PATH TO
HAZEL PAR

Cork Camogie

An Hour and a Half Remains

"**S**pores," Saoirse said as she ran at a full-out sprint, "these feckers are fast, cú."

The Leggy Trio laughed. All four of them were being hounded by simps—*FEAR TART!*

Together, the girls ran one big circle around the lawns in front of the stadium. The simps kept tripping over each other. They were really fast in one direction, but they weren't very agile—they'd trip over just about anything. Fanny, meanwhile, was posted up in front of the stadium, standing guard over the entry to Hazel Park with the contingent of ornery fear tart plugging the hallway that she'd kept back with the thin film.

"I still cannot believe that you'd leave us early," Leader said. "We told you five more minutes."

"And then took fifteen!" Saoirse said.

"It's not my fault—Two's makeup has lead," Hater said.

"I wouldn't put that poison on my face!"

"Then how come last time I stole some, I got a pimple?"

Leader scoffed. "Because you thought it was a good idea to binge-eat sausage!"

Everybody ducked Hater's lethal eye roll—except a simp who got hit and went down. "You're all feckin' stupid."

The trio looked strange—hurleys in hand, Two's on her back; holding up the hems of conservative dresses, their hair pulled back with claw clips. She was so used to their dance class outfits.

"You're all under arrest!" Fanny shouted as they ran.

Leader donned a wicked smile. "There's nothing illegal about a spot of hurling!" she called back.

"Leeeeegs!" the pack of pathetic, pimpled people-fae shrieked as they ran after them.

Hater smacked a few in the face with her hurley for fun. They fell, causing a small pile-up on the side of the peloton.

NO AGILITY AT ALL, FOLKS.

"Are they going to eat us?" Saoirse asked.

"Legs!" cried the fear tart.

"Worse." Two could really move on those crutches.

Hater pointed to the simps' long sticks, with sets of smoking blue orbs hanging from their ends by chains—so one sat a bit lower than the other: Blue Balls. "They'll unload their balls on you."

MESSAGE FROM ALL OF US TO YOU: DON'T YOU GET HIT!

She didn't intend to. They curved the edge of the lawn outside Hazel Park.

"If worst comes to worst, we'll sacrifice Two," Hater said.

"Hey!" Two protested.

"Nice plan, Two," Leader agreed. "Don't worry, Saoirse," Leader pulled the claw clip from her hair and handed it to Hater. "Clips and hips, A simp call if you please."

Hater tossed Leader her hurley, then hiked up her dress, took out her own clip, and used both to pin the fabric in place, showing bare legs.

THE FEAR TART GO WILD, FOLKS!

The hateful Leggy got her hurley back.

"I can't believe I'm having to do this." She pulled off from their group, cupping a hand around her mouth. She shouted to the fear tart, "Mama's proud of you! I'm so proud of you, big boy! Come, sit on my lap and let me comb your hair."

The whole pack ground to a halt. "Leegs?" they asked. "Legs? Legs? Legs?"

She, Leggy Leader, and Leggy Two also skidded to a stop—Leader and Two pincered Saoirse between their long skirts, blocking her legs from view.

"You're so good at that." Leader shook her head.

"I'll teach you sometime." Hater turned back to the pack, dangerously showing off one appendage, with a sappy, almost loving look that Saoirse didn't think Hater's face could make. "You're my special star."

"Leeeeeegs!" The fear tart took off after a cackling Hater Leggy.

Two raised a crutch. "Bust some balls, Hater!"

She did, as they watched, Hater leaped a low garden wall near the score zone and made—an explosion!

Boom!

The peloton of fear tart smacked into the wall and tripped, causing their balls to smack hard on the pavement, the wall, or each other. The sound was deafening, the smell was as much so. Several fear tart soared into the air from the result of the blast, slamming into each other and setting off more blue balls in a spore shower of degenerate shame.

Hater leaped the other wall and picked up the pack of fear tart congregating on the other side.

Leader placed a dainty hand on her chest. "This is quite a game of hurling."

"You think this is weird? Last time I had to fight a pack of wolves with pool noodles."

They both looked at her like she was mad.

"I won."

"You're silly, Silly Saoirse."

Nobody was ever going to believe that story, were they?

Hazel Park loomed behind them, the sounds of proper hurling coming from inside.

Satirical?

AN HOUR AND A HALF.

She was running out of time!

"Feck all this crutching is destroying my nipple," complained Two.

Leader was ignoring her for Fanny, "You know, Saoirse, I wish you'd mentioned the investigator on your case was the literal I of PÉNIS!" Leader said.

"Does it matter?"

"Yes! I would never let you come on your own. No wonder you were struggling."

"Struggling? I had my goals pulled off the line twice!"

Leader balked. "Against Captain Pressure?!"

"Who's that?" Two asked.

"Nah, her name is Fanny Burns."

"I'm sure it does now," said Leader, "but only because she was on fire when she was younger! Saoirse, many women change their name when they start working for PÉNIS."

It all clicked. "Fanny Burns is _Captain Fanny Pressure_?!" she shrieked. Aisling's favorite player—the woman who'd played pro camogie for only one year before disappearing. The one who famously never let a single shot go off inside her No-No Zone?! "Tuatha Dé Danann!"

"She's not as famous outside Cork, but we had a county-wide party when she was named investigator."

"That sounds fun!" said Two.

A heat rose inside Saoirse; she'd almost scored twice on Captain Pressure! She had to tell Aisling!

Hater sprinted around the lawn, barefoot, restarting her simp call when the fear tart started recovering from their explosion against the garden wall, leaving Fanny shaking her head.

"I get she's all super cool," Two said, "but aren't we, like, pressed for time and stuff?"

Leader asked, "How do we win your challenge?"

"It's strip hurling," Saoirse said. "But Fanny's play makes no sense. Fanny said that if she wins, she's declaring me a Good Girl. I have to be a Bad Girl, or the county won't get a second chance—but she won't even clear the sliotar past the statue. She's stalling for time, but I don't see why she wouldn't just win and arrest me."

"She's intentionally stalling?" Leader bit the tip of her thumb in concentration.

"Does it matter?" asked Two. "We still just gotta score, silly."

"I don't mean to suggest it isn't possible," Leader said, "but how exactly are we supposed to score on Captain Pressure?"

"Is she that good?" Two asked.

Saoirse was starting to wonder that herself. Her Whiskey seemed to be as free-wheeling as a Rage Boner, and Fanny herself was so physically capable it was a serious ask.

Across the lawn, Hater downed another simp with her hurley.

Saoirse smiled.

"What is it, Silly Saoirse?"

"We use their balls against them."

Two and Leader outright snorted.

"Feck! Everything is a dick joke!"

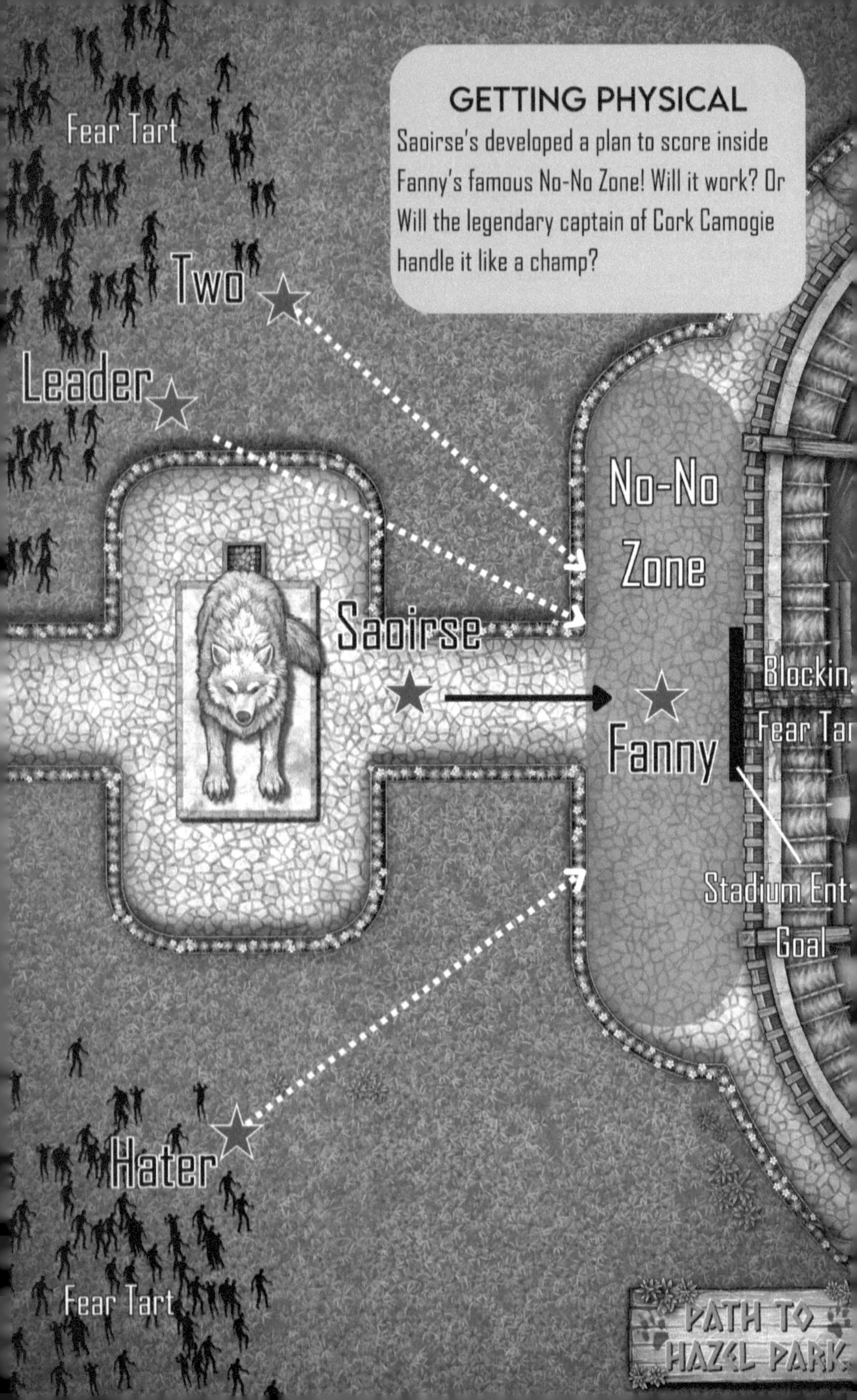

Fear Tart
Two
Leader
GETTING PHYSICAL
Saoirse's developed a plan to score inside
Fanny's famous No-No Zone! Will it work? Or
Will the legendary captain of Cork Camogie
handle it like a champ?
No-No
Zone
Saoirse
Blockin
Fear Tar
Fanny
Stadium Ent
Goal
Hater
Fear Tart
PATH TO
HAZEL PARK

Ball Knowledge

I f Saoirse couldn't beat Fanny into submission by herself, then they'd all beat Fanny together.

They tapped hurleys, and Two passed out hair ties.

Cue us in, Satirical.

WITH PLEASURE.

LADIES AND GENTLEMEN, IT'S SAOIRSE SATIRICAL BACK AGAIN, BRINGING YOU THE MATCH BEFORE THE MATCH OF THE CENTURY! WHAT DO I MEAN? WELL, LET'S JUST SAY IT'S A GOOD THING YOUR NUMBER TWENTY-SEVEN AND MINE GOT SOME TEAMMATES—NOW OUR TEAM IS ABSOLUTELY STACKED. ISN'T THAT RIGHT, LITTLE HURLER?

Little Hurler adjusted a mic shroom before opening her mouth as if she'd say something, then simply smiled instead.

SO TRUE! TURNS OUT HAVING A MUTE COMMENTATOR IS A REAL DRAWBACK, FOLKS. WHICH IS WHY I'M JUST GONNA DO IT MYSELF—RIGHT AFTER TONIGHT'S SPONSOR, SPUNK. ARE YOU HAVING TROUBLE KEEPING HATCH-SNATCHERS AWAY FROM YOUR BATCH? ARE YOUR EGGS UNFERTILIZED? DO YOU FIND YOURSELF HANKERING FOR A SALTY SNACK? SPUNK HAS THE ANSWER TO ALL OF THAT! THEIR PATENTED FORMULA GOES ON IN SPURTS AND COMES OFF IN STAINS. VISIT YOUR LOCAL APOTHECARY AND TRY SPUNK TODAY.

Leader and Two ran off to help Hater with the simps and fill her in on the plan. Saoirse returned to the pile of sliotars at the base of the statue. "Alright, Fanny," Saoirse said, balancing a fresh sliotar on her hurley, keeping an eye on the Leggy Trio. The three of them were each curling a different peloton of fear tart toward Fanny's box.

"All that time," Fanny said, "and your big plan is still just 'score?'"

"You can't stop me this time."

"I think I've made it clear I don't care. Just confess."

"Let's put that to the test."

GO! TWENTY-SEVEN!

Little Hurler charged. Saoirse contested, soloing the sliotar down the path. Fanny still came to meet her.

"Weird way to not care." Saoirse smiled.

"I'm in it for the love of the game."

Leader shouted, "Now!"

Saoirse dropped the sliotar and threw herself into Fanny's walls as all three Leggies leaped the low garden boxes into the main path. Hater and Leader, each having yoinked pairs of lethal sliotars off some simps, their blue glow juggled at the ends of their hurleys.

Boom!

Fast, but not agile, the fear tart crashed calf-long into the flower boxes and piled up on each other in a comic display.

THEY'RE FLYING OVER THE FIELD! IT'S RAINING MEN... FEAR TART.

Simps!

"Trying to Blue Ball me!?" Fanny shouted, backing deeper into her zone, twisting out of the way of a flying simp.

Boom!

Saoirse kept her honest with another attempt on goal. "Blue Balls are harmless."

Despite what Fanny said about not caring, the investigator still blocked her shot.

"Tell that to my favorite sundress!" Two bellowed. A fear tart crushed her to the pavers. "No!"

They surrounded Fanny, leaving her stranded in the center of her No-No Zone. "This only further proves you're a Good Girl!"

"Objection!" Leader shouted with gusto.

Boom!

Everybody froze with a start.

AND NOT FROM THE FLYING FEAR TART, FOLKS. WHOA, THAT WAS A CLOSE ONE!

"What?" Leader asked, sharing looks with them across Fanny's box, then became sad. "Oh, come on, are you serious? Do none of you listen to courtroom recitations?"

"Romance." Hater actually flushed.

"Slags at the Beach or The Suitor," squealed Two from under the tart.

"CSI."

"You're all so trashy!" Leader cried.

"Nobody for Mallhark?" Fanny asked.

"Shut up, Fanny." Saoirse slammed her weight into the investigator. And it was back on. "Two, switch!"

She shoved off the fae. "Gotcha, Silly Saoirse."

Boom!

Two tossed a crutch aside and took her hurley from her back. Saoirse hand-passed her the regular sliotar. Despite Two being unable to move well, if Fanny really didn't want to lose clothes, she'd have to pay some attention to her.

Several simps rolled through the No-No Zone. "...legs..."

Which meant she, Hater, and Leggy Leader were free to drive their Blue Balls at Fanny's face. Saoirse ran to fetch herself her own pair of Blue Balls from the simp pile at the flower wall.

"You think I'm that easy?" Fanny roared, leaping to dis-sliotar Two, who was unnaturally agile.

"Sorry," chimed Two. She dodged easily.

Saoirse squeezed a blue ball, and its contents gushed all over her hands.

Gross.

Little Hurler squirmed.

DISGUSTING, LADIES AND GENTLEMEN.

Hater took aim. She had her balls by the chain; she knocked one free and drove it at Fanny. "The feck do you know about straw?!"

It was a blistering strike, but the investigator dodged adeptly. "No-no."

Saoirse found a non-greasy simp and began wiping her hands off on his shirt. Tuatha Dé Danann, she should have used her hurley. What an awful smell.

Her whole crowd dumped what was left of their nachos in disgust.

"Try this delu-lu-lusional strike!" Leader struck a blue ball at Fanny, who spun on her heels again, up to the task. "Shite."

Boom!

Saoirse ducked the impending flying fear tart, but they never came; in fact, the fear tart in question merely climbed atop the pile himself and then jumped off as if he'd exploded properly. "What the?"

"Pathetic," Fanny smirked.

Saoirse finally got it all off her fingers. Some of it was still sticky. So gross. She needed a shower. She attacked the chain on a simp's balls, attempting to bust them loose. When that didn't work, she stepped on them. The fae groaned with pleasure.

Tuatha Dé!

Is he smiling, folks?

What was wrong with these creatures?

"Hater, catch!" Leader struck her other ball right for her, before tackling Fanny to the ground—but Hater dodged it with a look of audacity. "I don't believe in that catching shit."

"Really!?" Leader was exasperated.

"Get their balls and feckin' drive it."

"You want me to pull first time!?" Leader shrieked.

"Pull every time!"

Leave it to the oldest rivalry in hurling, folks.

Saoirse spun round with a full flail in one hand, a hurley in the other, ready for action. "Aaaah!" but nobody paid her any mind.

"Typical Tipperary," Leader and Fanny shook their heads.

Little Hurler was still back at the pile, smacking balls.

"Hey, Fanny!?" Two asked, from right next to the goal. When had she gotten there? The bucktoothed, innocent Leggy was right in front of the cling-wrap-stopped simps with the regular sliotar. "Show us how bad you are."

She struck for a goal.

Saoirse cheered. "Yes, Two!"

Two struck, slick with it.

Fanny's eyes went wide, hand out toward the goal line. "Tulip Grip!" She sucked the ball right off the edge.

"Awe!" Two stomped with her good foot. "I had that one."

So, Fanny didn't want to lose. *Interesting.*

Fanny hand-passed her the ball. Saoirse caught it.

"I'm getting tired of waiting, Little Gale," Fanny started jawing from back in her zone. "Give up. Confess. The President thinks your sentence could be spankings."

"The President of PÉNIS?"

"Don't listen to her, Saoirse." Two cautioned. "She's just trying to pull you into her game."

"You're lucky I missed the chance to arrest you on sabotage," Fanny continued. "It was a well-known fact among those I investigated in Croaghgorm that you didn't want to participate in *The Violet Intercourse*." Fanny gave it the proper gravitas. "I had my suspicions after I flirted with the team in front of you. Your reactions were ever so sweet. You must really love them."

"I do!"

"Saoirse," Hater bapped her with her hurley.

"Look at you—your dad's in custody."

Dad.

"Don't fall for it," Leader said.

"We found the loaded Magic Eight Ball."

They couldn't have.

"Silly Saoirse!"

"Aisling said you'd planned it together!"

Hold up.

Little Hurler raised two brows and a bean snack. She was hungry.

Fanny just lied.

"Great Goddess Danu," Saoirse whispered. "An Dagda, Manannán, The Morrígan. It can't be."

"What can't be? Saoirse?" Leader was concerned.

Aisling didn't even know what she and her dad were planning. They didn't want to risk her being implicated with Triple K. Why would Fanny be trying so hard to prove she was innocent unless—

What is, 'it's my job, Triple K.'

"You three handle the simps," Saoirse told the others.

"What are you talking about?" Leader asked.

What's in the sliotars for four hundred, Triple K.

Why would she remove the restriction? Was she really using Saoirse to get to the donors?

Saoirse played the sliotar out to her hurley.

If Fanny clears the sliotar, stripping is the only way I can prove my innocence—a transgression...

But not by PÉNIS.

THE VIOLET INTERCOURSE.

Fanny always said the name of the rite with the proper gravitas.

Saoirse started slowly up the walk, slipping the simps.

It couldn't be.

"Finally, I was getting tired of waiting," Fanny said.

Only the guilty trip.

Only one color played Chastity!

Saoirse sped up—slower, jogging—

Fanny played for one year, then she just disappeared.

Till she was at a full sprint. "My truth is!" she shouted it.

Fanny took a ready position. "Feck off."

"As a womb-bearing being!" Saoirse yelled.

"I hate that phrase!" The investigator shouted.

"THAT I AM SHAMROCK VIOLET!"

Fanny froze, and Saoirse put a lovely strike right down her hallway.

Lightning flashed.

Thunder rumbled.

The rain came in sheets.

A geas coalesced on the back of Fanny's palm. For the first time since their battle had started, Fanny Pressure, the once-great captain of Cork Camogie, truly entered the fray.

Fear like she'd never known washed over her. If this was the real investigator she could never beat her physically. There was only one choice: Saoirse would have to FINGER her.

FINGERING Fanny

Less than an Hour Remains

*P*ÉNIS *Therapy Advanced Module – FINGERING: a specialized therapeutic technique—not for normal athletes, but problem cases who needed to be broken open, stretched beyond their structure, and strategically dismantled from the inside.*

Saoirse could think of a woman who fit that description: Fanny Pressure. Fanny wasn't trying to arrest her on behalf of PÉNIS. A purple triskele flashed on the back of the investigator's hand. She was stalling her for Triple K. Fanny was Shamrock Violet. Too tight, too defensive, too contained within herself to be beaten in open play. Now it was up to her to pull those walls apart.

YOU GOT LUCKY WITH LORCAN!

Maybe I'll get lucky here, too.

YOU'RE NOT A REAL THERAPIST!

It was pouring rain.

Fanny's knotty hurley, her refusal to clear—the investigator only cared about playing defense. Even inside.

HOW DO YOU KNOW THAT?

Fanny. Saoirse smiled. It was her turn. Saoirse recalled the Druid's recitation: *to dismantle your rigid teammate's problems with pressure, penetration, inside-out destabilization, and controlled overstimulation of their weak points, take the following steps...*

Saoirse held her hurley at the ready. She'd broken open Lorcan and found a prize inside. Now she knew Fanny's secret. She had to get inside her as well.

I GIVE UP, FOLKS. DO YOUR BEST, TWENTY-SEVEN.

"Shamrock Violet," Saoirse faced one of *those women* through the pouring rain.

"You figured it out." Fanny sneered. "Congratulations."

"It's illegal to be emotionally involved in a case. I know that from CSI! No wonder this doesn't make sense—your challenge only works to prove I'm guilty of trespassing against our Color! You couldn't care less about PÉNIS!"

"So what?"

Fanny hadn't taken anything off. She was abandoning the rite—*THAT'S SO DANGER-OUS, FOLKS*. She'd be saddled with an enormous amount of cosmic bad luck. Enough to kill.

Saoirse pulled herself a new sliotar.

The Leggies had taken the simps on the run around the field outside Hazel Park. The only ones left were those still stuffed into the hallway and held back with the thin film. It was just her and Fanny now. The boys could wait no longer. Saoirse would win!

F — Find the opening. No matter how strong-walled she is, every woman has a gap in her defenses. Locate the weakness, probe gently, then commit.

Saoirse soloed along the edge of the scoring zone—what she now knew was Fanny's No-No Zone. She'd probably designed the challenge that way on purpose. "What happened? You were Fanny Pressure!" Saoirse called through the rain. "Aisling has your player stave in her room! You're my best friend's hero!"

Lightning split the sky.

"You should know." The investigator strode to meet her. "I rolled a 'Yes' on the Magic Eight Ball, and now it's Fanny Burns."

Thunder rumbled through.

Fanny lunged for her. Saoirse rolled out of the way. Fanny had her pair of pink fuzzy cuffs, but the rain slicked them down. She escaped—but dropped her solo.

"You participated in *The Violet Intercourse*?!" But of course she did—the investigator was old—but then why the geas?

"Participated? I was *the Violet Intercourse*! I was the only woman the Magic Eight Ball picked that year."

The only one? The only one they violated? Saoirse might be sick. "They outlawed that!"

"Because of me."

STOP, TWENTY-SEVEN, YOU DON'T KNOW WHAT YOU'RE DOING—YOU MIGHT MAKE IT WORSE!

I — Insert pressure where she's tightest. Hit the point of tension—pride, rage, memory, fear. Tight muscles break before they bend.

"The gods must have thought you deserved it."

"You're salm right I did!" Was that tears or rain? Spores, Fanny was so angry. Saoirse started to second-guess herself. Was she supposed to use her MOUTH when FINGER-ING a woman? Maybe Satirical was right, but right now she didn't have the time to second-guess her choice; the team's last day was almost over!

Fanny tried to cuff her again. Saoirse leaped the garden wall, backing into the open field.

"What do you think's going to happen, Little Gale?" Fanny asked, marching through the mud. "Do you think your team will welcome you with open arms? Be happy to make space for you? The Wolves won't support you. They don't want to help you dance—they don't need your goals!"

She'd heard this before from Kate back in the Library of Lived Experience, the Sisterhood Healing session, and the Gratitude Circle. "Yes, they do!" The sky flashed.

N — Navigate the interior. Stay inside her rhythm. Feel her pulse. Defeating her means knowing the battlefield from within.

Both women tossed their hurleys aside.

Against her better judgment, Saoirse let herself get sucked into a warm, wet Fanny. Fanny reached to seize her, but Saoirse got the investigator's wrists, holding them in front of her as they fought over nothing.

"Keep sticking your fingers where they don't belong," Fanny grunted.

Saoirse could see cellulite through Fanny's leggings. Dents developed from the pressure—from all the weight she'd carried in her mind.

"I dare you," Fanny spat. "I play better when I'm wet."

Thunder rolled.

It was just like breathing with Lorcan, only more difficult, more dangerous. Saoirse wriggled inside Fanny, careful not to let her cuff her. She had to pick at the crack. She had to break Fanny open. It was the only way past her defenses—the only way to get inside and save the team! "The Violet would have let you play pro."

"Who cares about going pro?!" Fanny shrieked. "Women are meant to work. They're meant to be the breadwinners of their family. It's girls like you that stop the Violet from succeeding in dismantling the paddyarchy!"

"I don't want to fight the paddyarchy! I just want to be free."

"Sunshine Hurler!!"

"Skank!"

Fanny tackled her. They rolled, leg-locked, through the mud and grass. Saoirse pressed into her thighs, pushing the dents deeper. She would break this woman!

"Gods, they look like they're having fun," Leader ran by.

"Get a room, you two!" Hater.

"Me, Two?" asked Two.

"You two. Not you too, Two," Leader tried.

"I didn't bring mine," said Two.

This wasn't enough. How was she supposed to pick at Fanny's cracks from in front of her? The rain poured on top of them. She was getting so drenched she could hardly see the investigator.

She had to break this rock apart. To crack her open and find what was at the core of her hate. It'd worked for Lorcan. It would work again! If she got through to her. If she could show her the error of her ways, she could call off the simps. Saoirse could get into the arena and save County Tyrconnell!

G — Grind down resistance. Don't give space. Don't release pressure. Wear down her composure until she quivers.

Saoirse pinned Fanny with her hips. "I'm not some puritan. I'm not going to sit here and say all girls should do the opposite of the Violet and aim for a lofty ideal nobody can reach. Tuatha Dé Danann, the gods only know—even before all this began, before I even knew what *The Violet Intercourse* meant, the only men I'd ever have wanted to *Intercourse* with were my team! But that's not enough to convince me to act like you."

Saoirse heard something tear. What was that?

Fanny flipped her. "You idiot, that still makes you sound like a Good Girl!"

"Does not." She flipped back.

"Does too." Flipped again.

"Does not!" Flip.

The rains came heavier now.

E — Expand the breach. Get in there with all you've got. Open her up to change.

"That's why you don't clear the ball!" Saoirse pulled herself, squelching, from between Fanny's wet thighs and pinned her. "The same reason you won't strip beyond what you're already wearing—you're afraid to put it out there!"

"I don't know what you're talking about!" the investigator bellowed.

"You think if you put yourself out there that you'll crack—just like your hurley! Look!" Leader sent a goal down the hall.

Fanny's eyes went wide. Another tearing sound ripped through the rain.

Saoirse used Fanny's line against her. "Show me how bad you are."

"How dare you!"

NONE OF THAT SOUNDED LIKE THE LETTER E! TWENTY-SEVEN, YOU'RE RIPPING HER APART!

Saoirse was bucked off. Fanny snatched her hurley and cuffs and ran for the zone. The dents in her legs were deeper. Saoirse poured on the pressure. "You know what happens if you break a rite?"

"I'm not doing it!" Fanny shouted, huffing back to defend her zone.

The Spectators were on their feet, hollering, booing— *'Cheating Fanny!'*

In Saoirse's estimate, therapy was improved with a physical component. Fanny was weak—she'd beaten down her resistance.

THE WRONG WAY!

Now it was time to put Blue Balls in her face.

R — Rotate positions & apply varied stimulation. One angle won't break her—movement will. Switch tempo, pressure, partners if needed.

"Leader!" Saoirse pointed. "You and Hater play out front."

They did.

"I'll play out high!" shouted Two.

"I'll take her back." Saoirse said.

"You can't pincer me!" Fanny roared.

"We already are."

The Leggies dumped the simps on the flower boxes once more.

Saoirse sprinted for Fanny's backside. Together, the four of them passed the sliotar back and forth, spreading Fanny out to where she couldn't defend them all at once—even with repeated use of her Whiskey. That didn't stop her from trying.

"Whiskey! Whiskey! WHISKEY! Tulip Grip!" A split formed at the tip of Fanny's bas.

Fanny was ragged, panting, her lips just hanging there as she knelt on the pavers.

They scored. The ripping sound came a third time. What was that tear?

STOP, SAOIRSE, PLEASE! YOUR FEAR'S DRIVING YOU TO DO BAD THINGS!

Two kicked another sliotar into play. One more goal, and Fanny would have to expose everything she was hiding. She'd be in the nip. Her rock split open.

Fanny huddled over her hurley, "No, please no." It'd split right up the bas.

This was it. They needed to apply more pressure. "If I was wrong, then do it," she said.

"Whiskey!" Fanny's hurley split ran deeper. "Fine, you want me to do it, I'll do it!" Was she... crying?

YOU'RE MISSING SOMETHING!

One last push.

They watched. Fanny wriggled limply at a pair of wet pants. They seemed stuck. The investigator rolled awkwardly around, trying to free herself. Spores, she knew the embarrassment of that feeling—but this was for her own good.

HOW CAN YOU SAY THAT? IT WASN'T FOR YOUR OWN GOOD.

She'd pushed Lorcan to the point of assaulting her.

Getting hit was the price you paid to score.

BUT SHE'S NOT HITTING YOU, IS SHE?

Eventually, they came free. Fanny tossed them aside. "See? I'm better than you. I'm going to make you quit. When this match ends, you're going to a dungeon."

The last crack.

She'd found it.

"You!" Saoirse said excitedly. "You're only upset because I had the guts to get away with what you never even tried!"

The Leggies laughed.

Her stadium roared.

Hurler hit a celebratory flip!

NO, TWENTY-SEVEN!!!

Lightning crashed behind a scared little girl—a tiny Fanny.

"No!" The words came out soft. Saoirse's eyes grew wide.

Fanny had curled up on the pavers, shaking.

Tears welled up inside. This wasn't how her therapy needed to go!

Something ripped.

Fanny's hurley split right through the bas.

Fanny wasn't a rock in the river—she was a pool noodle, dented from the pressure of carrying too heavy a burden!

Satirical was right. She'd used the wrong therapy.

Fanny was in tears.

Saoirse was in tears; she'd wanted to score so bad that she'd just ripped her in half.

The rain slowed to a sprits. The final sound of tearing came with, "Leeeeegs!"

Simps started flooding through the torn film that had held them in the hallway. She hadn't been FINGERING her at all—she'd been tearing Fanny's Box apart, and left her no better than Triple K, and _The Violet Intercourse_: with simps flooding the investigator's No-No Zone.

Malice leered at her from two halves of a torn soul. Fanny said, "Execute order: 69."

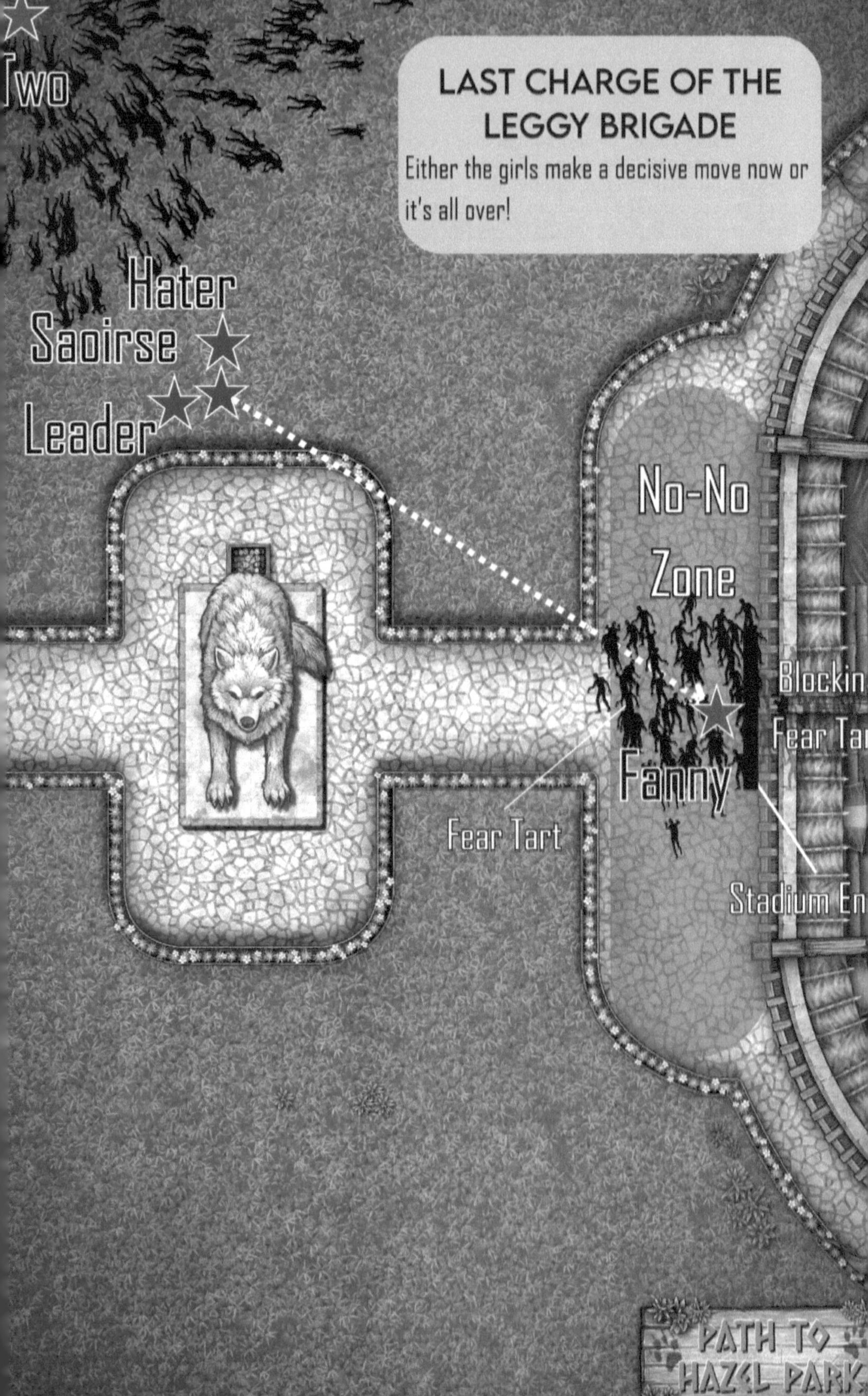
Two
LAST CHARGE OF THE LEGGY BRIGADE
Either the girls make a decisive move now or it's all over!
Hater
Saoirse
Leader
No-No Zone
Blockin
Fear Ta
Fanny
Fear Tart
Stadium En
PATH TO HAZEL PARK

Bad Girl

S aoirse fought her tears. She'd not meant well by the therapy at all. She'd swung her hurley to score and broken a soul barely hanging on. *Those women...* of course, they had that attitude, that dead-eyed stare. Fanny participated in *The Violet Intercourse* as the only woman. One month of being gang raped against guaranteed death. It was more of a miracle that Fanny even had the strength of will to make it through.

YOU SHOULD HAVE STOPPED.

Sorry, didn't cut it—but sorry also didn't get her into the stadium. She was gonna be sick. Saoirse cried. She cried for Fanny. She cried for what she'd done; cried for *The Violet Intercourse*. *Tuatha Dé Danann!*

"SAOIRSE STORM!" Hands seized her. "Run!" Leader screamed.

She did, following the Leggies up the path through a haze of tears and rain.

I tore her! I tore her apart! Just like the noodle! I was trying to stretch Fanny into a shape that worked for me instead of seeing her for what she really was. I've caused her so much pain!

TWENTY-SEVEN...

The entire herd of fear tart sprinted after them with an intense hunger in their eyes, and they were gaining.

"There's too many!" Hater scowled.

They passed the sliotars, passed Melak's statue, into the open field beyond.

"We need something to draw all the fear tart," Leader said. "Then you'll have a shot."

"I guess it's time, isn't it?" Hater asked.

"Hater?" Saoirse asked.

"Hater, you can't!" said Two.

"She can if she wants to," Leader poshed.

"I'm sorry, Saoirse, Leader," Hater sniffed.

"Two?" asked Two.

"Somebody's got to go down," Hater shared a meaningful look with all of them as they ran from the simps. "And it's not gonna be me. Run!" She smiled and seized Two's crutches.

"Ha!" Leader shouted.

Two tumbled forward immediately, doing her best to protect her injured leg. "Hater, you slag!"

"Two!" Saoirse screeched. "Two!"

"Saoirse! Quick! Stiff Spearman's Fall!" Leader threw her between her and Hater. They fell back in the Daughters of Dagda trademark fall. The others unclipped their dresses. The garments unfurled to cover their legs—and hers—as the whole pack turned for Two. Both of them were laughing. Why were they laughing?!

"Two!"

It was an ungodly sight.

Innumerable simps crawled on each other, piling onto her defenseless friend, congealing into a displeasing mound of pimples, pustules, and poor hygiene twenty-seven feet high.

They raised their balls.

"TWO!!!"

And struck.

Boom.

Punctuated by distant thunder, their Blue Balls exploded, their gunk unloaded, their stench eroded... the grass as the thirsty fae flew backward, landing in a starburst around the mushroom cloud of fucky, gunky spulunky that took her favorite dancer. At the center could only be... but she couldn't—

"Two...." Saoirse whimpered and threw Leader, dying of hysterics, off of her. She raced through the stench and sky-blue slime, the others fast behind her. "Two!" she said—but didn't fall to her knees in the slime.

Gross.

Hater arrived a moment later and, unceremoniously, kicked Two's dead body so it rolled once.

"Hater!" Saoirse said. Why were they so blasé about this?!

"What? Now it's slime-free." She indicated the spot where Two's body had been lying.

Saoirse flopped down in the slime-free grass. "Two...?"

She leaned over the vaguely human-shaped pile of plasma—and heard a sudden gasp for air.

Two raised a shaky hand. "Hiya, Silly Saoirse."

"Oh! Two!" she seized up halfway into a hug. "Maybe later."

"Saoirse, I don't have much time. I'll be paralyzed."

"Temporarily," Hater assured her, leaning over Saoirse's side, Leggy Leader on the other, both their mouths covered.

Saoirse followed suit. "But..." Saoirse asked, "The chafing?"

"Don't worry. They didn't get me that bad," Two choked through the gunk, reaching a shaking hand to reveal a bare breast. "I only have one nipple!"

With that, Two succumbed to the stench.

Saoirse stood, too apprehensive to touch her. The residue was nasty. "I don't understand. There was an explosion."

"Oh," Leader waved dismissively, "simps are just really dramatic."

"She'll be fine," Hater agreed. "I mean, as fine as anybody with a brain like hers can be." Hater finished using a foot to cross Two's arms in a heroic fashion. "How many different puns do you think you can get out of that scene based on the phrase 'two to the chest'?"

"Tuatha Dé, Hater!" Saoirse couldn't believe it. "She sacrificed herself for us."

"Oh, come on, it was funny. Besides, it was Two's idea."

"Really?"

Leader nodded. "Yeah, she'll do just about anything as long as she has plausible deniability."

"But she hates simps!"

"Well, sure—who wouldn't after what happened to her?" Leader said, a posh hand to her chest. "I mean, she was in the forest alone one time..."

"You made her re-live that trauma!?"

"I know." Both Hater and Leader dabbed away tears. "All those balls—and they left her completely unsatisfied!"

Both Leggies laughed.

Saoirse just shook her head.

"Simps," Hater spat.

"Fear... tart..." Two creaked.

The three of them gingerly stepped their way out of Two's fairly noble sacrifice. Saoirse was reminded of how awful she'd just been to her investigator. She was there, standing, rage twisting her face.

Poor Fanny.

Even Spirit Stadium had stopped cheering.

Little Hurler had her jersey over her nose for the stench.

"We're a long way away now," Hater rapped her hurley against the walk. A few of the simps had avoided the pile up or were held back in reserve. They'd packed back into the hallway, but it was weak.

"Talk about not playing by the rules of the engagement." Leader stretched out with her hurley held high above her.

"She's a bad woman, that Fanny," Hater said.

"We have to stop her therapy," Saoirse looked to the others.

Hater did a hair flip. "Now?"

"We're not picking at her cracks. We're ripping her apart."

"Then what's the proper procedure?"

Saoirse sighed and faced the entrance to the stadium resolutely. "We have to see Fanny for who she is. Not what we want her to be."

I DON'T MEAN TO BE A NEGATIVE THINKER HERE, BUT THE NEXT LETTER IS I.

Shite.

When they got back to the pile of sliotars at the base of Melak's statue, Fanny called to them. "Done chatting?"

Satirical?

MAYBE HALF AN HOUR.

Then there was no choice. "I'm sorry," Saoirse said.

Fanny balked.

Saoirse couldn't blame her. But it also turned out she couldn't stop the therapy, even though she wanted to. There were only a few minutes left in what might be the last day ever for the Wolves. Saoirse gave Leader a look.

The Leggy placed a dainty hand to her chest at the implications. "Tuatha Dé."

Saoirse gave Hater the same.

Hater cracked her neck. "Salm, that's a lot of balls."

"I'm sure it would be for you," Leader laughed.

"It's okay?" Saoirse asked.

Both women stared down doom.

"Saoirse, your team needs you," Leader said.

"Yeah, more than you know," Hater agreed.

"What's going on? What are you doing?" Fanny asked, voice shaking.

"Risking bad luck." Saorise said.

Fanny's eyes widened.

The Leggy duo shared one last look before Leader adjusted her ponytail. "You swear you won't tell anybody about this?"

Saoirse nodded. "Absolutely."

I THINK YOU'RE GOING TO NEED TO BRACE FOR IMPACT, FOLKS.

Emergency shroombrellas were passed around Spirit Stadium.

The Leggy pair ripped off their skirts, revealing a green, white, and orange thong and—

They all marveled at Hater.

"We were in a rush." She shrugged.

"That was this morning!" Leader said.

"LEEEEEGS!"

"You can't be serious!" Fanny shouted, holding her split hurley shakily in front of her eyes.

The fear tart, barely contained behind a poorly repaired bit of film, screamed, "LEEEEEGS!"

"Saoirse, feel helpless?" Leader held her hurley out like a spear.

"Helpless and needing help are different things." She added hers to the point.

"Whatever." Hater put up hers.

Together they made a three-hurley point.

Yeah, definitely brace. Oh, this is going to be nasty.

"Leggies!" Saoirse called.

"Saoirse!" they responded.

"I need that creed!"

The three of them set the point and their determination. "The Daughters of Dagda are here to help, not hinder!"

"You wouldn't dare!" Fanny fell back.

"I can't believe we're doing this," Leader whimpered.

"Not your speed?" Hater asked.

"No, thank you," Leader said.

"How do you like it?"

"The back of the thigh."

"Salm, you're vanilla."

Saoirse screamed, "A Bad Girl wouldn't follow any of the rules!"

I — Invade the core. Push past her outer shell into the soft center. That's where champions fall apart.

"CHARGE!"

They did. Together, all three broke into a wild sprint. Little Hurler ran with them. Spirit Stadium was up, shroombrellas added to the point.

Even Satirical put out her mic, her distant voice screeching in the back of her mind. *CHARGE!*

Leader was shrieking.

Hater was screeching.

The remaining simps got scared. "Legs..?"

"This proves nothing!" Fanny shouted, falling away. "You get in that stadium, I'm guaranteed to get you, you hear!"

They hit.

"Legs!"

Simps slipped off their hurl-spears like sins in the Shannon.

"Go!" Saoirse shouted.

"We are here to help, not hinder!" Leader roared.

"Give me these," Hater said.

"You heathen!" Fanny cried.

"Leeeeegs!"

The simps got Hater.

"Hater!" Saoirse shouted.

"I knew you'd go down first. Typical Tipperary!"

"Leeeeegs!"

Then the simps swallowed Leader.

"Leader!"

"So... many... balls..!"

'Saoirse!' her Spectators cried.

DUCK, TWENTY-SEVEN.

Little Hurler led her right.

She spun, and with one last leap, Saoirse popped through the last of the simps, narrowly avoiding a pair of Blue Balls by a hair, and found herself, untouched, standing on the field in a circle of empty space surrounded by all of the team.

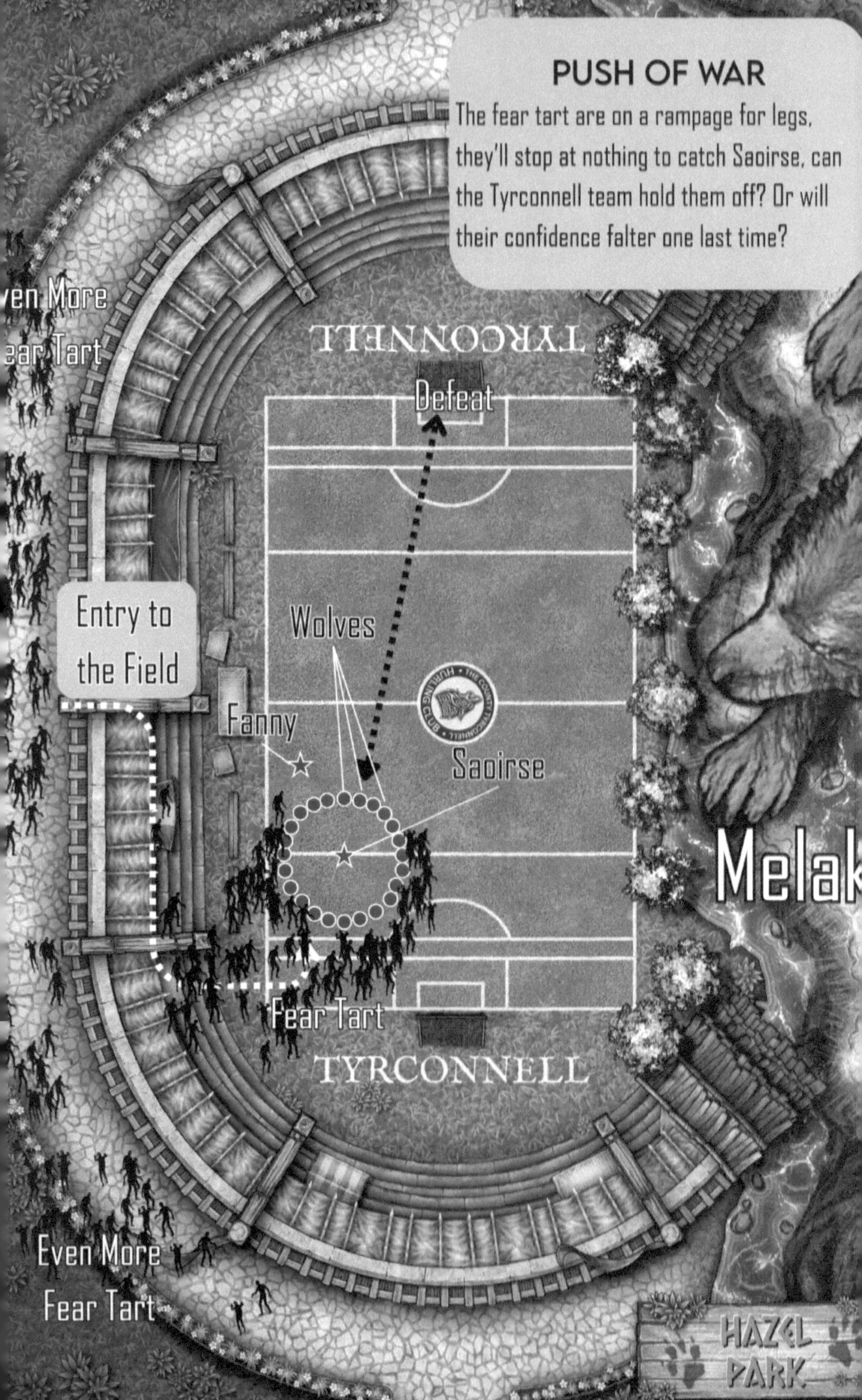
PUSH OF WAR
The fear tart are on a rampage for legs, they'll stop at nothing to catch Saoirse, can the Tyrconnell team hold them off? Or will their confidence falter one last time?
Even More Fear Tart
TYRCONNELL
Defeat
Entry to the Field
Wolves
Fanny
Saoirse
Melak
Fear Tart
TYRCONNELL
Even More Fear Tart
HAZEL PARK

Making Space
A Half-Hour Remains

"**H**old them off, lads!" called a man's voice.

"Tuatha Dé, there's a lot of them." Another.

"Feckin' simps!" a third.

FEAR TART!

Saoirse clutched her chest.

The County Tyrconnell hurling club had been waiting for them at the end of the hall. The Spectators bellowed their approval, several shaking out wet shroombrellas.

Lorcan was at the team's head, along with the original lineup, including fish-eyed Fiachra from free ball—but no Finley. They had their hurleys up, forming a defensive circle around her. The simps mindlessly crashed against the sticks. The boys held them at bay, but the half-fae were so numerous that their circle was pushed back, closer and closer to the Wolves' home goal.

"Hold strong!" Lorcan snarled.

The team gave a collective grunt. Together they threw renewed vigor into the effort, their hurleys braced—but their boots kept slipping, pushed through the pitch.

Where did all these simps keep coming from?

FEAR TART!

"Team?" Saoirse asked.

"We should have realized you were a Good Girl sooner," Sean said, blonde locks caught in the spore light.

"I'm sorry, I thought you were a stunt!" Fiachra shouted, fish-face, fully focused. "Forgive me."

"Good Girls are deadly, cú," Nolan, the other assistant captain, grumbled, his broad back holding back an outrageous number.

But it didn't make sense. "How did you know to wait for me? How did you know I was pushing for the stadium?"

"You've been mic'd to the stadium speakers," Lorcan growled and punched a simp in the face, popping his pustules with a sickening burst.

Saoirse checked her bra. The fuzzy black spore Fanny gave her to capture her confession was being broadcast through the stadium!? Now she looked it was the same one Lorcan had been using all trials! How many people had heard everything? She looked up. A lot.

The whole section down midfield was packed—donors. It looked like half the business owners in the county!

"Tuatha Dé Danann!" Her stomach rocked in waves. Spectators held on for dear life, most glad they'd already finished their nachos.

Yeah, seat belts for the Spectators. Right after my next kelpie.

"It's okay," Lorcan said. "We'll figure this out. We all know Fanny's trying to frame you on your Color."

"But... I made you all flaccid."

Sean shook his locks. "It's not your fault what our Wives did to you."

Orla's words came back now: *Maybe they'd make space for you if you were the kind of woman worth making space for.*

Are you that woman?

Or am I a lie?

"YOU BLASPHEMING LITTLE STRUMPET!" Fanny shrieked as she managed her way through a pack of simps. She was quickly losing control over them, and it wasn't hard to see why. She was only wearing her sports bra and heels, one hand cupped around her no-no zone.

And after all she'd been through! She was already mad, and this would make it so much harder to finish fingering her.

I thought we'd given up on that?

She couldn't. What if finishing her off was what mattered? "What happened to you?" Saoirse asked.

"You can thank that Tipp bitch, Hater!" Fanny shrieked.

Gods salm it, Hater. Saoirse could see it from here. Fanny was like Lorcan. There was no light in the back of her eyes.

"Saoirse Storm," said a voice she knew all too well—a voice that sounded as if it was always complaining—the voice of Mother Uilefaoimo O'Gasm, the middle head of the three-headed triantess that ran Shamrock Violet, the Kwality Kontrol Kouncil, Triple K. The nine-foot-tall Mothers Superior towered over the simps in their violet habit. "Come to join *The Violet Intercourse*?"

The simps pushed their circle back.

"No thanks," she said.

"Triple K!" Fanny whimpered the moment she saw the giantess. "A robe. Please."

"You haven't made the team," Mother Uilefaoimo, her head a pudgy, lopsided blob, said from beneath a bandeau with the symbol of the feminine upside down. "Your geas is active."

"Triple K. Please." Fanny tried again.

Saoirse spared a look for Fanny, but the triantess didn't seem bothered. "You and I both know I've got another way."

That didn't shake the Mothers Superior at all. "And you won't be able to use it."

The circle was pushed back.

"What? I found the answer to Finley's stave!"

Triple K gripped Fanny's wrist and yanked forward. The purple triskele of a death pact formed on the back of her hand.

"Fanny must get you to participate in *The Violet Intercourse*. If she doesn't, she dies."

"No!" Saoirse said.

"Saoirse, don't do it," Lorcan growled. "We'll find another way to get you out."

She smiled. He was so kind, but geas didn't have loopholes. "Thank you for coming to the door."

"I knew you couldn't be a Bad Girl."

That stung. He didn't know. He didn't know who she was. Not who she really was. If he did, he wouldn't help her. "Yeah..."

Twenty-Seven?

"Please... Triple K?" Fanny pleaded.

The triantess finally addressed the investigator. "Stop complaining. You couldn't even get her confession, Fanny!"

The simps continued to jaw at the team. Their circle was closing on their own goal line. She didn't know why, but Saoirse knew she couldn't let them get the team there with their confidence issues. If the simps 'scored a goal,' the team would never recover again.

"I will," Fanny said. "Please, Mothers."

The Mothers didn't heed Fanny's request for decency. They just left her standing there in her blasphemy, dooming Fanny's immortal soul.

It broke Saoirse's heart. It broke Little Hurler, too. Her once battle-hardened heart had taken her helmet off, big eyes wide with tears for Fanny's fate.

If I hadn't picked at her... if I'd approached her as a noodle... "Let her get dressed, Triple K!" Saoirse said.

The triantess sneered. "Why? You've only a few precious moments before both of you die!"

"Triple K, I'm trying," Fanny said. "I was about to secure it!"

"That's not what it sounded like in the stadium!" Mother Uilefaoimo complained in a shriek. "You want a robe? Make it happen!"

"But, Mothers!"

"Do it!" they snapped.

Tuatha Dé Danann.

This is awful. What do we do?

What did they do? Now that hard wouldn't save her, now that she'd ruined the trials. The only thing she could do. Try to save Fanny's soul. "I'm sorry, Fanny," Saoirse said.

"You're sorry?"

"It was wrong for me to have assumed when I said that. When I attacked you..."

It was only because you were attacking yourself.

Saoirse shuddered.

"Saoirse?" Lorcan asked—and their circle pushed back. The goal line was so close.

She faced Fanny—the pain she'd caused—and did what she should have done the first time. She asked, "Did you try?"

Fanny went pink. "Of course not."

That's not going to work—she's afraid of Triple K.

"I've seen firsthand how women change years after they do *The Violet Intercourse*," Saoirse said. "It isn't pretty. The hate from the ugly girls who wait and get nothing. The older woman, once pretty, who never realized it would end. I don't want to look back on my life with that regret. I don't want to be one of *those women*."

"No woman dislikes our way of being," Mother O'Gasm laughed.

Saoirse saw Fanny's eyes dart about the pitch as if searching for the lie in her words.

When the investigator's head snapped up, so did she. "They still want me!"

"But do they keep you?"

"Keep?" Triple K's heads bellowed. "You've been out of Croaghgorm less than a week, and the paddyarchy's already rotted your brain!"

Triple K could speak, but Saoirse was watching Fanny's eyes.

"That's right!" the investigator said. "I'm free!"

"You're not free—you're being used," Saoirse said. "Can't you see Triple K doesn't have your best interest at heart? There's no reason for her to put us in geas if we'd pick the rite willingly. There is no reason to ban dance. It doesn't even trigger the pact! I've been dancing at Social Suicide all week. I've been doing it my whole life. You said you'd tried experimenting."

"As a way to improve my hurling!" Fanny crumbled under the angry gaze of Mother Karen About.

"Don't be afraid to put the ball in play!" Saoirse shouted.

"That's rich," Fanny said, "coming from a *Bad Girl*."

The boys sagged a bit.

"What's she talking about?" Lorcan growled. "I thought she was declaring you innocent?"

WHAT INDEED?

She'd been here before—sat in a river of hate behind a crumbling rock, trying to prove her Chastity!. Only this time, she already knew what kind of men she'd find inside—and how to break them out.

With the truth.

N — Nullify boundaries: Break her structure—the play, the plan, the walls she hides behind. Raw contact beats strategy every time.

"I'm just trying to understand you," Saoirse said.

She needed to see Fanny for who she was—not what she wanted her to be, not as a hurler, not as a woman who wanted to dance—but as a woman trapped in the Violet, convinced it was the best way.

"No, you're not," Fanny said.

Noodles didn't want to hold weight. They dented. The stress of Fanny's past was already self-evident in her thighs. Saoirse needed to take that weight off her—give her a place to be free of the burden she believed she had to carry.

"Then let's do a Sisterhood Healing Session. Here. A Gratitude Circle—just you and me."

"You think I'd waltz up to you and explain my trauma?" Fanny balked.

"Fanny," Saoirse said, "I'm grateful for you. I'm grateful for all the help you gave the hurlers during our practices."

"That's not going to work," Triple K laughed.

"For the time you let me fondle balls—and even take the team to Social Suicide despite knowing full well it was part of *The Violet Intercourse.*"

"You what?!" Triple K bellowed at the investigator.

"I'm grateful for the fact we got to 'get out and hurl'."

"Liar!" Fanny screamed. "I'm not going to say my truth is!"

"I am."

ARE YOU SURE YOU CAN?

I love you, Satirical. I love you, Little Hurler. "I love you, Fanny."

The circle pushed back.

"My truth is, as a hurling being," Saoirse spoke, voice amplified by the stadium's loudspeakers, "THAT I DID CONSPIRE TO THROW THE MATCH!"

YOU FINALLY SAID IT.

The donors stood in shock, their gasps echoing around Hazel Park.

Her circle collapsed, the last of the team's rocks crumbling into the river. They slid back, back, back.

"Don't fold!" Lorcan howled. "We've already misjudged her more than enough. Let's let the lady share her story!"

The wall locked down—not with renewed strength, but disbelief—the backs of their toes right on the edge of their goal line, Saoirse trapped in the net.

She should have scored on that night versus Tyrone.

Her Spectators couldn't believe it.

Saoirse stared down Fanny through the gap between her soon-to-be shields and the simps.

"I conspired. A man came to my village—he knew my secret practice spot. He offered to trade with my dad for a loaded Magic Eight Ball. When we lost, we'd swap out the usual for the new one. We'd roll it after I lost, and it would say 'No!'"

"That's what happened?" Lorcan asked.

"I didn't try to sabotage anything." She fixed her focus on Fanny. On those dead eyes. "I know now that you know what it's like to be Shamrock Violet—to have a spear pointed to your neck, in a death pact from birth, to choose between death or being defiled."

Fanny looked away.

"Tuatha Dé Danann!" Sean shouted.

"I didn't know Violet was like that!" Lorcan howled.

The team slammed a half-step forward.

"I chose a hidden third option. I chose to defy," she said. "I didn't know about the laws that would cause the hurling team to fold. I just figured I'd win next season. Twenty-seven is my lucky number."

"Touching." Triple K barked a dark, hollow laugh. "But that admission makes you guilty both by your Color and PÉNIS. Fanny! Sentence this strumpet!"

Every eye in Hazel Park and Spirit Stadium focused on the lead investigator for PÉNIS. Only the simps, their manic drive for legs, tried to push for their goal.

"I..." Fanny stumbled. "I..."

"Tell us your truth, Fanny," Saoirse cried. "Tell us who you really are!"

"Enough—she's guilty. Arrest her!"

"Fanny, your truth is—"

"My truth is..."

"As a woman, as a girl—"

"My truth is..."

"What you're doing is pathetic," Triple K complained at Fanny. "You look pathetic."

"Fanny?" Saoirse asked. "Are you a Mallhark girl or aren't you!?"

That one got her. "My truth is!" Fanny set her stance. "My truth is that I tried out for Cork Hurling! I did trials for the Rebels!"

"You did what!?" Triple K looked ready to kill.

Fanny faced her. "I tried out for Cork. I failed. I wouldn't dance. I told myself I had to be the perfect Shamrock Violet—so my defense faltered." She turned to Saoirse. "By the time I realized my mistake, nobody wanted to make space for me. They didn't want to work to integrate my dancing style. One failed attempt at a role I was unfamiliar with—and they gave up on me. My corner-backs collapsed. Every round they'd come in my box. It was easy points over the bar."

"You could have danced! You could have made space for them!" Saoirse encouraged.

"I've heard enough," Mother Mai Kleetoris spat. Triple K seized Fanny by her bra, lifting her up to their considerable height. "Arrest her, or that rule I made after your first time doing _The Violet Intercourse_, I'll repeal it!"

She ripped the bra, and Fanny dropped, with a snap, into a pair of broken business heels. The Mothers Superior shoved her and her split hurley, tumbling into the Tyrconnell circle.

Saoirse caught her.

"Here." Triple K threw a pair of fuzzy cuffs in after the disgraced woman. "Arrest her."

"Fanny?" Saoirse asked.

Fanny stumbled to her feet, unable to bring herself to cover anything. She grabbed the cuffs—a slow, misshapen mess of tears.

"Fanny." Saoirse tried.

Fanny made a weak attempt at her wrists.

Saoirse dodged. "Fanny."

Attempt. Dodge. "Fanny, please."

"You are hereby..."

G — Go until she collapses.

"...under arrest."

Do not stop early. The only successful fingering is the one that leaves her unable to stand.

"Oh, gods, Fanny!" Saoirse threw herself into a hug. "It's okay. Everything will be okay."

"Useless!" Triple K said.

The team gained a half-step.

Saoirse pulled the hair from the inspector's face and tucked it past her ear. Little Hurler hugged Fanny's heart.

"You never even asked me why I liked the team," she said, speaking the words just for Fanny but making sure the team could hear. "Even they assumed I hated them."

TELL HER GOOD.

The Spectators leaned in.

Saoirse let a bit of her dust flow free, rubbing Fanny as she held her—a golden hand job for the soul.

"My entire life was a war against the Magic Eight Ball. It has never once rolled me the outcome I wanted. And now, for the last four years, every day—day after day—it rolled 'Yes' on my participation in *The Violet Intercourse.* No matter what I did, no matter how I played, it was always a 'Yes.' I didn't think there was anybody who could understand my pain. But then there was Tyrconnell."

The boys listened with keen interest, the simps faltering more and more.

"What a mess! What losers! The Wolves had been failing since before I was born!" They came to the edge of the line—one blade from the paint.

"But I never saw them cry. I never saw them fold. If anything, they always came back harder—pushed more—dug deeper. Now I know what they were going through off the field. It all makes sense. I love them for the very reason the Violet don't—because they lose, and they never give up!"

Fanny collapsed. Saoirse let her go.

"That's why you listen, men," Lorcan said.

The team pushed back against the simps with renewed resolve, reclaiming much of the goal box.

Saoirse turned to face the Triple K. "The days of you stopping women from being who they want to be end today."

"Brainwashed by the paddyarchy," Uilefaoimo complained.

"I want out of my geas—but I want Fanny out of hers, too. If I don't win right here, right now, I'll participate in *The Violet Intercourse* forever!"

"Deal." Triple K reached a hand over the simps. Saoirse took it—mist wrapped around them, coalescing into purple triskeles on the backs of their palms.

"Rite of Ritual Hurling," Saoirse said.

"One shot wins," Triple K spoke together. "No falls."

Saoirse nodded.

"No matter what you do here, you're headed for the dungeons!" Triple K held a hurley made for a triantess high. "Whiskey!" The pitch began to warp and darken. "Violet Letter!"

Saoirse shook her head. A soft smile worked its way across her face. She'd never been the kind of girl who could do what Fiadh did, not for herself, not for the boys—but for Fanny? "You think that scares me?" she asked. "I've always known I was bound for a PÉNIS dungeon. I've known that, but Tuatha Dé Danann, so help me, I will not go before I get my whole team hard!" She spiked her hurley into the dirt, reached up—*for Fanny*—and pulled off her bra.

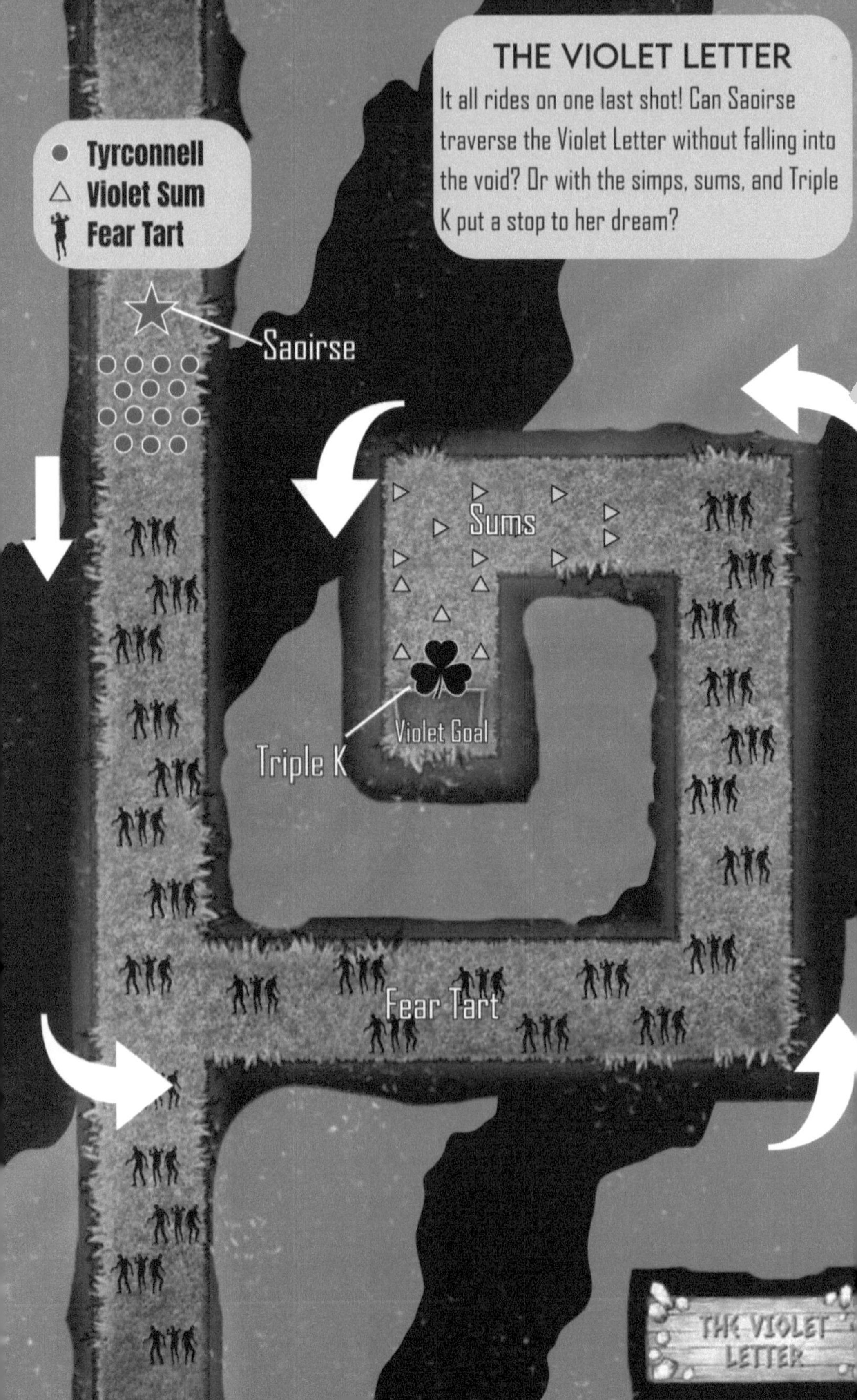

Tyrconnell
Violet Sum
Fear Tart
THE VIOLET LETTER
It all rides on one last shot! Can Saoirse traverse the Violet Letter without falling into the void? Or with the simps, sums, and Triple K put a stop to her dream?
Saoirse
Sums
Triple K
Violet Goal
Fear Tart
THE VIOLET LETTER

The Violet Letter

County Tyrconnell's magic rose to life in the form of white—

Hurling belonged to glory.

Light.

Glory to the gods.

Brilliant. Blinding.

And the pitch to Saoirse.

An eruption of pride.

She couldn't miss.

A release of power.

A sexplosion!

"WHISKEY!!!"

Pa-plunk. A sliotar hit her in the side of the face.

The whole world went white.

She couldn't see much more than the grass at her feet, the sliotar, and—

"Fanny?" Saoirse knelt beside a girl curled up and crying, wearing only a pair of broken heels. She didn't have anything to say. Instead, she held her hand out to the side and asked, "Púca Súcca?"

With a loud snap, a robe of green, white, and orange appeared in her hands. She pulled it around the inspector, who clutched at it in desperation.

For a moment, their eyes met. She saw all she needed to see.

Saoirse stooped and roll-lifted the sliotar from the white void. She spared one last look for Fanny—and they both knew, as the light faded, it was time for her final—

Goooooooooooooooooooal! She's tits out for Tyrconnell! Breasts bouncing for the boys! Jugs jiggling for justice! Her pelt piggies are on parade!

Her Spectators roared.

Little Hurler yanked down her helmet.

It was time to end this.

The mists flooded onto the field, filling the boys' hurleys to beyond full with magical power, the ogham carvings on their shafts bristling. To a man, their mojo was back—and all it took was telling the truth... and a nice pair of tits.

WHAT A STRANGE WHISKEY, FOLKS. TRIPLE K'S MAGIC HAS WARPED THE PITCH. I'VE NEVER SEEN ANYTHING LIKE IT. A SQUARE SPIRAL OF GRASS, AND AT ITS CEN-TER—THE GOAL!

It was just like the fishhook symbol on the rocks in Beltany Circle.

She could hear voices...

Saoirse and the team were near one end of a long strip. An endless black void surrounded the entire pitch. The simps—*FEAR TART!*—clawed at each other, desperate not to fall off the edges of the five-meter-wide strip of violet grass.

"That's what she meant by no falls." Neither she nor Triple K could go into the void.

"What is this strange pitch?" asked a hurler.

"It's some kind of ogham," said another.

The blades seemed to hiss and snap at them. She swore she heard voices.

"It doesn't matter what it is!" Lorcan roared. "We make space for Saoirse!" He held his hurley high. "For our Dancer!"

"Yeah!" They said.

"Let's cut these simps!"

Saoirse threw her head back and howled, "Ahoooo."

The rest replied in kind: "For Tyrconnell! For the Wolves!"

"Leeeegs."

Saoirse shouted, "Charge!"

SLIOTAR IN HER SOLO, TYRCONNELL TAKES OFF INTO THE SIMPS! AND IT'S PIMPLE VS STICK, PUSTULE VS—WELL... STICK! THAT SHOULD BE A LOT OF RED CARDS, FOLKS, BUT THIS COMMENTATOR COULDN'T CARE LESS. BEAT 'EM BAD, BOYS! TWENTY-SEVEN!

The team surged forward, calling out Whiskey names in an explosion of magics she did not understand and sending innumerable simps to an endless doom. It would take a while to run the strange, elongated pitch. She was both so close and so far from the goal. It was just there to her left—but she knew if she shot the sliotar from here, it would get lost in the void. This was her one shot. She could not miss it.

They turned a corner on the strange violet pitch.

Triple K screamed from the goal. She and twelve lesser sums of Shamrock Violet stood ready at the center of the fishhook spiral. "She's been brainwashed by the paddyarchy!"

"I haven't even met a man named Paddy before!" Saoirse shouted back, staying in the space provided for her by the team.

"The paddyarchy is everywhere. It's oppressive."

"The only thing oppressing me right now is my Color. It's my body, my choice. I'd rather do *The Violet Intercourse* with men who never quit than become a jaded swamp hag who got passed over after like you!"

They turned another corner.

Saoirse ducked a pair of flying Blue Balls. Simps poured over the edge of the thin strip of violet grass. Her team could comfortably fit seven men across. She had two rows of protection.

"This is almost too easy!" Sean said.

Hurler had one eye on the grass.

Saoirse had to agree—for the head of a Color, Triple K didn't have a powerful Whiskey.

"It's time! Let them have it!" the Kwality Kontrol Kouncil urged their sums forward.

The women in violet habits fell into prayer, tracing shamrocks around themselves, whispering to the grass.

Then it happened.

Blades near the edge of the thin field grew in length, lashing at the ankles of simps and hurlers both. The men instinctively chopped at the blades, which let some simps through to the second line.

"What are you doing!?" Lorcan growled.

"Shite this grass, Lorcan!" said one.

One of the team was thrown into the abyss, followed by a tumble of far-flung simps in their business attire and pointed inflatable hats.

The voices came back, louder now.

"Grand. That's a way to score."

"Your fans would never."

"What would your Wives think?"

The grass was speaking!

"The grass!" yelled one, as a long purple blade lashed at their feet. "It's trying to guilt-trip us!"

That it was.

"Jump it!" said another.

"Leave your cares behind."

"Faith, trust, and golden dust!"

"I can fly." The grass bound his ankle. "Nope."

He was hurled into the abyss.

"Steadfast in yourself, lads," Lorcan called. "We can't leave her open!"

It was a nice thought—but they were overrun.

The guilt-tripping thinned the ranks of the Tyrconnell members. A number of simps managed to break their line. Saoirse shrieked and dropped her solo as she was engulfed by half-fae, by fear tart—a pus-ridden pile of guilt and shame. The grass started making sense:

You don't deserve it.

You think they'll like that?

You want their jersey—they don't need your goals.

Blue Balls rained down on her. She could feel their squishy juices strike her topless back. She had to fight it! She had to dance.

She grabbed her lucky hurley—but several simps had a grip on her shaft. There were just too many. She couldn't move—couldn't hop, slide, prance, or run. One reached for the sliotar even if grabbing off the ground was illegal...

No—if he gets it, we can't score!

But she didn't have the hope. She didn't have the hands.

It was over.

She didn't have a—

"WHISKEY!" The grass flashed white. "AWARENESS OF THE WOLF!"

—shield in her river.

Seven simps flew into the void.

Lorcan, his face contorted till it was almost a wolf's, tore through the simps with powerful claws, wielding his hurley like a staff, beating back the horde by himself. She sat at his back, in a bubble of space, safe.

He sent seven simps into the void at a time, almost like An Dagda himself, and looked down at her. "Are you unharmed, my lady?"

Ohhh, it was just like her dreams! "Pick my flowers?"

He grabbed her by the throat and pulled her to her feet—the opposite of the direction she was hoping for after that, but hey.

Keep it together.

A few more simps jumped off the edge for fun. She could see what Leader meant by dramatic.

"Run na Rince!" Seamus cried.

Instinctively, Saoirse went into her dance. Dancing, Seamus's Whiskey wouldn't affect her. The same could not be said for the simps, who hit the ground rolling like they'd been lit on fire, flinging themselves off the edges of the violet swirl.

Four men danced their way toward them: Sean, Nolan, Seamus, and Fiachra.

They were the most super-masculine kick line of doom.

"They can't take it!" said Seamus.

"They're falling off the ogham!" Fiachra cheered.

"Only real men can dance," Lorcan said, marching a simple, aggressive jig. The last of the simps rolled into the void.

"Boys," Saoirse tried.

"Save it," Sean said. "Not only because I want the whole team to hear, but because we've got company." He nodded back toward the team's goal, where more simps flooded onto the field, coming at them from behind.

"Simps are endless, cú," Nolan said.

Seriously, how many of these things are there?

The Spectators were going nuts.

"Go," Sean urged her. "We'll hold them off!"

"Saoirse," Lorcan cupped her chin. "We believe in you."

"Not as much as I believe in you."

SEE, THAT'S GOOD THERAPY.

He let her go and joined the kick line facing the other direction—toward the oncoming fear tart.

Saoirse restarted her solo with a simple flick. She stared across the void at Triple K. The long blades of grass didn't attack her.

"How!?" Uilefaoimo O'Gasm complained. "How can you be immune to my Whiskey!?"

She rapped the sliotar a few times.

Little Hurler had her own sliotar ready in her heart—a golden apple embroidered with silver branches and purple leaves.

Mist rose from the violet grass.

"Because..." Saoirse said.

I LOVE YOU, TWENTY-SEVEN.

"I may have thrown the match—but I'm not guilty."

Crack!

A gigantic bolt of purple lightning struck just behind Saoirse.

The world went black.

Crystal. Clarity. Presence.

"What was that!?" The triantess's Whiskey symbol fell away, the whole pitch dropped out beneath them, sinking into the abyss—leaving them floating. The boys kept dancing as if nothing had changed. Saoirse watched them go until they disappeared into battle against thirst.

Her spirit—our rhythm.
Her soul—our people's percussion.

"No!" Uile complained. "No, you can't!"

Crystals shot across the sky like stars, coming to rest at her feet and building into something greater.

"What's going on?" Saoirse asked. "Is this your Whiskey? Satirical? Hurler?"

Nothing.

Clack. Clack. Clack.

Orla???

Snap.

The last crystal snapped into place.

Percussion to her melody—ash wood and gold.

Saoirse's feet found purchase. She stood on a giant star-crystal version of her own lucky hurley.

Triple K hissed. "A True Whiskey!"

Saoirse stood at the tip, staring down the Color of guilt and shame. Lightning continued to flash around them, striking the hurley with powerful blasts.

Uilleann.
Forfeda.

She gripped her own hurley tight. It was hot to the touch—but her Heart compelled her to sink into the heat. Pipes sang around her: a robust set of uilleann.

"You pretty girls are all the same," Triple K said. "Think you're special just because you were born attractive. That all ends when we ruin you in the eyes of men to the point of disgust!"

"Beautiful choices make you beautiful."

"Liar! With you out of the way, the ugly girls have a chance."

"Every girl has a chance—they just don't want to be good women."

"No prince charming would ever pick me!"

"Have you tried giving one PÉNIS therapy?"

"Like I'd debase myself to a Paddy!"

"You gotta get over your ex, cú."

TWENTY-SEVEN?

Yeah?

YOU BETTER FUCKING SCORE.

> *Join the dance or don't indulge it—*
> *Half measures only make you fall.*

Stupid, foaming, bimbo sock-head?

Saoirse flicked the sliotar, sliding forward. She faced down the shaft, coming to a stop at the top of the grip—the hurley angled down a steep run to the net. She wasn't about to start putting shots over the bar. "How about I show you all something?"

To her surprise, a voice answered and echoed everywhere—the laughter of Sean. "Like what?"

She scanned the crystal hurley. Twelve sums stood between her and the head of Shamrock Violet: three at half-back, three at full-back, and the other six helping Triple K block her goal.

An amplified, distorted "LEGS!" resonated from the unseen simps.

Yeah, she had a line. Saoirse smiled. "A stunt."

Little Hurler?

Her heart's hair played in the sparkling wind. Sometimes, to win a game, a girl had to make the big play.

Her Color did not account for the Storm.

"Watch me."

SAOIRSE STORM!!!

> *The girl goes dancing there—*

She dove, sprinting down the decline, racing right—pulling the center half-back across the crystal toward the right half-defender.

The sums' violet habits flapped around them, reflecting in the hurley.

> *On the leaf-sown, new-mown, smooth—*

She skidded to a stop, kicking up diamonds.

> *Grass plot of the garden—*

With a smack, she slapped the sliotar down into the stars, where it bounced through the left half's legs. She spun off the confused defender, tapped the ball to her open palm, then dropped it again so it rolled through the center half's legs as well, down the hurley.

The two women dog-piled each other off the side.

> *Escaped from bitter youth—*

Lightning followed her, carving the spell into the crystal, burning it into her ash.

Saoirse stormed after her free ball. It rolled toward a portly sum—the right corner-back, closing fast.

> *Escaped out of her crowd—*

Instead of a jab-lift, she leaped to the other side of the ball, sliding backward, letting the sliotar roll up her stick with its own momentum.

> *Or out of her black cloud—*

She felt the first sum at her back, saw the other closing for a tackle...

> *Ah, dancer—*

...And hit the splits.

> *Ah, sweet dancer.*

Slamming into the crystal, Saoirse slipped between them at the knees. The two women collided above her and fell into the void. She spun, cradling the sliotar against the bas.

Only two sums remained. Rings in their noses, they charged like bulls from the back corners.

When they lowered their bandeaus for a tackle, Saoirse leaped between their shoulders—meters into the air, spinning off their back. The sum's ankles failed beneath them. They collided in a tangle heap of violet behind.

STILL SIX LEFT—HOW WILL SHE HANDLE IT, FOLKS!?

The grass left at Triple K's feet loomed ready to trip. This was no time for insecurity. She was halfway down her shaft!

"And after they made all that room for you." A voice echoed at first, then settled into a woman born of the darkness, landing on the crystal hurley next to her, running at speed. Her green, white, and orange robe was wide open, rippling behind her.

"Fanny!?"

"Told you I'd be there when you climaxed." It was Fanny indeed. She'd taken off her heels. "I've got enough in me for three. You'll have to do the rest yourself!"

"So, I'm not guilty?"

"I definitely have to arrest you, but I think with a name your punishment could be... a hundred spanks."

"See, I knew you were a Bad Girl." That voice! It couldn't be.

Appearing from out of the black, behind Fanny. Deep blue hair and devious features curled in a smile was—

"Finley!" she said. "You came back!!!"

'Finley!' The Spectators cheered.

He winked. "Take it home, Superspore."

"Whiskey!" he cried and clapped Fanny hard on her ass. She blushed. Mist congealed in his palm as if it were being sucked out of Fanny herself. "Trickster in the Tain! Hope you don't mind if I borrow this."

He ran to Saoirse's other side. The trio reached the base of her bas.

They turned to the last of the sum's hands outstretched. "TULIP GRIP!"

Three sums a piece soared into their arms, tackling them off the edge of the star-crystal and into the abyss.

Leaving her a clear shot at the goal. Just her and evil. She charged Triple K—her solo, ready for striking.

The KKK spoke together. "You cheating harlot!"

"Welcome to Chastity!" Saoirse yelled. "For today's daily triple, the category is Hurling."

"Shut up!"

"What girl is about to kick your ass?"

"You can't say that!"

"Yes, I can. I just did."

"Wield our light."

The voice from the game against Melak?

Saoirse braced herself against the crystal hurley. Strange heat, something more than just hope pushed through her thighs, a sensation she'd felt once before—a feat. In this moment, she could have fought a whole army on behalf of Ulster...

"Sing our spirit."

And won.

She leaped, erupting from the surface of the star crystal. She was higher than she'd ever imagined, soaring meters above the hurley as she was propelled by it, thrust forward by a golden geyser of crystal and light.

"The spirit of Éire!"

It was there this time. Saoirse held her hurley to the sky and roared with every fiber of her mind, body, and spirit.

"WHISKEY!!!"

A last bolt of lightning shot from the sky and connected with her lucky hurley.

Stars and shine.

Green, white, and orange.

The energy raced up her hurley, shattering with a crack—her stick alight with magic power.

She's earned a True Whiskey!

She roared, "AAAAAAAH!" skin bristling with heat, her mouth opening more, more, more till her jaw unhinged.

"If my Color, if my people, don't want to support my lifestyle!" she said, speaking clearly despite her maw. "Then I choose Social Suicide!

Her hurley is slippery yet sticky in her hand. She didn't need to read to know what was said.

You don't swing a hurley to escape a life!
You swing it to save one

"SHAMELESS STRIKE!!!!"

"NOOOOOOO!!!" screeched Triple K.

Three meters from the net. Only the worthless missed from three meters.

Her hurley flashed.

Let her finish her dance,

"Boom."

Let her finish her dance.

The sliotar shot of her hurley, translucent, trailing a tail of gold, and went right through Triple K's bas.

Ah, dancer, ah, sweet dancer!
~ W.B. Yeats.

Saoirse landed hard on regular green grass. A sensation like liquid gold swelled between her legs, warmth, connection, and love as she'd never known. She shook till her legs gave out, and collapsed into a convulsing puddle of pure joy.

"You worthless pick me," Mother Uilefaoimo O'Gasam spat from fatigued knees.

She'd won. It wouldn't be enough to keep them hard forever, but it would be enough for now. Her geas shattered for Finley, her geas shattered for Triple K. "Suck my sourdough starter, bitch."

"Saoirse Storm," said Fanny, binding her in a pair of fuzzy pink cuffs. "You are under arrest for conspiracy, match fixing, and sabotage. Though if you drop me a quick name, we can actually make use of the simps."

"Fear tart."

"You're a funny one," Fanny said, "I never brought the fae for you, only your confession."

It hit her, the stadium, the inexplicable end to the team, bringing in all the donors, Fanny planned this whole ordeal as a way to smoke out the conspirator who gave her the Magic Eight Dowel. "Some bushy eyebrow guy named Connor."

She gave the nod to her fae, who scrabbled off into the crowd, as the County Tyrconnell Hurling Club arrived with a robe and working whiskeys; she didn't have to guess what else was working as well.

"Saoirse Storm," Lorcan said, "I know we're only halfway done with the trials, but how about you play full-forward for the Wolves?"

He threw the robe around her and bound it tight.

"I'd love to."

Fanny escorted her off the pitch, as she found for the first time, the light was rising in the eyes of the team who'd take Tyrconnell Hurling to new horizons.

The End

Afterword
Please Leave A Review!

Dear reader,

Thank you. If you've read this far, it means the world to me. I hope you enjoyed your time with Saoirse and the rest of the wacky characters in *Hard to Win*. I don't know where the idea for this story came from; it's definitely unique. What I do know is I enjoyed writing it and think it's a blast. If you agree, I invite you to leave a review on Amazon, Goodreads, and anywhere else books get reviewed. And if you didn't enjoy it, go ahead and review it anyway. I'd rather people who think this book isn't for them let others know that. That way, they can spend their hard-earned money on a different experience they'd prefer. If you've left a review either way, you have my extra thanks.

When I set out to write books, I did it because I was convinced that climbing to the summit of this mountain was something the universe couldn't take away from me, like it did my last mountain. I'd be lying if I said that a part of me didn't work all this time and put in all the hours if it wasn't for my belief in the glory of it—and the tons of cash and women—but it's changed a lot since I started back at the base. Nowadays, I wish only for one thing: to give people a better day.

Maybe that's some corny shit. I recognize that people might feel that way. Lots of people think I'm not as happy as I say, not as positive as I purport to be, and that I'm compensating in my outlook—and hey, maybe I am. I've thought about it a lot. I try hard not to be fake. Maybe that in itself is fake? I'm sure my good friend and philosophical genius of the first water, Stas, will let me know when he reads this. I digress.

What I really want to say is that I'm grateful. No matter how you came by this book, no matter if you liked it or not, you gave it a chance—you gave me a chance—and perhaps that's a choice that is being second-guessed already, too. Ha! I'm not out to change your opinion or make up your mind for you on that. You may think whatever you wish. I am still going to be thankful for you all the same.

Stay crazy,

I. M. Price

About the Author

Thriving with a smile on his face and a song in his heart, I. M. Price is the living definition of a homeless man down by the river—provided that river is called Planet Fitness.

I. M. Price is just plain strange. He spends his days in his 'apartment in a parking space,' a broken van that's in a seriously nice location: access to a gym, good food, and all life's necessities are within a walking distance most Americans would be envious of; there are books to read; and he writes so much that the good people at the local Chick-fil-A and Panera Bread think he's crazy. Which, to be fair, he is. So fair play to them.

After attending and quitting university to pursue a career as a professional gamer, I. M. Price grazed the sun before his game of choice was struck by a comet that sent him into a spiral of depression that saw all his best years stolen from him, both physically and mentally, only to have his mind recover just in time for COVID, leading to him spending the better part of ten years essentially in prison. This mix of life experience has given him a very unique take on most worldly things—novels and stories included (as you no doubt noticed).

Thankfully, the universe hasn't seen fit to tow his car yet, or we might miss out on the rest of his books. And if you sarcastically said "what a loss" or something similar, don't worry—you're in good company; God and the Devil are both still flipping coins on whether or not that fact has been a bad bet.